"A fast and fascinating read."

—*Knoxville News-Sentinel* (TN)

"The plot is classic Clark, except the author tells her story from a first-person perspective. She pulls it off well."

—*Star Ledger* (NJ)

ON THE STREET WHERE YOU LIVE

"Is a reincarnated serial killer at work in a New Jersey resort town more than a century after he first drew blood? That's the catchy premise that supports Clark's 24th book. . . . [A] plot-driven novel."

—*Publishers Weekly*

"A suspenseful page-turner that will delight her many fans."

—*Booklist*

"The cleverly complex plot gallops along at a great clip, the little background details are *au courant,* and the identities of both murderers come as an enjoyable surprise. *On the Street Where You Live* just may be Clark's best in years."

—Amazon.com

BEFORE I SAY GOOD-BYE

"Mary Higgins Clark knows what she's doing. . . . This savvy author always comes up with something unexpected. . . . A hold-your-breath ending."

—*The New York Times Book Review*

MARY
HIGGINS
CLARK

A NOVEL

Nighttime
Is My
Time

POCKET BOOKS

New York   London   Toronto   Sydney

POCKET BOOKS, a division of Simon & Schuster, Inc.
1230 Avenue of the Americas, New York, NY 10020

This book is a work of fiction. Names, characters, places, and incidents are products of the author's imagination or are used fictitiously. Any resemblance to actual events or locales or persons, living or dead, is entirely coincidental.

ISBN 0-7434-1263-X

First Pocket Books paperback edition April 2005

10 9 8 7 6 5 4 3 2 1

POCKET and colophon are registered trademarks of Simon & Schuster, Inc.

Cover design by Jackie Seow
Front cover photo by Gary Isaacs/Photonica

Manufactured in the United States of America

For information regarding special discounts for bulk purchases, please contact Simon & Schuster Special Sales at 1-800-456-6798 or business@simonandschuster.com.

ACKNOWLEDGMENTS

I am frequently asked if the longer I write, the easier it gets. I wish that were true, but it simply isn't. Each story is a new challenge, a new landscape to fill with characters and events. That is why I am so grateful to those same people who are always there for me, especially when I'm beginning to wonder if I really can tell the tale the way I hope to tell it.

Michael Korda has been my editor ever since my first suspense fiction novel thirty years ago. He has been friend, mentor, and editor par excellence for three decades. Senior editor Chuck Adams has been part of our team for the last dozen years. I am grateful to both of them for everything they do to guide this writer along the way.

My literary agents, Eugene Winick and Sam Pinkus, are true friends, good critics, and great supporters. I love them. Dr. Ina Winick brings her psychological expertise to assist me on the workings of the human mind.

Lisl Cade, my publicist and dear friend, is always there for me.

Many thanks to Michael Goldstein, Esq., and Meyer Last, Esq., for their valuable assistance in answering my queries about adoption law and procedure.

Again and always a tip of the hat to Associate Director of Copyediting, Gypsy da Silva, and her team: Rose Ann Ferrick, Anthony Newfield, Bill Molesky, and Joshua Cohen, and to Detective Richard Murphy and Sgt. Steven Marron, Ret., for their continuing support and guidance.

Agnes Newton, Nadine Petry, and Irene Clark are always in my corner on my literary journeys.

The special joy is that after the story is told, I celebrate with my nearest and dearest, the children and grandchildren and, of course, "Himself," my marvelous husband, John Conheeney.

And now I hope you, my valued readers, enjoy the goings-on at a deadly twentieth class reunion in the beautiful Hudson Valley.

For Vincent Viola, a proud West Point graduate,

and his lovely wife, Theresa,

with affection and friendship.

The definition of an owl had always pleased him: A night bird of prey . . . sharp talons and soft plumage which permits noiseless flight . . . applied figuratively to a person of nocturnal habits. *"I am The Owl,"* he would whisper to himself after he had selected his prey, *"and nighttime is my time."*

It was the third time in a month he had come to Los Angeles to observe her daily activities. "I know your comings and goings," he whispered as he waited in the pool house. It was one minute of seven. The morning sun was filtering through the trees, causing the waterfall that spilled into the pool to sparkle and shimmer.

He wondered if Alison could sense that she had only one minute more of life on earth. Did she have an uneasy feeling, perhaps a subconscious urge to skip her swim this morning? Even if she did, it wouldn't do her any good. It was too late.

The sliding glass door opened, and she stepped onto the patio. Thirty-eight years old, she was infinitely more attractive than she had been twenty years ago. Her body, tanned and sleek, looked good in the bikini. Her hair, now honey blond, framed and softened her sharp chin.

She tossed the towel she was carrying onto a lounge chair. The blinding anger that had been simmering inside him escalated into rage, but then, just as quickly, was replaced by the satisfaction of knowing what he was about to do. He had seen an interview in which a daredevil stunt diver swore that the moment before he began to dive, knowing that he was risking his life, was an indescribable thrill, a sensation he needed to repeat over and over again.

For me it's different, he thought. The moment before I reveal myself to them is what gives me the thrill. I know they're going to die, and when they see me, they know, too. They understand what I am going to do to them.

Alison stepped onto the diving board and stretched. He watched as she bounced softly, testing the board, then positioned her arms in front of her.

He opened the door of the pool house just as her feet lifted from the board. He wanted her to see him when she was in midair. Just before she hit the water. He wanted her to understand how vulnerable she was.

In that split second, their eyes locked. He caught her expression as she plunged into the water. She was terrified, aware that she was incapable of flight.

He was in the pool before she had surfaced. He hugged her against his chest, laughing as she flailed about, kicking her feet. How foolish she was. She should simply accept the inevitable. "You're going to die," he whispered, his voice calm, even.

Her hair was in his face, blinding him. Impatiently he shook it away. He didn't want to be distracted from the pleasure of feeling her struggle.

The end was coming. In her craving for breath, she had opened her mouth and was gulping water. He felt her final frantic effort to break away from him, then the hopelessly feeble tremors as her body began to go limp. He pressed her close, wishing he could read her mind.

Was she praying? Was she begging God to save her? Was she seeing the light that people who have experienced a near-death event claim to have seen?

He waited a full three minutes before he released her. With a satisfied smile he watched as her body sank to the bottom of the pool.

It was five minutes after seven when he climbed out of the pool, pulled on a sweatshirt, shorts, sneakers, a cap, and dark glasses. He had already chosen the spot where he would leave the silent reminder of his visit, the calling card that everybody always missed.

At six minutes past seven he began to jog down the quiet street, another early morning fitness buff in a city of fitness buffs.

Sam Deegan had not intended to open the file on Karen Sommers that afternoon. He'd been fishing through the bottom drawer of his desk in search of the packet of cold pills he vaguely remembered having stashed there. When his fingers touched the well-worn and troublingly familiar folder, he hesitated and then, with a grimace, pulled it out and opened it. When he looked at the date on the first page, he realized that he had been subconsciously intending to find it. The anniversary of Karen Sommers' death was Columbus Day, twenty years ago next week.

The file ought to have been kept with the other unsolved cases, but three successive Orange County prosecutors had indulged his need to keep it at his fingertips. Twenty years ago Sam had been the first detective to arrive in response to the frantic phone call from a woman screaming that her daughter had been stabbed.

Minutes later, when he had arrived at the house on Mountain Road in Cornwall-on-Hudson, he had found the victim's bedroom crowded with shocked and horrified onlookers. One neighbor was bent over the bed uselessly trying to administer mouth-to-mouth resuscitation. Others were attempting to pull the hysterical parents away from the heartbreaking sight of their daughter's brutalized body.

Karen Sommers' shoulder-length hair was spilling onto the pillow. When he yanked the would-be rescuer back, Sam could see the vicious stab wounds in Karen's chest and heart that must have caused instant death and had drenched the sheets with her blood.

He remembered his initial thought had been that the young woman probably never even heard her attacker enter her room. She probably never woke up, he reflected, shaking his head as he opened the folder. The mother's screams had attracted not only neighbors but a landscaper and delivery man who were on the premises next door. The result was a thoroughly compromised crime scene.

There had been no signs of forced entry. Nothing was missing. Karen Sommers had been a twenty-two-year-old first-year medical student who surprised her parents by coming home for an overnight visit. The logical suspect was her ex-boyfriend, Cyrus Lindstrom, a third-year law student at Columbia. He admitted that Karen had told him she wanted both of them to start seeing other people, but he also insisted that he had agreed it was a good idea because neither one of them was ready for a serious commitment. His alibi—that he had been asleep in the apartment he shared with three other law students—was verified, although all three roommates admitted they had gone to bed by midnight and therefore did not know whether or not Lindstrom had left the apartment after that time. Karen's death was estimated to have taken place between two and three in the morning.

Lindstrom had visited the Sommers house a few times. He knew a spare key was kept under the fake rock near the back door. He knew that Karen's room was the first one to the right off the back staircase. But that wasn't proof that in the middle of the night he had driven fifty miles from Amsterdam Avenue and 104th Street in Manhattan to Cornwall-on-Hudson and killed her.

"A person of interest"—that's what we call people like Lindstrom today, Sam reflected. I always thought that guy was as guilty as sin. I could never understand why the Sommers family stood by him. God, you'd have thought they were defending their own son.

Impatiently, Sam dropped the file on his desk, got up, and walked to the window. From his perspective he could see the parking lot, and he remembered the time a prisoner on trial for murder had overpowered a guard, dropped out the window of the courthouse, raced across the lot, mugged a guy getting into his car, and driven away.

We got him in twenty minutes, Sam thought. So why in twenty years can't I find the animal who killed Karen Sommers? For my money, it's still Lindstrom.

Lindstrom was now a high-powered New York criminal attorney. He's a master at getting the murdering bums off, Sam thought. Appropriate, since he's one of them.

He shrugged. It was a rotten day, rainy and unusually

cold for early October. I used to love this job, he thought, but it's not the same anymore. I'm ready to retire. I'm fifty-eight years old; I've been at police work most of my life. I should just take the pension and run. Lose a little weight. Visit the kids and spend more time with the grandkids. Before you know it, they'll be in college.

He had a vague sense of a headache brewing as he ran a hand through his thinning hair. Kate used to tell me to stop doing that, he thought. She said I was weakening the roots.

With a half smile at his late wife's unscientific analysis of his approaching baldness, he went back to his desk and stared down again at the file marked "Karen Sommers."

He still regularly visited Karen's mother, Alice, who had moved to a condominium in town. He knew it comforted her to feel that they were still trying to find the person who had taken her daughter's life, but it was more than that. Sam had a feeling that someday Alice would mention something that had never occurred to her as being important, something that would be the first step toward finding out who had gone into Karen's room that night.

That's what has kept me in this job the last couple of years, he thought. I wanted so much to solve this case, but I can't wait any longer.

He went back to his desk, opened the bottom drawer, and then hesitated. He should let it go. It was time to put this folder with the other unsolved cases in the general file. He'd done his best. For the first twelve years after the murder, he'd gone to the cemetery on the anniversary. He'd stayed there all day, hidden behind a mausoleum, watching Karen's grave. He'd even wired the tombstone to catch anything a visitor might say. There'd been some cases where killers had been caught because they'd paid an anniversary visit to their victim's grave, even talking about the crime to their victim.

The only people who ever came to Karen's grave on the anniversary were her parents, and it had been a gut-wrenching intrusion of privacy to hear them reminisce about their only daughter. He'd given up going there eight years ago, after Michael Sommers died and Alice came alone to stand at the grave where her husband and daughter were now resting side by side. That was when he walked away, not wanting to be a witness to her grief. He'd never gone back.

Sam stood up and put the Karen Sommers file under his arm, his decision made. He wouldn't look at it again. And next week, on the twentieth anniversary of Karen's death, he'd put in his retirement papers.

And I'll stop by the cemetery, he thought. Just to let her know how sorry I am that I didn't do better by her.

It had taken nearly seven hours to drive from Washington through Maryland, Delaware, and New Jersey to the town of Cornwall-on-Hudson.

It was not a trip Jean Sheridan enjoyed making—not so much because of the distance, but because Cornwall, the town in which she had grown up, was filled with painful memories.

She had promised herself that no matter how persuasively charming Jack Emerson, the chairman of their twentieth high school reunion committee, attempted to be, she would plead work, other commitments, health—anything to avoid being part of it.

She had no desire to celebrate her graduation twenty years ago from Stonecroft Academy, even though she was grateful for the education she'd received there. She didn't even care about the "Distinguished Alumna" medal she'd be receiving, despite the fact that the scholarship to Stonecroft had been a stepping-stone to the scholarship to Bryn Mawr and then the doctorate at Princeton.

But now that a memorial for Alison had become part of the reunion schedule, it was impossible for her to refuse to attend.

Alison's death still seemed so unreal that Jean almost expected the phone to ring and hear that familiar voice, the words clipped and rushed as though everything had to be said in the space of ten seconds: "Jeannie. You haven't called lately. You've forgotten I'm alive. I hate you. No, I don't. I love you. I'm in awe of you. You're so damn smart. There's a premiere in New York next week. Curt Ballard is one of my clients. An absolutely terrible actor, but so gorgeous nobody cares. And his latest girlfriend is coming, too. You'd faint if I even whispered her name. Anyhow, can you make it next Tuesday, cocktails at six, the film, then a private dinner for twenty or thirty or fifty?"

Alison always did manage to get that kind of message across in about ten seconds, Jean thought, and Alison was always shocked when ninety percent of the time Jean couldn't drop everything and race to New York to join her.

Alison had been dead almost a month. Impossible as that was to believe, the fact that she might have been the victim of foul play was unbearable. But during her career she had made scores of enemies. No one got to head one of the largest talent agencies in the country without being hated. Besides, Alison's rapier-like wit and biting sarcasm had been compared to the stinging utterances of the legendary Dorothy Parker. Was someone whom she had ridiculed or fired been angry enough to kill her? Jean wondered.

I like to think that she had a fainting spell after she

dove into the pool. I don't want to believe that anyone held her under the water, she thought.

She glanced at the shoulder bag beside her on the passenger seat, and her mind raced to the envelope inside it. What am I going to do? Who sent it to me and why? How could anyone have found out about Lily? Is she in trouble? Oh, God, what shall I do? What *can* I do?

These questions had caused her weeks of sleepless nights ever since she had received the report from the laboratory.

She was at the turnoff that led from Route 9W to Cornwall. And near Cornwall was West Point. Jean swallowed over the lump in her throat and tried to concentrate on the beauty of the October afternoon. The trees were breathtaking with their autumn colors of gold and orange and fiery red. Above them, the mountains, as always, were serenely calm. The Hudson River Highlands. I'd forgotten how beautiful it is here, she thought.

But of course that thought led inevitably to the memory of Sunday afternoons at West Point, sitting on the steps of the monument on an afternoon such as this. She had begun her first book there, a history of West Point.

It took ten years to finish, she thought, mainly because for a long time I simply couldn't write about it.

Cadet Carroll Reed Thornton, Jr., from Maryland. Don't think about Reed now, Jean warned herself.

The turn from Route 9W onto Walnut Street was

still an automatic reaction rather than a considered decision. The Glen-Ridge House in Cornwall, named after one of the town's large boardinghouses of the mid-nineteenth century, was the hotel chosen for the reunion. There had been ninety students in her graduating class. According to the latest update she'd received, forty-two of them were planning to attend, plus wives and husbands or significant others, and children.

She hadn't had to make any of those extra reservations for herself.

It had been Jack Emerson's decision to have the reunion in October rather than June. He'd done a poll of the class and determined that June was when their own kids were graduating from high school or grammar school, making it more difficult for them to get away.

In the mail she'd received her ID badge with her senior class picture on top and her name emblazoned under it. It had come with the schedule of events for the weekend: Friday night, opening cocktail party and buffet. Saturday, breakfast buffet, tour of West Point, the Army-Princeton football game, and then cocktail party and black-tie dinner. Sunday was supposed to have concluded the reunion with a brunch at Stonecroft, but after Alison's death it had been decided to include a morning memorial service in her honor. She had been buried in the cemetery adjacent to the school, and the service would be at graveside.

In her will, Alison had left a large donation to the scholarship fund at Stonecroft, which was the primary reason for the hastily planned memorial ceremony.

Main Street doesn't feel very different, Jean thought as she drove slowly through the town. It had been many years since she'd been here. The summer she graduated from Stonecroft, her father and mother had finally split, sold the house, and gone their separate ways. Her father was now managing a hotel in Maui. Her mother had moved back to Cleveland where she had been raised and had married her high school sweetheart. "My biggest mistake was not marrying Eric thirty years ago," she'd gushed at the wedding.

And where does that leave me? That was the thought that ran through Jean's mind at that moment. But the breakup had at least meant the merciful end of her life in Cornwall.

She resisted the impulse to detour to Mountain Road and drive past her old home. Maybe I will sometime over the weekend, she thought, but not now. Three minutes later she was pulling into the driveway of the Glen-Ridge House, and the doorman, a professionally warm smile creasing his face, was opening the door of the car and saying, "Welcome home." Jean pushed the button for the trunk and watched as her garment bag and suitcase were scooped up.

"Go right to the check-in desk," the doorman urged. "We'll take care of the luggage."

The hotel lobby was clubby and warm, with deep carpeting and comfortable groupings of chairs. The front desk was to the left, and diagonally across from it Jean could see that the bar was already filling with pre–cocktail party celebrants.

A banner over the front desk welcomed the Stonecroft reunion class.

"Welcome home, Ms. Sheridan," said the clerk, a man in his sixties. His smile revealed glistening white teeth. His badly dyed hair exactly matched the finish on the cherrywood desk. As Jean gave him her credit card, she had the incongruous thought that he might have cut a chip from the desk to show his barber.

She wasn't ready to deal with any of her old classmates yet and hoped she could get to the elevator without being stopped. She wanted to have at least a quiet half hour while she showered and changed, before she had to put on her badge with the picture of the frightened and heartbroken eighteen-year-old girl she had been, and join her former classmates at the cocktail party.

As she took the room key and turned, the clerk said, "Oh, Ms. Sheridan, I almost forgot. I have a fax for you." He squinted at the name on the envelope. "Oh, sorry. I should be calling you Dr. Sheridan."

Without replying, Jean ripped open the envelope. The fax was from her secretary at Georgetown: "Dr. Sheridan, sorry to bother you. This is probably a joke or mistake, but I thought you'd want to see it." The "it" was a single sheet of paper that had been faxed to her office. It read, "Jean, I guess by now you've verified that I know Lily. Here's my problem. Do I kiss her or kill her? Just a joke. I'll be in touch."

For a moment Jean felt unable either to move or think. Kill her? Kill her? But why? Why?

He had been standing in the bar, watching, waiting for her to come in. Over the years he'd seen her picture on her book jackets, and every time he did, it was a shock to see that Jeannie Sheridan had acquired such a classy look.

At Stonecroft she'd been one of the smart but quiet ones. She'd even been nice to him in an offhand sort of way. He'd started to really like her until Alison told him how they'd all made fun of him. He knew who "they" were: Laura and Catherine and Debra and Cindy and Gloria and Alison and Jean. They used to sit at the same table at lunchtime.

Weren't they cute? he thought as the bile rose in his throat. Now Catherine and Debra and Cindy and Gloria and Alison were gone. He'd saved Laura for last. The funny part was that he still wasn't sure about Jean. For some reason he wavered about killing her. He still remembered the time when he was a freshman and had tried out for the baseball team. He'd been cut right away and had started to cry, those baby tears that he never could hold back.

Crybaby. Crybaby.

He'd run off the field, and a little later Jeannie had caught up with him. "I didn't make the cheerleader squad," she said. "So what?"

He knew she had followed him because she felt sorry for him. That's why something told him that she hadn't been one of the ones who made fun of him for wanting to take Laura to the prom. But then she had hurt him in a different way

Laura had always been the prettiest girl in the class—golden blond, china blue eyes, great body, noticeable even in the Stonecroft skirt and blouse. She was always sure of her power over the guys. The words "come hither" had been meant for her to utter.

Alison had always been mean. As a writer for the school paper, her "Behind the Scenes" column was supposed to be about school activities, but she always managed to find a way to take a dig at someone, like in a review for the school play when she'd written, "To everyone's surprise, Romeo, a.k.a. Joel Nieman, managed to remember most of his lines." Back then the popular kids thought Alison was a riot. The nerds stayed away from her.

Nerds like me, he thought, savoring the memory of the look of terror on Alison's face when she saw him coming toward her from the pool house.

Jean had been popular, but she hadn't seemed like the other girls. She'd been elected to the student council, where she'd been so quiet you'd think she couldn't talk, but anytime she opened her mouth, whether there or in class, she always had the right answer. Even then she'd been a history buff. What surprised him was how much prettier she was now. Her stringy light brown hair was darker and fuller, and cut like a cap around her face. She was slim, but not painfully thin anymore. Somewhere along the way she'd also learned how to dress. Her jacket and slacks were well cut. Wishing he could see the expression on her face, he watched as she shoved a fax into her shoulder bag.

"I am the owl, and I live in a tree."

In his head he could hear Laura imitating him. "She has you down pat," Alison had screeched that night twenty years ago. "And she told us you wet your pants, too."

He could imagine them all making fun of him; he could hear their shrill gales of mocking laughter.

It had happened way back in the second grade when he was seven years old. He'd been in the school play. That was his line, the only thing he had to say. But he couldn't get it out. He'd stuttered so much that all the kids on stage and even some of the parents began to snicker.

"I ammm th-th-the oooooowwwwwlllll, and, and I livvvvve in aaaaaa . . ."

He never did get the word "tree" out. That was when he burst out crying and ran off the stage holding the tree branch in his hand. His father had slapped him for being a sissy. His mother had said, "Leave him alone. He's a dopey kid. What can you expect? Look at him. He's wet his pants again."

The memory of that shame mingled with the imagined laughter of the girls and swirled in his head as he watched Jean Sheridan get into the elevator. Why should I spare you? he thought. Maybe Laura first, then you. Then you can all have a good laugh at me, all of you together, in hell.

He heard his name being called and turned his head. Dick Gormley, the big baseball hero of their class, was standing beside him in the bar, staring at his ID. "Great to see you," Dick said heartily.

You're lying, he thought, and it's *not* great to see you.

Laura had barely put her key in the door of the room when the bellman appeared with her luggage: a garment bag, two large suitcases, and an overnight satchel. She could sense what the man was thinking: *Lady, the reunion lasts for forty-eight hours, not two weeks.*

What he said was "Ms. Wilcox, my wife and I used to watch *Henderson County* every Tuesday night. We thought you were great in it. Any chance it will be coming back?"

Not the chance of a snowball in hell, Laura thought, but the man's obvious sincerity gave her a much-needed lift. "Not *Henderson County,* but I've done a pilot for Maximum Channel," she said. "It's scheduled to go on the air after the first of the year."

Not the truth, but close to the truth. Maximum had okayed the pilot and announced it was optioning the series. Then two days before she died, Alison had phoned. "Laura, honey, I don't know how to tell you this, but there's a problem. Maximum wants someone younger to play Emmie."

"Younger?" she had shouted. "For God's sake, Alison, I'm thirty-eight. The mother in the series has a twelve-year-old daughter. And I look good. You know I do."

"Don't yell at me," Alison had shouted back. "I'm doing my best to convince them to keep you. As for looking good, between laser-surgery and botox and face-lifts, everybody in this business looks good. That's why it's so hard to cast anyone as a grandmother. Nobody looks like one anymore."

We agreed to come to the reunion together, Laura thought. Alison told me that, according to the list of classmates who'd responded yes, Gordon Amory would be here, and apparently he just bought into Maximum. She said that he had enough influence to help me keep the job, assuming he could be convinced to use his power.

She had pushed and pushed Alison to call Gordie right away and make him force Maximum to accept her for the role. Finally Alison had said, "First of all, don't call him Gordie. He hates it. Second, I was trying to be tactful, something as you well know I rarely trouble to be. I'll say it straight. You're still beautiful, but you're not much of an actress. The people at Maximum think this series could turn out to be a real hit, but not with you in it. Maybe Gordon can change their minds. You can charm him. He had a crush on you, didn't he?"

The bellman had gone down the hall to fill the ice bucket. Now he tapped on the door and came back in. Without even thinking, Laura had already opened her purse and pulled out a twenty-dollar bill. His fervent "Thanks so much, Ms. Wilcox," made her wince. Once again she had played the big shot. Ten bucks would have been plenty.

Gordie Amory had been one of the guys who'd had a really big crush on her when they were at Stonecroft. Who'd have guessed that he'd end up such a big shot? God, you never know, Laura thought as she unzipped the garment bag. We should all have a crystal ball to look into the future.

The closet was small. Small room. Small windows. Dark brown carpet, brown upholstered chair, bed-spread in tones of pumpkin and brown. Impatiently, Laura pulled out the cocktail dresses and evening suit she'd carried in the garment bag. She already knew that she'd wear the Chanel tonight. Go for glitter. Knock them dead. Look successful, even if you are behind in your taxes and the IRS has a lien on the house.

Alison had said that Gordie Amory was divorced. Her final advice rang in Laura's ears: "Look, honey, if you can't talk him into using you in the series, maybe you can get him to marry you. I understand he's mighty impressive. Forget what a nerd he was at Stonecroft."

"Anything else I can do for you, Dr. Sheridan?" the bellman asked.

Jean shook her head.

"You feel all right, Doctor? You look kind of pale."

"I'm fine. Thank you."

"Well, you just let us know if there's anything we can do for you."

At last the door closed behind him, and Jean could sink down on the edge of the bed. She had jammed the fax into the side panel of her shoulder bag. Now she grabbed it and reread the cryptic sentences: "Jean, I guess by now you've verified that I know Lily. Here's my problem. Do I kiss her or kill her? Just a joke. I'll be in touch."

Twenty years ago Dr. Connors had been the physician in Cornwall to whom she had confided her pregnancy. He had reluctantly agreed with her that involving her parents would be a mistake. "I'm going to give up the baby for adoption no matter what they say. I'm eighteen, and it's my decision. But they'll be upset and angry and make my life even more miserable than it is," she had said, weeping.

Dr. Connors told her about the couple who had finally given up hope that they would have their own child and who were planning to adopt. "If you're sure you're not going to keep the baby, I can promise you they will give it a wonderful, loving home."

He had arranged for her to work in a nursing home in Chicago until the baby was due. Then he flew to Chicago, delivered it, and took the baby from her. The following September she began college, and ten years later learned that Dr. Connors died of a heart attack after a fire consumed his medical offices. Jean had heard that all his records were lost.

But perhaps they weren't lost. And if not, who found them, and why after all these years is that person contacting me? Jean agonized.

Lily—that was the name she'd given to the baby whom she'd carried for nine months and then had known for only four hours. Three weeks before Reed's graduation from West Point and hers from Stonecroft, she had realized she was pregnant. They had both been frightened but agreed that they would get married immediately after graduation.

"My parents will love you, Jeannie," Reed had insisted. But she knew he was worried about their reaction. He admitted that his father had warned him about getting serious with anyone until he was at least twenty-five. He never got to tell them about her. A week before graduation he'd been killed by a hit-and-run driver on the West Point campus who'd been speeding along the narrow road on which he was walking. Instead of watching Reed graduate fifth in his class, General, now retired, and Mrs. Carroll Reed Thornton accepted the diploma and sword of their late son in a special presentation at the graduation ceremony.

They never knew they had a granddaughter.

Even if someone had salvaged the record of her adoption, how would he or she have gotten close enough to Lily to take her hairbrush, with long, golden strands of her hair still caught in its bristles? Jean wondered.

That first terrifying communication had contained the brush and a note telling her to "Check the DNA—it's your kid." Stunned, Jean had submitted strands from the lock of hair she had kept from her baby, along with her own DNA sample and strands from the brush to a private DNA laboratory. The report had unequivocally confirmed her worst fears—the hairs on the brush had come from her now nineteen-and-a-half-year-old daughter.

Or is it possible that the wonderful, caring couple who adopted her know who I am, and this is a buildup to asking me for money?

There had been a lot of publicity when her book about Abigail Adams became a best-seller and then a very successful film.

Let it be only about money, Jean prayed as she stood up and reached for the suitcase that it was time to unpack.

6

Carter Stewart threw his garment bag on the bed. Besides underwear and socks, it contained a couple of Armani jackets and several pairs of slacks. On impulse he decided to go to the first-night party in the jeans and sweater he was wearing.

In school he'd been a scrawny, untidy kid, the child of a scrawny, untidy mother. When she did remember to throw clothes in the washer, as often as not she was out of detergent. Then she'd toss in bleach, ruining whatever garments were in the machine. Until he started hiding his clothes from her and then laundering them himself, he'd gone to school in slightly soiled or freakish-looking attire.

Being too dressed up when he first met his former classmates might bring on remarks about how he used to look. Now what would they see when they looked at him? Not the shrimp he'd been most of the high school years but now of average height with a disciplined body. Unlike some of the others he'd spotted in the lobby, he had no gray strands in his full head of well-barbered dark brown hair. His ID showed him with shaggy hair and his eyes almost shut. A columnist had recently referred to his "dark brown eyes that suddenly flicker with a hint of yellow flames when he is angry."

Impatiently he looked around the room. He'd worked in this hotel the summer of his junior year at Stonecroft. He'd probably been in this dumpy room any number of times, carrying room service trays to businessmen, to ladies on a tour of the Hudson Valley, or to parents visiting their kids at West Point—or, he thought, even to trysting couples who were sneaking away from their homes and families. I could always spot those, he thought. He used to smirk and ask those couples, "Would this be a honeymoon?" when he brought up their breakfasts. The guilty expression on their faces had been priceless.

He'd hated this place then and he hated it now, but since he was here, he might as well go downstairs and start the backslapping, "great-to-see-you" ritual.

Making sure he was carrying the piece of plastic that passed for a room key, he left the room and walked down the corridor to the elevator.

The Hudson Valley Suite where the opening cocktail party was being held was on the mezzanine floor. When he stepped off the elevator, he could hear the electronically enhanced music and the voices trying to yell above it. There looked to be about forty or fifty people already gathered there. Two waiters with trays holding glasses of wine were standing at the entrance. He took a glass of the red and sampled it. Lousy merlot. He might have guessed.

He started into the suite, then felt a tap on his shoulder. "Mr. Stewart, I'm Jake Perkins, and I'm covering the reunion for the *Stonecroft Gazette*. May I ask you a few questions?"

Sourly, Stewart turned and looked at the nervously eager redheaded kid standing inches away from him. The first thing you learn when you want something is not to get in the other guy's face, he thought irritably as he tried to step back and felt his shoulders brush against the wall. "I would suggest we step outside and find a quiet spot unless you can read lips, Jake."

"That's not my talent, I'm afraid, sir. Outside is a good idea. Just follow me."

After a split second's consideration, Stewart decided not to abandon the wine. Shrugging, he turned and followed the student down the corridor.

"Before we begin, Mr. Stewart, may I tell you how much I enjoy your plays. I want to be a writer myself. I mean, I guess I am a writer, but I want to be a successful one like you."

Oh, God, Stewart thought. "Everyone who interviews me says the same thing. Most, if not all of you, won't make it."

He waited for the expression of anger or embarrassment that usually followed that statement. Instead, to his disappointment, the baby-faced Jake Perkins smiled cheerfully. "But I will," he said. "I'm absolutely sure of that. Mr. Stewart, I've done a lot of research on you and the others who are being honored. You all have one thing in common. The three women were achievers when they were here, but not one of you four men created much of a stir at Stonecroft. I mean, in your own case, I couldn't find a single activity listed in your yearbook, and your marks were only mediocre. You didn't write for the school paper or—"

The nerve of this kid, Stewart thought. "In my day, the school paper was amateurish even for a school paper," he snapped, "as I'm sure it still is. I was never athletic, and my writing was restricted to a personal journal."

"Is that journal the basis for any of your plays?"

"Perhaps."

"They're all pretty dark."

"I have no illusions about life, nor did I have any when I was a student here."

"Then would you say that your years at Stonecroft were not happy?"

Carter Stewart took a sip of the merlot. "They were not happy," he said evenly.

"Then what brought you back to the reunion?"

Stewart smiled coldly. "The opportunity to be interviewed by you. Now if you'll excuse me, I see Laura Wilcox, the glamour queen of our class, getting out of the elevator. Let's see if she recognizes me."

He ignored the sheet of paper that Perkins was trying to hand him.

"If you'd just give me one minute more, Mr. Stewart. I have a list here that I think you'll find of great interest."

Perkins studied the back of Carter Stewart's lean frame as he walked with swift strides to catch up with the glamorous blonde now walking into the Hudson

Valley Suite. Nasty to me, Perkins thought, jeans and sweater and sneakers to show his contempt for everyone here who's all duded-up for the night. He's not the kind to show up just to collect some crummy, meaningless medal. So what really brings him here anyhow?

It was the question he'd ask in the last sentence of his article. He'd already done plenty of research on Carter Stewart. He'd started writing in college, offbeat one-act plays that were performed by the drama department and that led to a postgraduate stint at Yale. That was when he dropped his first name, Howard—or Howie, as he'd been called at Stonecroft. He had his first Broadway hit before he was thirty. He was reputed to be a loner who escaped to one of his four homes around the country when he was working on a play. Withdrawn, unpleasant, perfectionist, genius—those were some of the words used to describe him in articles. I have a few others I could add, Jake Perkins thought grimly. And I will.

7

It took Mark Fleischman longer than he had expected to drive from Boston to Cornwall. He had hoped to have a couple of hours in which to walk around the town before having to face his former classmates. He wanted to have a chance to figure out the difference between his perception of himself as it had been when he was growing up there and the reality, as he understood it, of who he was now. Am I hoping to exorcise my own demons? he wondered.

As he drove with maddening slowness down the congested Connecticut Turnpike, he kept thinking of the statement he'd heard that morning from the father of one of his patients: "Doctor, you know as well as I do that kids are cruel. They were cruel in my day, and they haven't changed. They're like a pride of lions stalking the wounded prey. That's what they're doing to my kid now. That's what they did to me when I was his age. And you know what, Doctor? I'm a pretty successful guy, but when I go to an occasional reunion at my prep school, in ten seconds I'm not the CEO of a Fortune 500 company. I'm back to feeling like the clumsy nerd everyone else had fun picking on. Crazy, isn't it?"

As the car once again slowed to a crawl, Mark decided that, in hospital terminology, the Connecticut Turnpike was in a constant state of intensive care. There was always a huge construction project going on somewhere along the way, the kind of project that meant cramming three lanes into only one, causing inevitable traffic jams.

He found himself comparing the turnpike problems to problems he saw in patients, such as the boy whose father had come in for the conference. The child had attempted suicide last year. Another kid, ignored and tormented as he had been, might have gotten a gun and turned it on his classmates. Anger and hurt and humiliation were squeezed together and forced into one outlet. Some people tried to destroy themselves when that happened; others tried to destroy their tormentors.

A psychiatrist who specialized in adolescents, Mark had an advice and call-in television program that had recently become syndicated. The response had been gratifying. "Tall, lanky, cheerful, funny, and wise, Dr. Mark Fleischman brings a no-nonsense approach to helping solve the problems of that painful rite-of-passage called adolescence"—that's what one critic had written about the show.

Maybe I can put it all behind me after this weekend, he thought.

He hadn't taken time for lunch, so after he finally got to the hotel, he went into the bar and ordered a sandwich and a light beer. When the bar suddenly began to fill up with reunion attendees, he quickly got his check, left half the sandwich uneaten, and made his way up to his room.

It was a quarter of five, and the shadows were heavy and closing in. For a few minutes he stood at the window. The knowledge of what he had to do weighed heavily on him. But after that, I'll put it all behind me, he thought. The slate will be clean. Then I really will be able to be cheerful and funny—and maybe even wise.

He felt his eyes begin to moisten and abruptly turned from the window.

———

Gordon Amory went down in the elevator with his ID in his pocket. He would slip it on when he got to the party. For now, it was amusing to stand unrecognized by his former classmates and glance at their names and pictures as, floor by floor, they got into the elevator.

Jenny Adams was the last one to get on. She'd been a bovine kid, and while she had slimmed down some, she was still a big woman. There was something unmistakably small-town suburban in the cheap brocade suit and off-the-pushcart costume jewelry she was wearing. She was accompanied by a burly guy whose beefy arms were straining the seams of his too-tight jacket. Both were smiling broadly and said a general hello to the occupants of the elevator.

Gordon did not reply. The half-dozen others, all wearing their tags, sent out a chorus of greetings. Trish

Canon, whom Gordon remembered as being on the track team and who was still beanpole thin, squealed, "Jenny! You look marvelous!"

"Trish Canon!" Jenny's arms flew around her former classmate. "Herb, Trish and I used to pass each other notes in math. Trish, this is my husband, Herb."

"And my husband, Barclay," Trish said. "And—"

The elevator stopped at the mezzanine. As they stepped out, Gordon reluctantly took out his ID and put it on. Expensive plastic surgery had made sure that he no longer looked like the weasel-faced kid in the school picture. His nose was now straight, his formerly heavy-lidded eyes now wide. His chin was sculpted, and his ears lay flat against his head. Implants and the artistry of a top colorist had transformed his formerly thin and drab brown hair into a thick chestnut mane. He knew he was now a handsome man. The only outward manifestation of the tortured kid he had been was that in moments of great stress he could not stop himself from biting his nails.

The Gordie they knew doesn't exist, he told himself as he started toward the Hudson Valley Suite. He felt a tap on his shoulder and turned.

"Mr. Amory."

A baby-faced, redheaded kid with a notebook was standing next to him.

"I'm Jake Perkins, a reporter for the *Stonecroft Gazette*. I'm interviewing the honorees. Could I just have a minute of your time?"

Gordon managed a warm smile. "Of course."

"May I begin by saying that you've changed a lot in the twenty years since your senior picture."

"I guess I have."

"You already owned the majority share of four cable television channels. Why did you buy into Maximum?"

"Maximum has a reputation for strong family programming. I decided it would round out our ability to reach a segment of the audience I wanted in our entertainment portfolio."

"There's been buzz about a new series and a rumor that your former classmate Laura Wilcox may be the star. Is that true?"

"There has been no casting yet on the series you mention."

"Your crime and punishment channel has been criticized as being too violent. Do you agree?"

"No, I do not. It offers genuine reality, not those made-up ludicrous situations that are the bread and butter of the commercial networks. Now if you'll excuse me."

"One more question, please. Would you just glance at this list?"

Impatiently, Gordon Amory took the sheet of paper from Perkins.

"Do you recognize those names?"

"They seem to be some of my former classmates."

"They are five women, members of this class, who have died or disappeared during these twenty years."

"I didn't realize that."

Perkins pointed. "I was astonished when I began my

research. It started with Catherine Kane nineteen years ago. Her car skidded into the Potomac when she was a freshman at George Washington University. Cindy Lang vanished when she was skiing at Snowbird. Gloria Martin was an apparent suicide. Debra Parker piloted her own plane, and six years ago it crashed, killing her. Last month, Alison Kendall drowned in her pool. Wouldn't you say it would be fair to call this a hard luck class, and maybe do a program on your network about it?"

"I would prefer to call it a 'tragedy-ridden' class, and, no, I would not want to do a program about it. Now if you'll excuse me."

"Of course. Just one more question. What does receiving this medal from Stonecroft mean to you?"

Gordon Amory smiled. *It means I can say a pox on your house. In spite of the misery I endured here, I've made it big—that's what he thought.* Instead he said, "It is the fulfillment of my dream to be considered a success in the eyes of my classmates."

8

Robby Brent had checked into the hotel on Thursday afternoon. He'd just finished a six-day engagement at the Trump Casino in Atlantic City where his famous comedy act had drawn its usual large audience. It made no sense to fly home to San Francisco only to come right back, and he hadn't felt like staying in Atlantic City or stopping in New York.

It had been a satisfactory decision, he decided as he dressed for the cocktail party. He reached in the closet for a dark blue jacket. Putting it on, he looked at himself critically in the mirror on the closet door. Lousy lighting, he thought, but he still looked okay. He'd been compared to Don Rickles, not only because of his swift-paced comedy act, but because of his appearance as well. Round face, shiny dome, a bit stocky — he could understand the comparison. Still, his looks hadn't stopped women from being attracted to him. Post Stonecroft, he added to himself, definitely post Stonecroft.

He still had a couple of minutes before it was time to go down. He walked over to the window and looked out, thinking about how yesterday, after he'd checked in, he'd walked around town, picking out the homes of the kids who, like him, were honorees at the reunion.

He'd passed Jeannie Sheridan's house. He'd thought about how a couple of times the cops had been called by the neighbors because her parents were scuffling with each other in the driveway. He had heard they divorced years ago. Probably lucky they had. People used to predict that one or the other would end up getting hurt during one of their fights.

Laura Wilcox's first house was right next to Jeannie's. Then her father inherited some money, and the family moved to the big house on Concord Avenue when they were sophomores. He remembered walking past Laura's first house when he was a kid, hoping she'd happen to come out so he could start a conversation with her.

A family named Sommers had bought Laura's house. Their daughter had been murdered in it. They'd sold it eventually. Most people don't hang around a place where their kid has been stabbed to death. That had been on Columbus Day weekend, he reflected.

The invitation to the reunion lay on the bed. He glanced at it. The names of the honorees and their bios were included in the packet. Carter Stewart. How long after Stonecroft did it take him to drop being called Howie? Robby wondered. Howie's mother had called herself an artist and was always seen around town with her sketch pad. Occasionally she'd persuade the art gallery to show some of her stuff. Really bad, Robby remembered. Howie's father had been a bully, always whacking him around. No wonder his plays were so dark. Howie used to run out of the house and hide from his old man in the neighbors' backyards. He may be successful, but inside he has to be the same sneak who used to peep in people's windows. Thought he got away with it, but I caught him a couple of times. He had a crush on Laura so intense it practically oozed from his pores.

As did I, Robby admitted, sneering down at the picture of Gordie Amory, the plastic surgery kid. Mr. Cover Boy himself. Yesterday, during his walk, he'd looked up Gordie's house and saw that it had been totally renovated. Originally an odd shade of blue, it was now twice the size and sparkling white—like Gordie's new teeth, Robby thought.

Gordie's first house had burned down when they were juniors. The joke in town was that it was the only way it could be thoroughly cleaned. Gordie's mother had kept the place looking like a pigpen. A lot of people thought that Gordie deliberately set the fire. I wouldn't have put it past him, Robby thought. He was always weird. Robby reminded himself to call Gordie "Gordon" when they met at the cocktail party. Over the years he'd run into him a few times—uptight as they come and another one who'd been crazy about Laura.

So was Mark Fleischman, the other guy being honored. At school Mark had never said boo to anyone, but you got the feeling there was a lot going on inside him. He'd always been in the shadow of his older brother, Dennis, who'd been an all-around big man at Stonecroft, top student, outstanding athlete. Everyone in town knew him. He'd been killed in a car accident the summer before their class began its freshman year. Different as day and night, the two brothers. It was well known around town that if God had to take one of their sons, Mark's parents would have preferred that he and not Dennis had been chosen. He had so much resentment built up inside him that it's a wonder the top of his head didn't come off, Robby thought grimly.

He reached for his room key, finally ready to face the crowd below, and then opened the door of his room. I either disliked or hated just about all of my classmates, he thought. Then why did I accept the invitation to come here? He pushed the button for the elevator. I'll get plenty of new material for the act, he promised himself. There was another reason of course, but he quickly pushed it out of his mind. I won't go there, he thought as the elevator door opened. At least not now.

9

As they arrived at the cocktail party, Jack Emerson, the chairman of the reunion committee, invited the honorees to step into the alcove at the end of the Hudson Valley Suite. A florid-faced man with the look of a drinker, indicated by the broken capillaries in his face, he was the only member of the class who had elected to stay in Cornwall and therefore was in place to do hands-on planning for this weekend. "When we introduce the class individually, I want to save you and the others for last," he explained.

Jean walked into the alcove in time to hear Gordon Amory observe, "Jack, I gather that we have you to thank that we're the ones to be honored."

"It was my idea," Emerson said heartily. "And you deserve it, one and all. Gordie, I mean Gordon, you're an outstanding figure in cable television. Mark is a psychiatrist with a reputation for being an expert in adolescent behavior. Robby is an outstanding comedian and mimic. Howie, I mean Carter Stewart, is a major playwright. Jean Sheridan—oh, here you are, Jean, so good to see you—is a dean and professor of history at Georgetown, and now she's a best-selling author. Laura Wilcox was the star of a long-running sitcom. And Alison

Kendall became head of a major talent agency. As you know, she would have been the seventh recipient. We'll send her plaque to her parents. They are very pleased to know that she is being honored by her graduating class."

The hard luck class, Jean thought with a stab of pain as Emerson rushed over to plant a kiss on her cheek. That had been the term that school reporter Jake Perkins had suggested when he'd grabbed her for an interview. What he'd told her had been a shock. I lost track of everyone except Alison and Laura after graduation, she remembered. The year Catherine died, I was in Chicago, supposedly choosing to work for a year before college. I knew that Debby Parker's plane crashed, but I didn't know about Cindy Lang and Gloria Martin. And only last month, Alison. Dear God, we all used to sit at the same table.

And now only Laura and I are left, she thought. What kind of karma is hanging over us?

Laura had phoned to say she'd meet her at the party. "Jeannie, I know we were talking about getting together earlier, but I'm not nearly ready. I have to make an entrance with all flags flying," she'd explained. "My object for the weekend is to woo and win Gordie Amory so that I can play the lead in his new TV series."

Instead of being disappointed, Jean realized she had been relieved. The respite had given her time to phone Alice Sommers, who had been their next-door neighbor years ago. Mrs. Sommers now lived in a townhouse near the parkway. The Sommerses had moved to Cornwall about two years before their daughter Karen was murdered. Jean never forgot the time when she'd been picked up at school by Mrs. Sommers. "Jean, why don't you come shopping with me?" she'd suggested. "I don't think you should go home right now."

That day she'd been spared the cringing embarrassment of seeing a squad car in front of her house and her parents being handcuffed. She never knew Karen Sommers well. Karen had been in Columbia Medical School in Manhattan, and the Sommerses kept an apartment in Manhattan. That was where they spent time with their daughter. In fact, until the night of her death, Karen had rarely come to Cornwall.

We've always kept in touch, Jean thought. When they came to Washington, they always called to invite me to dinner. Michael Sommers had died years ago, but Alice had learned about the reunion and called to say that Jean must come over for a ten o'clock breakfast before the scheduled visit to West Point.

In the time she might have visited with Laura, Jean had made up her mind. Tomorrow when she saw Alice, she would tell her about Lily and show her the faxes and the original letter with the hairbrush and strands of Lily's hair. Whoever knew about the baby must have seen Dr. Connors' records, she thought. It has to be someone who was around here at that time or who knew someone from around here who could get hold of the records. Alice might help me find the right person to talk to in law enforcement here. She had always said that they were still trying to find her Karen's murderer.

"Jean, it's good to see you again." Mark Fleischman

had been speaking to Robby Brent, but now he came over to her. "You look lovely, but upset. Did that kid reporter grab you?"

She nodded. "Yes, he did. Mark, I was shocked. I didn't know about anyone's death except Debby's and then, of course, Alison's."

Fleischman nodded. "Neither did I. In fact, I hadn't heard about Debby. I've never bothered with any of the stuff that came from Stonecroft until Jack Emerson contacted me."

"What did Perkins ask you?"

"Specifically, he wanted to know if since none of the five died together in some sort of multiple accident, wouldn't I, as a psychiatrist, find that many deaths in so small a group an unusually high number? I told him I didn't have to look up anything to know that the number was out of the ball park. Of course it was."

Jean nodded. "He told me that according to his research, that kind of statistic is much more likely to happen in wartime, but he said there are examples of families or classmates or members of a team that seem to be jinxed. Mark, I don't think it's jinxed. I think it's eerie."

Jack Emerson had overheard. The smile he'd worn while listing their accomplishments vanished and was replaced by a look of irritated concern. "I asked that Perkins kid to stop showing that list around," he said.

Carter Stewart came into the alcove with Laura Wilcox in time to hear Emerson. "I can assure you, he's showing it around," he said shortly. "My suggestion to anyone who has not yet been pounced upon by that young man is to tell him you do not wish to see it. It worked for me."

Jean was standing to the side of the entry, and Laura did not spot her when she walked in. "OK if I join you?" she joked. "Or have I wandered into the men's club by mistake?"

Smiling, she moved from one man to the other, closely examining their tags, then kissing each one of them on the cheek. "Mark Fleischman, Gordon Amory, Robby Brent, Jack Emerson. And, of course, Carter, whom I used to know as Howie and who hasn't kissed me yet. You all look marvelous. You see, there's the difference. I was at my peak at sixteen, and after that it was all downhill. You four and Howie, I mean Carter, were just starting up the hill in those days."

Then she spotted Jean and rushed to embrace her.

It was the icebreaker they needed. Mark Fleischman could see the notable relaxation as polite expressions became amused smiles and the better wines they'd put aside for the honorees began to be sipped.

Laura's still a knockout, he thought. Thirty-eight or -nine like the rest of us, but could pass for thirty. The cocktail suit she was wearing was clearly pricey, very pricey. The television series she'd been on had been cancelled a couple of years ago. He wondered how much work she'd had since then. He knew she'd had a messy divorce, with claims and counterclaims; he'd read about it on Page Six of the New York Post. He smiled to himself as she kissed Gordie a second time. "You used to have a crush on me," she teased him.

Then it was his turn. "Mark Fleischman," she said breathlessly. "I swear you were jealous when I was dating Barry Diamond. Am I right?"

He smiled. "Yes, you're right, Laura. But that was a long time ago."

"I know, but I haven't forgotten." Her smile was radiant.

He had once read that the Duchess of Windsor had the capacity to make every man she spoke to feel like the only man in the room. He watched as she turned to another familiar face.

"I haven't forgotten either, Laura," he said quietly. "Never for one *minute* have I forgotten."

10

It amused him to note that at the cocktail party Laura was, as usual, the center of attention, even though she was the least deserving of all the honorees. On the television series that had been the one feather in her cap, she had played a shallow blonde who only cared about the person she saw reflected in the mirror. The ultimate in typecasting, he thought.

There was no denying that she still looked damn good, but she was enjoying that final bloom before the change begins to take place. Already there were fine lines around her eyes and mouth. He remembered that her mother had that same papery skin, the kind that ages fast and hard. If Laura lived another ten years, even plastic surgery could only do so much for her.

But of course, she wasn't going to live another ten years.

Sometimes, even for months at a time, The Owl retreated to a secret spot deep inside him. During those times he was almost able to believe that all the things The Owl had done had been a dream. Other times, though, like now, he could feel it living inside him. He could see The Owl's head, its dark eyes surrounded by pools of yellow. He could feel how its talons grasp the limb of a tree. He could feel the touch of its soft velvety plumage, causing him to shiver inwardly. He could feel the rush of air beneath its wings as it swooped down on its prey.

Seeing Laura had brought The Owl rushing from its perch. Why had he waited so long to come to her? The Owl demanded to know, but he was afraid to answer. Was it, he wondered, because when Laura and Jean were finally destroyed, The Owl's power over life and death would vanish with them? Laura should have been dead twenty years ago. But that mistake had liberated him.

That mistake, that accident of fate, had transformed him from the stuttering crybaby—"I ammm th-th-the oooooowwwwwlllll and I livvvvve in aaaa . . ."—into The Owl, the predator, powerful and unflinching.

Someone was studying his ID, a guy with glasses and thinning hair, dressed in a reasonably expensive dark gray suit. Then the man smiled and held out his hand. "Joel Nieman," he said.

Joel Nieman. Oh, sure, he had been Romeo in the senior play. He was the one Alison had written about in her column: "To everyone's surprise, Romeo, a.k.a. Joel Nieman, managed to remember most of his lines."

"Did you give up on acting?" The Owl asked, smiling back.

Nieman looked surprised. "You have a good memory. I thought the stage could do without me," he said.

"I remember the review Alison wrote about you."

Nieman laughed. "So do I. I was going to tell her she did me a favor. I took up accounting, and it was a better way to go. Terrible shame about her, isn't it?"

"Terrible," The Owl agreed.

"I read that initially there was some question of a possible homicide investigation, but the police now pretty much believe that she passed out as she hit the water."

"Then I think the police are stupid."

Joel Nieman's expression became curious. "You think Alison was *murdered*?"

The Owl realized suddenly that perhaps he looked and sounded too vehement. "From what I read, she made a lot of enemies along the way," he said carefully. "But who knows? The police are probably right. That's why they always say that no one should go swimming alone."

"Romeo, my Romeo," a voice squealed.

Marcy Rogers, who had been Juliet in the school play, was tapping Nieman's shoulder. He spun around.

Marcy still wore her chestnut hair in a mass of tangled curls, but now it was highlighted with random streaks of gold. She struck a theatrical pose. "And all the world shall be in love with night."

"I can't believe it. It's Juliet!" Joel Nieman exclaimed, beaming.

Marcy glanced at The Owl. "Oh, hi." She turned back to Nieman. "You've got to meet my real life Romeo. He's over at the bar."

Dismissal. Just the way he'd always experienced it at

Stonecroft. Marcy hadn't even bothered to look at his ID. She simply wasn't interested in him.

The Owl looked around. Jean Sheridan and Laura Wilcox were standing next to each other on the buffet line. He studied Jean's profile. Unlike Laura, she was the kind of woman who got better looking as she aged. She looked decidedly different, although her features certainly hadn't changed. What had changed was her poise, her voice, the way she held herself. Oh, sure, her hair and clothes made a difference, but the change in her was more interior than outward. Growing up, she had to have been embarrassed by the way her parents carried on. A couple of times the cops had been exasperated enough to cuff them.

The Owl walked over to the buffet line and picked up a plate. He realized that he was beginning to understand his ambivalence toward Jean. During the years at Stonecroft, a couple of times, such as when he didn't make the football team, she'd gone out of her way to be nice to him. In fact, in the spring of senior year he'd actually considered asking her for a date. He had been sure she wasn't going out with anyone. Sometimes, on warm Saturday nights, he would hide behind a tree in lovers' lane and wait for the cars to drive there after the movies. He never saw Jean in one of them.

Positive thoughts aside, it was too late to change course now. Only a couple of hours ago, seeing her come into the hotel, he'd finally made up his mind to kill her, too. At this moment he understood why he had made that irrevocable decision. His mother used to say "still waters run deep." Jeannie may have acted nice to him a couple of times, but she was probably just like Laura underneath, snickering about the poor dope who had wet his pants and cried and stuttered.

He helped himself to salad. And so what if she hadn't been in lovers' lane with one of the jerks in their class, he reflected. Instead, Miss "Butter-Wouldn't-Melt-in-Her-Mouth" Jeannie had been romancing a West Point cadet—he knew all about that.

Fury lashed through him, alerting him that soon he would have to release The Owl.

He skipped the pasta, selected poached salmon and green beans with ham, and looked around. Laura and Jean had just settled at the honoree table. Jean caught his eye and waved him over. Lily looks just like you, he thought. The resemblance is really striking.

The thought sharpened his hunger.

11

At two o'clock, Jean gave up the attempt to sleep, turned on the light, and opened a book. But after reading for an hour and realizing that she had not absorbed one word, she restlessly put the book down and turned off the light again. Every muscle in her body felt wired and taut, and she had the beginning of a headache. She knew that the effort to socialize all evening, despite the constant gnawing worry that Lily might be in danger, had exhausted her. She realized that she was counting the hours until ten o'clock when she would visit Alice Sommers and tell her about Lily.

The same thoughts kept racing through her mind. *In all these years I've never mentioned her to a soul. The adoption was private. Dr. Connors is dead, and his records were destroyed. Who could have found out about her? Is it possible that her adoptive parents know my name and have kept track of me? Maybe they told someone else, and that person is the one contacting me now. But why?*

The window facing the back of the hotel was open, and the room was getting cold. After a moment's debate Jean sighed and pushed back the covers. *If I have any hope of getting some sleep, I'd better close it,* she thought. She got out of bed and padded across the room. Shivering as she cranked in the open panel, she happened to glance down. A car without its lights on was pulling into the self-parking area of the hotel parking lot. Curious, she watched as the figure of a man stepped out and began walking quickly toward the back entrance of the hotel.

His coat collar was up, but when he opened the door to the lobby, his face was clearly visible. Turning away from the window, Jean thought, I wonder what in the name of God one of our distinguished dinner partners found to do until this hour of the night.

12

The call came into police headquarters in Goshen at 3:00 A.M. Helen Whelan of Surrey Meadows was missing. A single woman in her early forties, she had last been seen by a neighbor. Whelan had been walking her German shepherd, Brutus, at or about midnight. At 3:00 A.M. a couple living a few blocks away at the edge of the county park were awakened by the howling and barking of a dog. They investigated and found a German shepherd trying to struggle to its feet. It had been savagely beaten on the head and back with a heavy instrument. A woman's size seven shoe was found on the road nearby.

———

At 4:00 A.M., Sam Deegan had been called in and assigned to the team of detectives investigating the disappearance. He stopped first to talk to Dr. Siegel, the veterinarian who had treated the wounded animal. "My guess is that he was knocked out for a couple of hours by the blows to his head," Siegel told Deegan. "They came from something about the size and weight of a tire iron."

Sam could visualize the scenario. Helen Whelan had let her dog off the leash for a run in the park. Someone seeing her standing alone in the road had tried to drag her into a car. The German shepherd had rushed to protect her and had been beaten senseless.

He drove to the street where the animal had been found and began ringing doorbells. At the fourth house an elderly man claimed he heard a dog barking frantically at about 12:30 A.M.

Helen Whelan was, or had been, a popular physical education teacher at Surrey Meadows High. Sam learned from several fellow teachers that her habit of walking her dog late at night was well known. "She was never nervous about it. She'd tell us that Brutus would be dead before he'd let anyone hurt her," the principal of her school said sadly.

"She was right," Sam told him. "The vet had to put Brutus down."

By ten o'clock that morning he could see that this case was not going to be an easy one to solve. According to her distraught sister who lived in nearby Newburgh, Helen had no enemies. She had been seeing a fellow teacher for several years, but he was on a sabbatical in Spain this semester.

Missing or dead? Sam was sure that anyone who had so savagely injured a dog would have no mercy on a woman. The difficult investigation would begin, and he would commence his share of it in Helen's neighborhood and at her school. There was always the chance that one of the weirdo teenagers the schools were spitting out today held a grudge against her. From her picture he could tell that she was a very attractive woman. Maybe some neighbor had fallen in love and been rejected.

He only hoped it wouldn't turn out to be one of those random crimes, committed by a stranger on a stranger, whose only fault was to be in the wrong place at the wrong time. That kind of crime was the hardest to investigate, and often went unsolved, something he hated.

That train of thought inevitably brought him to Karen Sommers. But her death wasn't hard to *solve*, Sam thought; it was only hard to *prove*.

Karen's killer was Cyrus Lindstrom, the boyfriend she dumped twenty years ago—of that he was sure. But as of next week, when I turn in my papers, I'll be off that case, Sam reminded himself.

And I'll be off yours, too, he thought, as with compassionate eyes he studied a recent picture of blue-eyed, auburn-haired Helen Whelan, who was now officially listed as "missing, presumed dead."

13

Laura had been tempted to sleep in and save her energy for the pre-game luncheon at West Point, but when she awoke on Saturday morning, she changed her mind. Her goal of romancing Gordie Amory had achieved only middling success at the dinner after the cocktail party. The honorees had sat together, and Jack Emerson had joined them. At first Gordie was quiet, but eventually he had warmed up some and even paid her a compliment. "I think every guy in our class had a crush on you at some point, Laura," he said.

"Why past tense?" she had teased.

His answer had been promising: "Why indeed?"

And then the evening provided an unexpected bonus. Robby Brent told the group that he'd been asked to do a situation comedy on HBO and he liked the script. "The public is finally getting sick of all the reality shows," he said, "and is ready to laugh. Think about the classic comedies: *I Love Lucy, All in the Family, The Honeymooners, The Mary Tyler Moore Show.* They had real humor, and, trust me, real humor is about to make a comeback." Then he'd looked at her. "You know, Laura, you really ought to read for the part of my wife. I have a feeling you'd be good."

She wasn't sure if he was kidding, since Robby made his living as a comic. On the other hand, if he *wasn't* kidding and if she didn't get to first base with Gordie, it might be yet another chance at grabbing the golden ring—perhaps her last chance.

"Last chance." Unintentionally, she whispered the words aloud. They gave her a funny, queasy feeling. All night she'd had troubled dreams. She'd dreamt of Jake Perkins, that pushy kid reporter who'd handed out the list of the girls who used to sit at their lunch table at Stonecroft and who had died since then. Catherine and Debra and Cindy and Gloria and Alison. Five of them. She'd dreamt that, one by one, he was crossing their names off the list, until now only she and Jeannie were still alive.

Separately we both stayed close to Alison, she thought, and now we're the only two left. Even though we lived next door to each other in school, Jeannie and I weren't enough alike to ever be really close. She's too nice. She never made fun of the guys the way the rest of us did.

Stop it! Laura warned herself. Don't think about a jinx or a curse. You have today and tomorrow to catch the golden ring. With one word from his newly sculpted lips, Gordie Amory could keep her on the series for Maximum. And suddenly Robby Brent was another one of the group who could make things happen. If he wasn't just pulling her leg about the series and if he decided he wanted her in his show, she'd have a real chance at the part. And I'm good at comedy, Laura told herself. Darn good.

And then there was Howie—no, Carter. He could open doors for her as well if he wanted to. Not in his plays, of course. God, they were all not only depressing but impossible to figure out. His artistic obscurity, however, didn't make him less powerful when it came to helping her career.

I wouldn't mind being in a hit play, she thought wistfully. Although, now that Alison was dead, she needed a new agent, too.

She glanced at her watch. It was time to get dressed. She knew she had lucked out with her choice of an outfit to wear for the day at West Point—the blue Armani suede with a Gucci scarf would be perfect for the chilly day that was forecast. According to the weather report, the temperature would only reach the low fifties.

An outdoor girl I'm not, Laura thought, but since everybody says they're going to the game, I'm not missing it.

Gordon, she reminded herself as she tied the scarf. Gordon, not Gordie. Carter, not Howie. At least Robby was still Robby, and Mark was still Mark. And Jack Emerson, the Donald Trump of Cornwall, New York, hadn't decided to be known as Jacques.

When she went down to the dining room, she was disappointed to see that only Mark Fleischman and Jean were at the honorees table.

"I'm just having coffee," Jean explained. "I'm meeting a friend for breakfast. I'll catch up with you at lunch."

"You'll go to the trooping of colors and the game?" Laura asked.

"Yes, I will."

"I never went up there much," Laura said. "But you did, Jeannie. You were always a history buff. Didn't one of the cadets you knew pretty well get killed before graduation? What was his name?"

Mark Fleischman took a sip of coffee and watched as Jean's eyes clouded with pain. She hesitated, and he clamped his lips firmly together. He had been about to answer for her. "Reed Thornton," she said. "Cadet Carroll Reed Thornton, Jr."

The most difficult week of the year for Alice Sommers was the one leading up to the anniversary of her daughter's death. This year it had been particularly hard.

Twenty years, she thought. Two decades. Karen would be forty-two years old now. She'd be a doctor, probably a cardiologist. That had been her goal when she started medical school. She'd probably be married and have a couple of children.

In her mind, Alice Sommers could see the grand-children she had never known. The boy, tall and blond, like Cyrus—she had always believed that he and Karen would end up together. The one thing about Sam Deegan that really upset her was his unshakable belief that Cyrus had caused Karen's death.

And what about their daughter? She would have looked like Karen, Alice had decided, fine-boned, with blue-green eyes and jet black hair. Of course, she would never really know.

Turn back the clock, Lord. Undo that terrible night. It was a prayer she had uttered thousands of times over the years.

Sam Deegan had told her that he didn't believe Karen ever woke up when the intruder came into her room. But Alice had always wondered. Had she opened her eyes? Had she sensed a presence? Had she seen an arm arcing over the bed? Had she felt the terrible thrusts of the knife that had taken her life?

It was something she could talk about to Sam, although she had never been able to express it to her husband. He had needed to believe that his only child had been spared that instant of terror and pain.

All this had been running through Alice Sommers' mind for days. On Saturday morning when she awoke, the heaviness and pain was lifted at the thought that Jeannie Sheridan was coming to see her.

At ten o'clock the bell rang. She opened the door and embraced Jean with fierce affection. It felt so good to hold the young woman in her arms. She knew her welcoming kiss was for Karen as well as Jean.

Over the years she had watched Jean evolve from the shy, reticent sixteen-year-old she had been when they became neighbors in Cornwall to the elegant, successful historian and writer she was now.

During the two years they'd lived next to each other before Jean graduated from high school, went to work in Chicago, and then went to Bryn Mawr, Alice had learned to both admire and pity the young girl. It seemed incredible that she was the child of her parents, people so caught up in their own contempt for each other that they never could see what effect their public brawls were having on their only child.

Even then she had shown so much dignity, Alice thought, as she held Jean out to inspect her and then hugged her again. "Do you realize it's been eight months since I've seen you?" she demanded. "Jeannie, I've *missed* you."

"I've missed you, too." Jean looked at the older woman with deep affection. Alice Sommers was a pretty woman with silver hair and blue eyes that always held a hint of sadness. Her smile, though, was warm and quick. "And you look wonderful."

"Not bad for sixty-three," she agreed. "I decided to stop supporting the hair salon, so what you see now is the real thing."

Arms linked, they walked from the vestibule to the living room of the townhouse. "I just realized, Jeannie, that you've never been here. We've always gotten together in New York or Washington. Let me show you around, starting with my fabulous view of the Hudson."

As they walked through the townhouse, Alice explained, "I don't know why we stayed in the house so long. I'm so much happier here. I think Richard felt that if we moved, in some way we'd be leaving Karen behind. He never got over losing her, you know."

Jean thought about the handsome Tudor-style house that she had admired so much when she was growing up. I knew it like the back of my hand, she thought. I was in and out of it when Laura lived there, and then Alice and Mr. Sommers were always so nice to me. I wish I had known Karen better. "Did anyone I might have known buy the house?" she asked.

"I don't think so. The people who bought it from us were from upstate. They sold it last year. I understand the new owner did some renovating and is planning to rent it furnished. A lot of people think that Jack Emerson is the real buyer. The rumor is that he's been picking up a lot of property in town. He has certainly come a long way from the kid who used to sweep out offices. He's quite the entrepreneur now."

"He's chairman of the reunion."

"And the driving force behind it. There's never been this much hoopla over a twentieth anniversary at Stonecroft." Alice Sommers shrugged. "But at least it got you here. I hope you're hungry. Waffles and strawberries are the breakfast menu."

It was over their second cup of coffee that Jean took out the faxes and the envelope with the brush and showed them to Alice, and told her about Lily. "Dr. Connors knew a couple who wanted a baby. They were patients of his, which means they must have lived in this area. Alice, I don't know whether to go to the police or get a private investigator. I don't know what to do."

"You mean you had a baby at age eighteen and never told anyone about it?" Alice reached across the table and took Jean's hand.

"You knew my mother and father. They'd have had a shouting match about whose fault it was that I got into trouble. I might as well have distributed flyers around town with the news."

"And you've never told anyone?"

"Not one single soul. I had heard that Dr. Connors helped people adopt babies. He wanted me to tell my parents, but I was of age and he said he had a patient who had learned she could not have a child. She and her husband were planning to adopt, and they were absolutely wonderful people. When he spoke to them, they immediately said they'd be thrilled to have the baby. He got me a job in the office of a nursing home in Chicago, which gave me the cover of being able to say that I wanted to work for a year before I entered Bryn Mawr."

"I remember how proud we were when we heard about your scholarship."

"I left for Chicago right after we graduated. I needed to get away. And it wasn't just because of the baby. I needed to grieve. I wish you could have known Reed. He was so special. I guess that's why I've never married." Tears welled in Jean's eyes. "I've never felt that way about anyone else." She shook her head and picked up the fax. "I thought of going to the police with this, but I live in Washington. What could they do? *'Do I kiss her or kill her? Just a joke.'* This isn't necessarily a threat, is it? But it stands to reason that whoever adopted Lily was living in this area because she was a patient of Dr. Connors. That's why I believe if I go to the police it should be in this town, or at least in this county. Alice, what do you think?"

"I think you're right and I know exactly the right person to contact," Alice said firmly. "Sam Deegan is an investigator for the district attorney's office. He was there the morning we found Karen and has never closed the file on her death. He's become a good friend. He'll find a way to help you."

15

The bus to West Point was scheduled to leave at ten. At nine-fifteen, Jack Emerson left the hotel and made a quick trip home to pick up the necktie he had forgotten to pack. Rita, his wife of fifteen years, was reading the newspaper as she sipped coffee at the breakfast table. When he came in, she looked up indifferently.

"How's the great reunion going, Jack?" The sarcasm that tinged every word she uttered to him was particularly apparent in her greeting.

"I would say it's going very well, Rita," he said amicably.

"Is your room comfortable at the hotel, or do you know?"

"The room is as comfortable as rooms at the Glen-Ridge get. Why don't you join me there and see for yourself?"

"I think I'll pass." Her eyes dropped back to the newspaper, dismissing him.

For a moment he stood looking at her. She was thirty-seven years old, but not one of those women who got better as she aged. Rita had always been reserved, but along the way her narrow lips had acquired an unattractive sullen droop. When she was in her twenties and her hair was loose around her shoulders, she had been genuinely attractive. Now, with her hair drawn tightly back and pinned in a French knot, her skin seemed taut. In fact, everything about her looked pinched and angry. Standing there, Jack realized how thoroughly he disliked her.

It infuriated him that he felt the need to explain his presence in his own home. "I don't have the tie I'll want for the dinner tonight," he snapped. "That's why I stopped by."

She put the paper down. "Jack, when I insisted that Sandy go to boarding school instead of your beloved Stonecroft, you must have known something was in the wind."

"I believe I did." Here it comes, he thought.

"I'm moving back to Connecticut. I've rented a house in Westport for the next six months or so until I see what I want to buy. We'll work out visitation for Sandy. In spite of the fact that you're a rotten husband, you've been a reasonably decent father, and it's better if we keep our separation amicable. I know exactly what you're worth, so let's not waste too much money on lawyers." She stood up. "Hail fellow, well met—jovial, wisecracking, community-minded, smart businessman, Jack Emerson. That's what a lot of people say about you, Jack. But even besides the womanizing, there's a lot festering inside of you. Out of idle curiosity I'd be interested to know what it is."

Jack Emerson smiled coldly. "Of course I knew that when you insisted on sending Sandy to Choate you were beginning your move back to Connecticut. I debated about trying to talk you out of it—that is, for ten seconds I debated. Then I celebrated."

And guess again if you think you know what I'm worth, he added mentally.

Rita Emerson shrugged. "You always said that you had to have the last word. You know something, Jack? Underneath what passes for veneer, you're still the same tacky little janitor who resented pushing mops after school. And if you don't play fair in the divorce, I might have to tell the authorities you confessed to me that you arranged to have that fire set in the medical building ten years ago."

He stared at her. "I never told you that."

"But they will believe me, won't they? You worked in that building and knew every inch of it, and you wanted that property for the mall you were planning. After the fire you were able to buy it cheap." She raised an eyebrow. "Run along and get your school tie, Jack. I'll be on my way out of here in a couple of hours. Maybe you can pick up one of your fellow classmates and have a real reunion here tonight. Be my guest."

16

The sense of finally beginning to take action gave Jean a measure of peace. Alice Sommers had promised to call Sam Deegan and try to arrange a meeting for Sunday afternoon. "He often stops by on Karen's anniversary anyhow," she said.

I don't have to go home tomorrow, Jean thought. I can stay at the hotel for at least a week. I'm good at research. Maybe I can find someone who worked in Dr. Connors' office, a nurse or secretary who can tell me where he registered the births of the babies whose adoptions he handled. Maybe he kept copies of his records elsewhere. Sam Deegan could help me find out how to get them, assuming they exist.

Dr. Connors had taken the baby from her in Chicago. Was it possible he had registered her birth there? Had the adoptive mother traveled with him to Chicago, or had he taken Lily back to Cornwall himself?

Anyone in the reunion group who was driving separately to West Point had been told to park in the lot near the Thayer Hotel. Jean felt a lump in her throat as she drove through the gate onto the grounds of the academy. As she had so often in the past few days, she thought of the last time she had been there, at the graduation of Reed's class, when she watched his mother and father accept his diploma and sword.

Most of the Stonecroft group were on tours of the Point. They were scheduled to meet at twelve-thirty for lunch at the Thayer. Then they would watch the trooping of colors before going to the game.

Before joining the others, Jean headed for the cemetery to visit Reed's grave. It was a long walk through the grounds, but she welcomed the time for reflection. I found so much peace here, she thought. What would my life have been like if Reed had lived, if my daughter were with me now, not somewhere with strangers? She had not dared go to Reed's funeral. It had taken place on her graduation day from Stonecroft. Her mother and father had never met Reed and knew virtually nothing about him. There was no way to explain that she could not go to her own graduation.

She walked past Cadet Chapel, remembering the concerts she had attended there, at first alone and then later a few times with Reed. She walked past the monuments that bore names emblazoned in history, as she wended her way to section 23 and stood in front of the headstone that bore his name, Lt. Carroll Reed Thornton, Jr. There was a single rose propped against the headstone with a small envelope attached to it. Jean gasped. Her name was written on the envelope. She picked up the rose and tore the card from the envelope. Her hands began to tremble as she read the few words it contained: "Jean, this is for you. Knew you'd stop by."

On the walk back to Thayer she tried to compose herself. It almost has to mean that someone at the reunion knows about Lily and is playing this cat-and-mouse game with me, she thought. Who else would have known I was going to be here today and would anticipate that I'd go to Reed's grave?

There are forty-two from our class here, she thought. That narrows the field of who might be contacting me from anyone in the world to one of forty-two. I'm going to find out who it is and where Lily is. Maybe she doesn't know she's adopted. I won't interfere with her life, but I need to know that she's all right. I'd just like to see her once, even from a distance.

Her footsteps quickened. There was only today and tomorrow to try to see everyone face-to-face, to try to learn who had been in the cemetery. I'll talk to Laura, she thought. She doesn't miss anything. If she was on the tour that included the cemetery, she might have noticed something.

The moment she stepped inside the room reserved for the Stonecroft luncheon, Mark Fleischman came up to her. "The tour was really interesting," he said. "I'm sorry you missed it. I'm ashamed to say that even when I was living in Cornwall, the only times I came down to West Point were to jog. But you were here pretty often in senior year, weren't you? I mean, I remember you wrote some articles about it for the school paper."

"Yes, I was," Jean said carefully. A kaleidoscope of memories rushed through her mind. Sunday afternoons in spring, walking down the footpath at Trophy Point and settling on one of the benches to write. The pink granite benches had been donated to the Point by the class of 1939. She could recite the words inscribed on them: DIGNITY, DISCIPLINE, COURAGE, INTEGRITY, LOYALTY. Even the lettering on those benches made me realize the pettiness of the life my parents were leading, she thought.

She wrenched her attention back to Mark. "Our leader, Jack Emerson, has decreed that the honorees are supposed to mingle and sit anywhere today" he was saying, "which is going to pose a problem for Laura. Did you notice how she's been spreading her charms? She was flirting with our television executive, Gordon, our playwright, Carter, and our comedian, Robby, at the dinner table last night. On the bus she was sitting next to Jack Emerson and making a fuss over *him*. He's become quite the real estate magnate, I gather."

"You're the one specializing in adolescent behavior, Mark. Laura always went for the guys who were successful. Don't you think that carries through into adulthood? And, anyhow, she might as well concentrate on those four. Her ex-boyfriends, such as Doug Hanover, are either not here or have their wives in tow." Jean had to sound amused.

Mark was smiling, but as she studied him, Jean saw a change in his expression, a tightening in his eyes. You, too? she wondered. And she realized that it was disappointing to think that Mark had been another one to have a crush on Laura, and maybe even still had one. Well, she wanted to have a chance to talk to Laura, and if he wanted to be with her, too, that was fine. "Let's sit with Laura," she suggested. "I always did in school." For a moment the image of the lunch table at Stonecroft surfaced vividly in her mind. She saw there Catherine and Debra and Cindy and Gloria and Alison.

And Laura and me.

And Laura . . . and me . . .

The Owl had expected that the disappearance of a woman in Surrey Meadows, New York, would not be reported in time to make the Saturday morning papers but was pleased that it was featured on both the radio and television. Before and after breakfast, as he soaked his arm, he watched and listened to the reports. The pain in his arm emanated from where the dog had sunk his teeth; he considered it a punishment for his carelessness. He should have noticed the leash in the woman's hand before he stopped the car and grabbed her. The German shepherd had appeared out of nowhere, leaping onto him, snarling as it attacked. Fortunately, he was able to grab the tire jack that he always kept on the front seat when he went on that kind of outing.

Now Jean was sitting across the luncheon table from him, and it was obvious that she had found the rose at the grave. He was sure she was hoping that Laura had noticed who in their group might have been carrying the flower or had slipped away during the cemetery tour. He wasn't worried. Laura hadn't noticed anything. He'd stake his own life on that. She'd been too busy trying to figure out which of us she had the best chance of using. She's broke and desperate, he thought triumphantly.

The accident of learning about Lily all those years ago had made him realize all the many ways in which it was possible to have power over other people. Sometimes it amused him to use that power. Other times, he just waited. His anonymous tip to the IRS three years ago had caused the audit of Laura's finances. Now she had a lien on her house. Soon it wouldn't matter anymore, but he had the satisfaction of knowing that even before he killed her, she had been worried about losing her home.

The idea of contacting Jean about Lily had only surfaced when he happened to meet the adoptive parents of her daughter. Even though I was ambivalent about killing Jean, I wanted to make her suffer, he thought, without regret.

Leaving the flower on the headstone had been a stroke of genius. At the lunch table in Thayer, he had seen the distress in Jean's eyes. At the trooping of the colors before the football game, he made it his business to sit next to her. "It's a marvelous sight, isn't it?" he'd asked her.

"Yes, it is."

He knew she was thinking about Reed Thornton.

The Hellcats drum and signal corps was marching past the stand where they were sitting. Take a good look, Jeannie, he thought. Your kid is the one on this end in the second row.

18

After they got back to the Glen-Ridge House in Cornwall, Jean made it her business to go up in the elevator with Laura and to follow her down to her room. "Laura, honey, I need to talk to you," she said.

"Oh, Jeannie, I've just got to have a hot bath and rest," Laura protested. "Tours of West Point and going to a football game may be all very well, but I'm not one for spending hours outdoors. Can we get together later?"

"No," Jean said firmly. "I need to talk to you now."

"Only because you're such a good friend," Laura said with a sigh. She slipped the plastic key into the lock. "Welcome to the Taj Mahal." She opened the door and flipped the light switch. The lamps at the side of the bed and on the desk went on, casting uncertain light on the room already falling into shadows from the late afternoon sun.

Jean sat on the edge of the bed. "Laura, this is really important. You went to the cemetery as part of your tour, didn't you?"

Laura began to unbutton the suede jacket she had worn to West Point. "Uh-huh. Jeannie, I know you used to go up there a lot when we were at Stonecroft, but this is the first time I went through the cemetery. God, when you think of all the famous people who are buried there. General Custer. I thought they'd figured he messed up that attack he led, but now I guess, thanks to his wife, they've decided he was a hero. Standing at his grave today I thought of something you told me a long time ago, that the Indians called Custer 'Chief Yellow Hair.' You always managed to come up with things like that."

"Did everyone go on the tour to the cemetery, Laura?"

"Everyone on the bus did. Some of the people who brought their kids had their own cars, and they kind of did their own tour. I mean, I saw them wandering off by themselves. When you were a kid, did you want to look at tombstones?" Laura hung up her jacket in the closet. "Jeannie, I love you, but I have got to lie down. You should, too. Tonight's our big night. We get the medal or the plaque or whatever it is we get. You don't think they'll make us sing the school song, do you?"

Jean got up and put her hands on Laura's shoulders. "Laura, this is important. Did you notice if anyone on the bus was carrying a rose, or did you see anyone take out a rose in the cemetery?"

"A rose? No, of course not. I mean I saw some other people putting flowers on some of the graves, but no one from our crowd. Who in our group knew someone who's buried there well enough to bring flowers?"

I should have known, Jean thought. Laura wasn't paying attention to anyone who wasn't important to her. "I'll get out of your way," she promised. "What time are we due downstairs?"

"Seven o'clock cocktails, dinner at eight. We get our medals at ten o'clock. Then tomorrow it's just the memorial service for Alison and the brunch at Stonecroft."

"Are you going right back to California, Laura?"

Impulsively, Laura hugged Jean. "My plans are not yet definite, but let's say I may have a better option. See you later, honey."

When the door closed behind Jean, Laura pulled her garment bag out of the closet. As soon as the dinner was over, they would slip away. As he had said, "I've had enough of the hotel, Laura. Have an overnight bag ready, and I'll put it in my car before dinner. But keep your mouth shut. It's nobody's business where we stay tonight. We'll make up for you not realizing how great I was twenty years ago."

As she packed a cashmere jacket to wear in the morning, Laura smiled to herself. *I did tell him that I definitely want to go to Alison's memorial, but I didn't care if we skipped brunch.*

Then she frowned. He'd replied, "*I* wouldn't dream of missing Alison's memorial," but of course he meant we'd be there together.

19

At three o'clock in the afternoon, Sam Deegan was surprised to receive a phone call from Alice Sommers. "Sam, are you by any chance free this evening to go to a black-tie dinner?" she asked.

Sam hesitated out of pure astonishment.

"I realize this is absolutely no notice," Alice said apologetically.

"No, not at all. The answer is that, yes, I'm free, and I do have a tuxedo hanging in my closet, cleaned and pressed."

"There's a gala tonight honoring some of the graduates of the twentieth reunion class at Stonecroft. People in town were asked to buy seats for the dinner. The whole thing is really a fund-raiser for the new addition they want to put on Stonecroft. I wasn't planning to go, but there's someone being honored I want you to meet. Her name is Jean Sheridan. She used to live next door to me, and I'm very fond of her. She has a serious problem and needs some advice, and my original plan was to ask you to stop by tomorrow to talk to her about it. Then I decided it would be lovely to be there when Jean receives her medal, and . . ."

Sam realized that Alice Sommers' invitation had

been impulsive, and she was becoming not only apologetic but perhaps was even regretting having made the phone call.

"Alice, I would enjoy going very much," he said emphatically. He did not tell her that he had been at work since 4:30 A.M. on the Helen Whelan case and had just returned home, planning to go to bed early. A nap of an hour or two will take the edge off, he thought. "I was planning to stop by tomorrow," he added.

Alice Sommers knew what he meant. "Somehow I expected that you would. If you can make it at seven at my place, I'll give you a drink first, then we'll start over to the hotel."

"It's a date. See you later, Alice." Sam hung up and sheepishly realized he was inordinately pleased to receive the invitation; then he considered the reason for it. What kind of problem could Alice's friend, Jean Sheridan, be having? he wondered. But no matter how serious, it couldn't compare with what had happened to Helen Whelan early this morning as she was walking her dog.

20

"This really is a big to-do, isn't it, Jean?" Gordon Amory asked.

He was sitting to her right, on the second tier of the dais where the honorees had been placed. Below them, the local congressman, the mayor of Cornwall-on-Hudson, the sponsors of the dinner, the president of Stonecroft, and several trustees were observing the packed ballroom with satisfaction.

"Yes, it is," she agreed.

"Did it occur to you to invite your mother and father to this grand occasion?"

If there had not been a wry note in Gordon's voice, Jean would have been angry, but at his touch of humor, she responded in kind. "No. Did it occur to you to invite *yours?*"

"Of course not. As a matter of fact, you've probably noticed that not one of our fellow honorees seems to have brought a beaming parent to share this moment of triumph."

"From what I understand, most of our parents have moved away. Mine were gone the summer I graduated from Stonecroft. Gone and split, as you may know," Jean added.

"As are mine. When I consider the six of us sitting here, supposedly the pride of our graduating class, I've decided that of all of us, Laura was probably the only one who enjoyed growing up here. I think you were quite unhappy, as was I, as were Robby and Mark and Carter. Robby was an indifferent student in a family of intellectuals, and was always being threatened with the loss of his scholarship to Stonecroft. Humor became his armor and his retreat. Mark's parents let the world know that they wished his brother had been spared, and that Mark had been the son who died. His reaction was to become a psychiatrist treating adolescents. I wonder if he has been trying to treat the adolescent inside."

Physician, heal thyself, Jean thought, and suspected that Gordon might be right.

"Howie, or Carter as he insists on being called, had a father who used to whack him and his mother around," Gordon continued. "Howie stayed out of the house as much as possible. You knew that he used to be caught peeking in windows. What was he trying to do, get a glimpse of normal home life? Don't you think that might be why his plays are so dark?"

Jean decided to sidestep that one. "That leaves you and me," she said quietly.

"My mother was a slovenly housekeeper. You may remember that when our house caught on fire, the joke in town was that that was the only way to really clean it. I now have three homes and confess to being positively obsessed with the need for cleanliness in every one of them, which is why my marriage failed. But then, that was a mistake from the beginning."

"And my mother and father had public brawls. Isn't that what you're remembering about me, Gordon?" She knew that was exactly what he was thinking.

"I was remembering how easily kids get embarrassed and that with the exception of Laura, who was always the golden girl of our class, you and Carter and Robby and Mark and I had a tough row to hoe. We certainly didn't need our parents to make it harder for us, but one way or the other, they all did. Look, Jean, I wanted to change so much, I got myself a whole new face. But when the chips are down, I sometimes wake up to find I'm still Gordie the nerd, the dopey-looking kid it was fun to pick on. You've made a name for yourself in academic circles, and now you've written a book that is not only critically acclaimed but a best-seller. But who are you inside?"

Who indeed? Inside, I'm still too often the needy outsider, Jean thought, but she was saved from answering when Gordon suddenly smiled boyishly and said, "One should never get too philosophical over dinner. Maybe I'll feel differently after they hang that medal on me. What do you think, Laura?"

He turned to speak to her, and Jean turned to Jack Emerson who was on her left.

"That seems to be an intense discussion you've been having with Gordon," he observed.

Jean noted the naked curiosity on his face. The last thing she wanted to do was continue with him the conversation she had been having with Gordon. "Oh, we were just gossiping about growing up here, Jack," she said glibly.

I was so unsure of myself, she thought. I was so thin and awkward. My hair was stringy. I was always waiting for my mother and father to start blasting at each other again. I felt so guilty when they told me that the only reason they were staying together was for *my* sake. All I wanted to do was grow up and get as far away as possible. And I did.

"Cornwall was a great place to grow up," Jack said heartily. "Never could understand why more of you didn't settle here or at least buy a country retreat for yourselves around here, now that you're all so successful. Incidentally, if you ever decide you want one, Jeannie, I have some properties listed that I can promise you are little jewels."

Jean remembered that Alice Sommers had told her the rumor was that Jack Emerson was the new owner of Alice's former home. "Any in my old neighborhood?" she asked.

He shook his head. "No. I'm talking about places with drop-dead river views. When can I take you around and show them to you?"

Never, Jean thought. I'm not coming back here to live. I just want to get out of here. First, though, I have to find out who is contacting me about Lily. It's just a hunch, but I'd stake my life that that person is sitting in this room right now. I want this dinner to be over so that I can meet Alice and the detective she has brought here tonight. I have to believe that somehow he will be able to help me find Lily and remove any threat to her safety. And when I am sure that she is well and happy, I need to go back to my adult world. Being here for twenty-four hours has already made me realize that, for better or for worse, whatever I have become was because of the life I led here, and I have to make peace with that.

"Oh, I don't think I'm in the market for a home in Cornwall," she told Jack Emerson.

"Maybe not now, Jeannie," he said, his eyes twinkling, "but I bet that someday soon I'll find a place for you to stay. In fact, I'm *sure* of it."

21

At these dinners the honorees are usually introduced in increasing order of importance, The Owl thought sardonically as Laura's name was called. She was the first to receive her medal, jointly presented by the mayor of Cornwall and the president of Stonecroft.

Laura's garment bag and small suitcase were in his car. He'd sneaked them down the backstairs, out the service entrance, and into the trunk without being observed. As a precaution he'd broken the light over the service entrance and worn a cap and jacket that could vaguely have passed for a uniform if anyone happened to see him, even from a distance.

Predictably, Laura looked beautiful. She was wearing a gold dinner gown that, as the well-worn saying went, "left nothing to the imagination." Her makeup was flawless. Her diamond necklace was probably fake but looked good. Her diamond earrings might be genuine. They were probably the last, or near the last, of the jewelry she'd received from her second husband. A little talent, helped by her spectacular good looks, had given Laura her fifteen minutes of fame. And, face it, she had an engaging personality—that is, if you weren't on the receiving end of her trashing.

Now she was thanking the mayor, the president of Stonecroft, and the dinner guests. "Cornwall-on-Hudson was a wonderful place to grow up," she gushed. "And the four years at Stonecroft were the happiest of my life."

With a thrill of anticipation, he imagined the moment when they got to the house, when he closed the door behind her and saw the terror begin to come into her eyes, the moment when she understood that she was trapped.

They were applauding Laura's speech, and then the mayor was announcing the next honoree.

Finally it was over, and they could get up to leave. He sensed that Laura was looking at him, but he did not meet her glance. They had agreed that they would mingle for a little while, then go to their rooms separately while everyone was saying good night. Then she would meet him at the car.

The others would be checking out in the morning and driving in their own cars to the memorial service at Alison's grave, and then on to the farewell brunch. Laura wouldn't be missed until then, and the supposition might easily be that she'd simply had enough of the reunion and had headed home early.

"Congratulations are in order, I suppose," Jean said, resting her hand a few inches above his wrist. She had touched the deepest and most ragged of the dog bites. The Owl felt a spurt of blood from the wound dampen his jacket and realized that the sleeve of Jean's royal blue dinner gown was in contact with it.

With a tremendous effort he managed not to give any hint of the pain that shot through his arm. Obviously Jean did not realize what had happened, and she turned to greet a couple in their early sixties who were approaching her.

For an instant, The Owl thought of the blood that had dripped onto the street when the dog bit him. DNA. It concerned him that it was the first time he'd ever left physical evidence behind—except, of course, for his symbol, but over the years everyone everywhere had missed that. In a way he'd been disappointed by their stupidity, but in another way he'd been glad. If the deaths of all those women were linked, it would make it harder for him to continue. *If* he chose to continue after Laura and Jean.

Even if Jean realized the spot on her sleeve was blood, she wouldn't have any idea where it had come from and how she had come in contact with it. Besides, no detective, not even Sherlock Holmes, would connect a spot on the sleeve of an honoree of Stonecroft Academy with blood found in the street twenty miles away.

Never in a million years, The Owl thought, dismissing the idea as absurd.

22

From the moment she met Sam Deegan, Jean understood why Alice had spoken so highly of him. She liked his looks: a strong face enhanced by clear dark blue eyes. She also liked the warmth of his smile and his firm handshake.

"I told Sam about Lily and about the fax you received yesterday," Alice said, her voice low.

"There's been another one," Jean whispered. "Alice, I'm so frightened for Lily. I almost couldn't make myself come down to dinner. It's been so hard to try to make conversation when I don't know what may be happening to her."

Before Alice could reply, Jean felt a tug on her sleeve as a cheery voice cried, "Jean Sheridan. My, how happy I am to see you! You used to baby-sit for my kids when you were thirteen."

Jean managed a smile. "Oh, Mrs. Rhodeen, it's so good to see you again."

"Jean, people want to talk to you," Sam said. "Alice and I will go over and get a table in the cocktail lounge. Join us as soon as you can."

It was fifteen minutes before she could break away

from the local people who had attended the dinner and who remembered her growing up or who had read her books and wanted to talk to her about them. But at last she was with Alice and Sam at a corner table where they could speak without being overheard.

As they sipped the champagne Sam had ordered, she told them about the flower and note she had found in the cemetery. "The rose couldn't have been there long," she said nervously. "It almost has to have been put there by someone in the reunion group who knew I was going to West Point and was sure I'd stop at Reed's grave. But why is he or she playing this game? Why these vague threats? Why not come out with the reason for being in touch with me now?"

"May I be in touch with you now?" Mark Fleischman asked pleasantly. He was standing at the empty chair beside her, a glass in his hand.

"I was looking to ask you to have a nightcap, Jean," he explained. "I couldn't find you, then I spotted you over here."

He saw the hesitation on the faces of the people at the table, and acknowledged to himself that he had expected it. He had been perfectly aware that they were in a serious discussion, but he wanted to know whom Jean was with and what they were talking about.

"Of course, join us," Jean said, trying to sound welcoming. How much did he overhear? she wondered as she introduced him to Alice and Sam.

"Mark Fleischman," Sam said. "Dr. Mark Fleischman. I've seen your program and like it very much.

You give darn good advice. I especially admire the way you handle teenagers. When they're your guests, you have a way of letting them vent their feelings and feel comfortable about doing it. If more kids opened up and got decent advice, they would realize they were not alone and their problems wouldn't seem so overwhelming."

Jean watched as Mark Fleischman's face brightened with a pleased smile at the obvious sincerity of Sam Deegan's praise.

He was so quiet as a kid, she thought. He was always so shy. I never would have guessed that he'd end up a television personality. Was Gordon right that Mark became a psychiatrist specializing in adolescents because of his own problem after his brother's death?

"I know you grew up here, Mark. Do you still have family in town?" Alice Sommers asked.

"My father. He's never moved from the old homestead. Retired, but does a lot of traveling, I gather."

Jean was startled. "At dinner, Gordon and I were talking about the fact that none of us has roots here anymore."

"I don't have roots here, Jean," Mark said quietly. "I haven't been in touch with my father in years. Although he clearly must realize from all the publicity about this reunion and the fact that I'm here as one of the honorees, I haven't heard from him."

He caught the note of bitterness that had crept into his voice, and was ashamed of it. What made me open up like that to two perfect strangers and to Jeannie

Sheridan? he wondered. I'm supposed to be the listener. "Tall, lanky, cheerful, funny, and wise, Dr. Mark Fleischman" was how they introduced him on TV.

"Perhaps your father is out of town," Alice suggested softly.

"If he is, then he's wasting a lot of electricity. His lights were on last night." Mark shrugged, then smiled. "I *am* sorry. I didn't mean to pour out my soul. I came barging over here because I wanted to congratulate Jean on her remarks at the podium. She was sweet and natural and thankfully made up for the antics of a couple of our fellow honorees."

"And so did you," Alice Sommers said heartily. "I thought Robby Brent was absolutely out of order and that Gordon Amory and Carter Stewart sounded downright bitter. But if you're going to congratulate Jeannie, be sure to mention how lovely she looks."

"I seriously doubt that with Laura up there, anybody noticed me," Jean said, but she realized how pleased she was by Mark's unexpected compliment.

"I'm sure everyone noticed you and would agree you look lovely," Mark said as he stood up. "I also wanted to be sure to tell you that it's been good to see you again, Jeannie, in case we don't get a chance to visit tomorrow. I'll go to Alison's memorial service, but I may not be able to stay for the brunch."

He smiled at Alice Sommers and extended his hand to Sam Deegan. "I've enjoyed meeting you. Now I see a couple of people I want to catch in case I miss them in the morning." With long strides he was across the room.

"That man is very attractive, Jean," Alice Sommers said emphatically. "And it's obvious that he has an eye for you."

But that may not be the only reason he dropped by, Sam Deegan thought. He'd been watching us from the bar. He wanted to know what we were talking about.

I wonder why it was so important to him.

The Owl was almost out of the cage. He was separating from it. He could always tell when total separation was taking place. His own kind, gentle self—the person he might have become under different circumstances— began to recede. He heard and saw himself smiling and joking and accepting the kisses on the cheek from some of the women in the reunion group.

And then he slipped away. He could feel the velvety softness of his plumage when, twenty minutes later, he sat in the car waiting for Laura. He watched as she slipped out the back entrance of the hotel, taking care to look around and avoid running into anyone. She had even been smart enough to wear a hooded raincoat over her gown.

Then she was at the car door, opening it. She slid onto the seat beside him. "Take me away, honey," she said laughing. "Isn't this fun?"

Jake Perkins stayed up late to write his report about the banquet for the *Stonecroft Academy Gazette*. His home on Riverbank Lane looked over the Hudson, and he valued that view as he valued few things in his life. At age sixteen he already considered himself something of a philosopher as well as a good writer and a keen student of human behavior.

In a moment of profound thinking, he had decided that the tides and currents of the river symbolized to him the passions and moods of human beings. He liked to get that kind of depth into his news stories. He knew, of course, that the columns he wanted to write would never get by Mr. Holland, the English teacher who was the adviser and censor of the *Gazette*, but to amuse himself, Jake wrote the column he wished he could print before he got down to the one that he'd submit.

> The somewhat shabby ballroom of the stuffy Glen-Ridge House was somewhat brightened with blue and white Stonecroft

banners and centerpieces. The food was predictably dreadful, beginning with what passed for a seafood cocktail followed by filet mignon done to a crisp, yet only slightly warm, pan-roasted potatoes that could have been lethal weapons, and wilted string beans almondine. Melted ice cream with chocolate sauce completed the chef's attempt at gourmet dining.

The townspeople supported the event by turning out to honor the graduates, all of whom were once residents of Cornwall. It is generally known that Jack Emerson, the chairman and driving force behind the reunion, has a purpose behind his effort not connected with embracing his fellow classmates. The banquet was also the kickoff for the building project at Stonecroft, a new addition that will be erected on land presently owned by Emerson and built by the contractor acknowledged to be in Emerson's pocket.

The six honorees were seated at the dais together with Mayor Walter Carlson, Stonecroft president Alfred Downes, and trustees . . .

Their names don't matter in this version of the story, Jake decided.

Laura Wilcox was the first to receive the Distinguished Alumna medal. Her gold lamé dress had most of the men in the assembly unaware of what she was babbling, something to the effect of how happy her life had been in this town. Since she had never come back and since no one could ever picture the glamorous Ms. Wilcox strolling down Main Street or stopping by for a tattoo at our recently opened tattoo emporium, her remarks were greeted with polite applause and a few whistles.

Dr. Mark Fleischman, psychiatrist and now television personality, gave a low-key, well-received address in which he cautioned parents and teachers to build up their kids' morale. "The world will be happy to beat them down," he said. "It's your job to make them feel good about themselves even while you give them appropriate limits."

Carter Stewart, the playwright, gave a two-level speech in which he said he was sure that the townspeople and the students who have become prototypes for many of the characters in his plays were present at the banquet. He also said that contrary to Dr. Fleischman's remarks, his father believed in the old chestnut that to spare the rod was to spoil the child. He then thanked his late father for having been that kind of parent because it gave him a dark view on life which has served him well.

Stewart's remarks were greeted with nervous laughter and little applause.

Comedian Robby Brent broke up the audience with his vividly funny imitation of the teachers who were always threatening to fail him, which would have caused him to lose his scholarship to Stonecroft. One of those teachers was present and smiled gamely at Brent's merciless parody of her gestures and mannerisms and dead-on imitation of her voice. But Miss Ella Bender, the rock of the mathematics department, was close to tears as Brent devastated the audience with a perfect parody of her high-pitched tone and nervous giggle.

"I was the last and dumbest of the Brents," Robby concluded. "You never let me forget it. My defense was humor, and for that I thank you."

He then blinked his eyes and puckered his lips exactly as President Downes blinks his eyes and puckers his lips, and handed him a check for $1, his contribution toward the building fund.

Then, as the audience gasped, he yelled, "Just kidding," and waved a check for $10,000, which he ceremoniously handed over.

Some in the audience thought he was sidesplittingly funny. Others, like Dr. Jean Sheridan, were distressed by Brent's antics. She was later overheard telling someone that she did not believe humor should be cruel.

Gordon Amory, our cable television czar, was next to speak. "I never made any team I tried for at Stonecroft," he said. "You can't imagine how hard I prayed that I'd get just one chance to be a jock—which proves the old adage, 'Be careful what you pray for. You may get it.' Instead I became a television addict, then began analyzing the stuff I was watching. Before long, I realized I could tell why some programs or specials or situation comedies or docudramas worked and why others were worthless. That was the beginning of my career. It was founded on rejection, disappointment, and pain. And, oh yes, before I leave, let me set a rumor to rest. I did not deliberately set fire to my parents' home. I was smoking a cigarette and did not notice after I turned off the television and went up to bed that the live butt had slipped behind the empty pizza box my mother had left on the couch."

Before the audience had time to react, Mr. Amory then presented a check for $100,000 to the building fund and joked to President Downes, "May the great work of molding minds and hearts at Stonecroft Academy continue well into the future."

He might as well have been saying go jump in a lake, Jake thought, remembering how Amory had settled at his place on the dais with a self-satisfied smile.

The last honoree, Dr. Jean Sheridan, spoke about growing up in Cornwall, the town that had been the enclave of the wealthy and the privileged nearly 150 years ago. "As a scholarship student, I know I received a superb education at Stonecroft. But outside the school grounds there was another learning place, in this town and countryside. Here and in the area around us, I acquired an appreciation of history that has shaped my life and career. For that I am eternally grateful."

Dr. Sheridan did not say that she was happy here, or mention that all the old-timers would remember her parents' domestic disputes that enlivened the town, Jake Perkins thought, or that she was known to break down and cry in class after some of her parents' more publicized episodes.

Well, tomorrow's the end of it, Jake thought as he stretched and walked over to the window. The lights from Cold Spring, the town across the Hudson, were less visible since a fog was setting in. Hope it lifts tomorrow, Jake thought. He'd cover the memorial service at Alison Kendall's grave and then catch a movie in the afternoon. He had heard that the names of the four other graduates who had died were also going to be read at the memorial.

Jake went back to his desk and looked at the picture he'd dug out of the files. In an almost unbelievable twist of fate, all five of the dead graduates had not only shared the luncheon table in senior year with two of the honorees, Laura Wilcox and Jean Sheridan, but they had died in the order in which they were seated.

Which means Laura Wilcox is probably next, Jake thought. Can this be just a bizarre coincidence, or should someone be looking into it? But that's crazy. Those women died over a period of twenty years, in totally different ways, all across the country. One of them was even skiing when she must have gotten caught in an avalanche.

Fate, that's what it was, Jake concluded. Nothing but fate.

"**I**'m planning to stay on for a few extra days," Jean told the front-desk clerk who answered the phone on Sunday morning. "Will that be a problem?"

She knew it wouldn't be a problem. All the other reunion guests would undoubtedly be on their way home after the brunch at Stonecroft, so there'd be many empty rooms.

Although it was only eight-fifteen, she was already up and dressed and had sipped the coffee and juice and nibbled at a muffin from the continental breakfast she had ordered. She had arranged to go back to Alice Sommers' house after the Stonecroft brunch. Sam Deegan would be there, and they would be able to talk without fear of interruption. Sam had told her that no matter how private the adoption was, it had to have been registered, and a lawyer must have drawn up papers. He had asked Jean if she had a copy of the document she had signed, giving up her rights to the baby.

"Dr. Connors didn't leave me any papers," she explained. "Or maybe I didn't want to have any reminder of what I was doing. I really don't remember. I was numb. I felt as if my heart was being torn out of my body when he took her from me."

But that conversation had opened another avenue of thought. She had been planning to go to the nine o'clock Mass at St. Thomas of Canterbury on Sunday morning, before the memorial service for Alison. St. Thomas had been her parish when she was growing up, but in talking to Sam Deegan, she had remembered that Dr. Connors had been a parishioner there as well. In the midst of one of her sleepless periods during the night, it had occurred to her that it was at least possible the people who adopted the baby had been parishioners of St. Thomas as well.

I told Dr. Connors that I wanted Lily to be raised Catholic, she remembered. And if the adoptive parents were Catholic and were members of St. Thomas of Canterbury at that time, it would have made sense for Lily to be baptized there. If I could look at the records of baptisms between late March and mid-June of that year, it would be a start in searching for Lily.

When she woke at six, it was to feel tears running down her cheeks and to hear herself whispering the prayer that now was becoming a part of her subconscious: "Don't let anyone hurt her. Take care of her, please."

She knew that the office of the church wouldn't be open on Sunday. Even so, maybe this morning, after Mass, she could talk to the pastor and make an appointment to see him. I've got to feel as though I'm doing *something*, she thought. Maybe there's even a priest who was at the parish twenty years ago and who might just remember a parishioner adopting a baby girl at that time.

A sense of something imminent, a growing certainty that Lily was in immediate danger, had become so strong that Jean knew she could not go through the day without taking some kind of action.

At eight-thirty she went downstairs to the parking lot and got in her car. It was a five-minute drive to the church. She had decided that the best time to speak to a priest was after Mass when he would be standing outside, greeting people as they exited.

She started to drive to Hudson Street, realized she was at least twenty minutes early, and impulsively turned the car toward Mountain Road to look at the house where she had grown up.

The house was almost halfway up the winding street. When she had lived there, the exterior had been brown siding with beige shutters. The people who owned the house now had not only enlarged it but refinished it with white shingles and a forest green trim on the shutters. The new owner obviously understood how trees and plants could frame and beautify a relatively modest home. It looked almost jewel-like in the early morning mist.

The brick and stucco house where the Sommerses had lived also looked well cared for, Jean thought, even though it was obvious no one was living there now. The shades were drawn in all the windows, but the trim was freshly painted, the hedges neatly clipped, and the long bluestone walkway from the front door to the driveway was new.

I always loved this house, she thought as she stopped

the car for a better look. Laura's father and mother kept it up when they lived there, and then the Sommerses did as well. I remember when we were nine or ten, Laura said that she thought our house was ugly. I thought the brown was ugly, too, but I wouldn't give her the satisfaction of admitting it. I wonder if she would approve of it now.

Not that it mattered. Jean turned the car around and began to drive down the hill toward Hudson Street. Laura never deliberately meant to hurt me, she thought. She was taught to be self-centered, and I don't think, in the long run, it's done her much good. The last time I talked to Alison, she said that she was trying to get Laura a job on a new sitcom, but that it was tough to make it happen.

She said that Gordie—then she laughed and changed it to Gordon—could make it happen but that she didn't think he would, Jean recalled. Laura has always been the golden girl. It was almost pathetic to see her playing up to all the guys, even, for God's sake, to Jack Emerson. There's something downright *unattractive* about him, she thought with a shiver. What makes him so certain that I'll buy a house around here someday?

Earlier it had looked as though the mist would clear, but in the way of October weather, the clouds had become stronger and the mist was now a wet, cold drizzle. Jean realized that it was the same kind of weather as the day when she realized she was pregnant. Her mother and father had been having another of their arguments, although this one ended in what passed for peace. Jean was going to college on a scholarship. There was no need for them to have to put up with each other anymore. They had done their duty as parents, and now it was time for them to lead their own lives.

Put the house on the market—with luck, they'd be rid of it by August.

Jean thought of how she had come silently down the stairs, slipped out of the house, and walked and walked and walked. I didn't know what Reed would say, she thought. I did know that he would feel he had betrayed his father's expectations for him.

Twenty years ago Reed's father had been a lieutenant general stationed at the Pentagon. That was one of the reasons we never mingled with his classmates, Jean thought. Reed didn't want it to get back to his father that he was seriously dating anyone.

And I didn't want him to meet my parents.

If he had lived and we had married, would it have lasted? It was a question she had asked herself many times in the last twenty years, and she always came to the same answer: It would have lasted. In spite of his family's disapproval, in spite of the fact that it probably would have taken me years to get the education I knew I had to have, it would have lasted.

I knew him such a short time, Jean thought as she drove into the church parking lot. I'd never even had a boyfriend before him. And then one day when I was sitting on the steps of the monument at West Point, he sat down beside me. My name was on the cover of the notebook I'd brought with me. He said, "Jean Sheridan," and then he said, "I like Stephen Foster's music, and do you know what song I'm thinking of now?" Of course I didn't, and he said, "It begins like this: 'I dream of Jeannie with the light brown hair . . .'"

Jean parked the car. Three months later he was dead, she thought, and I was carrying his child. And when I saw Dr. Connors in this church and remembered having heard that he handled adoptions, it was like a gift, telling me what to do.

I need a gift like that again.

26

Jake Perkins figured the number of mourners at Alison Kendall's grave at less than thirty. The others had all elected to go directly to the brunch. Not that he blamed them. The rain was picking up. His feet were sinking into the soft, muddy grass. There's nothing worse than being dead on a rainy day, he thought, and hoped he'd remember to jot down that bit of wisdom later.

The mayor had skipped this event, but President Downes, who had already extolled the generosity and talent of Alison Kendall, was now offering a generic prayer that was sure to satisfy everyone except an out-and-out atheist, if one happened to be present.

She may have been talented, Jake thought, but it was her generosity that has us out here risking pneumonia. I know one person who *didn't* risk it. He looked around to be sure he had not missed Laura Wilcox, but she definitely wasn't there. All the other honorees were present. Jean Sheridan was standing near President Downes, and there was no question she was genuinely sad. A couple of times she dabbed at her eyes with a handkerchief. Everyone else in the group looked as if they wished Downes would wrap it up quickly so they could get inside and have a Bloody Mary.

"We remember also Alison's classmates and friends who have been called home," Downes said soberly: "Catherine Kane, Debra Parker, Cindy Lang, and Gloria Martin. This graduating class of twenty years ago produced many great achievers, but also never before has one class known such great loss."

Amen, Jake thought, and decided he would definitely use the picture of the seven girls at the lunch table with his story on the reunion. He already had the caption—Downes had just handed it to him: "Never before has one class known such great loss."

At the beginning of the ceremony a couple of students had handed a rose to each of the people who came to the memorial service. Now, after Downes concluded his remarks, one by one everyone placed the rose at the foot of the tombstone and started to walk across the cemetery to the adjacent school grounds. The farther they got away from the grave, the faster they moved. Jake could read their minds: "Well, thank God that's over. I thought I'd freeze."

The last one to leave was Jean Sheridan. She stood there, looking not just sad but deep in thought. Jake noticed that Dr. Fleischman had stopped and was waiting for her. Sheridan reached down and touched Alison's name on the tombstone, then turned, and Jake could see that she seemed glad to see Dr. Fleischman. They began to walk toward the school together.

Before he could stop her, the sophomore who was handing out the roses had given him one. Jake wasn't much for ceremonies, but he decided to leave his rose with the others. As he was about to put it down, he noticed something on the ground. He bent down and picked it up.

It was a pewter lapel pin in the shape of an owl, about an inch long. Jake could see at a glance that it wasn't worth more than a couple of bucks. It looked like something a kid or some nature lover who was on a crusade to save owls might wear. Jake was about to toss it away, then changed his mind. He brushed it off and put it in his pocket. It would soon be Halloween. He'd give it to his kid cousin and tell him that he had dug it out of a grave just for him.

27

Jean was disappointed that Laura had not bothered to attend the memorial service for Alison, but she also realized that she was not surprised. Laura had never put herself out for anyone, and it was silly to think that she might begin at this stage of her life. Knowing Laura, she wasn't going to stand out in the cold and rain—she'd go directly to the brunch.

But by the time the brunch was half over and Laura had not appeared, Jean felt the beginning of deep unease. She confided that feeling to Gordon Amory. "Gordon, I know you were talking to Laura a lot yesterday. Did she say anything to you about not showing up today?"

"We talked at lunch yesterday and at the game," he corrected. "She was campaigning to get me to make her the lead in our new sitcom. I told her that I never interfere with the people I hire to cast my programs. When she continued to persist, I rather unkindly emphasized that I never made exceptions, particularly for minimally talented school chums. At that point she used a rather unladylike expression and turned her charms on our insufferable chairman, Jack Emerson. As you may know, he has been bragging about his considerable financial assets. Also, last night he gleefully announced that his wife had just left him, so he was fair game for Laura, I guess."

Laura seemed to be in wonderful spirits at dinner, Jean thought. And she was fine when I tried to talk to her in her room before dinner. Did anything go wrong later last night? Or did she just decide to sleep in this morning?

I can at least check on that, she thought. She was sitting next to Gordon and Carter Stewart at the luncheon table. With a murmured "Back in a minute," she walked between the rows of tables, taking care not to make eye contact with anyone. The brunch was being held in the auditorium. She slipped into the corridor that led to the homeroom of the freshman class and dialed the hotel.

Laura did not answer the phone in her room. Jean hesitated and then asked to be switched to the front desk. She identified herself and asked if by any chance Laura Wilcox had checked out. "I'm a little concerned," she explained. "Ms. Wilcox was supposed to meet a group of us and hasn't shown up."

"Well, she hasn't checked out," the clerk said genially. "Why don't I send someone up to see if she's overslept, Dr. Sheridan. But you take the blame if she gets mad."

He's the guy whose hair matches the top of the desk, Jean thought, recognizing both the voice and the tone. "I'll take responsibility," she assured him.

As she waited, Jean glanced around the corridor. God, I feel as though I never left this place, she thought.

Ms. Clemens was the homeroom teacher when we were freshmen, and my desk was the second seat in the fourth row. She heard the door from the auditorium open and turned to see Jake Perkins, the reporter from the school newspaper.

"Dr. Sheridan." The clerk's voice had lost its jocular tone.

"Yes." Jean realized she was gripping the phone. Something's wrong, she thought. *Something's wrong.*

"The maid went into Ms. Wilcox's room. The bed hasn't been slept in. Her clothes are still in the closet, but the maid did notice that some of her toiletries that were on the vanity are gone. Do you think there's a problem?"

"Oh, if she took some things with her, I would say not. Thank you."

That's all Laura would need, Jean thought, for me to be asking questions about her if she went off with somebody. She pushed the button on the cell phone to end the call and snapped the cover closed. But who would she have been with? she wondered. If Gordon was to be believed, he had brushed her off. He said that she'd been flirting with Jack Emerson, but she certainly hadn't neglected Mark or Robby or Carter, either. Yesterday at lunch she was joking with Mark about how successful his show was and saying that maybe she should go into therapy with him. I heard her telling Carter she'd love to do a Broadway show, and later she was in the bar with Robby for a nightcap.

"Dr. Sheridan, may I have a word with you?"

Startled, Jean spun around. She'd forgotten about Jake Perkins. "I'm sorry to bother you," he said unapologetically, "but I wonder if you can tell me if Ms. Wilcox is planning to show up here today."

"I don't know her plans," Jean said, smiling dismissively. "Now I really must get back to the table."

Laura probably got friendly with one of the guys at the dinner last night and went to his place with him, she thought. If she hasn't checked out, she's bound to show up at the hotel later.

———

Jake Perkins studied Jean's expression as she passed him. She's worried, he thought. Could it be because Laura Wilcox didn't show up? My God, is it possible that she's missing? He pulled out his own cell phone, dialed the Glen-Ridge House, and asked for the front desk. "I have a flower delivery for Ms. Laura Wilcox," he said, "but I was asked to make sure that she hadn't checked out."

"No, she hasn't checked out," the clerk told him, "but she didn't stay here last night, so I'm not sure when she'll be back to pick up her bags."

"Was she planning to stay through the weekend?" Jake asked, trying to sound indifferent.

"She was supposed to check out by two. She ordered a car to take her to the airport at two-fifteen, so I don't know what to tell you about your flowers, sonny."

"I guess I'll check with my customer. Thanks."

Jake turned off his cell phone and slipped it back into his pocket. I know exactly where I'm going to be at two o'clock, he thought—I'll be in the lobby of the Glen-Ridge, waiting to see if Laura Wilcox is there to check out.

He started to walk back down the corridor to the auditorium. Suppose she never *does* show up, he thought. Suppose she just disappears. If she does . . . He felt a thrill of nervous anticipation shoot through him. He understood what it was—a newsman's nose for a hot story. It's too big for the *Stonecroft Academy Gazette*, Jake thought. But the *New York Post* would love it. I'll get the lunch table picture enlarged and have it ready to run with the story. He could see the headline: "Hard Luck Class Claims Another Victim." Pretty good.

Or maybe even, "And Then There Was One." Even better!

I took a couple of really good pictures of Dr. Sheridan, he thought. I'll have them ready to show the *Post* as well.

As he opened the door of the auditorium, the first lines of the school song were being sung by the assembled guests. "We hail thee, dear Stonecroft; the place of our dreams . . ."

The reunion of the twentieth-anniversary graduates was over at last.

28

"I guess this is good-bye, Jean. It's been good to see you again." Mark Fleischman was holding his card in his hand. "I'll give you mine if you'll give me yours," he said, smiling.

"Of course." Jean dug into her bag and pulled a card out of her wallet. "I'm glad you were able to make the brunch after all."

"I am, too. When do you leave?"

"I'm staying at the hotel for a few days more. A little research project." Jean tried to sound casual.

"I tape some shows in Boston tomorrow. Otherwise I'd stay and ask you to join me for a quiet dinner tonight." He hesitated, then bent down and kissed her cheek. "Again, as people say, it's been good to see you."

"Good-bye, Mark." Jean caught herself before adding, "Give me a call if you plan to be in Washington." For an instant their hands lingered together, then he was gone.

Carter Stewart and Gordon Amory were standing together, saying final good-byes to the dispersing classmates. Jean walked over to them. Before she could speak, Gordon asked, "Have you heard from Laura?"

"Not yet."

"Laura's unreliable. That's another reason her career has tanked. She has a history of keeping people waiting, but Alison had been moving heaven and earth to get her a job. Too bad that Laura couldn't remember that today."

"Well . . ." Jean decided not to agree or disagree. She turned to Carter Stewart. "Are you heading back to New York, Carter?"

"As a matter of fact, I'm not. I'm checking out of the Glen-Ridge and into the Hudson Valley Hotel across town. Pierce Ellison is directing my new play. He lives only ten minutes away in Highland Falls. We need to go over the script together, and he suggested we could work quietly at his place if I stayed over a few days. I'm not staying at the Glen-Ridge, though. They haven't spent a nickel on improvements at that place in fifty years."

"I can vouch for that," Amory agreed. "I have too many memories of being a busboy and then a room-service waiter there. I'm heading over to the country club. Some of my people are coming in. We're looking for a corporate headquarters in this area."

"Talk to Jack Emerson," Stewart said sarcastically.

"Anyone but him. My people have lined up some places for me to see."

"Then this may not be good-bye," Jean said. "We may be bumping into one another in town. Whether or not, it's been good to be with you."

She did not see Robby Brent or Jack Emerson, but didn't want to wait any longer. She had agreed to meet

Sam Deegan at Alice Sommers' home at two o'clock, and it was nearly that time now.

With a final smile and a murmured good-bye to the classmates she passed on the way out, she walked quickly to the parking lot. As she got into her car, she looked across the school grounds to the cemetery. The unreality of Alison's death hit her again. It seemed so strange to leave her here on this cold, wet day. I used to tell Alison that she should have been born in California, Jean thought as she turned the key in the ignition. She hated the cold. Her idea of heaven was to get out of bed in the morning, open the door, and go for a swim.

That was what Alison was doing the morning she died.

It was the thought that accompanied Jean as she drove to Alice Sommers' home.

29

Carter Stewart had reserved a suite at the new Hudson Valley Hotel near Storm King State Park. Perched on the side of the mountain overlooking the Hudson, with its center building and twin towers, it reminded him of an eagle with outstretched wings.

The eagle, symbol of life and light and power and majesty.

The tentative title for his new play was *The Eagle and the Owl.*

The owl. Symbol of darkness and death. Bird of prey. Pierce Ellison, his director, liked the title. I'm not sure, Stewart thought, as he pulled up at the entrance of the hotel and stepped out of the car. I'm just not sure.

Is it too obvious? Symbols are meant to be noted by the profound thinker, not served on a platter to the Wednesday matinee bridge club. Not that that group rushed to buy tickets to his plays.

"We'll take care of your bags, sir."

Carter Stewart pressed a five-dollar bill into the doorman's hand. At least he didn't say, "Welcome home," he thought.

Five minutes later, a scotch from the mini-bar in his hand, he was standing at a window in his suite. The

Hudson was brooding and restless. Only mid-afternoon in October and there was already a winter feel in the air. But at least, thank God, the reunion was over. I even quite liked seeing a few of those people again, Carter thought, if only to remind me of how far I've come since I left there.

Pierce Ellison felt that they needed to strengthen the character of Gwendolyn in the play. "Get someone who really is a ditsy blonde," he'd been urging. "Not an actress *playing* a ditsy blonde."

Carter Stewart chuckled aloud as he thought of Laura. "My, my, how she would have fit the bill," he said aloud. "I'll drink to that, even though in one hundred thousand years it would never have happened."

30

Robby Brent had not missed the fact that many of his former classmates shunned him after his speech at the dinner. A few others had paid him the barbed compliment of saying that he was a marvelous mimic, even if he had been a little hard on their old teachers and the principal. It also got back to him that Jean Sheridan said humor should not be cruel.

All of which was intensely satisfying to Robby Brent. Miss Ella Bender, the math teacher, had apparently been seen crying in the ladies room after the dinner. You seem to forget, Miss Bender, how frequently you reminded me that I didn't have one-tenth the ability for higher mathematics that my brothers and sisters did. I was your whipping boy, Miss Bender. The last and least of the Brents. And now you have the nerve to be offended when I show your prissy ways and unfortunate habit of frequently licking your lips with your tongue. Too bad.

He had hinted to Jack Emerson that he might be in the market to invest in property, and Emerson had buttonholed him after the brunch. Emerson was a blowhard in a lot of ways, Robby thought as he turned into the Glen-Ridge driveway, but he did make sense when they talked about real estate and the advisability of investing in this area.

"Land," Emerson had expounded. "Around here it does nothing but go up in value. Taxes are low when it's undeveloped. Sit on it for twenty years, and you'll be worth a fortune. Get in on it before it goes out of sight, Robby. I have a few listings on some fabulous parcels, all with views of the Hudson, and some of them waterfront. They'll knock your socks off. I'd buy them myself, but I have plenty. Don't want to make my kid too rich when he grows up. Stay over and I'll take you around tomorrow."

"It's the land, Katie Scarlett, it's the land." Robby grinned, remembering the bewildered look on Emerson's face when he quoted that line from *Gone With the Wind* to him. But then he'd latched onto it when he explained that what Scarlett's father meant was that land was the basis for security and wealth.

"Gotta remember that, Robby. That's great and it's true. Land is real money, real value. Land doesn't go away."

Next time I'll try a quote from Plato on him, Robby thought as he stopped the car at the entrance to the Glen-Ridge. Might as well let the valet do the parking today, he thought. I'm not going anywhere until tomorrow, and then I'll be in Emerson's car.

Jack Emerson should only know how much property I already have, he thought. W. C. Fields used to leave money in banks in towns all over the country, wherever he was performing. I buy undeveloped land all over the country and then have it posted with NO TRESPASSING signs.

All my life growing up, I lived in a rented house, he thought. Even back then, those intellectual wizards, my mother and father, couldn't scrape together enough money for a down payment on a real home. Now, besides my home base in Vegas, if I wanted, I could build a house on my property in Santa Barbara or Minneapolis or Atlanta or Boston or the Hamptons or New Orleans or Palm Beach or Aspen, to say nothing of acres and acres in Washington. Land is my secret, Robby thought smugly as he walked into the lobby of the Glen-Ridge.

And land holds my secrets.

31

"I was at the cemetery this morning," Alice Sommers told Jean. "I could see the Stonecroft group at the memorial service. Karen's grave isn't terribly far from where Alison Kendall is buried."

"Not as many people attended as I would have expected," Jean said. "Much of the class went directly to the breakfast."

They were sitting in the cozy den of Alice Sommers' townhouse. She had started the fire, and the leaping flames not only warmed the room but elevated their spirits as well. It was clear to Jean that Alice Sommers had been weeping for a long time. Her eyes were swollen and puffy, but there was an expression of peace on her face that had not been there yesterday.

As though she could read her thoughts, Alice said, "You know, as I told you yesterday, the days leading up to the anniversary are the worst. I go over every minute of that last day, wondering if there was something we could have done to keep Karen safe. Of course, twenty years ago we didn't have an alarm system. Now, most of us wouldn't dream of going to bed without setting an alarm in the house."

She reached for the teapot and refilled their cups. "But now I'll be okay again," she said briskly. "In fact, I've decided that retirement may not be such a good thing. One of my friends has a flower shop and needs help. She's asked me to work for her a couple of days a week, and I'm going to do it."

"That's a great idea," Jean said sincerely. "I remember how beautiful your garden always looked."

"Michael used to tease me by saying that if I spent as much time in the kitchen as I did in the garden, I'd be a world-class chef," Alice said. She glanced out the window. "Oh, look, here's Sam. Right on time, as always."

Sam Deegan scraped his feet carefully on the mat before he rang the bell. He had stopped at Karen's grave on his way to meet Jean, then had found himself almost unable to say that he had to give up trying to find her killer. Something kept blocking the apology he had planned to offer her. Finally he had said, "Karen, I'm retiring. I have to. I'll talk your case over with one of the young guys. Maybe somebody smarter than I am can nab the guy who hurt you."

Alice was opening the door before his finger touched the bell. He did not comment on her swollen eyes, but gripped both her hands in his. "Let me just be sure I don't track mud into the house," he said.

He was at the cemetery, Alice thought gratefully. I

know he was. "Come on in," she told him. "Don't worry about a speck or two of dirt." There was something so strong and reassuring about Sam, she thought as she took his coat. *I was so right when I asked him to try to help Jean.*

He had brought a notebook with him, and after greeting Jean and accepting the offer of a cup of tea from Alice, he got down to business. "Jean, I've been doing a lot of thinking. We have to take seriously that whoever is writing you about Lily may be capable of hurting her. He was near enough to her to pick up her hairbrush, so it may be someone in the family who adopted her. He—and understand, it could just as easily be a *she*—may intend to try to extort money from you, which as you point out would be almost a relief. But that kind of situation could go on for years, too. So it's clear we've got to find this person as fast as possible."

"I went to St. Thomas of Canterbury this morning," Jean said, "but the priest who said Mass was one who only comes in on Sundays. He said I should go to the rectory office tomorrow and see the pastor about looking at the baptismal records. Since then I've been thinking about it. He might be pretty wary about opening them to me. He might think this is just my way of trying to find Lily."

She looked directly at Sam. "I'll bet that thought occurred to you."

"When Alice told me about it, it did occur to me," Sam said frankly. "Having met you, though, I absolutely believe that the situation is exactly as you describe it.

But you're right—the priest would have to be very careful, which is why I think it should be me going to him instead of you. He'd probably be a lot more willing to talk to me if he knows of an adopted baby who was baptized at that time."

"I've thought of that, too," Jean said quietly. "You know, for these twenty years I've wondered if I shouldn't have kept Lily. It wasn't all that many generations ago that an eighteen-year-old with a baby was the norm. Now that I have to find her, I realize that if I could see her even from a distance, I'd be satisfied." She bit her lip. "Or at least I think I'd be satisfied," she said softly.

Sam looked from Jean to Alice. Two women who, each in a different way, had lost a child. The cadet was about to graduate and be commissioned. If he had not been killed in that accident, Jean would have married him and kept her baby. If Karen had not happened to come home for an overnight visit twenty years ago, Alice would still have her, and probably have grandchildren as well.

Life never has been fair, Sam thought, but some things we can try to make better. He hadn't been able to solve Karen's murder, but at least maybe he could help Jean now.

"Dr. Connors had to have worked with a lawyer to handle the adoption papers," he said. "Somebody is sure to know who that lawyer was. Does his wife or family still live around here?"

"I don't know," Jean said.

"Well, we'll start with that. Did you bring the hairbrush and faxes with you?"

"No, I didn't."

"I'd like to get them from you."

"The brush is one of those small ones that you carry in a purse," Jean said. "It's the kind you can get in a drugstore. The faxes don't have anything to identify the source, but of course you can have them both."

"When I speak to the pastor, it will help if I have them."

Jean and Sam left a few minutes later. They arranged that he would follow her in his car to the hotel. From the window, Alice watched them go, then reached in the pocket of her sweater. This morning she had found a trinket on Karen's grave that had undoubtedly been dropped by a child. When she was little, Karen had loved stuffed animals and had a variety of them. Alice thought of the owl that had been one of her favorites, as with a wistful smile she looked down at the inch-long pewter owl she was holding in the palm of her hand.

Jake Perkins sat in the lobby of the Glen-Ridge House, watching as the last of the reunion celebrants checked out and headed back to their private lives. The welcoming banner was gone, and he could see that the bar was empty. No last good-byes, he thought. By now they're probably all sick of one another.

The first thing he had done when he arrived was stop at the front desk and verify that Ms. Wilcox had not yet returned to check out, and that she had not cancelled the car that was to take her to the airport at two-fifteen.

At two-fifteen he watched as a uniformed driver came into the lobby and went to the desk. Jake rushed to stand next to him and hear for himself that the man expected to pick up Laura Wilcox.

At two-thirty the driver left, obviously disgruntled. Jake overheard his comment that it was too damn bad he hadn't been told that she wasn't going, because he could have had another job, and not to bother to call him the next time she needs a ride.

At four o'clock, Jake was still in the lobby. That was when Dr. Sheridan returned with the older man she'd been talking to after the dinner. They went directly to the front desk. She's asking about Laura Wilcox, Jake thought. His hunch was right—Laura Wilcox was missing.

He decided it wouldn't hurt to try to get a statement from Dr. Sheridan. He reached her side in time to hear the man she was with say, "Jean, I agree. I don't like the look of it, but Laura is an adult and has the right to change her mind about checking out of the hotel or catching a plane."

"Excuse me, sir. I'm Jake Perkins, a reporter for the Stonecroft paper," Jake broke in.

"Sam Deegan."

It was clear to Jake that his presence was not welcomed by either Dr. Sheridan or Sam Deegan. Get right to it, he thought. "Dr. Sheridan, I know you were concerned that Ms. Wilcox didn't show up for the brunch, and now she has missed her car to the airport. Do you think that anything may have happened to her—I mean, given the history of the women at your old lunch table at Stonecroft?"

He saw the startled glance Jean Sheridan gave to Sam Deegan. She hasn't told him about the lunch table group, Jake thought. He didn't know who this guy was, but it would be interesting to test his reaction to what Jake was now sure was a breaking story. He pulled out the picture of the girls at the lunch table from his pocket. "You see, sir, this was the group at Dr. Sheridan's lunch table in their senior year at Stonecroft. Over these twenty years since they graduated, five had died as of last month. Two of them were killed in accidents, one was a suicide, and one disappeared, supposedly caught in an avalanche in Snowbird. Last month, the fifth one, Alison Kendall, died in her swimming pool. From what I read, it seems to be a possibility that it was not an accidental death. Now Laura Wilcox seems to be missing. Don't you think that this is a pretty bizarre coincidence?"

Sam took the picture, and as he studied it, the expression on his face became grim. "I don't believe in coincidence of this magnitude," he said brusquely. "Now if you'll excuse us, Mr. Perkins."

"Oh, don't worry about me. I'm going to wait around to see if Ms. Wilcox shows up. I'd like to have a final interview with her."

Ignoring him, Sam took out his card and handed it to the desk clerk. "I want a list of the employees who were on duty last night," he said, his voice commanding and forceful.

"I thought I'd be gone by now, but I had a whole bunch of messages waiting for me when I got back from the brunch," Gordon Amory explained to Jean. "We're shooting one episode of our new series in Canada, and some major problems have developed. I've been on the phone the last two hours."

His bags at his side, he had come up to the front desk as the clerk was showing Sam the worksheets of the hotel employees. Then he studied Jean's face. "Jean, is something wrong?"

"Laura is missing," Jean said, hearing the tremor in her own voice. "She was supposed to have been picked up at two-fifteen to go to the airport. The bed in her room wasn't slept in, and the maid said that some of her toiletries seem to be gone. Maybe she just decided to stay with someone and is perfectly all right, but she was so definite about being with us this morning that I'm terribly worried now."

"She was certainly definite about being at the brunch when she was talking to Jack Emerson last night," Gordon said. "As I told you, she was pretty cool to me after I told her she didn't have the faintest chance of being cast in the upcoming series, but in the bar after dinner I overheard what she said to Jack."

Sam had been listening to their conversation. He turned to Gordon and introduced himself. "We have to realize that Laura Wilcox is an adult. She has every right in the world to go off by herself or with a friend, and to change her mind about checking out. Nevertheless, I think it would be wise to follow up and see if anyone, either a hotel employee or a friend, knew her plans."

"I'm sorry to have kept you waiting, Mr. Amory," the clerk said. "I have your bill ready."

Gordon Amory hesitated, then looked at Jean. "You think something may have happened to Laura, don't you?"

"Yes, I do. Laura was very close to Alison. She simply wouldn't deliberately skip the memorial, no matter what plans she had for last night."

"Is my room still free?" Amory asked the clerk.

"Yes, of course, sir."

"Then I'm going to stay at least until we know more about Ms. Wilcox." He turned to Jean, and for an instant, even in the midst of her concern about Laura, she was struck by the realization of what a handsome man Gordon Amory had become. I used to feel so sorry for him, she thought. He was a pathetic loser back then, and look what he's made of himself.

"Jean, I know I hurt Laura last night, and it was lousy of me—kind of a payback, I guess, for the way she used to brush me off when we were kids. I could have

promised her a part even if it wasn't the lead in that series. I have a feeling she may be desperate. That could
explain why she didn't show up this morning. I bet she'll
be back with or without an explanation for where she's
been, and when she is, I'm going to offer her a job. And
I'm going to hang around to do it personally."

34

Jake Perkins stayed in the lobby of the Glen-Ridge, watching as, one after another, the employees who had been on duty Saturday night went into the small office behind the desk and talked to Sam Deegan. When they came out, he managed to buttonhole enough of them to learn that they got the impression that Deegan was also going down the list and phoning anyone who was off today but had been around last night.

The upshot from what he heard was that no one had seen Laura Wilcox leave the hotel. The doorman and the valet parkers were absolutely certain that she had not left by the front door.

He correctly guessed that the young woman in a maid's uniform might be the one who cleaned Laura's room. When she emerged from talking to Deegan, Jake followed her across the lobby, jumped in the elevator behind her, and got off at the fourth floor with her. "I'm a reporter for the Stonecroft newspaper," he explained as he handed her his card, "and I'm also a stringer for the *New York Post*." Close to the truth, he thought. Before much longer, I will be.

It wasn't hard to get her talking. Her name was Myrna Robinson. She was a student at the community college and worked part-time at the hotel. She's kind of naïve, Jake thought smugly as he observed her absolutely thrilled expression at the excitement of having been questioned by a detective.

He opened his notebook. "What exactly did Detective Deegan ask you, Myrna?"

"He wanted to know if I was sure that some of Laura Wilcox's cosmetics were missing and I told him I was absolutely positive," she confided breathlessly. "I said, 'Mr. Deegan, you have no idea how much stuff she managed to get on top of that skinny vanity in the bathroom, and half of it's gone. I mean, things like cleanser and moisturizer and a toothbrush and her cosmetic bag.'"

"The kind of stuff any woman carries when she goes away overnight," Jake said helpfully. "What about clothes?"

"I didn't talk about clothes to Mr. Deegan," Myrna said hesitantly. Nervously she twisted the top button on her black uniform dress. "I mean, I told him I was sure one of her suitcases was missing, but I didn't want him to think I was nosy or anything, so I didn't mention that her blue cashmere jacket and slacks and ankle-top boots weren't in the closet."

Myrna was about Laura's size. Dollars to doughnuts she had been trying on the clothes, Jake thought. A suit and slacks were missing—probably what Laura planned to wear to the memorial service and brunch. "You told Mr. Deegan about a suitcase that isn't in her room?"

"Uh-huh. She brought a lot of luggage with her. Honest, you'd think she was on a round-the-world trip. Anyway, the smaller suitcase wasn't there this morning. It was different from the others. It's a Louis Vuitton — that's how I noticed it wasn't there. I love that pattern, don't you? So distinctive. The two big ones she had are creamy-colored leather."

Jake prided himself on his ear for French, so he winced inwardly at Myrna's pronunciation of "Vuitton." "Myrna, is there any chance I could get a look at Laura's room?" he asked. "I swear I won't touch a thing."

He had gone too far. He could see an alarmed expression replace the excitement on her face. She looked past him down the corridor, and he could read her thoughts. If the housekeeper ever caught her bringing someone into a guest's room, she'd be fired. Quickly he backtracked. "Myrna, I shouldn't have asked you that. Forget it. Listen, you have my card. It would be worth twenty bucks to me if you take my number and give me a call if you hear anything about Laura. How about it? Want to be a girl reporter?"

Myrna bit her lip as she considered the offer. "It's not the money," she began.

"Of course not," Jake agreed.

"If you put the story in the *Post*, I'd have to be an unnamed source."

She's smarter than she looks, Jake thought, as he nodded eagerly. They shook hands on the deal.

It was nearly six o'clock. When he went back to the

lobby, it was almost deserted. Jake went up to the desk clerk and inquired if Mr. Deegan had left the hotel.

The clerk looked tired and distressed. "Look, sonny, he's gone, and unless you want to rent a room, I'd suggest you go home, too."

"I'm sure he asked you to let him know if Ms. Wilcox returns or if you hear from her," Jake suggested. "May I give you my card? I became friendly with Ms. Wilcox during the course of the weekend, and I'm concerned about her, too."

The clerk took the card and studied it. "Reporter for the *Stonecroft Academy Gazette* and writer-journalist-at-large, huh?" He tore the card in half. "You're too big for your breeches, sonny. Do me a favor and get lost."

35

The body of Helen Whelan was discovered at 5:30 P.M. on Sunday afternoon in a wooded area in Washingtonville, a town about fifteen miles from Surrey Meadows. The discovery was made by a twelve-year-old boy who was cutting through the woods, taking a shortcut to his friend's home.

Sam got the message as he was finishing his interviews of the employees at the Glen-Ridge House. He called Jean in her room. She had gone upstairs to phone Mark Fleischman, Carter Stewart, and Jack Emerson, in the hope that one of them might have known Laura's plans. She had already seen Robby Brent in the lobby, and he had disclaimed any knowledge of where Laura might be.

"Jean, I have to go," Sam explained. "Have you reached anyone yet?"

"I talked to Carter. He's very concerned but has no idea where Laura might be. I told him that Gordon and I are having dinner, and he's going to join us. Maybe if we can make a list between us of the people Laura seemed to be spending time with, we might come up with something. Jack Emerson isn't home. I left word on his answering machine. Same with Mark Fleischman."

"That's about the best you can do for the moment," Sam said. "Our hands are legally tied. If no one has heard from her by tomorrow, I'll try to get a search warrant to go through her room and see if she left any indication of where she might have gone. Otherwise, sit tight."

"You will go over to the rectory in the morning?"

"Absolutely," Sam promised. He snapped closed his phone and hurried out to his car. There was no point in telling Jean that he was on his way to the crime scene where another woman who had disappeared had been found.

———•———

Helen Whelan had been struck with a blow on the back of her head and then had been stabbed repeatedly. "He probably hit her from behind with the same blunt weapon that he used on the dog," Cal Grey, the medical examiner, told Sam when he arrived at the crime scene. The body was in the process of being removed, and under floodlights investigators were combing the roped-off area for possible clues to the killer. "I can't be sure until I do the autopsy, but it looks to me as if the injury to her head might have knocked her out. The stab wounds happened after he got her here. One can only hope that she didn't know what was happening to her."

Sam watched as the slender body was lifted into a body bag. "Her clothes don't look disturbed."

"They're not. My guess is that whoever grabbed her brought her directly here and killed her. She still has the dog's leash around her wrist."

"Hold it a minute," Sam snapped to the attendant who was opening the stretcher. He squatted down and felt his feet sink into the muddy ground. "Let me have your flashlight, Cal."

"What do you see?"

"There's a smear of blood on the side of her slacks. I doubt she got it from the wounds in her chest and neck. My guess is that the killer was bleeding pretty heavily, probably from a dog bite." He straightened up. "Which means he may have needed to go to an emergency room. I'll get an alert out to all the hospitals in the area to report any dog bites they may have treated over the weekend or that may come up in the next few days. And make sure the lab runs tests on the blood. I'll meet you back at your place, Cal."

On the drive to the medical examiner's office, the waste of the life of Helen Whelan hit Sam with intensity, catching him in the pit of his stomach. It happened whenever he encountered this kind of violence. I want that guy, he thought, and I want to be the one who cuffs him. I hope to God that wherever that dog bit him, he's in misery right now.

That train of thought gave him another idea. Maybe he's too smart to go to an emergency room, but he'll still have to take care of that bite. It's like looking for a needle in a haystack, but it might be worth notifying all the pharmacies in the area to watch out for someone buying items such as peroxide and bandages and antibacterial ointments.

But if he's smart enough to avoid a hospital, he's probably smart enough to shop for stuff like that in one of the big drugstores where there's a long line at the cash register and no one is paying attention to what's in the basket except to scan it.

Still, it's worth a try, Sam decided grimly, remembering the smiling picture of Helen Whelan he had seen in her apartment. She was twenty years older than Karen Sommers had been, he thought, but she died the same way—savagely stabbed to death.

The mist that had come and gone all day had turned into a driving rain. Sam frowned as he switched on the windshield wipers. There couldn't be any connection between those cases, though, he thought. There hadn't been a similar stabbing in this area in twenty years. Karen had been in her home. Helen Whelan had been outside walking her dog. But, then again, was it possible that some maniac had been lying low all these years?

Anything was possible, Sam decided. Please let him have gotten careless, he thought. Let him have dropped something that would lead us to him. Hopefully we'll have his DNA. That must be his blood on the dog's whiskers and maybe also the smear on her slacks.

Arriving at the medical examiner's office, he pulled into the parking area, got out of his car, locked it, and went inside. It was going to be a long night and a longer day tomorrow. He had to see the pastor at St. Thomas and persuade him to open the records of baptisms that had taken place nearly twenty years ago. He had to get in touch with the families of the five women from Stonecroft who had died in the order in which they sat at the lunch table—he needed to know more about the details of their deaths. And he needed to find out what had happened to Laura Wilcox. If it weren't for the deaths of the other five from her class, I'd say she just took off with a guy, he thought. From what I understand she's pretty lively and has never been without a man for long if she can help it.

The medical examiner and the ambulance with Helen Whelan's body arrived seconds behind him. Half an hour later Sam was studying the effects that had been removed from the body. Her watch and a ring were her only jewelry. She had probably not been carrying a handbag because her house key and a handkerchief were in the pocket on the right side of her jacket.

Lying on the table next to the house key was one other object: a pewter owl a little over an inch long. Sam reached for the tweezers that the attendant had used in handling the keys and the owl, picked up the owl and examined it closely. The unwinking eyes, cold and wide, met his gaze.

"It was way down in the pocket of her slacks," the attendant explained. "I almost missed it."

Sam remembered there had been a pumpkin outside the door of Helen Whelan's garden apartment and a paper skeleton in a box in the hall that she must have been planning to hang up somewhere. "She was decorating for Halloween," he said. "This was probably part of the stuff she had. Bag everything, and I'll take it to the lab."

Forty minutes later, he was watching as the clothing of Helen Whelan was checked under a microscope for anything that might help identify her killer. Another attendant was examining the car keys for fingerprints.

"These are all hers," he commented, as with tweezers in his hand he reached for the owl. A moment later he said, "That's funny. There aren't any fingerprints on this thing, not even smudges. How do you figure that one? It didn't walk into her pocket. It had to have been put there by someone wearing gloves."

Sam thought for a minute. Had the killer left the owl deliberately? He was sure of it. "We're keeping this quiet," he snapped. Taking the tweezers from the attendant, he picked up the owl and stared at it. "You're going to lead me to this guy," he vowed. "I don't know how yet, but you *will*."

36

They had agreed to meet at seven o'clock in the dining room. At the last minute Jean decided to change into dark blue slacks and a light blue sweater with a floppy wide collar that she had bought at an Escada sale. All day she had been unable to shake off the chill of the cemetery. Even the jacket and slacks she had been wearing seemed to retain the cold and dampness she had felt there.

Ridiculous, of course, she told herself as she touched up her makeup and brushed her hair. While standing in front of the bathroom mirror, she paused for a moment, holding the brush and staring at it. Who had been so close to Lily that he or she had managed to take her brush from her home or handbag, she wondered.

Or was it possible that Lily managed to trace me and is punishing me for giving her up? Jean asked herself, agonized by the thought. She's nineteen and a half now. What kind of life has she led? Have the people who adopted her been the wonderful couple Dr. Connors described to me, or did they turn out to be bad parents once they had the baby?

But instinct immediately told Jean that Lily wasn't playing games to torment her. This is someone else, someone who wants to hurt *me*. Ask for money, she pleaded silently. I'll give you money, but don't hurt *her*.

She looked back into the mirror and studied her reflection. Several times she had been told that she resembled the *Today* show host Katie Couric, and she felt flattered at the comparison. Does Lily look like me? she wondered. Or is she more like Reed? Those strands of hair are so blond, and he used to joke that his mother said his hair was the color of winter wheat. That means she has his hair. Reed's eyes were blue and so are mine, so she certainly has blue eyes.

This line of speculation was familiar territory. Shaking her head, Jean laid the brush on the counter, turned off the bathroom light, reached for her purse, and went down to meet the others for dinner.

Gordon Amory, Robby Brent, and Jack Emerson were already at the table in the nearly empty dining room. As they stood up to greet her, she was aware of the marked contrast in the way they looked and dressed. Amory was wearing a cashmere open-necked shirt and expensive tweed jacket. He looked every inch the successful executive. Robby Brent had changed from the cableknit sweater he had worn to the brunch. To Jean, the turtleneck shirt he was wearing now emphasized his short neck and squat body. A hint of perspiration on his forehead and cheeks gave him a glistening appearance that she found off-putting. Jack Emerson's corduroy jacket was well cut, but cheapened by the red-and-white-checked shirt and bright multicolored tie he wore. The thought went through her mind that with his fleshy florid face, Jack Emerson embodied the old anti-Nixon political ad with the slogan "Would you buy a used car from this man?"

Jack pulled out the empty chair beside his own and patted her arm as she stepped around it. In a reflex action, Jean stiffened and pulled her arm away from him.

"We've ordered drinks, Jeannie," Emerson told her. "I took a chance and ordered a chardonnay for you."

"That's fine. Are you guys early, or am I late?"

"We're a bit early. You're exactly on time, and Carter isn't here yet."

Twenty minutes later, as they were debating whether or not to order, Carter arrived. "Sorry to keep you waiting, but I didn't expect another reunion quite this soon," he observed dryly as he joined them. He was now wearing jeans and a hooded sweatshirt.

"None of us did," Gordon Amory said in agreement. "Why don't you order a drink, and then I suggest we get down to the reason we're here now."

Carter nodded. He caught the waiter's eye and pointed to the martini Emerson was drinking. "Continue," he said to Gordon, his tone dry.

"Let me start by saying that after some consideration, I believe and hope that our concern for Laura may be unnecessary. I remember hearing that a few years ago she accepted an invitation to visit some big bucks guy, who shall be nameless, at his Palm Beach estate, and she reportedly left in the middle of a dinner party to go away with him on his private plane. That time, as far as anyone could gather, she didn't even bother to bring her own toothbrush, never mind her cosmetics."

"I don't think anyone returned to Stonecroft in a private plane," Robby Brent observed. "In fact, I think from the looks of some of them, they probably backpacked to get here."

"Come on, Robby," Jack Emerson protested. "A lot of our graduates have done mighty well. That's why quite a few of them have bought property around here for an eventual second home."

"Let's skip the sales pitch for tonight, Jack," Gordon said irritably. "Listen, you have big bucks, and you're the only one, as far as we know, who has a house in town and could have invited Laura to join you for your own quiet reunion."

Jack Emerson's already florid face darkened. "I hope that's supposed to be funny, Gordon."

"I don't want to displace Robby as our comedian in residence," Gordon said as he helped himself to an olive from the dish the waiter had placed on the table. "Of course I was joking about you and Laura, but not about the sales pitch."

Jean decided it was time to try to redirect the conversation. "I left a message for Mark on his cell phone," she said. "He called me back just before I came downstairs. If we haven't heard from Laura by tomorrow, he's going to rearrange his schedule and come back."

"He always had a thing for Laura when we were kids," Robby observed. "I wouldn't be surprised if he still does. He made it a point to sit next to her on the dais last night. He even changed place cards to make it happen."

So that's why he's rushing back, Jean thought, realizing she had read too much into his phone call. "Jeannie," he had said, "I want to believe that Laura is okay, but if anything has happened to her, it could mean that there is a terrible pattern to the loss of the girls at your lunch table. You've got to realize that."

And I assumed he was worrying about me, she thought. I was even thinking of telling him about Lily. Since he's a psychiatrist, I thought maybe he'd have some insight into what kind of person is contacting me about her.

It was a relief when the waiter, a slight, elderly man, began passing out menus. "May I tell you our specials for this evening?" he asked.

Robby looked up at the waiter with a hopeful smile. "Can't wait," he murmured.

"Filet mignon with mushrooms, filet of sole stuffed with crabmeat . . ."

When he had finished the recitation, Robby asked, "May I ask you a question?"

"Of course, sir."

"Is it a habit of this establishment to make last night's leftovers today's specials?"

"Oh, sir, I assure you," the waiter began, his voice flustered and apologetic, "I've been here forty years, and we're very proud of our cuisine."

"Never mind, never mind. Just a little humor to lighten the table talk. Jean, you first."

"The caesar salad and rack of lamb, medium-rare,"

Jean said quietly. Robby isn't just sarcastic, she thought; he's nasty and cruel. He likes to hurt people who can't strike back, people like Miss Bender, the math teacher at the dinner last night, and now this poor guy. He talks about Mark having a crush on Laura. But no one had a bigger crush on her than he did.

Suddenly, a disquieting thought occurred to her. Robby's made a lot of money now. He's famous. If he invited Laura to meet him somewhere, she would go, I know she would. Jean was aghast to realize that she was seriously considering the fact that Robby might have lured Laura away and then harmed her.

Jack Emerson was the last to order. As he handed the menu back to the waiter, he said, "I promised some friends that I'd drop in for a nightcap, so I think it would be a good idea to start discussing who we think Laura might have paid a lot of attention to over the weekend." He shot a glance at Gordon. "Besides you, of course, Gordie. You were at the top of her A-list."

Dear God, Jean thought, they'll all be at each other's throats if this keeps up. She turned to Carter Stewart. "Carter, why don't we start with you. Any suggestions?"

"I saw her talking a lot to Joel Nieman, better known as the Romeo who forgot half his lines in the school play. His wife was here only for the cocktail party and dinner Friday night, then went home. She's an executive with Target and was flying to Hong Kong Saturday morning."

"Don't they live somewhere around here, Jack?" Gordon asked.

"They live in Rye."

"That's not that far away."

"I was talking to Joel and his wife at the party Friday night," Jean said. "He doesn't look at all like the kind of guy who would ask Laura to go home with him the minute his wife is out of town."

"He may not look like it, but I happen to know he's had a couple of girlfriends," Emerson said. "Also that he was damn near indicted for some shady deals his accounting firm was involved in. That's why we passed on making him an honoree."

"How about our missing honoree, Mark Fleischman?" Robby Brent asked. "He may be, as his introduction at the dinner quoted, 'tall, lanky, cheerful, funny, and wise,' but he also was hanging around Laura every minute he could. He broke his neck rushing to sit next to her on the bus to West Point."

Jack Emerson finished his martini and signaled the waiter for a refill. Then he raised his eyebrows. "Just occurred to me. Mark would have a place to invite Laura. I know for a fact that his father's out of town. I met Cliff Fleischman in the post office last week and asked him if he was coming to see his son honored. He told me he had long-standing plans to visit some friends in Chicago but that he'd give Mark a call. Maybe he offered him the house. Cliff won't be back till Tuesday."

"Then I think Mr. Fleischman must have changed his mind," Jean said. "Mark told me that he'd passed his old house and there were a lot of lights on. He didn't say anything about hearing from his father."

"Cliff Fleischman leaves a bunch of lights on whenever he's away," Emerson replied. "His house was burglarized when he was on vacation about ten years ago. He blamed it on the fact that it was so dark. He said it was a dead giveaway that there was no one home."

Gordon broke off a bread stick. "I got the feeling Mark was estranged from his father."

"He is, and I know why," Emerson said. "After Mark's mother died, his father gave up the housekeeper, and she came to work for us for a while. She was a real gossip and gave us the lowdown on the Fleischmans. Everybody knew that Dennis, the older son, was the apple of his mother's eye. She never got over losing him, and blamed Mark for the accident. The car was at the top of that long driveway, and Mark was always pestering Dennis to teach him to drive. Mark was only thirteen and wasn't allowed to start the car unless Dennis was with him. That afternoon he'd started it and then forgotten to put on the parking brake before he left the car. When the car started to roll down the hill, Dennis never saw it coming."

"How did she find out?" Jean asked.

"According to the housekeeper, one night shortly before she died, something happened and she turned completely against Mark. He didn't even come to her funeral. She cut him out of her will, too; she had big bucks from her mother's family. Mark was in medical school at that time."

"But he was only thirteen years old at the time of the accident," Jean said in protest.

"And always jealous of his brother," Carter Stewart said quietly. "You can bet that. But maybe he has been in touch with the father, and maybe he still has a key to the house, and maybe he knew the father was away."

Did Mark lie about having to go back to Boston? Jean wondered. He went out of his way to stop at the table in the bar when I was with Alice and Sam to tell us about walking past his father's house. Could he still be right here in town with Laura?

I don't want to believe that, she acknowledged to herself, as Gordon Amory volunteered, "We're all assuming that Laura went *with* someone. It's also possible she went *to* someone. We're not that far from Greenwich and Bedford and Westport, where a lot of her celebrity friends have homes."

Jack Emerson had brought a list of the people who attended the reunion. In the end, they decided that each of them would take names to call, explain why they were concerned, and ask for their thoughts as to where Laura might have gone.

When they left the dining room, after promising to be in touch in the morning, Carter Stewart and Jack Emerson headed for their cars. In the lobby, Jean told Gordon Amory and Robby Brent that she was going to stop at the desk.

"Then I'll say good night," Gordon told her. "I still have some phone calls to make."

"It's Sunday night, Gordie," Robby Brent said. "What could be so important it can't wait till morning?"

Gordon Amory stared at Robby's deceptively innocent face. "As you know, I prefer to be addressed as 'Gordon,'" he said quietly. "Good night, Jean."

"He is so full of himself," Robby said as he watched Gordon walk across the lobby and press the button for the elevator. "I bet he goes up and turns on the television. Tonight's the opening of a new series on one of his channels. Or maybe he just wants to look in the mirror at his pretty new face. Honest to God, Jeannie, that plastic surgeon must be a genius. Remember what a dorky-looking kid Gordie used to be?"

I don't care why he's going up to his room, Jean thought. I just want to check to see if by any chance Laura has phoned and then go up to bed myself. "More power to Gordon that he was able to turn his life around. He had a pretty nasty time growing up."

"Like all of us," Robby said dismissively. "Except of course, for our missing beauty queen." He shrugged. "I'm going to grab a jacket and go out for a while. I'm a health nut and except for a couple of walks, I haven't had any exercise all weekend. The gym in this place is the pits."

"Is there anything about this town or this hotel or the people you've been meeting that isn't the pits in your opinion?" Jean asked, not caring if her voice sounded sharp.

"Very little," Robby said cheerfully, "except for you, of course, Jeannie. I was sorry to see that you looked kind of upset when we talked about Mark hanging around Laura this weekend. For the record, I could see that Mark was playing up to you, too. He's a hard guy to figure out, but then most psychiatrists are more nuts than their patients. If Mark did release the brake on the car that killed his brother, I wonder if consciously or unconsciously it was deliberate. After all, it was his brother's new car, a gift from Mommy and Daddy for graduation from Stonecroft. Think about that."

With a wink and a wave of his hand he was on his way to the bank of elevators. Furious and humiliated that he had so correctly diagnosed her reaction to the comments about Mark and Laura, Jean walked over to the desk. The clerk on duty was Amy Sachs, a small soft-voiced woman with short graying hair and oversized glasses that hung loosely over the bridge of her nose.

"No, we definitely have not heard from Ms. Wilcox," she told Jean. "But a fax came in for you, Dr. Sheridan." She turned and reached for an envelope on the shelf behind the desk.

Jean felt her mouth go dry. As she told herself that she should wait and read the contents upstairs, she ripped open the envelope.

The message it contained consisted of eight words: LILIES THAT FESTER SMELL FAR WORSE THAN WEEDS.

Lilies that fester, Jean thought. *Dead lilies.*

"Is anything wrong, Dr. Sheridan?" the mousy clerk asked anxiously. "I hope that isn't bad news."

"What? Oh . . . no . . . it's quite all right, thank you." In a daze, Jean made her way upstairs, went to her room, opened her purse, and ransacked her wallet for Sam Deegan's cell phone number. His terse, "Sam Deegan" made her realize that it was nearly ten o'clock and that he might have been asleep. "Sam, I probably woke you up—"

"No, you didn't," he interrupted. "What is it, Jean? Did you hear from Laura?"

"No, it's Lily. Another fax."

"Read it to me."

Her voice trembling, she read the eight words to him. "Sam, that's a quote from a Shakespeare sonnet. He's referring to dead lilies. Sam, whoever sent this is threatening to kill my child." Jean heard the rising hysteria in her voice as she cried, "What can I do to *stop* him? What can I *do*?"

37

She probably had the fax by now. He still didn't know why he enjoyed taunting Jean, especially now that he had decided he was going to kill her. Why twist the knife by threatening Meredith, or Lily, as Jean called the girl? For nearly twenty years his secret knowledge of her birth and of her adoptive parents had been one of those little facts that seem useless, like gifts that cannot be returned but will never be taken from the shelf.

It was only when he met her parents at a luncheon last year and realized who they were that he had made it his business to be friendly with them. In August he had even invited them to spend a long weekend with him and to bring Meredith who was home on vacation with them. That was when the idea of taking something that would be proof of her DNA occurred to him.

The opportunity to steal her brush had been handed to him on a platter. They were all at the pool, and her cell phone rang while she was brushing her hair after a swim. She answered the call and walked away to talk privately. He slipped the brush into his pocket and then began circulating among his other guests. The next day he sent the brush and the first message to Jean.

The power of life and death—so far he had exercised it over five of the lunch room girls as well as over many other women, chosen at random. He wondered how soon it would be before they found the body of Helen Whelan. Had it been a mistake to leave the owl in her pocket? Until now he had left his symbol hidden, unobtrusive, unnoticeable. Like last month, when he had slipped one of them into a kitchen drawer in the pool house where he had waited for Alison.

The lights in the house were off. He took the night vision glasses from his pocket, put them on, put his key in the lock, opened the back door, and went inside. He closed and locked the door and walked through the kitchen to the back staircase, then padded noiselessly up the stairs.

Laura was in the bedroom that had been hers before her family moved to Concord Avenue when she was sixteen. He had tied her hands and feet and put a gag on her mouth. She was lying on top of the bed, her gold evening gown glittering in the dark.

She had not heard him come into the room, and when he bent over her, he could hear her terrified gasp. "I'm back, Laura," he whispered. "Aren't you glad?"

She tried to shrink away from him.

"I ammmm an owwlllll annnnd I livvvvve in in in a tree," he whispered. "You thought it was funny to mimic me, didn't you? Do you think it's funny now, Laura? Do you?"

With the night glasses, he could see the terror in her

eyes. Whimpering sounds came from her throat as she shook her head from side to side.

"That's not the right answer, Laura. You do think it's funny. All of you girls think it's funny. Show me you think it's funny. Show me."

She began to shake her head up and down. In a quick movement, he untied the gag. "Don't raise your voice, Laura," he whispered. "No one will hear you, and if you do cry out, I will hold this pillow over your face. Do you understand me?"

"Please," Laura whispered. "Please . . ."

"No, Laura I don't want you to say 'please.' I want you to mimic me, giving my line onstage, and then I want you to laugh."

"I . . . I ammmm an owl annnd I llllivvve livvvvve innnnn aaaa treeee."

He nodded approvingly. "That's the way. You're a very good mimic. Now pretend that you're with the girls at the lunch table and giggle and snicker and cackle and laugh. I want to see how amused all of them were after you ridiculed me."

"I can't . . . I'm sorry . . ."

He lifted the pillow and held it over her face.

Desperately, Laura began to laugh, shrill, high-pitched, hysterical bleating sounds. "Ha . . . ha . . . ha . . ." Tears spilled from her eyes. "Please . . ."

He put his hand over her mouth. "You were about to use my name. That is forbidden. You may only call me 'The Owl.' You will have to practice imitating the girls being amused. Now I am going to untie your hands and let you eat. I brought you soup and a roll. Wasn't that good of me? Then I will permit you to use the bathroom.

"After that, when you are back in a safe sleep position, I am going to dial the hotel on my cell phone. You will tell the desk clerk that you are with friends, that your plans are indefinite, and to hold your room for you.

"Do you understand that, Laura?"

Her answer was barely audible: "Yes."

"If you attempt in any way to seek help, you will die immediately. You do understand that?"

"Y-e-s."

"Very well."

Twenty minutes later the computerized answering system at the Glen-Ridge House was responding to a caller who had pushed "3" for reservations.

The phone at the front desk rang. The clerk picked it up and identified herself. "Front desk, Amy speaking." Then she gasped. "Ms. Wilcox, how good to hear from you. We've all been so concerned about you. Oh, your friends will be so happy to hear that you've called. Of course we'll hold the room for you. Are you sure you're all right?"

The Owl broke the connection. "You did that very well, Laura. Some stress in your voice, but that's natural, I suppose. Maybe you do have the makings of an actress." He tied the gag over her mouth. "I'll be back eventually. Try to get some sleep. You have my permission to dream about me."

38

Jake Perkins knew that the clerk who had booted him out of the Glen-Ridge went off duty at 8:00 P.M. That meant he could go back to the hotel anytime after eight and hang around the desk with the other clerk, Amy Sachs, to see if anything had developed.

After dinner with his parents, who were enthralled with his account of what was going on at the hotel, he went over the notes he would be giving to the *Post*. He had decided to wait until the morning to call the newspaper. By then Laura Wilcox would have been missing a full day.

At ten o'clock he was back at the Glen-Ridge, entering the deserted hotel lobby. You could fly a plane through this place and not hit anyone, he thought as he walked to the front desk. Amy Sachs was there.

Amy liked him. He knew that. Last spring when he had been covering a luncheon for Stonecroft, she had said he reminded her of her kid brother. "The only difference is Danny is forty-six and you're sixteen," she'd said, then she'd laughed. "He always wanted to be in publishing, too, and in a way I guess he is. He owns a trucking company that delivers newspapers."

Jake wondered how many people realized that

under her timid, anxious-to-please exterior, Amy had a good sense of humor and was pretty sharp.

She welcomed him with a timid smile. "Hi, Jake."

"Hi, Amy. Just thought I'd stop by and see if you'd heard from Laura Wilcox."

"Not a word." Just then the phone at her elbow rang, and she picked up the receiver. "Front desk, Amy speaking," she whispered.

Then as Jake watched, Amy's face changed and she gasped, "Oh, Ms. Wilcox . . ."

Jake leaned over the desk and motioned to Amy to hold the receiver away from her ear so that he could listen, too. He caught Laura saying that she was with friends, her plans were indefinite, and to please hold her room for her.

She doesn't sound like herself, he thought. She's upset. Her voice is trembling.

The conversation lasted only twenty seconds. When Amy replaced the receiver, she and Jake looked at each other. "Wherever she is, she's not having a good time," he said flatly.

"Or maybe she's just hungover," Amy suggested. "I read an article about her in *People* magazine last year, and it said she'd been in rehab for a drinking problem."

"That would explain it, I guess," Jake agreed. He shrugged. So much for my big story, he thought. "Where do you think she went, Amy?" he asked. "You were on duty all weekend. Did you notice her hanging around with anyone specially?"

Amy Sachs' oversized glasses wiggled when she

frowned. "I saw her arm in arm with Dr. Fleischman a couple of times," she said. "And he was the first to check out Sunday morning, even before that brunch at Stonecroft. Maybe he'd left her sobering up somewhere and was anxious to get back to her."

She opened a drawer and took out a card. "I promised that detective, Mr. Deegan, that I'd phone him if we heard from Ms. Wilcox."

"I'm on my way," Jake said. "I'll see you, Amy." With a wave of his hand he started for the front door as she dialed. He went outside, stood indecisively on the pavement, walked halfway to his car, and then returned to the desk.

"Did you reach Mr. Deegan?" he asked.

"Yes. I told him that I'd heard from her. He said that was good news and to let him know when she actually comes back for her bags."

"That's what I was afraid of. Amy, give me Sam Deegan's number."

She looked alarmed. "Why?"

"Because I think Laura Wilcox sounded scared rather than hungover, and I think Mr. Deegan should know that."

"If anyone finds out I let you listen in on her call, I'll lose my job."

"No, you won't. I'll say I grabbed the receiver when you mentioned her name and turned it so I could hear, too. Amy, five of Laura's friends are dead. If she's being held against her will, she may not have much time, either."

Sam Deegan had barely hung up after speaking to Jean when he received the telephone call from the Glen-Ridge clerk. His immediate reaction was that Laura Wilcox was a remarkably selfish woman to have missed her friend's memorial service, worried her other friends, and cost the limousine driver another fare by not cancelling. But even that reaction had been tempered by the unsettling fact that there was something suspicious about the vague story she had told the clerk and the clerk's assessment that she had sounded either nervous or hungover.

Jake Perkins' follow-up phone call cemented that impression, especially since Jake was emphatic that he thought Wilcox sounded frightened. "Do you agree with Ms. Sachs that it was exactly ten-thirty when Laura Wilcox called the hotel?" Sam asked him.

"At exactly ten-thirty," Jake confirmed. "Are you thinking of tracing it, Mr. Deegan? I mean, if she used her cell phone, you'd be able to trace the area where the call was made, isn't that right?"

"Yes, that's right," Sam said irritably. This kid was a know-it-all. But he was only trying to be helpful, so Sam was inclined to cut him some slack.

"I'll be happy to continue to keep my ear to the ground for you," Jake said, his voice now cheerful. The thought that Laura Wilcox might be in danger and that he was assisting the investigation to locate her filled him with a feeling of importance.

"Do that," Sam said, then reluctantly added, "and thanks, Jake."

Sam pushed the end button on his phone, sat up, and swung his legs out of the bed. He knew that at least for the next few hours there was no question of sleep. He had to let Jean know that Laura had been in contact with the hotel, and he had to get an order from a judge to look at the hotel's telephone records. He knew that the Glen-Ridge had caller ID. When he got the phone number, he would subpoena the phone company to find out the name of the subscriber and the locale of the antenna that had carried the call.

Judge Hagen in Goshen was probably the nearest judge in Orange County authorized to issue the order. As he dialed the district attorney's office to get Hagen's phone number, Sam realized it was some measure of the level of his own unease about Laura that he was now planning to disturb the sleep of a notoriously cantankerous judge rather than wait until morning to start trying to trace the missing woman.

39

Jean had set the volume of her cell phone at the highest level, afraid that when she went to bed she might miss a call. Sam had suggested that whoever was contacting her about Lily might go one step further and call her. "Hang on to the idea that this may be all about money," he said. "Somebody wants you to believe that Lily is in danger. Let's hope his next move might be to speak to you. If he does, we can trace the call."

He had managed to calm her down somewhat. "Jean, if you let yourself get paralyzed with worry, you're going to be your own worst enemy. You tell me that you confided to no one that you had a baby and that in Chicago you were known by your mother's maiden name. But somebody found out nonetheless, and that may have happened recently or it may have happened nineteen and a half years ago when the baby was born. Who knows? You've got to help yourself now. Try to remember if you saw anyone in Dr. Connors' office when you consulted him, maybe a nurse or secretary who figured out why you were there and who was nosy enough to find out where your baby was taken. Don't forget, you've become a celebrity now, with your best-selling book. Your new contract with your publisher was brought up during your interviews. My bet is that somebody who has access to Lily has decided to blackmail you by threatening her. I'll go to see the pastor of St. Thomas in the morning, and you start making a list of anyone you got friendly with at that time, especially anyone who might have had access to your records."

Sam's calm reasoning had the effect of snapping Jean's growing panic. After she said good-bye to him, she sat at the desk with a pen and notepad and wrote on the first page: DR. CONNORS' OFFICE.

His nurse had been a cheerful heavyset woman of about fifty, she remembered. Peggy. That was her name. Her last name was Irish and began with a K. Kelly . . . Kennedy . . . Keegan . . . It will come to me, I know it will, she thought.

It was a beginning.

The sharp ring of her cell phone made her jump. She glanced at the clock as she picked it up. It was almost eleven. Laura, she thought. Maybe she's come back.

Sam's message that Laura had called the desk clerk should have been reassuring, but Jean heard the concern in his voice. "You're not sure that she's all right, are you?" she asked.

"Not yet, but at least she did call."

Which means that she's still alive, Jean thought. That's what he's saying. She chose her words carefully. "Do you think that for some reason Laura may not be able to come back here?"

NightTime Is My Time

"Jean, I meant for this call to reassure you about Laura, but I guess I'd better level with you. The fact is that two people who heard the call have confirmed that she sounded distressed. Laura and you are the only two lunch table girls still alive. Until we know exactly where she is and who she's with, you've got to be very, very careful."

40

She knew he was going to kill her. It was only a question of when. Incredibly, after he left, she had fallen asleep. Light was flickering through the closed blinds, so it must be morning. Is it Monday or Tuesday? Laura wondered as she tried not to become fully awake.

Saturday night when they'd gotten here, he had poured champagne for them and toasted her. Then he'd said, "Halloween is coming soon. Want to see the mask I bought?"

He was wearing the face of an owl, each enlarged eye with a wide black pupil set in a sickly yellow iris, and edged with tufts of grayish down that darkened into deep brown around the pointed beak and narrow mouth. I laughed, Laura remembered, because I thought that was what he was expecting. But I could sense then that something had happened to him—he had changed. Even before he took off the mask and grabbed my hands, I knew I was trapped.

He dragged her upstairs, tied her wrists and her ankles together, and covered her mouth with a gag, being careful to leave it loose enough to be sure she didn't choke. Then he tied a rope across her waist and fastened it to the frame of the bed. "Did you ever read

Mommie Dearest?" he'd asked. "Joan Crawford used to tie her kids to the bed to make sure they didn't get up at night. She called it 'safe sleep.' "

Then he'd made her begin to recite the line about the owl in the tree, the line from that grade-school play. Over and over again he made her say it, and then he made her imitate the girls at the lunch table, laughing at him. And each time, she could see the murderous anger building in his eyes. "You all laughed at me," he said. "I despise you, Laura. The sight of you revolts me."

When he left her, he deliberately put his cell phone on the top of the dresser. "Just think, Laura. If you could reach this phone, you could call for help. But don't do it. The cords will tighten if you try to open them. Take my word for it."

She had tried anyway, and now her wrists and ankles were throbbing with pain. Her mouth was parched. Laura tried to moisten her lips. Her tongue touched the rough cloth of the sock he had taped over her mouth, and she felt bile rise in her throat. If she got sick, she would choke. Oh, God, please help me, she thought, panicking as she fought back the wave of nausea.

The first time he reappeared, there was some light in the room. It must have been Sunday afternoon, she figured. He untied my wrists and gave me soup and a roll. And he let me go to the bathroom. Then he came back a long time later. It was so dark, it must have been night. That was when he had me make the phone call. Why is he *doing* this to me? Why doesn't he just kill me and get it over with?

Her head was clearing. As she tried to move her wrists and ankles, the dull throbbing became intense pain. Saturday night. Sunday morning. Sunday night. It had to be Monday morning now. She stared at the cell phone. There was no way she could reach it. If he let her call anyone again, should she try to shout his name?

She could imagine the pillow muffling the sound before it escaped her throat, imagine the pillow pressing over her nostrils and mouth, choking life from her. I can't, Laura thought. I can't. Maybe if I don't upset him, someone will realize that I may be in trouble and try to find me. They can trace calls from cell phones. I *know* they can. They can find out who owns his phone.

That hope was the only chance she had, but it gave her the faintest trickle of relief. Jean, she thought. He intends to kill her, too. They say people can project thoughts. I'm going to try to send mine to Jean. She closed her eyes and imagined Jean as she had looked at the dinner, dressed in her royal blue evening gown. Moving her lips under the tape, she began to say his name aloud. "Jean, I'm with him. He killed the other girls. He's going to kill us. Help me, Jean. I'm in my old house. Find me, Jean!" Over and over she whispered his name.

"I forbade you to use my name."

She had not heard him come back. Even with the gag over her mouth, Laura's scream broke the silence of the room that had been hers for the first sixteen years of her life.

41

Monday morning, around dawn, Jean finally drifted off into a heavy but fitful sleep in which vague, undefined dreams of urgency and helplessness pulled her to momentary consciousness. But when she became fully awake, she was shocked to see that it was almost nine-thirty.

She considered ordering room service, then vetoed the idea of having even a continental breakfast in this room. It felt cramped and depressing, and the gloomy colors of the walls, bedspread, and window drapery made her long for her comfortable home in Alexandria. Ten years ago, in an estate sale, she had bought a seventy-year-old Federal-style, two-story house that had been owned by the same recluse for forty years. It had been dirty and neglected and cluttered, but she had fallen in love with it. Her friends had tried to dissuade her, saying such an undertaking was a bottomless pit of financial woes, but now they confessed that they'd been wrong.

Beyond mouse droppings, peeling wallpaper, the soiled carpet, dripping sinks, and the filthy stove and refrigerator, she had seen the high ceilings, oversized windows, and generous rooms, and the spectacular view of the Potomac that was then obscured by overgrown trees.

She'd gone for broke, buying the house and having the roof replaced. After that she had done the minor repairs herself, scrubbing and painting and wallpapering. She'd even sanded the parquet floors that had been an unexpected bonus, discovered when she pulled up the ragged carpet.

Working on the house was therapeutic for me, Jean thought as she showered, washed her hair, and toweled it dry. It was the place I dreamed of living in when I was growing up. Her mother had been allergic to flowers and plants. With an unconscious smile, she thought of the conservatory off her kitchen where every day fresh flowers bloomed.

The colors she had used throughout the house were those that to her meant cheer and warmth: yellows and blues and greens and reds. Not a single beige wall, her friends joked. The advance on her last contract had made it possible for her to panel her library and office as well as remodel the kitchen and bathrooms. Her home was her haven, her retreat, her sense of accomplishment. Because it was not far from Mount Vernon, she had jokingly named it Mount Vernon, Jr.

Being here in this hotel, even totally aside from her need to find Lily, had brought back the painful memory of all the years she had lived in Cornwall. It had made her feel once again like the girl whose father and mother were the joke of the town.

It made her remember how it felt to be desperately

in love with Reed and then have to hide the grief of his death from everyone. All these years I've wondered if I made a mistake in giving up Lily, she thought. Coming back here, I'm beginning to understand that without my parents helping me, it would have been just about impossible to keep her and care for her properly.

As she dried and brushed her hair, she realized that she believed Sam Deegan's premise that the threat to Lily was all about money. "Jean," he had said, "think about this. Is there one single person who has a reason to want to hurt you? Have you ever gotten a job someone else wanted? Have you ever 'skunked' anyone, as the kids would say?"

"Never" had been her honest reply.

Sam had somehow managed to convince her that whoever was contacting her would soon demand money. But if it *is* about money, I believe that someone from around here learned I was pregnant, Jean thought, and that person was able to find out who adopted my baby. And maybe because there was a lot of talk about the reunion and publicity noting that I was one of the honorees, that person decided it was the right time to contact me.

As she looked in the bathroom mirror, she realized that she was startlingly pale. She ordinarily wore little makeup in the daytime, but now she touched her cheeks with blush and deliberately selected a lip color a little deeper than usual.

The realization that she was probably going to be staying in Cornwall for at least a few days meant that she had brought several changes of clothing. She decided today to wear a favorite cranberry turtleneck sweater over dark gray slacks.

Her determination to take action to find Lily had removed some of her terrible sense of helplessness. She clipped on earrings and gave a final brush to her hair. She put the brush down on the dresser, realizing it was the same size and shape as the one she had received in the mail with the strands of Lily's hair.

At that moment the name of the nurse who had been in Dr. Connors' office passed through her mind: Peggy Kimball.

Jean yanked open the drawer of the night table and pulled out the phone book. A quick look disclosed several Kimballs, but she decided that the one she would try first was the listing "Kimball, Stephen and Margaret." It wasn't too early to call. A woman's voice was on the answering machine: "Hi. Steve and Peggy aren't here now. At the tone please leave a message with your phone number, and we'll get back to you."

Can you remember a voice after twenty years, or am I just hoping I remember that voice? Jean asked herself as she carefully chose her words. "Peggy, I'm Jean Sheridan. If you were a nurse in Dr. Connors' office twenty years ago, it's terribly important that I speak with you. Will you please call me at this number as soon as possible."

While the phone book was open, she turned to the "C" listings. Dr. Edward Connors would have been at least seventy-five by now if he had lived. The odds were his wife was somewhere around that age as well. Sam

Deegan was going to ask the pastor of St. Thomas about her, but maybe she was still listed. The doctor had lived on Winding Way; there was a Mrs. Dorothy Connors listed on Winding Way. Feeling hopeful, Jean dialed the number. The silvery voice of an older woman answered. When she hung up the phone a few minutes later, Jean had an appointment to visit Mrs. Dorothy Connors at eleven-thirty that morning.

42

On Monday morning at ten-thirty, Sam Deegan was in the office of Rich Stevens, the district attorney of Orange County, filling him in on the missing Laura Wilcox and the threat to Lily.

"I served the order for the telephone records of the Glen-Ridge House at one this morning," he said. "Both the clerk and that kid from Stonecroft are positive that it was Laura Wilcox who made the call, but they also agree that she sounded distressed. The hotel records showed that it was a 917 number on the ID, so we know she called from a cell phone. The judge was very unhappy at having his sleep interrupted last night.

"I served the subpoena for the subscriber's name and address, but I had to wait until 9:00 A.M. when the telephone business office was open."

"What did you find out from the records?" Stevens asked.

"The kind of information that makes me sure Wilcox is in trouble. The phone was one of those that are bought with one hundred minutes of available calling time and then discarded."

"The kind used by drug dealers and terrorists," Stevens snapped.

"Or, in this case, maybe a kidnapper. The cell site is Beacon in Dutchess County, and you know how wide an area that covers. I've already talked to our tech guys, and they tell me there are two more power stations in Woodbury and New Windsor. If a new call comes in, we can triangulate it and pinpoint the location it's being made from. We could also do that if the power was left on, but unfortunately it's been turned off."

"I never turn off the power on my cell phone," Stevens commented.

"Neither do I. Most people don't. That's another reason to believe that Laura Wilcox was forced to make that phone call. She has her own phone registered to her name. Why wouldn't she use that, and why isn't it on now?"

He then laid out his suggested course of action. "I want to get rap sheets on all the graduates who attended the reunion," he said, "both men and women. A lot of them haven't been back here in twenty years. Maybe we'll come up with something from someone's past, find someone who has a history of violence or has been institutionalized. I want the relatives of the five dead women from the lunch table to be contacted to see if there was anything suspicious about their deaths. We're also trying to contact Laura's parents. They're on a cruise."

"Five from one lunch table and a sixth one missing," Stevens said incredulously. "If there isn't something suspicious, it's because it wasn't noticed. If I were you, I'd start with the last one. It's so recent that if the cops in L.A. know about the other women, they may take a hard look at labeling Alison Kendall's death a drowning accident. We'll send for all of the police reports in all of those cases."

"The office at Stonecroft is sending over a list of the graduates who attended the reunion, as well as a list of the other people who were at the dinner," Sam said. "They have addresses and phone numbers of all the graduates and at least some of the townspeople who attended. Of course, some people bought a table and didn't provide names of guests, so it will take extra time to find out who they are." Exhausted, Sam could not conceal a yawn.

It was an acknowledgment of the sense of urgency he had communicated to the district attorney that Rich Stevens did not suggest his veteran investigator catch some sleep. Instead he said, "Get some of the other guys started on doing the follow-up, Sam. Where are you going now?"

Sam's smile was rueful. "I have an appointment with a priest," he said, "and I'm hoping he'll be the one to do the confessing."

43

The discovery of the body of Helen Whelan became a major story for the media. The disappearance of the popular teacher forty-eight hours earlier had already been given heavy coverage, but now the confirmation of her murder was a prime interest story because it had also triggered alarm throughout the small towns of the Hudson Valley.

The fact that her dog had been savagely attacked and his leash was still wrapped around the victim's wrist when her body was found gave added spice to the possibility that a random or serial killer was on the loose in this area that was normally drenched in history and tradition.

The Owl had dozed intermittently throughout Sunday night. After his first visit to Laura at ten-thirty, he'd managed to catch a few hours of rest. Then his dawn visit had given him the satisfaction of reducing her to trembling pleas for mercy—mercy she had denied him in their school years together, he had reminded her. After that second visit he had showered for a long time, hoping that the hot water would help relieve the terrible throbbing in his arm. The wound from the dog bite was festering. He had stopped at the old drugstore in town, where he used to shop as a kid, but then he'd walked out immediately. He had been about to pick up peroxide and antibiotic salves and bandages. Then it had occurred to him that the cops weren't necessarily stupid. They might have put a notice out to local pharmacies to watch for someone buying those kinds of medical supplies.

Instead he went to one of the big chains and bought shaving supplies, toothpaste, vitamins, crackers and pretzels and sodas, and then, in a moment of inspiration, he'd added cosmetics, cold cream, moisturizing lotion, and deodorant. Only then had he thrown into the mix the supplies he needed, the peroxide, bandages, salves.

He hoped he wasn't getting a fever. His body felt warm, and he knew his face was flushed. With all the useless camouflage items he had tossed into the basket at the drugstore, he had managed to forget to include aspirin. But that he could safely buy anywhere. Most of the time, most of the world has a headache, he thought, smiling to himself at the mental image conjured up by that reasoning.

He turned up the volume on the television. They were showing pictures of the crime scene. He observed intently how muddy it seemed. He hadn't remembered the area as being that swampy. That meant the tires of his rental car were probably embedded with dirt from that area. It would be wise to leave the car in the garage of the house where so far he was allowing Laura to continue to live. He'd rent another mid-priced, mid-sized, unobtrusive black sedan. That way, if for any reason anyone started to nose around and check the cars of the reunion group, his would be passed over.

As The Owl was selecting a jacket from the closet, a breaking story came across the screen: "Young reporter from Stonecroft Academy in Cornwall-on-Hudson reveals the disappearance of actress Laura Wilcox may be linked to a fiend he calls 'The Lunch Table Serial Killer.'"

44

"Monsignor, I cannot emphasize sufficiently the urgency of our request," Sam Deegan told Monsignor Robert Dillon, pastor of the Church of St. Thomas of Canterbury. They were in the rectory office. The monsignor, a thin man with prematurely white hair and rimless glasses that illuminated intelligent gray eyes, was behind his desk. The faxes Jean had received were spread out in front of him. In a chair directly across from the desk, Sam was putting Lily's hairbrush back in a plastic bag.

"As you can see, the latest communication suggests that Dr. Jean Sheridan's daughter is in grave danger. We intend to try to trace her original birth certificate, but we are not even sure if it was registered here or in Chicago where the baby was born," Sam continued.

Even as he spoke, he felt the hopelessness of trying to make a quick breakthrough. Monsignor Dillon couldn't be more than in his early forties. Clearly he had not been around twenty years ago when Lily might have been baptized in this church, and, of course, her adoptive parents would have registered her under their surname and her new first name.

"I do understand the urgency, and I'm sure you understand that I must be cautious," Monsignor Dillon said slowly. "But, Sam, the biggest problem is that people don't necessarily baptize babies within a few weeks or even months anymore. It used to be that an infant was baptized within six weeks of its birth. Now we see them toddling in to receive the sacrament. We don't approve of that trend, but it does exist and *did* exist even twenty years ago. This is a fairly large and busy parish, and not only our own parishioners but frequently the grandchildren of parishioners are baptized here."

"I understand, but perhaps if you could start with the three months after Lily's birth, we could at least try to track those baby girls. Most people aren't secretive about adoptions, are they?"

"No, as a rule, they're proud of the fact they're adoptive parents."

"Then unless the adoptive parents themselves are behind these faxes to Dr. Sheridan, I think they would want to know of a possible threat to their daughter."

"Yes, they would. I'll have my secretary compile the list, but you do understand that before I give it to you, I will have to contact all the people listed personally and explain only that a girl adopted at that time may be in danger."

"Monsignor, that could take time, and that's just what we may not have," Sam protested.

"Father Arella can work with me. I'll have my secretary make the calls, and while I'm speaking with one party, she'll alert the next to stand by to hear from me. It shouldn't take that long."

"And what about the ones you don't reach? Monsignor, this nineteen-year-old girl may be in grave danger."

Monsignor Dillon picked up the fax, his expression deepening with concern as he studied it. "Sam, as you say, this last communication is frightening, but you can understand why we have to be careful. To protect us from possible legal problems, get a subpoena. That way we can release the names to you immediately. But I would suggest that you allow me to talk to as many of these families as possible."

"Thank you, sir. I won't take any more of your time right now."

They both stood up. "It occurred to me that your correspondent is something of a Shakespearean scholar," Monsignor Dillon observed. "Not too many people would have used a fairly obscure quote like this one about the lilies."

"That occurred to me as well, Monsignor." Sam paused. "I should have thought to ask this immediately: Are any of the priests who were assigned here at the time Jean's baby might have been baptized still with the diocese?"

"Father Doyle was the assistant pastor, and he died years ago. Monsignor Sullivan was the pastor at that time. He moved to Florida with his sister and brother-in-law. I can give you the latest address we have for him."

"I'd like to have that."

"It's right here in my file drawer. I'll give it to you

now." He opened the drawer, pulled out a folder, glanced in it, and wrote a name, address, and phone number on a slip of paper. He handed it to Sam, saying, "Dr. Connors' widow is a parishioner. If you wish, I can call and ask her to see you. She might remember something about that adoption."

"Thanks, but that won't be necessary. I spoke to Jean Sheridan just before coming here. She found Mrs. Connors' address in the phone book and is probably on her way to see her right now."

As they walked to the door, Monsignor Dillon said, "Sam, I just remembered something. Alice Sommers is our parishioner also. Are you the investigator who has continued to work on her daughter's case?"

"Yes, I am."

"She has told me about you. I hope you know how much comfort it has given her to know that you haven't stopped trying to find Karen's murderer."

"I'm glad that it's helped her. Alice Sommers is a very brave woman."

They stood at the door. "I was shocked to hear on the radio this morning that the body of the woman who was walking her dog has been found," Monsignor Dillon commented. "Is your office involved with that case?"

"Yes, we are."

"I understand that, like Karen Sommers, it appears to be a random killing and that she was also stabbed to death. I know it seems implausible, but do you think there is any chance that there is a connection between those murders?"

"Monsignor, Karen Sommers died twenty years ago," Sam said carefully. He did not want to share the fact that the same possibility had been preying on his mind, particularly since the stab wounds had been in exactly the same area of the chest.

The Monsignor shook his head. "I guess I'd better leave the detecting to you. It was just a thought that occurred to me, and because you're so close to the Sommers case, I felt I should mention it." He opened the front door and shook Sam's hand. "God bless you, Sam. I'll pray for Lily, and I'll get back to you with the names as fast as we can put them together."

"Thank you, sir. Do pray for Lily, and while you're at it, remember Laura Wilcox."

"The actress?"

"Yes. We're afraid she's in trouble, too. No one has seen her since Saturday night."

Monsignor Dillon stared at Sam's retreating back. Laura Wilcox was at the Stonecroft reunion, he thought incredulously. Has something happened to her as well? Dear God, what's going on here?

With a fervent silent prayer for the safety of both Lily and Laura, he returned to his office and dialed his secretary. "Janet, please drop everything else you're doing and get out the baptismal records of nineteen years ago, from March through June. As soon as Father Arella returns, tell him I have a job for him and to cancel any other plans he may have made for the day."

"Of course, Monsignor." Janet hung up the phone

and looked longingly at the grilled cheese and bacon sandwich and container of coffee that had just been delivered to her desk. As she pushed back her chair and begrudgingly got to her feet, she mumbled to herself, "My God, from the tone of his voice you'd think it was a matter of life and death."

45

Dorothy Connors was a frail septuagenarian who Jean could see at first glance suffered from rheumatoid arthritis. She moved slowly, and the joints of her fingers were swollen. Her face showed lines of pain, and she wore her white hair very short, probably, Jean thought, because raising her arms was a distinct effort.

Her home was one of the desirable high-up properties that overlooked the Hudson. She invited Jean to the sunroom off the living room where, as she explained, she spent most of her waking time.

Her vivid brown eyes brightened when she talked about her husband. "Edward was the most wonderful man and husband and doctor who ever walked the face of the earth," she said. "It was that dreadful fire that killed him, the loss of his office and all his records. It brought on his heart attack."

"Mrs. Connors, I explained to you on the phone that I've been getting threats about my daughter. She would be nineteen and a half now. I am frantic to find her adoptive parents and warn them about the possible danger to her. I was a girl from this town. Please help me. Did Dr. Connors talk to you about me? I could see where he would. My mother and father were the town

joke, with their public quarrels, and they only stayed together long enough to shove me into college. That was
why your husband understood I could never go to them
for help. He arranged the cover-up story, establishing
my reason for going to Chicago. He even came out and
delivered the baby himself in the emergency section of
the nursing home."

"Yes, he did that for a number of girls. He wanted to
help them maintain their privacy. Jean, fifty years ago it
wasn't easy for a girl to have a baby out of wedlock. Do
you know that the actress Ingrid Bergman was de-
nounced in Congress when she gave birth to an illegiti-
mate child? Standards of behavior change—for better
or worse, you decide. Today most of the world doesn't
think a thing about an unmarried woman bearing and
raising a child, but my husband was old-fashioned.
Twenty years ago he was deeply concerned about protecting his young pregnant mothers' privacy, even with
me. Until you told me, I never even knew that you had
been his patient."

"But you *did* know about my parents."

Dorothy Conners looked at Jean for a long moment.
"I knew they had problems. I also saw them at church
and chatted with them a number of times. My guess, my
dear, is that you only remember the bad times. They
were also attractive, intelligent people who unfortunately were ill-suited to each other."

Jean felt the sting of a rebuke and in an odd way
sensed that she had been put on the defensive. "I can
guarantee you that they were ill-suited to each other,"

she said, hoping that the anger she felt was not reflected in her voice. "Mrs. Connors, I *do* appreciate that you let me visit you on such short notice, but now I'll be brief. My daughter may be in very real danger. I know that you fiercely guard Dr. Connors' memory, but if you know anything about where he might have placed her, you owe it to me and to her to be honest with me."

"Before God, Edward never discussed patients in your situation with me, and I never heard your name mentioned by him."

"And he kept no records at home, and all his office records are gone?"

"Yes, they are. The entire building was so totally destroyed that arson has always been suspected but never proved. Certainly no records survived."

Clearly Dorothy Connors could give her no help. Jean rose to go. "I remember that Peggy Kimball was the office nurse when I saw Dr. Connors. I've left a message for her and hope she'll call me. Maybe she'll know something. Thank you, Mrs. Connors. Please don't get up. I'll find my way out."

She offered her hand to Dorothy Connors and then was shocked to see that the expression on the other woman's face could only be construed as extreme alarm.

46

Mark Fleischman checked into the Glen-Ridge House at one o'clock, dropped off his bag, phoned Jean's room but got no answer, and then went down to the dining room. He was surprised and pleased to see Jean sitting alone at a corner table, and with quick strides, he hurried over to her.

"Are you waiting for anyone, or would you like company?" he asked, then watched as the somber expression on her face was replaced by a warm smile.

"Mark, I didn't expect to see you! Of course, sit down. I was just about to order lunch, and nobody's planning to join me."

"Then consider yourself joined." He settled on the chair opposite her. "I put my briefcase with my cell phone in the trunk of the car by mistake," he said, "so I didn't get your message till I unpacked last night. I called the hotel early this morning, and the operator told me that Laura wasn't back and that the police were checking phone records. That's when I decided to rearrange my schedule and come back. I flew down and rented a car."

"That was very nice of you," Jean said sincerely. "We're all terribly worried about Laura." Quickly she gave him a rundown of what had transpired since he had left after the brunch the day before.

"You say you came back to the hotel with Sam Deegan, that man you were having a drink with the other night, and when you knew Laura was missing, he began an investigation?" Mark queried.

"Yes," Jean said, realizing she had awakened Mark's curiosity as to why Sam Deegan had been with her in the first place. "Sam followed me to the hotel because I was giving him something that our friend Alice Sommers is interested in seeing."

Alice *is* interested in seeing the faxes, she told herself, so it's not a complete fabrication. Looking across the table at Mark and seeing the concern in his eyes made her want to tell him about Lily, to ask him as a psychiatrist if he thought the threats were genuine, or whether someone was only setting her up for blackmail.

"Ready for menus?" the waitress chirped.

"Yes, thank you."

They both decided on a club sandwich and tea. "Coffee for breakfast, tea for lunch, and a glass of wine to start dinner," Mark said. "I've noticed that seems to be your routine, too, Jeannie."

"I guess it is."

"I've noticed a lot of things about you this weekend, and they reminded me of the years we were at Stonecroft."

"Such as?"

"Well, you always were very smart in school. You were also very quiet. And I remember that you were very sweet—that hasn't changed. Then I thought about one time during the freshman year when I was really down and you were very kind to me."

"I don't remember that."

"I won't go into it, but you were, and I also admired the way you held your head high when you were upset about your parents."

"Not always." Jean cringed inwardly, remembering the times she had started crying in class from the stress of the arguments at home.

It was as though he could read her mind, Jean realized, as Mark Fleischman continued. "I tried to hand you my handkerchief one day when you were upset, but you just shook your head and dabbed furiously at your eyes with a soggy Kleenex. I wanted to help you then, and I want to help you now. Coming from the airport I heard on the radio that the reporter kid who hounded us at the reunion is talking to the media about what he calls 'The Lunch Table Serial Killer.' Even if you're not worried about that possibility, I am. And with Laura missing, you're the only one of those girls left."

"I wish I was just worried about myself," Jean said.

"Then what are you worried about? Come on, Jean, tell me. I am trained to spot stress in people, and if I've seen anyone under stress, it was you the other night when you were talking to Sam Deegan, who you now tell me is an investigator from the district attorney's office."

The busboy was pouring water into their glasses. It gave Jean a moment to think. I *do* remember when Mark wanted to give me his handkerchief, she thought. I was so angry at myself for crying, and equally angry at him for noticing. He wanted to help me then. He wants to help me now. Should I tell him about Lily?

She saw him studying her and knew he was waiting her out. He wants me to talk to him. Should I? She looked directly back at him. He's one of those men who looks as good with glasses as without them, she thought. He has wonderful brown eyes. Those little specks of yellow in them are like sunlight.

She shrugged and raised her eyebrows. "You remind me of a professor I had in college who, when he asked a question, would just stare at you until he got an answer."

"That's exactly what I'm doing, Jean. One of my patients calls it my wise owl look."

The waitress came to the table with the sandwiches. "Right back with your tea," she said cheerfully.

Jean waited until the tea was poured, then said quietly, "Your wise owl look has convinced me, Mark. I guess I will tell you about Lily."

47

Sam Deegan's first act upon arriving at his office was to call the district attorney in Los Angeles and ask to be put in touch with Carmen Russo, the investigator who had headed the inquiry into the death of Alison Kendall.

"Death by accidental drowning was the determination, and we're sticking by that," Russo told him. "Her friends agree that she went for an early swim every morning. Door was open to the house, but nothing was taken. Pricey jewelry on top of her vanity. Five hundred dollars cash and credit cards in her wallet. She was extremely neat. Nothing out of place anywhere in the house, on the grounds, or in the pool house. Except for being dead, she was in perfect health. Her heart was strong. No sign of alcohol or drugs."

"Any suggestion at all of violence?" Sam asked.

"A slight bruise on her shoulder, but that was it. Without more evidence, it's not enough to suggest that it was a homicide. We took photographs, of course, but then released the body."

"Yes, I know. Her ashes are buried here in the family plot," Sam said. "Thanks, Carmen." He realized he was reluctant to break the connection. "What is going on with her home?"

"Her parents live in Palm Springs. They're up in years. From what I understand, they have Kendall's housekeeper still taking care of the place until they can bring themselves to have an estate sale. They can't be hungry for money. In that location the house has to be worth a couple of million bucks."

Discouraged, Sam hung up the phone. His every instinct told him that Alison Kendall had not died a natural death. By pointing out that the five dead women from the same class at Stonecroft had shared the same lunch table, Jake Perkins had latched onto something. Sam was sure of it. But if Kendall's death hadn't raised suspicion, how much luck would he have in trying to establish a pattern of murder with the four others who had died over a stretch of nearly twenty years?

His phone rang—it was Rich Stevens, the district attorney. "Sam, thanks to that bigmouth Perkins, we've had to call a press conference to make some kind of statement. Come on in here, and we'll figure out what to say."

Five minutes later, in Stevens' office, they debated the best way to defuse the media onslaught. "We believe we may have a serial killer. We've got to make this guy feel secure," Sam argued. "We tell it like it is. Alison Kendall's death was the result of accidental drowning. Even knowing that four other women who were once close friends have died, the Los Angeles police find nothing suspicious about her death. Laura Wilcox phoned the hotel to say her plans were indefinite. It is nothing more than a matter of conjecture on the part of a hotel employee that she sounded nervous. She is an adult with the right to privacy and should be treated as such. We are making inquiries into the deaths of the other women who shared the lunch table years ago, but it is obvious the accidents that claimed their lives—or, in the case of Gloria Martin, her suicide—indicate no pattern that suggests a serial killer."

"I think a statement like this makes us look pretty damn naïve," Rich Stevens said flatly.

"I *want* us to look naïve," Sam shot back. "I want whoever is out there to think we're a bunch of dopes. If Laura is still alive, I don't want him to panic before we have a chance to save her."

There was a tap at the door. One of the young new investigators on the staff was obviously excited. "Sir, we're going through the student personnel folders of the Stonecroft graduates who attended the reunion and may have something on one of them, Joel Nieman.

"What about him?" Stevens asked.

"When he was a senior, he was questioned about the fact that Alison Kimball's locker was tampered with. The screws had been removed from the hinges so that when she opened the door, it fell on her and knocked her down. She suffered a mild concussion."

"Why was he questioned?" Sam asked.

"Because he was really upset about something she had written in the school newspaper. The senior year school play was *Romeo and Juliet*. Nieman had the part of Romeo, and Kendall wrote something really nasty about him not being able to remember his lines. He prided himself on memorizing Shakespeare, and went around the school saying what he'd like to do to her. He told everybody the problem had been a couple of seconds of stage fright and was not a case of him forgetting lines. Right after that, she got bowled over by the locker door.

"There's other stuff, too. He has a lousy temper and has been hauled in after a couple of bar fights. He was almost indicted last year for some imaginative accounting practices, and his wife is away most of the time, like right now."

Monsignor Dillon and I both caught the fact that the guy who's contacting Jean about Lily quoted an obscure sonnet from Shakespeare, Sam thought.

He stood up. "Romeo, Romeo, wherefore art thou, Romeo?"

As Rich Stevens and the young investigator stared at him, Sam said, "That's exactly what I'm going to find out right now. Then we'll see what other lines from Shakespeare Joel Nieman might be able to quote for us."

48

At six-thirty The Owl returned to the house and crept up the stairs. This time Laura had obviously sensed his presence or had anticipated that he would be visiting, because when he entered the room and turned the flashlight on her, he could see that she was already trembling.

"Hello, Laura," he whispered. "Are you glad I'm back?"

Her breathing was harsh and shallow. He watched as she tried to shrink back against the mattress.

"Laura, you must answer me. Here, let me loosen the tape. Better than that, I'll take it off. I brought you something to eat. Now, are you glad I'm back?"

"Ye-yes, I'm glad," she whispered.

"Laura, you're stuttering. I'm surprised at you. You ridicule people who stutter. Show me how you ridicule them. No, never mind. I can't stay too long. I brought you a peanut butter and jelly sandwich and a glass of milk. You used to eat that every day in grammar school. Do you remember that?"

"Yes . . . yes."

"I'm glad you remember. It's important that we don't forget the past. Now I'll allow you to use the bathroom. Then you may eat your sandwich and drink the milk."

With a quick gesture he pulled her to a sitting position and cut the cords on her wrists. The movement was so fast that Laura swayed and reached out her hand. Inadvertently she grasped The Owl's arm.

He gasped with pain and clenched his fist, ready to strike her, but then he stopped. "You couldn't have known that my arm is very sore, so I must not hold it against you. But never touch that arm again. Understand?"

Laura nodded.

"Stand up. After you have visited the bathroom, I will permit you to sit in the chair and eat."

With tentative, unsteady steps, Laura obeyed. The night light in the bathroom made it possible for her to see the taps on the sink and turn them on. With a hurried gesture she splashed water on her face and hands and smoothed back her hair. If I can only stay alive, she thought. They've got to be looking for me. Please God, let them be looking for me.

The handle of the bathroom door turned. "Laura, it's time."

Time! Was he going to kill her now? God . . . please . . .

The door opened. The Owl pointed to the chair beside the dresser. Silently, Laura shuffled over to it and sat down.

"Go ahead," he urged. "Start to eat." He picked up the flashlight and directed the light on her neck so that he could watch her expression without blinding her. He was pleased to see that she was crying again.

"Laura, you're so afraid, aren't you? And I bet you're wondering how I knew that you ridiculed me. Let me tell you a story. Twenty years ago this weekend a bunch of us were home from our different colleges and got together one night. There was a party. Now, as you know, I was never part of the crowd, of the inner circle. Far from it, in fact. But for some reason I was invited to that party, and you were there. Lovely Laura. That night you were sitting on the lap of your latest conquest, Dick Gormley, our erstwhile baseball star. I was eating my heart out, Laura, that's how much of a crush I still had on you.

"Alison was at the party, of course. Quite drunk. She came over to me. I never liked her. Frankly, I was afraid of that tongue of hers—razor-sharp when she turned it on you. She reminded me that early in senior year I had had the temerity to ask you to go on a date. 'You . . .' she said with a sneer and laughed. 'The owl asking Laura out.' And then Alison demonstrated for me how you mimicked me when we were in the second-grade school play. 'I am annnnnn . . . ow . . . owwwlll . . . and . . . and . . . I . . . live . . . in . . . a . . . a . . .'

"Laura, your imitation of me must have been superb. Alison assured me that the girls at your lunch table screamed with laughter every time they thought of it. And then you reminded them that I had been dopey enough to wet my pants onstage before I ran off. You even told them that."

Laura had been taking bites of the sandwich. Now he watched as she dropped it onto her lap. "I'm sorry. . . ."

"Laura, you still don't understand that you have lived twenty years too long. Let me tell you about it. The night of that party, I was drunk, too. I was so drunk that I forgot you had moved. I came here that night to kill you. I knew where your family kept the extra key under that fake rabbit in the backyard. The new people kept it there, too. I came into this house and up to this room. I saw the flow of hair on the pillow and thought it was you. Laura, I made a mistake when I stabbed Karen Sommers. I was killing *you*, Laura. I was killing *you!*

"The next morning I woke up vaguely remembering that I'd been here. Then I found out what had happened and realized that I was famous." The Owl's voice became rushed with excitement at the memory. "I didn't know Karen Sommers. No one even dreamed of connecting me to her, but that mistake liberated me. That morning I understood that I have the power of life and death. And I've been exercising it ever since. Ever since, Laura. Women all over the country."

He stood up. Laura's eyes were wide with fear; her mouth hung open; the sandwich lay in her lap. He leaned toward her. "Now I have to go, but think about me, Laura. Think how lucky you have been to have enjoyed a bonus twenty years of life."

In savagely quick movements, he tied her hands, taped her mouth, pulled her up from the chair, pushed her back on the bed, and fastened the long rope over her body.

"It began in this room, and it will end in this room, Laura," he said. "The final stage of the plan is about to unfold. Try to guess what it might be."

He was gone. Outside the moon was rising, and from the bed Laura could see the faint outline of the cell phone on top of the dresser.

49

At six-thirty Jean was in her hotel room when she finally received the call she'd been hoping would come. It was from Peggy Kimball, the nurse who had been in Dr. Connors' office when she was his patient. "That's a pretty urgent message you left, Ms. Sheridan," Kimball said briskly. "What's going on?"

"Peggy, we met twenty years ago. I was a patient of Dr. Connors, and he arranged a private adoption for my baby. I need to talk to you about it."

For a long moment Peggy Kimball did not say anything. Jean could hear the voices of children in the background. "I'm sorry, Ms. Sheridan," Kimball said, a note of finality in her voice. "I simply cannot discuss the adoptions Dr. Connors handled. If you want to begin to trace your child, there are legal ways of going about it."

Jean could sense that Kimball was about to break the connection. "I've already been in touch with Sam Deegan, an investigator from the district attorney's office," she said hurriedly. "I have received three communications that can only be construed as threats to my daughter. Her adoptive parents have got to be warned to watch out for her. Please, Peggy. You were so kind to me then. Help me now, I beg you."

She was interrupted by Peggy Kimball's alarmed shout: "Tommy, I warn you. Don't throw that dish!"

Jean heard the sound of glass breaking.

"Oh, my God," Peggy Kimball said with a sigh. "Look, Ms. Sheridan, I'm baby-sitting my grandkids. I can't talk now."

"Peggy, can I meet you tomorrow? I'll show you the faxes I've received threatening my daughter. You can check on me. I'm a dean and professor of history at Georgetown. I'll give you the number of the president of the college. I'll give you Sam Deegan's number."

"Tommy, Betsy, don't go near that glass! Wait a minute. . . . by any chance are you the Jean Sheridan who wrote the book about Abigail Adams?"

"Yes."

"Oh, for heaven's sake! I loved it. I know all about you. I saw you on the *Today* show with Katie Couric. You two could be sisters. Will you still be at the Glen-Ridge tomorrow morning?"

"Yes, I will."

"I work in neonatal at the hospital. The Glen-Ridge is on the way there. I don't think I'll be any help to you, but do you want to have a cup of coffee around ten?"

"I would love to," Jean said. "Peggy, thank you, thank you."

"I'll call you from the lobby," Peggy Kimball said

hurriedly, then her voice became alarmed. "Betsy, I warn you. Don't pull Tommy's hair! Oh, my God! Sorry, Jean, it's becoming a free-for-all here. See you to-morrow."

Jean replaced the receiver slowly. That sounds like mayhem, she thought, but in a crazy way, I envy Peggy Kimball. I envy her the normal problems of normal people. People who mind their grandkids and have to clean up messy babies and spilled food and broken dishes. People who can see and touch their daughters and tell them to drive carefully and be home by mid-night.

She had been sitting at the desk of her room in the hotel when Kimball phoned. Scattered in front of her were the lists she had been trying to compile, mostly the names of people in the nursing home who had be-friended her and also the professors at the University of Chicago where she had spent all her spare time taking extracurricular courses.

Now she massaged her temples, hoping to rub away the beginnings of a headache. In an hour, at seven-thirty, at Sam's request, they would be having dinner to-gether in a private dining room on the hotel's mezzanine floor. The guests included the honorees, Gordon and Carter and Robby and Mark and me, Jean thought, and, of course, Jack, the chairman of the godforsaken re-union. What is Sam hoping to accomplish by getting all of us together again?

She realized that unburdening herself to Mark had been a mixed blessing. There was astonishment in his eyes when he said, "You mean that on graduation day at age eighteen, when you were tripping up to the stage to accept the History medal and a scholarship to Bryn Mawr, you were aware that you were expecting a baby and that the guy you loved was lying in a casket?"

"I don't expect either praise or blame for that," she had told him.

"For God's sake, Jean. I'm neither praising nor blaming you," he'd said. "But what an ordeal. I used to go to West Point to jog and had seen you once or twice with Reed Thornton, but I had no idea it was more than a casual friendship. What did you do after the graduation ceremony?"

"My mother and father and I had lunch. It was a really festive lunch. They had done their Christian duty by me and could now separate with a clear conscience. After we left the restaurant, I drove to West Point. Reed's funeral Mass had been that morning. I put the flowers my parents gave me at the graduation ceremony on Reed's grave."

"And shortly after that you saw Dr. Connors for the first time?"

"The next week."

"Jeannie," Mark had said, "I always felt that, like me, you were a survivor, but I can't imagine what you must have been going through, being alone at a time like that."

"Not alone. I gather somebody must have known about it or found out about it even then."

He had nodded and then said, "I've read up on your professional life, but what about your personal life? Is there someone special, or has there been someone special you might have confided in?"

Jean thought of the answer she had given him. "Mark, remember the words of the Robert Frost poem. 'But I have promises to keep, / And miles to go before I sleep. . . .' In a way I feel like that. Until now, when I've had to talk about her, there's never been a single soul I've ever wanted to tell about Lily. My life is very full. I love my job and love writing. I have plenty of friends, both men and women. But I'll be honest. I've always had a feeling that there is something unresolved in my life that has to be settled, a sense that in a way my life itself has been held in abeyance. Something needs to be finished before I can put this behind me. I think I'm beginning to understand the reason for that. I still wonder if I shouldn't have kept my baby, and now that she may need me I'm so helpless, I want to turn back the clock and have the chance to keep her this time."

Then she had seen the look on Mark's face. *Or are you setting up a manufactured scenario because of your need to find her?* He might as well have shouted the question. Instead he had said, "Jean, of course you must pursue this, and I'm glad Sam Deegan is helping you since you're obviously dealing with an unbalanced individual. However, as a psychiatrist, I warn you that you must be very careful. If because of these implied threats you are able to access confidential records, you may intrude into the life of a young woman who isn't ready or willing to meet *you.*"

"You think that I have been sending those faxes to myself, don't you?" Jean winced, remembering how angry she had been when she realized that some people jumped to that conclusion.

"Of course I don't," Mark had said promptly. "But answer me this: If you received a call right now asking you to meet Lily, would you go?"

"Yes, I would."

"Jean, listen to what I'm saying. Someone who somehow found out about Lily may be deliberately getting you into a fever pitch so that you'll be vulnerable to rushing off to meet her. Jean, you've got to be careful. Laura is missing. The other girls at your table are dead."

He had left it at that.

Now Jean stood up. She was due downstairs for dinner in forty minutes. Maybe an aspirin would prevent the oncoming headache she sensed, and a hot bath would revive her, she thought.

The phone rang at seven-ten as she was stepping out of the tub. For a moment she debated about letting it ring, then grabbed a towel and rushed into the bedroom. "Hello."

"Hi, Jeannie," a smiling voice said.

Laura! It was Laura.

"Laura, where are you?"

"Where I'm having a lot of fun. Jeannie, tell those cops to pick up their jacks and go home. I'm having the time of my life. I'll call you soon. Bye, dear."

50

Late Monday afternoon Sam went to interview Joel Nieman at his office in Rye, New York.

After keeping him waiting in the reception area for nearly half an hour, Nieman invited him into his decidedly upscale private suite. His entire manner suggested ill-concealed annoyance at the interruption.

Doesn't look much like Romeo to me, Sam thought as he studied Nieman's pudgy features and dyed reddish brown hair.

Nieman airily dismissed the suggestion that he had made a date with Laura during the reunion. "I heard that nonsense about the lunch table killer on the radio," he volunteered. "That school reporter, Perkins, started it, I gather. They ought to put a net over his head and cart him away until he grows up. Listen, I was in class with those girls. I knew them all. The idea that their deaths are related is nonsense. Just start with Catherine Kane. Her car skidded into the Potomac when we were college freshmen. Cath was always a fast driver. Look up the number of speeding tickets she got in Cornwall during her senior year, and you'll see what I mean."

"That may be," Sam said, "but don't you think it's a

remarkable case of lightning striking in the same place, not twice but *five* times?"

"Sure, it's pretty creepy that five girls from the same table died, but I could introduce you to the guy who services our computers. His mother and his grandmother dropped dead of heart attacks on the same day thirty years apart. Day after Christmas. Maybe they realized how much they spent for presents, and it got to them. Could be, don't you think?"

Sam looked at Joel Nieman with acute distaste but also with the sense that underneath his show of disdain there was a sense of unease. "I understand your wife left the reunion on Saturday morning to go on a business trip."

"That's right."

"Were you alone at your home on Saturday night after the reunion dinner, Mr. Nieman?"

"As a matter of fact, I was. Those long-winded affairs make me sleepy."

This guy isn't the kind who goes home alone when his wife is away, Sam thought. He took a shot in the dark. "Mr. Nieman, you were observed leaving the parking lot with a woman in the car."

Joel Nieman raised his eyebrows. "Well, perhaps I did leave with a woman, but she wasn't pushing forty years old. Mr. Deegan, if you're on a fishing expedition with me because Laura took off with some guy and hasn't resurfaced, I suggest you call my lawyer. And now, if you'll excuse me, I have a number of phone calls to make."

Sam got to his feet and ambled toward the door, obviously in no haste. As he passed the bookcase, he paused and looked at the middle shelf. "You have quite a collection of Shakespeare, Mr. Nieman."

"I have always enjoyed the Bard."

"I understand you were Romeo in your senior play at Stonecroft."

"That's right."

Sam chose his words carefully. "Wasn't Alison Kendall critical of your performance?"

"She said I forgot my lines. I didn't forget them. I had a moment or two of stage fright. Period."

"Alison had an accident in school a few days after the play, didn't she?"

"I remember that. The door of her locker fell on her. All the guys were questioned about it. I always thought that they should have been talking to the girls. A lot of them couldn't stand her. Look, this is going to get you nowhere. As I told you, I would bet my bottom dollar the other four lunch table deaths were accidents. There's absolutely no pattern to them. On the other hand, Alison was a mean kid. She trampled on people. From what I read about her, she never changed. I could see where someone might decide she'd been swimming long enough the day she drowned."

He walked to the door and pointedly opened it. "Speed the parting guest," he said. "That's Shakespeare, too."

Sam hoped he was professional enough not to allow his face to show exactly what he thought of Nieman and his cavalier dismissal of Alison Kendall's death. "There's also a Danish proverb that says fish and guests smell after three days," he observed. Especially dead guests, he thought.

"That was more famously paraphrased by Benjamin Franklin," Joel Nieman said quickly.

"Are you familiar with the Shakespeare quote about dead lilies?" Sam asked. "It's somewhat in the same vein."

Nieman's laugh was an unpleasant, mirthless bark. " 'Lilies that fester smell far worse than weeds.' That's a line from one of his sonnets. Sure, I know it. In fact, it's one I think about a lot. My mother-in-law's name is Lily."

Sam drove from Rye to the Glen-Ridge House faster than he approved, allowing the speedometer to climb. He had asked the honorees and Jack Emerson to meet him for dinner at seven-thirty. His gut instinct had been that one of the five men—Carter Stewart, Robby Brent, Mark Fleischman, Gordon Amory, or Emerson—held the key to Laura's disappearance. Now, after interviewing Joel Nieman, he wasn't as sure.

In effect, Nieman had admitted that he did not go home alone the night of the dinner. At Stonecroft he had been the prime suspect in the locker incident. He'd almost gone to jail for assaulting another man in a bar fight. He made no attempt to conceal his satisfaction that Alison Kendall was dead.

At the very least, Joel Nieman could use a great deal more scrutiny, Sam reasoned.

It was exactly seven-thirty when Sam entered the Glen-Ridge House. On the way into the private room, he passed the omnipresent Jake Perkins, sprawled on a chair in the lobby. Perkins jumped to his feet. "Any new developments, sir?" he asked cheerfully.

If there were, you'd be the last to know, Sam thought, but he managed not to let his annoyance show in his voice. "Nothing to report, Jake. Why don't you go home?"

"Pretty soon I'll be on my way. Oh, here's Dr. Sheridan. I'd like to catch her for a minute."

Jean was coming out of the elevator. Even from a distance Sam could see that there was something about her that suggested distress. It was the way she walked so quickly across the lobby toward the dining room. That sense of urgency made his own step quicken to catch up with her.

They met at the door of the dining room. Jean started to say, "Sam, I heard from—" Then, noticing Jake Perkins, she closed her lips.

Perkins had overheard. "Who did you hear from, Dr. Sheridan? Was it Laura Wilcox?"

"Go away," Sam said firmly. He took Jean's arm, propelled her through the dining room door, and closed it firmly.

Carter Stewart, Gordon Amory, Mark Fleischman,

"It never crossed my mind that you were worried about her, Carter," Robby Brent commented. "I think that other than Jean, the only person who really might be concerned is our chairman, Jack Emerson. Right, Jack?"

"What's this?" Sam wondered aloud.

Robby smiled innocently. "Jack and I had a date this morning to look at some real estate that I might invest in, or at least might have considered investing in were it not so wildly overpriced. Jack was on the phone when I got to his place, and while I waited for him to talk to yet another few potential suckers, I looked over the collection of pictures in his den. There was a pretty sentimental inscription on one of Laura, dated exactly two weeks ago. 'Love and kisses and hugs to my favorite classmate.' It makes me wonder, Jack. How many hugs and kisses did she give you over the weekend, and is she still giving them to you?"

For an instant Jean thought that Jack Emerson would physically attack Robby Brent. Emerson bolted up, slapped both hands on the table, and stared across at Robby. Then, in a visible effort to control himself, he clenched his teeth and slowly lowered himself back into the chair. "There is a lady present," he said quietly. "Otherwise, I'd be using the kind of language you understand best, you miserable little toad. Maybe you've made a good living ridiculing people who managed to accomplish something in their lives, but as far as I'm concerned, you're still the same birdbrained dope who couldn't find his way to the bathroom at Stonecroft."

Dismayed at the exchange of raw hostility, Jean's eyes swept the room to be sure there was no waiter present to overhear Jack Emerson's outburst. When her gaze reached the door, she could see that it was partly open. She had no doubt as to who was on the other side, taking in every word of the conversation.

She exchanged glances with Sam Deegan. Sam stood up. "If you'll excuse me, I think I'd better skip coffee," he said. "I have a phone call to trace."

51

Peggy Kimball was a generously sized woman of about sixty who emanated an air of warmth and intelligence. Her salt-and-pepper hair had a natural wave; her complexion was smooth except for the fine lines around her mouth and eyes. Jean had the immediate impression that Peggy was a no-nonsense person and that it would take a lot to faze her.

They both waved away menus and ordered coffee. "My daughter picked up her kids an hour ago," Peggy said. "I had cornflakes and cocoa with them at seven o'clock, or was it at six-thirty?" She smiled. "You must have thought you were listening to Armageddon on the phone last night."

"I teach a college freshman class," Jean said. "Sometimes I think those students sound younger than toddlers, and they certainly can be noisier."

The waiter poured the coffee. Peggy Kimball looked directly at Jean, her bantering demeanor gone. "I do remember you, Jean," she said. "Dr. Connors handled many adoptions for young girls in your position. I felt sorry for you because you were one of the very few who ever came to the office alone. Most of the girls were accompanied by a parent or some other concerned adult, sometimes even by the baby's father, who was usually just another scared teenage kid."

"Be that as it may," Jean said quietly, "we're here because I am a concerned adult worrying about the nineteen-year-old girl who is my daughter and who may need help."

Sam Deegan had taken the original faxes, but she had made copies of them along with the DNA report, which verified that the strands of hair on the brush were Lily's. She took them out of her bag and showed them to Kimball. "Peggy, suppose it was your daughter," she said. "Wouldn't you be upset? Wouldn't you construe all this as a threat?" She looked Peggy in the eye.

"Yes, I would."

"Peggy, do you know who adopted Lily?"

"No, I do not."

"A lawyer had to have handled the paperwork. Do you know what lawyer or law firm Dr. Connors used?"

Peggy Kimball hesitated, then said slowly, "I doubt there was a lawyer involved in your case, Jean."

There's something she's afraid to tell me, Jean thought. "Peggy, Dr. Connors flew out to Chicago a few days before my due date, induced labor, and took Lily from me hours after she was born. Do you know if he registered her birth in Chicago or back here?"

Kimball stared reflectively at the coffee cup she was holding, then looked back at Jean. "I don't know about you specifically, Jean, but I do know that sometimes Dr. Connors registered a birth directly to the adoptive par-

ents, as though the woman had been the natural
mother."

"But that's *illegal*," Jean protested. "He had no right
to do that."

"I know he didn't, but Dr. Connors had a friend who
knew he was adopted and spent his adult life trying to
track his birth family. It became an obsession with him,
even though he was deeply loved by the adoptive parents and was treated exactly as they treated their birth
children. Dr. Connors said it was a damn shame that he
ever was told he was adopted."

"Then you're saying that maybe there was no original birth certificate, and no lawyer involved. Lily may
believe that the people who adopted her are her natural
parents!"

"It's possible, especially since Dr. Connors flew to
Chicago to deliver your baby himself. Over the years he
sent several girls to that nursing home in Chicago. It
usually meant he was bypassing registering the birth
with the natural mother's name on the certificate. Jean,
there's something else you must realize. Lily's birth may
not necessarily have been registered either here or in
Chicago. It might have been treated as an 'at-home
birth' in Connecticut or New Jersey, for example. Dr.
Connors was well known throughout the area for ar-
ranging private adoptions."

She reached across the table and impulsively
grasped Jean's hand. "Jean, you talked to me at that
time. I remember that you said you wanted your baby to
be happy and to be loved, and you hoped that it would

grow up with a mother and father who were crazy about each other and who also thought the sun rose and set on their child. I'm sure you told Dr. Connors the same thing. Maybe, in a way, he thought he was carrying out your wishes by sparing Lily the longing to find you."

Jean felt as though huge metal doors had slammed shut right in front of her face. "Except now I *have* to find her," she said slowly, the words catching in her throat. "I *have* to find her. Peggy, you did imply that Dr. Connors didn't treat all his adoptions that way."

"No, he did not."

"Then he used a lawyer for some of them?"

"Yes, he did. That would be Craig Michaelson. He's still practicing, but he moved to Highland Falls years ago. You know where that is, I'm sure."

Highland Falls was the town nearest to West Point. "Yes, I know where it is," Jean said.

Peggy took a final sip of coffee. "I have to leave—I'm due at the hospital in half an hour," she said. "I wish I could have been more help, Jean."

"Maybe you can be," Jean said. "The fact remains that somebody found out about Lily, and maybe that happened at the time I was pregnant. Is there anyone else who was working in Dr. Connors' office who might have had access to the records?"

"No," Peggy said. "Dr. Connors kept those files under lock and key."

The waiter laid the check on the table. Jean signed it, and together the women walked into the lobby. Jack Emerson was sitting in a chair near the front desk, a newspaper on his lap. He nodded to Jean as she stood at the door saying good-bye to Peggy, then he stopped her as she passed him on the way to the elevator.

"Jean, any further word from Laura?"

"No." She was curious why Jack Emerson was in the hotel. Surely after that ugly exchange at the dinner table last night, he wouldn't want to run into Robby Brent. Then when he spoke she wondered if he could read her mind.

"I want to apologize for that exchange with Robby last night," Emerson said. "I hope you realize that was a lousy insinuation he made. I didn't ask Laura for that picture. I had written asking her to be an honoree at the reunion, and she sent it with her note of acceptance. She probably mailed out a thousand of those publicity pictures and inscribed all of them with hugs and kisses and love."

Was Jack Emerson studying her to see if she bought that explanation of the picture in his den? Jean wondered. She couldn't be certain. "You're probably right," she said dismissively. "Well, if you'll excuse me, I've got to run." Then she paused, her curiosity getting the better of her. "You look as though you're waiting for someone."

"Gordie, I mean *Gordon*, did ask me to take him around and look at some property after all. He didn't like anything the hot shots from the country club showed him yesterday. I have exclusives on a couple of sites that would be perfect for corporate headquarters."

"Good luck. Oh, here's the elevator. See you, Jack."

Jean walked rapidly to the elevator and waited as some people exited. Gordon Amory was the last to get out. "Did you hear any more from Laura?" he asked hurriedly.

"No."

"All right. Keep me posted."

Jean stepped into the elevator and pushed the number of her floor. Craig Michaelson, she thought. I'll call him the minute I get to the room.

Outside the hotel, Peggy Kimball got into her car and fastened her seat belt. Frowning in concentration, she tried to place the man who had nodded to Jean Sheridan in the lobby. Of course, she thought. That was Jack Emerson, the real estate guy who bought the property after our building burned down ten years ago.

She put the key in the ignition and turned it. Jack Emerson, she thought contemptuously. There had been a suggestion at the time that he might have had something to do with that fire. He not only wanted that property, but it had come out that he knew the building like the back of his hand. In high school he had made his spending money working a couple of evenings a week on the cleaning crew there. Was he working in the building when Jean was seeing Dr. Connors? Peggy wondered. We always scheduled girls like her in the evening so that they wouldn't run into other patients.

Emerson might have spotted her and put two and two together.

She began to back out of the parking space. Jean wanted to know about anyone who might have been working in the office, she thought. It might be worth mentioning Jack Emerson to her, even though she was absolutely certain that neither he nor anyone else could have gotten into those locked files.

52

Sam Deegan's subpoena for the telephone records that would show the area where Laura's phone call to Jean had originated produced exactly the same results as the one he'd gotten a day earlier. The second call from Laura had been made from the same kind of cell phone—the kind that could be purchased with one hundred minutes of available calling time and did not require a subscriber's name.

At eleven-fifteen on Tuesday morning, Sam was in the district attorney's office giving him an update. "It's not the same phone Wilcox used Sunday night," he told Rich Stevens. "This one was purchased in Orange County. It has an 845 exchange. Eddie Zarro is out checking the places in the Cornwall area that sell them. Of course, it's been turned off, just like the one Wilcox used to phone the Glen-Ridge desk clerk Sunday evening."

The district attorney spun a pen in his fingers. "Jean Sheridan can't be one hundred percent certain she was talking to Laura Wilcox."

"No, sir, she can't."

"And the nurse—what's her name, Peggy Kimball?—

told Sheridan that Dr. Connors may have arranged an illegal private adoption for her baby?"

"That's what Mrs. Kimball thinks."

"Have you heard anything from the priest at St. Thomas about baptismal records?"

"So far they're drawing a blank. They've been pretty successful reaching people who had baby girls baptized within that three-month period, but they haven't come up with one single instance of anyone admitting that their child had been adopted. The pastor, Monsignor Dillon, is smart. He called in some of the long-timers on the parish council who were around twenty years ago. They knew of families who had adopted children, but not one of them has a girl who's nineteen and a half now."

"Is Monsignor Dillon still working on it?"

Sam rubbed his hand over his head and thought again of how Kate used to tell him that he was weakening the roots of his hair. He decided it was a sign of his fatigue that from thoughts of Kate his mind jumped to Alice Sommers. It seemed more like two weeks than two days since he had seen her. But then, since early Saturday morning when Helen Whelan was reported missing, everything had been spinning out of control.

"Is Monsignor Dillon still searching through the files, Sam?" Rich Stevens asked again.

"Sorry, Rich. I guess I was woolgathering there for a minute. The answer is yes, and he's also called some of the neighboring parishes and asked them to do a discreet check on their own. If they think they have anything, Monsignor Dillon will let us know, and we can subpoena their records."

"And is Jean Sheridan following up on Craig Michaelson, the lawyer who handled some of Dr. Connors' adoptions?"

"She's seeing him at two o'clock."

"What's your next step, Sam?"

They were interrupted by the ringing of Sam's cell phone. He grabbed it from his pocket, glanced at the ID, and the fatigue suddenly dropped from his expression. "It's Eddie Zarro," he said as he pushed the talk button. "What have you got, Eddie?" he snapped.

As the district attorney watched, Sam's mouth dropped. "You've got to be kidding me. God, I feel so dumb. Why didn't I think of that, and what is that little weasel up to? Okay. I'll meet you at the Glen-Ridge. Let's hope he didn't decide to take off today."

Sam closed the phone and looked at his boss. "A cell phone with one hundred minutes on it was bought at the drugstore on Main Street in Cornwall a few minutes after seven last night. The clerk remembers distinctly the man who made the purchase because he's seen him on television. It was Robby Brent."

"The comedian? Do you think he and Laura Wilcox are together?"

"No, sir, I don't. The clerk in the drugstore watched Brent after he left. Brent stood on the sidewalk and made a phone call. According to him, it was at exactly the same time that Jean Sheridan received the call supposedly from Laura Wilcox."

"You mean that you think—"

Sam interrupted. "Robby Brent is a comedian by some standards, but by everyone's standard he's a first-class mimic. My guess is the guy was imitating Laura's voice on that call to Jean Sheridan. I'm on my way to the Glen-Ridge. I'm going to find that jerk and make him explain to me what he was up to."

"Do that," Rich Stevens snapped. "He'd better have a damn good story, or else let's slap him with a charge for hindering a police investigation."

53

How long had it been? Laura had the sense that she was lapsing in and out of something that was more than sleep. How long had it been since The Owl was here? She wasn't sure. Last night, around the time she had sensed he would be coming back, something had happened. She'd heard sounds on the stairs, then a voice — a voice she knew.

"*Don't!*" Then he had shouted the name she had been forbidden to even whisper.

It was Robby Brent who had shouted, and he sounded terrified.

Did The Owl hurt Robby Brent last night?

I think so, Laura decided, as she willed herself to slip once more into a world where she didn't have to remember that The Owl might come back and that one of the times he returned he would pick up the pillow, hold it over her face, press it down, and . . .

What had happened to Robby? Some time after she heard his voice last night, The Owl had come to her and given her something to eat. He had been angry, so angry that his voice had trembled as he told her that Robby Brent had imitated her voice.

"I had to sit through dinner wondering if somehow

you had gotten to the phone, but then my common sense told me that, of course, if you had been able to reach the phone, you would have called the police, not Jean, to say that you were fine. I was suspicious of Brent, Laura, but then that nosy kid reporter was there, and I thought maybe he was up to some trick. Robby was so stupid, Laura, so stupid. He followed me here. I left the door open, and he came in. Oh, Laura, he was so stupid."

Did I dream that? Laura wondered hazily. Did I make that up?

She heard a click. Was it the door? She squeezed her eyes shut as raw panic raced through her body.

"Wake up, Laura. Raise your head to show that you're glad I'm back. I must talk to you, and I want to feel that you care about everything I tell you." The Owl's voice became hurried, high-pitched. "Robby suspected me and tried to set a trap for me. I don't know where I let my guard down, but I took care of him. I told you that. Now Jean is getting too close to the truth, Laura, but I know what I can do to lead her astray and then ensnare her. You do want to help me, don't you?

"Don't you?" he repeated loudly.

"Yes," Laura whispered as she tried to make her voice audible through the gag.

The Owl seemed appeased. "Laura, I know you're hungry. I've brought you something to eat. But first I have to tell you about Jean's daughter, Lily, and explain to you why you have been sending Jean threatening notes about her. You do remember sending those notes, don't you, Laura?"

Jean? A daughter? Laura stared up at him.

The Owl had turned on the small flashlight and laid it on the bedside table facing her. The light was shining across her neck and penetrating the darkness immediately around her. Looking up, she could see that he was staring back down at her, motionless now. Then he raised his arms.

"I remember." She mouthed the words, trying to make them audible to him.

Slowly his arms lowered to his sides. Laura closed her eyes, weak with relief. It had almost been the end. She had not responded quickly enough.

"Laura," he whispered. "You still don't understand. I am a bird of prey. When I have been disturbed, there is only one way I know to make myself whole. Don't tempt me with your obstinacy. Now tell me what we are going to do."

Laura's throat was parched. The gag was pressing against her tongue. Beneath the numbness in her hands and feet, the throbbing was intensifying as every muscle tightened with fear. She closed her eyes, struggling to concentrate. "Jean . . . her daughter. . . . I sent notes."

After she opened her eyes, the flashlight was turned off. He was no longer hovering over her. She heard the click of the door. He was gone.

From somewhere nearby she could catch the faint aroma of the coffee he had forgotten to give her.

The office of Craig Michaelson, Attorney at Law, was located on Old State Road, only two blocks past the motel where Jean and Cadet Carroll Reed Thornton had spent their few nights together. As Jean approached the motel, she slowed down and blinked back tears.

Her mental image of Reed was so strong, her memory of their time together so intense. She felt that if she slipped into room 108, he would be there, waiting for her. Reed with his blond hair and blue eyes, his strong arms that wrapped around her, making her feel a kind of happiness that in all her eighteen years of life she had never imagined possible.

"I dream of Jeannie . . ."

For a long time after Reed died, she would wake up with the music of that song drifting through her mind. We were so in love, Jean thought. He was Prince Charming to my Cinderella. He was kind and smart, and he had a maturity far beyond his twenty-two years. He loved the military life. He encouraged me as a writer. He teased me that someday when he was a general, I'd be writing his biography. When I told him I was pregnant, he was worried because he knew what his father's reaction would be to an early marriage. But then he said, "We'll just move up our plans, Jeannie, that's all. Early marriages are not exactly unheard of in my family. My grandfather got married the day he graduated from West Point, and my grandmother was only nineteen."

"But you told me your grandparents knew each other from the time they were babies," she had pointed out. "That's a lot different. They'll see me as a townie who got pregnant so that I could get you to marry me."

Reed had covered her mouth with his hand. "I won't listen to that kind of talk," he'd said firmly. "Once they know you, my parents will love you. But on the same subject, you'd better introduce me to your mother and father pretty soon."

I had wanted to be a student at Bryn Mawr when I met Reed's parents, Jean thought. By then my mother and father would have split. If his parents had met them separately, they probably would have liked them well enough. They wouldn't necessarily have learned about their problems.

If Reed had lived.

Or even if he had to die young, if it had happened after we were married, I still could have kept Lily. Reed was an only child. His parents might have been angry about our marriage, but they surely would have been thrilled to have a grandchild.

We all lost big-time, Jean thought achingly as she put her foot down on the accelerator and sped past the motel.

Craig Michaelson's office occupied an entire floor of a building that Jean knew had not been there when she and Reed were dating. His reception area was attractive with paneled walls and wide chairs that had been upholstered in an antique tapestry pattern. Jean decided that at least on the surface it would seem that the Michaelson firm was prosperous.

She had not been sure what to expect. On the drive to Highland Falls from Cornwall she had decided that if Michaelson had been part of Dr. Connors' system of improperly registering births, he would be something of a charlatan and surely very much on the defensive.

After she had waited ten minutes, Craig Michaelson came out to the reception area himself and personally escorted her into his private office. He was a tall man in his early sixties, with a big frame and slightly sloping shoulders. His full head of hair, more dark gray than silver, looked as though he might have just left the barber. His dark gray suit was well cut, and his tie was a subdued gray-and-blue print. Everything about his appearance as well as the tasteful furnishings and paintings in his office suggested a reserved and conservative man.

Jean realized that she was not sure if that wasn't the worst possible scenario. If Craig Michaelson was *not* involved in Lily's adoption, then this was going to be another dead end in her search to find her.

She looked directly at the lawyer as she told him

about Lily and showed him the copies of the faxes and the DNA report. She sketched out her own background, reluctantly emphasizing her academic standing, the honors and awards she had received, and the fact that because of her best-selling book her financial success was a matter of public record.

Michaelson never took his eyes off her face except when he examined the faxes. She knew he was sizing her up, trying to decide if what she was telling him was the truth or just an elaborate hoax.

"Because of Dr. Connors' nurse, Peggy Kimball, I know that some of the adoptions the doctor arranged were illegal," she said. "What I need to know, what I beg you to tell me, is this: Did you handle my child's adoption yourself, or do you know who adopted her?"

"Dr. Sheridan, let me start by telling you that I never had any part in an adoption that was not handled to the strictest letter of the law. If at any time Dr. Connors was bypassing the law, he did so without my knowledge or involvement."

"Then if you did handle my baby's adoption, are you telling me that it was registered with my name as the mother and the name of Carroll Reed Thornton as the father?"

"I am saying that any adoption I handled was legal."

Years of teaching students, a small percentage of whom had been adept at dissembling and half-truths, had made Jean feel capable of spotting that practice whenever she encountered it. She knew she was encountering it now.

"Mr. Michaelson, a nineteen-and-a-half-year-old girl may be in danger. If you handled the adoption, you know who adopted her. You could try to protect her now. In fact, in my opinion, you have a moral obligation to try to protect her."

It was the wrong thing to say. Behind silver-framed glasses, Craig Michaelson's eyes turned frosty. "Dr. Sheridan, you have demanded that I see you today. You have come in with a story for the truth of which I have only your word. You have virtually suggested that I might have broken the law in the past, and now you are *demanding* that I break the law in order to help you. There are legal ways to have birth records released. You should go to the district attorney's office. I believe that they would petition the court to open those records. I can assure you that is the only way you should be going about this inquiry. As you yourself point out, it is possible that at the time you were expecting the baby someone might have seen you in Dr. Connors' office and somehow got into your file. You also pointed out that this may be all about money. Frankly, my guess is that you're right. Someone knows who your daughter is and suspects you will pay for the knowledge."

He stood up.

For a moment Jean remained seated. "Mr. Michaelson, I have pretty good instincts, and my instinct is that you handled my daughter's adoption and that you probably did it legally. My other very strong instinct is that whoever is writing to me and is close enough to Lily to steal her hairbrush is dangerous. I am going to go to court to try to get the records released. The fact remains, though, that in the interval, something might happen to my child because you are stonewalling me now. If it does, and I find out about it, I don't think I'll be responsible for what I'll do to you."

Jean could not control the tears that were spilling from her eyes. She turned and hurried from the room, not caring that the receptionist and several people in the reception area looked up at her in astonishment as she ran past them. When she reached her car, she flung open the door, got in, and buried her face in her hands.

And then she went deadly cold. As clearly as though Laura were in the car with her, she could hear her voice pleading, "Jean, help me! Please, Jean, help me!"

55

From the front window of his office, his face drawn with concern, Craig Michaelson watched Jean Sheridan as she rushed to her car. She's on the level, he thought. This isn't about a woman obsessed to find her child and fabricating a wild story. Should I warn Charles and Gano? If anything happened to Meredith, it would destroy them both.

He would not, could not, reveal Jean Sheridan's identity to them, but he could at least make Charles aware of the threats to his adopted daughter. It should be his decision as to what he might tell Meredith or how he might try to protect her. If the story about the hairbrush was true, maybe Meredith would remember where she was when she mislaid it or lost it. It might be one way to try to trace the sender of the faxes.

Jean Sheridan had said that if anything happened to her daughter, something I could have prevented, she wouldn't be responsible for what she would do to me, he recalled. Charles and Gano would feel exactly the same way.

His decision made, Craig Michaelson went to his desk and picked up the phone. He did not need to look up the number. Crazy coincidence, he thought as he dialed. Jean Sheridan doesn't live far from Charles and Gano. She's in Alexandria. They're in Chevy Chase.

The phone was picked up on the first ring. "General Buckley's office," a crisp voice said.

"This is Craig Michaelson, a close friend of General Buckley. I need to speak to him on a matter of great importance. Is he there?"

"I'm sorry, sir. The General is abroad on official business. Can someone else help you?"

"No, I'm afraid not. Will you be hearing from the General?"

"Yes, sir. The office is in touch with him regularly."

"Then tell him it is most urgent that he call me as soon as possible." Craig spelled his name and gave the number of his cell phone as well as his office number. He hesitated, then decided not to say that it concerned Meredith. Charles would respond to an urgent message as soon as he received it—he was confident of that.

And, anyhow, Craig Michaelson thought as he replaced the receiver, Meredith is safer at West Point than she would be almost anyplace else.

Then the unwelcome thought came to him that even being at West Point had not been enough to prevent the death of Meredith's natural father, Cadet Carroll Reed Thornton, Jr.

56

The first person Carter Stewart saw when he walked into the Glen-Ridge House at three-thirty was Jake Perkins, who was, as usual, sprawled on a chair in the lobby. Doesn't that kid have a home? Stewart wondered, as he walked to the phone at the end of the front desk and dialed Robby Brent's room.

There was no answer. "Robby, I thought we were supposed to get together at three-thirty," Stewart snapped in response to the computerized suggestion to leave a voice message. "I'll be in the lobby for another fifteen minutes or so."

As he hung up, he spotted the investigator Sam Deegan sitting in the office behind the front desk. Their eyes met, and Deegan got up, clearly on his way to talk to him. There was something decisive in the way Deegan moved which made Stewart aware that this would not be an idle conversation.

They stood across the desk from each other.

"Mr. Stewart," Sam said. "I'm glad to see you. I left a message for you at your hotel and was hoping to hear back from you."

"I've been working with my director on the script for my new play," Carter Stewart said, his tone abrupt.

"I see you were on the house phone. Are you meeting someone now?"

Stewart found himself resenting Sam Deegan's question. None of your business, he wanted to say, but something about Deegan's attitude made the remark die on his lips. "I have an appointment with Robby Brent at three-thirty. Before you ask me why I have an appointment, which is clearly your next question, let me satisfy your curiosity. Brent has agreed to star in a new sitcom. He has seen the first few scripts and feels they are off-target—that, in fact, they fall flat—and he asked me to take a look at them and give him my professional opinion as to whether or not they can be salvaged."

"Mr. Stewart, you've been compared to literary playwrights like Tennessee Williams and Edward Albee," Sam said sharply. "I'm just a run-of-the-mill kind of guy, but most of those situation comedies are insults to the intelligence. I'm surprised that you'd be interested in judging one of them."

"It was not my choice." Stewart's tone was icy. "After dinner last night, Robby Brent asked me to look at the scripts. He offered to bring them to my hotel, but as you can understand, that would have involved my having to dislodge him from my suite after I'd glanced at the material. It was much easier to stop by here on the way back from my director's home. And even though I do not *write* sitcoms, I am a very good judge of writing in *any* form. Do you know if Robby is expected soon?"

"I have no idea of his plans," Sam said. "I came here to talk to him also. I didn't get a response when I called him, and then realized that no one had seen him all day, so I had the maid go into his room. His bed had not been slept in. It appears that Mr. Brent is missing."

Sam was not sure that he wanted to give that much information to Carter Stewart, but his instinct told him to divulge it and watch for Stewart's reaction. It turned out to be stronger than he had anticipated.

"*Missing!* Oh, come now, Mr. Deegan. Don't you think this scenario has played itself out long enough? Let me explain: There is a part in this proposed series for a sexy blonde not unlike the vanished Laura Wilcox. The other day at West Point, specifically at the lunch table, Brent was telling Laura that she might be perfect for that part. I am beginning to think that the entire three-ring circus surrounding her disappearance is nothing more than a publicity stunt. And now, if you'll excuse me, I won't waste any more of my time waiting around for Robby."

I don't like that guy, Sam thought as he watched Carter Stewart leave. Stewart was wearing a somewhat tattered dark gray sweatsuit and dirty sneakers, a hobo's outfit that Sam figured had probably cost a fortune.

My feelings for him aside, has he put his finger on everything that's going on? Sam wondered. In the more than three hours that he had been sitting in the office, he had been doing some hard thinking and in the process had become more and more irritated.

We know Brent made the phone call impersonating

Laura, he reasoned. He bought a cell phone that appears to be the one that the call to Jean was made on. The clerk who sold it to him saw him dialing at exactly the time Jean thought Laura was talking to her. I'm beginning to think Stewart may be right, that all this is a way of getting publicity. And, in that case, why am I wasting my time here when I have a killer loose in Orange County who dragged an innocent woman into his car and stabbed her to death?

When he had arrived at the Glen-Ridge House, Eddie Zarro was waiting for him, but Sam sent him back to the office, saying there was no need for the two of them to hang out in the lobby waiting for Brent. Sam debated, then decided that now he'd get Zarro to relieve him and go home. I need a decent night's sleep, he decided. I'm so tired I can't think straight.

As he opened his cell phone to call the office, he realized that Amy Sachs, the desk clerk, was at his elbow. "Mr. Deegan," she began, her voice little more than a whisper, "you've been here since before noon, and I know you haven't had a single thing to eat. May I order coffee and a sandwich for you?"

"That's very kind, but I'll be leaving soon," Sam told her. As he spoke, he wondered how close Amy Sachs had been when he was talking to Stewart. She didn't appear to make any sound when she walked, and she made very little when she opened her mouth. Why do I bet her hearing is acute? Sam wondered sardonically as he watched her exchange a glance with Jake Perkins. And why do I bet that the minute I'm out of sight, she fills Jake in on the fact that Brent isn't around and that Stewart thinks all this hoopla is a publicity stunt?

Sam went back into the office. From there he had a good view of the main entrance. A few minutes later he saw Gordon Amory come in, and he hurried to catch him before he got on the elevator.

Amory was clearly not in the mood to talk about Robby Brent. "I have not spoken to him since that vulgar display last night," he said. "As a matter of fact, since you witnessed it, Mr. Deegan, and also heard Robby's attack on Jack Emerson, I think you should know that I have been out since ten o'clock this morning with Emerson, looking at real estate. He is the exclusive agent on some genuinely fine parcels of land. He also showed me the properties he had offered Robby for consideration. I must tell you, they were fairly priced and, in my opinion, excellent long-range investments—which is to say that anything Robby Brent insinuates, says, or does should be examined for motivation beyond the obvious. Now, if you'll excuse me, I have a number of phone calls to make."

The elevator door was opening. Before Amory could step into it, Sam said, "Another moment, please, Mr. Amory."

With a resigned smile that was almost a sneer, Amory turned back to him.

"Mr. Amory, Robby Brent did not sleep in his room last night. We believe it was he who imitated Laura Wilcox on the phone call to Jean Sheridan. Your colleague, Mr. Stewart, feels that Brent and Wilcox may be carrying on a hoax for publicity for Mr. Brent's new television series. What do you think?"

Gordon Amory raised an eyebrow. For an instant he looked dumbstruck; then a look of amusement came over his face. "A publicity stunt! Of course, that makes sense. In fact, if you look at Page Six of the *New York Post*, they're already suggesting that very thing about Laura's disappearance. Now Robby vanishes, and you tell me that he made the phone call to Jean last night. And the whole time we're all sitting around worrying about them."

"Then you think it's possible we're all wasting our time worrying about Laura?"

"*Au contraire*, it has not been a waste, Mr. Deegan. The one positive thing is that Laura's supposed disappearance has proven to me that I still have the milk of human kindness flowing in my breast. I was so concerned about her that I was planning to offer her a role in my new series. I'll bet you're right. The dear girl has other fish to fry and is doing it most successfully. And now I really must go."

"I assume you'll be checking out soon," Sam suggested.

"No, I'm still looking at property. But I guess I won't be seeing you around, since now you can get back to solving real crimes. Good-bye."

Sam watched Amory get into the elevator. Another one who thinks he's intellectually superior to an investigator, he thought. Well, let's just wait and see. Sam could feel his nerves fraying as he walked back across the lobby.

Whether or not Laura's disappearance is a publicity stunt, the fact still remains that five women from the lunch table are dead.

He had been hoping Jean would get back before he left, so he was delighted to see her standing at the front desk. He hurried to her side, anxious to hear about her meeting with the lawyer.

She was asking about messages. Always afraid she'll get another fax about Lily, Sam thought. And who can blame her? He put his hand on her arm. When she turned, he could see that her eyes looked as if she might have been crying. "Buy you a cup of coffee?" he offered.

"A cup of tea would be great."

"Ms. Sachs, when Mr. Zarro returns, please ask him to join us in the coffee shop," Sam said to the room clerk.

In the coffee shop he waited until Jean's tea and his coffee had been served before he spoke again. It seemed to him that Jean was still trying to regain her composure. Finally he said, "I gather it didn't go well with the attorney Craig Michaelson."

"It did and it didn't," Jean said slowly. "Sam, I would stake my life that Michaelson handled the adoption and may know where Lily is now. I was rude to him. I practically threatened him. On the way back here I pulled the car over to the side of the road and called to apologize to him. I also pointed out that if he does know where she is, she might remember where she lost her hairbrush, and that might be a direct link to whoever is threatening her."

"What did Michaelson say to that?"

"It was odd. He said that that had already occurred to him. Sam, I'm telling you he knows where Lily is, or at least how to trace where she is. He did say, using the words 'I urge you most strongly,' that I should have you or at least the district attorney's office petition a judge to open the records immediately and warn her parents of this situation."

"Then I would say that he obviously takes seriously what you told him."

Jean nodded in agreement. "I didn't think he did when I was in his office, but maybe my outburst—I swear I was on the verge of throwing something at him—may have convinced him. His attitude had done a one-hundred-and-eighty-degree turn when I talked to him twenty minutes later on the phone." She glanced up. "Oh, look, here's Mark."

Mark Fleischman was making his way to their table. "I told Mark about Lily," Jean said hurriedly, "so you can talk in front of him."

"You did, Jean? Why?" Sam was dismayed.

"He's a psychiatrist. I thought he might be able to offer some input into whether or not these faxes are real threats."

As Mark Fleischman came nearer, Sam saw that Jean's smile became genuinely pleased. Be careful, Jeannie, he wanted to warn her. In my book this guy is carrying a lot of baggage. There's a tension bubbling under the surface in him that a cop like me can feel.

Sam also did not miss the way Fleischman momentarily covered Jean's hand with his at her invitation for him to join them.

"I'm not interfering?" Mark asked, looking at Sam for reassurance.

"As a matter of fact, I'm glad to catch you," Sam told him. "I was about to ask Jean if she had heard from Robby Brent today. Now I can ask you both."

Jean shook her head. "I haven't."

"Nor, thankfully, have I," Fleischman said. "Is there any reason you thought we might have heard from him?"

"I was about to tell you, Jean. Robby Brent must have left the hotel after dinner last night. So far he has not come back. We've pretty much determined that the call you thought came from Laura was made on a prepaid cellular phone that Brent had just bought, and we're also fairly confident that the voice you heard was actually his. As you know, he's a superb mimic."

Jean looked at Sam, astonishment and distress reflected in her face. "But *why?*"

"At the luncheon at West Point on Saturday, did you hear Brent talk to Laura about possibly being on his new television series?"

"I did," Mark Fleischman said. "But I didn't know whether or not he was joking."

"He did say there was a part Laura might want to play," Jean confirmed.

"Both Carter Stewart and Gordon Amory think Brent and Laura may be pulling a hoax on us. What do you think?" Sam's eyes narrowed as he looked at Mark Fleischman.

Behind his glasses, Mark's eyes became thoughtful. He looked past Sam, then directly at him. "I think it's entirely possible," he said slowly.

"I disagree," Jean said emphatically. "I absolutely disagree. Laura is in trouble—I feel it; I know it." She hesitated, then decided against telling them that she felt as if she had heard Laura's plea for help. "Please, Sam, don't think like that," she begged. "Don't give up trying to find Laura. I don't know what Robby Brent is up to, but maybe he was just trying to throw us off the track by pretending to be her and saying she was fine. She's *not* fine. Really, I know she's not fine."

"Take it easy, Jeannie," Mark said gently.

Sam stood up. "Jean, we'll talk again first thing in the morning. I'll want you to come to my office on that other matter we were discussing."

Ten minutes later, with Eddie Zarro waiting in case Robby Brent returned to the hotel, Sam wearily got into his car. He turned on the engine, hesitated, thought for a moment, then dialed Alice Sommers. When she answered, he was struck once more by the silvery tone of her voice. "Any chance you have a glass of sherry for a tired detective?" he asked.

Half an hour later he was sitting in a deep leather chair, his feet on the ottoman, facing the fire in Alice Sommers' den. Taking the last sip of sherry, he put the glass on the table beside him. It had not taken too much persuasive power to have Alice convince him to catnap while she prepared an early dinner. "You have to eat," she pointed out. "Then you can go straight home and get a decent night's sleep."

As his eyes began to close, Sam gave a sleepy glance at the curio cabinet beside the fireplace. He was asleep before whatever object he saw there had triggered a startled response in his subconscious.

57

Amy Sachs went off duty at four o'clock, shortly after Sam Deegan left the Glen-Ridge House. She and Jake Perkins had arranged to meet at a McDonald's about a mile away. Now, over hamburgers, she was filling him in on Sam Deegan's activities and the conversation she had managed to overhear between him and, as she described him, "that uppity playwright, Carter Stewart."

"Mr. Deegan came to the hotel looking for Mr. Brent," she explained. "Eddie Zarro, the other investigator, was waiting for him. They both looked kind of mad. The minute Mr. Deegan couldn't reach Brent on the phone, he made Pete, the bellman, take them up to Brent's room. When Brent didn't answer the door, Mr. Deegan told Pete to open it. That's when they found out that Mr. Brent hadn't come back last night."

Between bites of hamburger, Jake was jotting in his notebook. "I thought Carter Stewart checked out after the reunion," he said. "What made him come back this afternoon? Who was he meeting?"

"Stewart told Mr. Deegan that he had agreed to go over scripts for Robby Brent's new television show. Then they were talking about a cell phone. I couldn't get all of it because Mr. Deegan doesn't speak loud. Mr. Stewart isn't all that loud, either, but his voice carries, and I've been blessed with good hearing. In fact, Jake, they said my grandmother, even at age ninety, could hear a worm slither through the grass."

"My grandmother is always telling me I mumble," Jake said.

"Actually, you *do* mumble," Amy Sachs whispered. "But, anyhow, Jake, when Mr. Deegan asked Mr. Stewart if he thought all this was a publicity trick by Laura Wilcox and Robby Brent, Mr. Stewart seemed to think it was. And maybe I missed something, but didn't Dr. Sheridan get a call from Laura Wilcox last night?"

Jake was practically salivating with the unexpected torrent of information. All afternoon he felt as if he had been watching a silent movie. He sat in the hotel lobby observing the activity but not daring to hang around the desk or obviously try to overhear the conversations. "Yes, Dr. Sheridan *did* get a call from Laura Wilcox. I happened to be around when they were talking about it in the small dining room."

"Jake, I don't think I've got this all straight. You know how it is—you hear part of one thing, then part of another. You can get only so near to people without seeming to be too near, but I get the impression that Robby Brent may have made that call last night and pretended to be Laura Wilcox."

Jake's hand was in midair, firmly grasping the uneaten portion of the hamburger. Slowly he lowered it to the plate. It was obvious he was mentally computing what Amy had just told him. "Robby Brent made that call and now he's not around, and they think all this is just a publicity stunt for some new television series?"

Amy's oversized glasses bobbled on her nose as she nodded happily. "Sounds like a reality series, doesn't it?" she asked. "Do you think that maybe there are hidden cameras filming in the hotel now?"

"It's something to wonder about," Jake agreed. "You're a sharp lady, Amy. When I open my own newspaper, I'm going to make you a columnist. Anything else you've noticed?"

She pursed her lips. "Just one thing. Mark Fleischman—you know, the really cute honoree who's a psychiatrist—"

"Sure, I know him. What about him?"

"I *swear* he has a crush on Dr. Sheridan. He went out early this morning, and when he came back, the first thing he did was come rushing to the desk and phone Dr. Sheridan. I overheard him."

"Of course," Jake said, grinning.

"I told him she was in the coffee shop. He thanked me, but before he hightailed it into the coffee shop, he asked if Dr. Sheridan had received any more faxes today. He looked almost disappointed when I said no, and he asked me if I was *sure* she hadn't gotten one. Even if he does have a crush on her, I think it's a little nervy of him to ask about her mail, don't you?"

"In a way I do, yes."

"But he is nice, and I asked him just casually if he'd had a pleasant day. He said yes, he'd been looking up some old friends at West Point."

58

After Sam Deegan left, Jean Sheridan and Mark Fleischman sat for nearly an hour at the table in the coffee shop. He reached over and covered her hand with his as she told him about meeting Craig Michaelson, about becoming convinced that Michaelson had handled Lily's adoption, and about verbally attacking him when she felt he was refusing to understand that Lily might be in genuine danger.

"I did call to apologize," she explained. "When I did, I pointed out that it's just possible Lily might remember where she was when her hairbrush disappeared. That could be a direct link to who might have taken it, unless, of course, her adoptive parents are behind all this."

"That's a real possibility," Mark agreed. "Are you taking Michaelson's advice to petition the court to open the file?"

"Absolutely. I'm meeting Sam Deegan in his office tomorrow morning."

"I think that's smart. Jean, what about Laura? You don't believe this is just some publicity stunt, do you?"

"No, I don't." Jean hesitated. It was nearly four-thirty, and the late afternoon sun was sending slanting shadows through the almost deserted coffee shop. She looked across the table at Mark. He was wearing an open sport shirt and dark green sweater. He's one of those men who'll always have a boyish look, she thought—except for his eyes. "Who was that teacher we had who called you an 'old soul'?" she asked.

"That was Mr. Hastings. And what brought that up?"

"He said you were wise beyond your years."

"I'm not sure it was meant as a compliment. You're leading up to something, Jeannie."

"I guess I am. My understanding of old souls is that they have great insight. When I got in the car after I left Craig Michaelson's office, I was upset. I told you that. But then, Mark, if Laura had been in the car with me, I couldn't have heard her speak more clearly. I heard her voice saying, 'Jean, help me. Please, Jean, help me.' "

She scrutinized his expression. "You don't believe me, or you think I'm crazy," she said defensively.

"That's not true, Jeannie. If anyone believes in the power of the mind to communicate, I do. But if Laura is really in trouble, where does Robby Brent fit into the picture?"

"I have no idea." Jean raised her hand in a gesture of helplessness, then lowered it as she looked around. "We'd better get out of here. They're already setting the tables for dinner."

Mark signaled for the check. "I wish I could ask you to have dinner with me, but tonight I have the unique privilege of breaking bread with my father."

Jean looked at him closely, not sure of how to respond. The expression on his face was inscrutable. Finally she said, "I know you've been estranged from him. Did he call you?"

"I walked past the house today. His car was there. Impulsively, quite impulsively, I went up and rang the bell. We had a long talk—not long enough to settle anything, but he did ask me to meet him for dinner. I said I would, on the condition that he would be prepared to answer certain questions I was going to ask him."

"And he agreed?"

"Yes, he did. Let's see if he keeps his word."

"I hope whatever you have to work out can be worked out."

"So do I, Jeannie, but I'm not counting on it."

They got in the elevator together. Mark punched the buttons for the fourth and sixth floors.

"I hope your view is better than mine," Jean said. "I overlook the back parking lot."

"Then it is better," he agreed. "I'm facing the front. If I'm in the room at the right time, I get to see the sunset."

"And if I happen to be awake, I get to see who comes rolling in around daybreak," Jean said as the elevator stopped at the fourth floor. "I'll see you, Mark."

The message signal on the phone in her room was blinking. The call was from Peggy Kimball and had come in only a few minutes earlier. "Jean, I'm on my break at the hospital, so I'll make this fast. After I left you, it occurred to me that Jack Emerson worked for the clean-up crew in our office building around the time

you were seeing Dr. Connors. I told you Dr. Connors always kept his file keys in his pocket, but he must have
had a spare hidden somewhere because I remember
that one day he forgot to bring his key ring to the office
but still was able to open the files. So maybe Emerson
or someone like him *did* get a look at your records. Anyhow, I thought you should know. Good luck."

Jack Emerson, Jean thought as she replaced the receiver and sank down on the bed. Could he be the one
who's doing this to me? He's always lived in this town. If
the people who adopted Lily live here, too, he may know
them.

She heard a sound and turned in time to see a
manila envelope being slid under the door. She hurried
across the room and yanked the door open.

An apologetic bellman was trying to straighten up.
"Dr. Sheridan, a fax came for you right after a whole
stack came for one of the other guests. Your fax got put
in with his material. He just came across it and brought
it down to the desk."

"It's all right," Jean said softly, fear almost closing
her throat. She closed the door and picked up the envelope. Her hand shaking, she ripped it open. It's going to
be about Lily, she thought.

It *was* about Lily. The fax read:

Jean, I am so terribly ashamed. I always knew
about Lily, and I know the people who adopted
her. She's a wonderful girl. She's smart; a college
sophomore and very happy. I didn't mean to

make you think I was threatening her. I need money desperately and thought I could get it this way. Don't worry about Lily, please. She is fine. I will be in touch with you soon. Forgive me and please let people know that I'm all right. The publicity stunt was Robby Brent's idea. He's going to try to straighten it out. He wants to talk to his producers before he has to make a statement to the press.

Laura

Her knees weak, Jean sank onto the bed. Then, crying with relief and joy, she dialed Sam's cell phone.

Jean's call jolted Sam from the peaceful nap he had been enjoying while Alice Sommers busied herself in the kitchen. "Another fax, Jean? Take it easy. Read it to me." He listened. "My God," he said. "I can't believe that woman would do this to you."

"You're talking to Jean? Is she all right?" Alice was standing in the doorway.

"Yes. Laura Wilcox has been sending the faxes about Lily. She's apologized, saying she never intended to hurt Lily."

Alice took the phone from him. "Jean, are you too upset to drive?" She listened. "Then come over here . . ."

When Jean arrived, Alice looked into Jean's face and saw the luminous joy she would have experienced herself if somehow years ago Karen had been spared. She put her arms around her. "Oh, Jean, I've been praying and praying."

Jean hugged her fiercely. "I know you have. I cannot believe that Laura has done this to me, but I am sure that Laura would never hurt Lily. And so it *was* all about money, Sam. My God, if Laura was that desperate, why didn't she just ask me straight out to help her? Half an hour ago I was ready to tell you that I thought Jack Emerson must be the one who knew about Lily."

"Jean, come in, sit down, and calm down. Have a glass of sherry and tell me what you mean by that. What does Jack Emerson have to do with this?"

"I just learned something that made me believe he was behind it." Obediently, Jean slipped off her coat, went into the den, sat on the chair nearest the fire, and, trying to keep her voice steady, told them about the call from Peggy Kimball. "Jack worked in that office at the time I was Dr. Connors' patient. He planned this reunion to get us all here. In his den he has that picture of Laura that Robby Brent talked about. It all seemed to fit—until the fax was delivered. Oh, I didn't tell you. The fax came in around noon but got mixed in with someone else's stuff."

"You should have received it at *noon?*" Sam asked quickly.

"Yes, and if I had, I wouldn't have gone to see Craig Michaelson. As soon as I got it, I tried to phone him so that in case he was planning to contact Lily's adoptive parents, I could tell him to hold off until I heard from

Laura again. There's no need now to alarm them or her."

"Have you told anyone else about this fax from Laura?" Sam asked quietly.

"No. I got it right after I went upstairs to my room. Mark and I sat and talked for at least an hour after you left us. Oh, I should call Mark now before he goes out to dinner. He'll be so glad to hear about this. He understands just as much as you two do how desperately worried I've been."

Dollars to doughnuts, Jean told Fleischman about the possibility that the hairbrush might be traced to the place where Lily lost it, or who she was with when she lost it, Sam thought grimly as he watched Jean reach for her cell phone.

He exchanged glances with Alice and saw they were sharing the same concern. Was this fax really from Laura, or was it one more bizarre twist in an ongoing nightmare?

Then there is another scenario, Sam thought. If Jean is right, and Craig Michaelson *did* handle the adoption, it's possible that Michaelson might already have contacted Lily's adoptive parents and discussed the missing brush.

Unless this communication from Laura was on the level, Lily had become a danger to whoever was sending the faxes. And whoever was doing it might have thought about the hairbrush being traced to him.

I'm not ready to accept that these faxes were from Laura, Sam thought. Not yet anyway. Jack Emerson worked in Dr. Connors' office, has always lived in town, and could easily be friends with a couple from Cornwall who might have adopted Lily.

Mark Fleischman may have won Jean's confidence, but I'm not convinced. There's something going on inside that guy that has nothing to do with going on television and giving advice to dysfunctional families, he decided.

Jean was leaving a message for Fleischman. "He's not in," she said, then sniffed and turned to Alice, a smile on her face. "Something smells wonderful. If you don't invite me to dinner, I'm going to invite myself. Oh, dear God, I'm so happy. *I'm so happy!*"

59

Nighttime is my time, The Owl thought as he frantically waited for darkness. He had been a fool to risk
going back to the house during the daytime—he might
have been seen. But then he had gotten the unsettling
feeling that maybe Robby Brent was not dead after all,
that, actor that he was, he had pretended to be unconscious. He could just picture him crawling out of his car
and making his way to the street—or maybe even going
up the stairs to find Laura and call 911.

The image of Robby alive and able to get help had
become so powerful that The Owl had no choice but to
go back to confirm for himself that he was indeed dead,
that he was exactly where he had left him, in the trunk
of his car.

It was almost like the first time he had taken a life,
that night in Laura's house, The Owl thought. Through
the haze of memory he recalled tiptoeing up the back
stairs, heading to the room where he had expected to
find Laura. That was twenty years ago.

Last night, knowing that Robby Brent was following
him, it hadn't been hard to outsmart him. But then he'd
had to dig in Robby's pocket for his keys so he could

drive his car into the garage. His first rental car, the one with the muddy tires, was occupying one space in the garage. He'd driven Robby Brent's car into the other space and then dragged Brent's body to it from the staircase where he had killed him.

Somehow he had revealed himself to Robby Brent. Somehow Robby had figured it out. What about the others? Was a circle closing so that soon he would no longer be able to escape into the night? He didn't like uncertainty. He needed reassurance — the reassurance that came only when he carried out the deed that reaffirmed his mastery over life and death.

At eleven o'clock he began to drive through Orange County. Not too near Cornwall, he thought. Not too near Washingtonville, where Helen Whelan's body was found. Maybe Highland Falls would be a good choice. Maybe somewhere in the vicinity of the motel where Jean Sheridan had stayed with the cadet would be the place to look.

Maybe one of the sidestreets near that motel would be the place where he was destined to find his victim.

At eleven-thirty, as he cruised down a tree-lined street, he observed two women standing on a porch beneath an overhead light. As he watched, one turned, went back inside, and closed the door. The other began to go down the porch stairs. The Owl pulled over to the curb, turned off the lights of the car, and waited for her as she cut across the lawn to the sidewalk.

She was looking down, walking swiftly, and did not hear him when he got out of the car and moved to the shadow of the tree. He stepped out as she passed him. He could feel The Owl spring from its cage as his hand covered her mouth, and he swiftly slid the rope around her neck.

"I'm sorry for you," he whispered, "but you have been chosen."

60

The body of Yvonne Tepper was discovered at 6:00 A.M. by Bessie Koch, a seventy-year-old widow who supplemented her Social Security check by delivering *The New York Times* to her customers in the Highland Falls area of Orange County.

She had been about to turn her car into Tepper's driveway, one of her sales pitches being her "no bare feet" policy. "People don't have to come down the driveway to get my papers," she explained in her flyers. "The paper is there when you open your door." The campaign was a loving tribute to her now deceased husband who typically went out in his bare feet to retrieve the morning newspaper from wherever their own delivery man had thrown it, usually nearer the curb than the front steps.

At first Bessie's mind did not accept the evidence of her eyes. There had been an overnight frost, and Yvonne Tepper was lying between two bushes, on grass that still glittered with shiny patches of icy moisture. Her legs were bent, and her hands were in the pockets of her navy blue parka. Her appearance was so neat and orderly that Bessie's first impression was that she must have just fallen.

When the reality hit, Bessie stopped the car with an abrupt slam of the brakes. Flinging open the door, she raced the few feet to Tepper's body. For a few moments she stood over it, numb with shock as she took in the woman's opened eyes, her slack mouth, and the cord that was twisted around her neck.

Bessie tried to call for help but was unable to force a sound past her throat and lips. Then she turned and stumbled back to the car and into the driver's seat. She leaned on the horn. In the nearby houses, lights flashed on, and annoyed residents rushed to their windows. Several men ran outside to see the cause of the commotion—ironically, all of them barefooted.

The husband of the neighbor Yvonne Tepper had been visiting when she was waylaid by The Owl jumped into the passenger seat of Bessie's car and firmly pulled her hands off the blaring horn.

That was when Bessie was finally able to scream.

61

Sam Deegan was weary enough to sleep the sleep of the just, even though the instinct that made him a good cop was not satisfied that the latest fax Jean had received was on the level.

The alarm woke him at 6:00 A.M., and he lay in bed briefly with his eyes closed. The fax was the first conscious thought in his mind. Too glib, he thought again. Covers everything. But it's doubtful that a judge would grant a rush order to open Lily's file now, he decided.

Maybe that had been the point of the fax. Maybe someone had panicked, fearing that if a judge allowed the file to be opened and Lily had been questioned about her missing hairbrush, it might have implicated him.

It was that scenario that worried Sam. He opened his eyes, sat up, and threw back the covers. On the other hand, he thought, mentally playing devil's advocate, it does make sense that Laura somehow learned years ago that Jean was pregnant. At dinner Jean had told Alice and him that, before she disappeared, Laura had made a reference to Reed Thornton. "I'm not sure if she used his name," Jean said. "But I was surprised that she even had known I was dating a cadet."

I don't trust that fax, and I still think it's too much of a coincidence that five women died in the order that they were sitting at a lunch table, Sam thought as he plodded into the kitchen, plugged in the coffee maker, and went into the bathroom and turned on the shower.

The coffee was ready when he got back to the kitchen, dressed for the office in a jacket and slacks. He poured orange juice into a glass and dropped an English muffin into the toaster. When Kate was alive, he always had oatmeal for breakfast. Even though he had tried to convince himself that it wasn't difficult—putting a third of a cup of oatmeal in a bowl, adding a cup of low-fat milk and sticking the bowl in the microwave for two minutes—it just never came out right. Kate's was so much better. After a while he'd given up trying to make it for himself.

It had been nearly three years since Kate lost her long battle with cancer. Fortunately, the house wasn't so big that, with the boys raised and out, he felt the need to sell it. You don't get to live in a big house on an investigator's salary, Sam thought. A lot of other women might have complained about that, but not Kate. She loved this house, he thought. She had made it a home, and no matter how rough his day had been, he'd been happy and grateful to return to it at night.

It's still the same house, Sam thought as he picked up the newspaper from outside the kitchen door and settled down at the breakfast table. But it feels a lot different without Kate. Last night, dozing in Alice's den, he'd had the same kind of feeling there that he used to have about this place. Comfortable. Warm. The sound of Alice preparing dinner. The mouthwatering smell of roast beef drifting into the den.

He then remembered that, as he had been dozing off, something had caught his attention. What was it? Did it have something to do with Alice's curio cabinet? Next time he dropped in, he'd take a look. Maybe it was the demitasse cups she collected. His mother had loved them, too. He still had some of hers in the china closet.

Should he put butter on the English muffin, or eat it dry? he wondered.

Reluctantly, Sam decided not to use butter. I sure went off my diet last night, he recalled. That Yorkshire pudding Alice made was terrific. Jean enjoyed it as much as I did. She had been about ready to break under the tension of worrying about Lily. It was good to see her really relax. She's been looking as if she was carrying the weight of the world on her shoulders.

Let's hope that fax was on the level and that we hear from Laura again soon.

The phone rang just as he opened the newspaper. It was Eddie Zarro. "Sam, we just heard from the police chief in Highland Falls. A woman was found strangled on her front lawn there. The D.A. wants all of us in his office ASAP."

There was something Eddie was holding back. "What else?" Sam snapped.

"There was one of those little pewter owls in her pocket. Sam, we've got a full-blown nut case out there. I've got to warn you also that it was on the radio this morning that the Laura Wilcox disappearance is a publicity stunt she dreamed up with that comedian, Robby Brent. Rich Stevens is a very unhappy guy about all the time we've wasted over Wilcox when he has a homicidal maniac in Orange County on his hands. So do yourself a favor and don't bring up her name."

62

When Jean awoke, she was astonished to see that it was nine o'clock. She shivered as she got out of bed. The window was open a few inches from the bottom, and a cold breeze was blowing through the room. She hurried over and closed the window, then opened the blinds. Outside the sun was breaking through the overhead clouds, reflecting, she decided, the way she was feeling. The sun was breaking through the clouds in her life, and she was filled with a sense of euphoria. Laura is the one who has been contacting me about Lily, she reasoned, and if there is anything I can stake my life on, it is that Laura would never harm her. This is all about her need for money.

Still, I hope she gets in touch with me again soon, Jean thought. I should despise her for what she has put me through, but I realize now how desperate she was. There was something frenetic about her behavior on Saturday evening. I remember how she acted when I tried to talk to her before the honoree dinner. I asked her if she had seen anyone carrying a rose at the cemetery. She kept trying to brush me off, and finally she practically threw me out of her room. Was it because she could see how upset I was and felt guilty about what she was doing to me? Jean wondered. I'll bet anything she put the rose on the tombstone. She would have guessed that I'd visit Reed's grave.

Jean's last conscious thought before she fell asleep last night had been that she must let Craig Michaelson know about the fax from Laura. If on his own he had chosen to contact Lily's adoptive parents, it simply wasn't fair to continue to worry them.

She slipped on her robe, went over to the desk, fished in her pocketbook for Michaelson's card, and phoned his office. He took her call immediately, and her heart sank at his reaction to what she told him.

"Dr. Sheridan," Craig Michaelson said, "have you verified that this latest communication is actually from Laura Wilcox?"

"No, and I can't. But do I believe she sent it? Absolutely. I confess that I was shocked to learn Laura knew about Lily and must have known I had been dating Reed. She certainly never let on at the time. Anyway, we also know, because of the cell phone Robby Brent bought and the time element of when I supposedly heard from Laura, that Robby must have made the phone call to me, imitating her voice. So I think we have two situations going here. Laura knows who Lily is, and she is broke and desperate for money. Then Robby concocted Laura's disappearance because he intends to use her on his new sitcom and was just trying to generate publicity. If you knew Robby Brent, you would understand it's the kind of performance—and sneaky trick—that he is utterly capable of carrying out."

Again she waited for reassurance from Craig Michaelson.

"Dr. Sheridan," he said finally, "I can understand your relief. As you very correctly surmised, when you came to my office yesterday, I was not at all convinced that you might not be concocting a story because you were obsessed with your need to locate your daughter. Frankly, your outburst was what convinced me that you were absolutely on the level. So I'm going to level with you now."

He did handle the adoption, Jean thought. He knows who Lily is and *where* she is.

"I considered the potential danger to your daughter serious enough to contact her adoptive father. He happens to be out of the country right now, but I'm sure I will hear from him shortly. I am going to tell him everything you have told me including who you are. As you know, you and I do not have an attorney-client privilege, and I feel I owe it to him and to his wife to make them aware that you are both believable and responsible."

"That is absolutely fine with me," Jean said. "But I don't want those people to go through the hell I've been going through these last few days. I don't want them to get the impression that Lily is in danger now, because I don't think she is anymore."

"I hope she is not, Dr. Sheridan, but I think until Ms. Wilcox comes forward, we should not be too sanguine about the fact that a serious problem may not still exist. Did you show this fax to the investigator you told me about?"

"Sam Deegan? Yes, I did. As a matter of fact, I gave it to him."

"May I have his phone number?"

"Of course." Jean had memorized Sam's number, but the continuing concern in Craig Michaelson's voice upset her enough that she could not be sure she remembered it. She looked it up, gave it to him, then said, "Mr. Michaelson, we seem to have reversed positions. Why are you so worried when I'm so relieved?"

"It's that hairbrush, Dr. Sheridan. If Lily remembers anything about the details of losing it—where she was, who she was with—it is a direct link to the person who sent it. If she recalls having been in the company of Laura Wilcox, then we can believe the contents of the recent fax are on the level. But knowing the adoptive parents and knowing Ms. Wilcox's rather well documented lifestyle, I find it a big stretch to think that your daughter was likely to be around her."

"I see," Jean said slowly, suddenly chilled by the logic of his reasoning. She ended the call with Michaelson, after agreeing to keep in touch. She then immediately dialed Sam's cell phone, but got no answer.

Her next call was to Alice Sommers. "Alice," she said, taking a deep breath. "Please be frank with me. Do you think there's any chance that the fax from Laura, or supposedly from Laura, was a ploy to slow us down, to keep me from contacting Lily's adoptive parents and asking about the hairbrush?"

The answer was the one she feared yet instinctively knew she was going to receive. "I didn't trust it at all, Jeannie," Alice said reluctantly. "Don't ask me why, but it didn't ring true to me, and I could tell Sam felt exactly the same way."

63

As Eddie Zarro had warned, District Attorney Rich Stevens was upset and angry. "These broken-down performers come into this county doing publicity stunts and waste our time when we have a maniac on our hands," he barked. "I'm going to issue a statement to the press to the effect that both Robby Brent and Laura Wilcox may face criminal charges for creating a hoax. Laura Wilcox has admitted that she's been sending those faxes threatening Dr. Sheridan's daughter. I don't care whether Dr. Sheridan is in a forgiving mood or not. I'm not. It's a crime to send threatening letters, and Laura Wilcox is going to answer for it."

Alarmed, Sam hastened to calm Stevens. "Wait, Rich," he said. "The press does not know about Dr. Sheridan's daughter or the threats to her. We can't let that out now."

"I'm aware of that, Sam," Rich Stevens snapped. "We're only going to refer to the publicity stunt that Wilcox confessed to in that last fax." He handed Sam the file on his desk. "Photos of the crime scene," he explained. "Take a look at them. Joy was the first one of our people to get there after the call came in. I know the rest of you have heard this already, but, Joy, fill Sam in on the victim and what the neighbor told you."

There were four other investigators in addition to Sam and Eddie Zarro in the district attorney's office. Joy Lacko, the only woman in the group, had been an investigator for less than a year, but Sam had enormous respect for her intelligence and ability to extract information from shocked or grief-stricken witnesses.

"The victim, Yvonne Tepper, was sixty-three years old, divorced, with two grown sons, both of whom are married and live in California." Joy had her notebook in her hand but did not consult it as she looked directly at Sam. "She owned her own hairdressing salon, was very well liked, and apparently had no enemies. Her former husband has remarried and lives in Illinois." She paused. "Sam, all of this is probably irrelevant, given the pewter owl we found in Tepper's pocket."

"No fingerprints on it, I assume?" Sam queried.

"No fingerprints. We know it has to be the same guy who grabbed Helen Whelan Friday night."

"What neighbor did you talk to?"

"Actually, everyone on the block, but the one who knows anything is the one Tepper had been visiting and had probably just left when she was waylaid. Her name is Rita Hall. Tepper and she were close friends. Tepper had brought some cosmetics from her salon for Mrs. Hall and ran over with them when she got home last night, sometime after ten o'clock. The two women visited for a while and watched the eleven o'clock news together. Hall's husband, Matthew, had already gone to bed. Incidentally, this morning he was the first person to reach Bessie Koch, the woman who found the body and was blowing the horn of her car to get help. He was smart enough to tell the other neighbors to keep away from the body and to call 911."

"Did Yvonne Tepper leave Mrs. Hall's house directly after the news was over?" Sam asked.

"Yes. Mrs. Hall walked her to the door and stepped out onto the porch with her. She remembered that she wanted to tell Tepper something she'd heard about a former neighbor. She said they didn't stand there longer than a minute and that the overhead light was on, so they could have been seen. She said she noticed a car slow down and pull over to the curb, but she didn't think anything of it. Apparently the people across the street have teenagers who are always coming and going."

"Does Mrs. Hall remember anything about the car?" Sam asked.

"Only that it was a medium-sized sedan, either dark blue or black. Mrs. Hall went back into her house and closed the door, and Mrs. Tepper cut across the lawn to the sidewalk."

"My guess is that she was dead less than a minute later," Rich Stevens said. "The motive wasn't robbery. Her handbag was on the sidewalk. She had two hundred bucks in her wallet and was wearing a diamond ring and diamond earrings. The only thing that guy wanted to do was kill her. He grabbed her, pulled her onto her own lawn, strangled her, left her body behind a bush, and drove away."

"He stayed long enough to drop the owl in her pocket," Sam observed.

Rich Stevens looked from one to the other of his investigators. "I've been turning over in my head whether or not to release the information about the owl to the papers. Maybe someone would know something about a guy who's obsessed with owls or possibly keeps them as a hobby."

"You can imagine what a field day the media would have if they knew about the owl being left in the victims' pockets," Sam said quickly. "If this nut is on an ego trip, and I think he is, we'll be feeding him what he wants, to say nothing about the possibility of setting a copycat killer loose."

"And it's not as though we'd be warning women by releasing that bit of information," Joy Lacko pointed out. "He leaves the owl *after* he kills his victim, not before."

At the end of the meeting it was agreed that the best course of action was to warn women against being alone on the street after dark and to acknowledge that evidence pointed to the fact that both Helen Whelan and Yvonne Tepper had been murdered by the same unknown person or persons.

As they got up to go, Joy Lacko said quietly, "What scares me is that right now some perfectly innocent woman is going about her business, not realizing that in the next few days, just because she happens to be in the wrong place at the wrong time when that guy comes cruising by, her life will be over."

"I am not conceding that yet," Rich Stevens said sharply.

I am, Sam thought. I am.

64

On Wednesday morning, Jake Perkins attended his scheduled classes, with the exception of the creative writing seminar, which he felt he was more equipped to teach than the current instructor. Just before the lunch break, in his capacity as a reporter for the *Stonecroft Gazette*, he went into the office of President Downes for his scheduled interview, in which Downes was supposed to give his comments on the glorious success of the reunion.

Alfred Downes, however, was clearly not in good temper. "Jake, I realize I had promised you this time, but actually it's quite inconvenient now."

"I can understand, sir," Jake responded soothingly. "I guess you've seen on the news that the district attorney may press criminal charges against two of our Stonecroft honorees because of this publicity hoax."

"I am aware of that," Downes said, his voice icy.

If Jake noticed the frosty tone, he did not show it. "Do you think that all this adverse publicity reflects badly on Stonecroft Academy?" he asked.

"I would think that's obvious, Jake," Downes snapped. "If you're going to waste my time asking stupid questions, then get out of here now."

"I don't mean to ask stupid questions," Jake said

quickly, his tone apologetic. "What I was leading up to is that at the dinner, Robby Brent gave a check for ten thousand dollars to our school. In light of his actions of the last few days, are you inclined to return that donation to him?"

It was a question that he was sure would make President Downes squirm. He knew how much Downes wanted a new addition to the school to be built during his term as president. It was common knowledge that, while Jack Emerson had dreamed up this reunion, along with the idea of the honorees, Alfred Downes had been delighted by the concept of it. It meant publicity for the school, a chance to show off the successful graduates— the message being, of course, that they learned everything they needed to know at good old Stonecroft—and it would also be a chance to wring donations from them and other alumni at the reunion.

Now the media were speculating about the eerie coincidence of five women from the same lunch table who had died since they graduated from Stonecroft, and Jake knew that wouldn't make anyone want to send their kids there. And now the Laura Wilcox and Robby Brent publicity scheme was another blow to the prestige of the school. His face set in earnest lines, his red hair sticking up even more than usual, Jake said, "Dr. Downes, as you know, my deadline for the *Gazette* is coming up. I just need a quote from you about the reunion."

Alfred Downes looked at his student with near loathing. "I am preparing a statement, and you will have a copy of it by tomorrow morning, Jake."

"Oh, thank you, sir." Jake felt a measure of sympathy for the man sitting across the desk from him. He's worried about his job, he thought. The board of trustees might give him the gate. They know Jack Emerson started the reunion fiasco because he owns the land they'll have to buy for a new addition, and that Downes went along with it. "Sir, I was thinking—"

"Don't think, Jake. Just be on your way."

"In a moment, sir, but please listen to this suggestion. I happen to know that Dr. Sheridan, Dr. Fleischman, and Gordon Amory are still at the Glen-Ridge and that Carter Stewart is staying across town at the Hudson Valley. Perhaps if you invited them to dinner and had some photos taken with them, it would be a way of putting Stonecroft back in a good light. Nobody could question any of *their* achievements, and pointing them out would offset the negative effect of the misconduct of the other two honorees."

Alfred Downes stared at Jake Perkins, thinking that in his thirty-five years of teaching he had never come across a student as nervy or as street-smart as he was. He leaned back in his chair and waited a long minute before responding. "When do you graduate, Jake?"

"I'll have enough credits by the end of this year, sir. As you know, every semester I've loaded up with extra classes. But my folks don't think I'll be ready to go off to college next year, so I'm happy to stay here and graduate with my class."

Jake looked at Dr. Downes and noted that he did not seem to share his happiness. "I have another idea for an article that you might like," he said. "I've done a lot of research on Laura Wilcox. I mean, I've gone over back issues of the *Gazette* and the *Cornwall Times* for the years she was here, and, as the *Times* reported, she was always the belle of the ball. Her family had money; her parents doted on her. I'm going to do a feature article for the *Gazette* to show how, with all the advantages Laura Wilcox enjoyed, she's the one who's having a hard time now."

Jake sensed that he was about to be interrupted, so he rushed on. "I think an article like that will serve two purposes, sir. It will show the kids at Stonecroft that having all the advantages doesn't guarantee success, and it will also show how the other honorees who had to struggle were better off for it. I mean, Stonecroft has both scholarship students and kids who work after school to help pay their tuition. That might motivate them, and besides, it looks good in print. The big-time media is looking for follow-up stories; it's the kind of thing they might pick up."

Gazing at the picture of himself on the wall behind Jake's head, Alfred Downes considered Jake's reasoning. "It's possible," he admitted reluctantly.

"I'm going to take pictures of the houses where Laura lived while she was growing up in Cornwall. The first one is empty now, but it was renovated recently and looks really good. The second house her family moved to on Concord Avenue is what I would call a tract mansion."

"A tract mansion?" Downes asked, bewildered.

"You know, it's one of a bunch of houses on one

block that are too big or too ostentatious for the neighborhood. They're sometimes called McMansions."

"I never heard either expression," Downes said, more to himself than to Jake.

Jake jumped to his feet. "Not important, sir. But I have to tell you, the more I think about it, the more I like the idea of doing a story on Laura with her homes in the background and pictures of her when she was here at Stonecroft and later ones when she became famous. Now I'll get out of your way, Dr. Downes. But maybe I should give you another piece of advice. If you can put that dinner together, I suggest you skip inviting Mr. Emerson. My impression is that none of the honorees can stand him."

65

At ten o'clock Craig Michaelson received the call he had been expecting. "General Buckley is on the line," his secretary announced.

Craig picked up the phone. "Charles, how are you?"

"I'm fine, Craig," a concerned voice answered. "But what about this matter of extreme urgency? What's wrong?"

Craig Michaelson drew in his breath. I should have known there was no way of beating around the bush with Charles, he thought. He didn't get to be a three-star general for no reason. "First of all, it may not be as worrisome as I thought," he said, "but I consider it a matter of genuine concern. As you probably suspected, it's about Meredith. Yesterday, Dr. Jean Sheridan came to see me. Have you ever heard of her?"

"The historian? Yes. Her first book was about West Point. I enjoyed it very much, and I believe I've read all her subsequent books. She's a good writer."

"She's more than that," Craig Michaelson said bluntly. "She's Meredith's natural mother, and I have called you because of something that she has brought to my attention."

"Jean Sheridan is Meredith's mother!"

General Charles Buckley listened intently as Michaelson told him what he knew of Jean Sheridan's history and of the Stonecroft reunion and the perceived threat to Meredith. He interrupted only occasionally, to clarify what he was hearing. Then he said, "Craig, as you know, Meredith is aware that she is adopted. Since she was a teenager, she has expressed interest in finding her natural mother. At the time you and Dr. Connors arranged the adoption, you told us that her father had been killed in an accident prior to his college graduation and her mother was an eighteen-year-old about to go to college on a scholarship. Meredith knows that much."

"Jean Sheridan is aware that I am revealing her identity to you. What I did not tell you twenty years ago is that Meredith's natural father was a cadet who died in a hit-and-run accident on the grounds of West Point. It would have made it too easy for you to determine who he was."

"A cadet! No, you didn't tell me that."

"His name was Carroll Reed Thornton, Jr."

"I know his father," Charles Buckley said quietly. "Carroll never got over his son's death. I can't believe that he is Meredith's grandfather."

"Trust me, he is, Charles. Now, Jean Sheridan is so relieved to believe that Laura Wilcox was the one contacting her about Lily, as she had called Meredith, that she's willing to accept this last fax with Laura's supposed apology as gospel. I don't."

"I can't imagine where Meredith would have met Laura Wilcox," Charles Buckley said slowly.

"Exactly my reaction. And there's something else. If Laura Wilcox is on the level about being behind these threats, I can tell you right now that the district attorney in this county is going to prosecute her."

"Is Jean Sheridan still in Cornwall?"

"Yes, she is. She's going to wait in the Glen-Ridge House until she hears from Laura again."

"I'm going to phone Meredith and ask her if she ever met Laura Wilcox and if she remembers where she left that hairbrush. There are meetings here at the Pentagon that I can't get out of today, but Gano and I will fly up to Cornwall tomorrow morning. Will you contact Jean Sheridan and say that her daughter's adoptive parents would like to meet her for dinner tomorrow evening?"

"Of course."

"I don't want to alarm Meredith, but I can ask her to promise me that she won't go outside the West Point grounds until we see her on Friday."

"Can you count on her keeping that promise?"

For the first time since they had begun speaking, Craig Michaelson heard his good friend General Charles Buckley sound relaxed. "Of course I can. I may be her father, but I'm also way up there in the chain of command. Now we know that Meredith is an army brat in both her natural and adoptive families, but remember, she's also a West Point cadet. When she gives her word to a senior officer, she doesn't break it."

I hope you're right, Craig Michaelson thought. "Let me know what she tells you, Charles."

"Of course."

———

An hour later General Charles Buckley called back. "Craig," he said, his voice troubled, "I'm afraid you're right to be skeptical about that fax. Meredith is absolutely certain that she never met Laura Wilcox, and she doesn't have the vaguest idea where she lost that hairbrush. I would have pressed her more, but she has a big exam in the morning and is terribly worried about it, so it absolutely wasn't the time to upset her. She's delighted that her mother and I"—he hesitated, then continued firmly—"that her mother and I are coming up to see her. Over the weekend, if all works out, we'll tell her about Jean Sheridan and give them a chance to meet each other. I asked Meredith to promise me to stay at the Academy until we saw her, and she laughed at me. She said she has another test on Friday and so much studying to do that she won't see the light of day until Saturday morning. But she did make the promise."

It sounds okay, Craig Michaelson thought as he replaced the receiver, but the cold hard fact is that Laura Wilcox did *not* send that fax, and Jean Sheridan has got to be made aware of that.

For easy access, he had placed Jean's card directly under the phone on his desk. He reached for it, picked up the phone, and started to dial Jean's number. Then he broke the connection. She wasn't the one to call, he decided. She had given him the number of that investigator from the district attorney's office. Where was it? What was his name? he wondered.

After a moment of rummaging around on the top of his desk, he saw the notation he had made: Sam Deegan, followed by a phone number. That's what I want, Michaelson thought, and he began to dial.

66

Last night—or was it this morning? she wondered—he had thrown a blanket over her. "You're cold, Laura," he said. "There's no need for that. I've been thoughtless."

He's being kind, Laura thought dully. He even brought jam with the roll and remembered that she liked skim milk in her coffee. He was so calm, she almost relaxed.

That was what she wanted to remember, not what he had told her as she sat in the chair, sipping the coffee, her legs still bound but her hands free.

"Laura, I wish you could understand the feeling I get when I'm driving along the quiet streets, watching for my prey. There is an art to it, Laura. Never drive too slowly. A patrol car watching for speeders is just as likely to pounce on the car that is not moving at an appropriate pace as one that's going too fast. You see people who know they've had too much to drink make the mistake of inching along the road, a sure sign that they don't trust their own judgment, and a sure sign to the police, too.

"Last night, Laura, I searched for prey. As a tribute to Jean, I decided to go to Highland Falls. That's where she had her little trysts with the cadet. Did you know about that, Laura?"

Laura shook her head in response. He became angry.

"Laura, speak up! Did you know that Jean was having an affair with that cadet?"

"I saw them together once when I went to a concert at West Point but didn't think much of it," Laura had told him. "Jeannie never said a word about him to any of us," she had explained. "We all knew she went up to the Point a lot because even then she was planning to write a book about it."

The Owl had nodded, satisfied with her answer. "I knew Jean often went up on Sundays with her notebook and sat on one of the benches overlooking the river," he had said. "I went looking for her one Sunday and saw him join her. I followed them when they went for a walk. When they thought they were alone, he kissed her. I kept track of them after that, Laura. Oh, they went to great pains not to be viewed as a couple. She didn't even go to the dances with him. That spring, I observed Jean carefully. I wish you could have seen the expression on her face when they were together and away from other people. It was *luminous!* Jean, quiet, kind Jean, whom I felt was my fellow sufferer, given her tumultuous home life, my soul mate—she was living a life from which she had *excluded* me."

I thought he had a crush on me, Laura reasoned, and that he hated me for making fun of him. But he really loved Jeannie. The horror of what he had told her was still seeping into her consciousness.

"Reed Thornton's death wasn't an accident, Laura," he said. "I was driving through the grounds that last Sunday in May, twenty years ago, just on the chance that I might see them. Handsome, golden-haired Reed was walking alone on the road that leads to the picnic grounds. Maybe they were meeting there. Did I mean to kill him? Of course I did. He had everything I didn't have—looks and background and a promising future. And he had Jeannie's love. It wasn't fair. Agree with me, Laura! *It wasn't fair!*"

She stammered a reply, anxious to agree with him and avoid his anger. Then he told her in detail about the woman he had killed the night before. He said he had apologized to her, but when it was Laura's time to die, and Jean's, there wouldn't be any apologies.

He said that Meredith would be the last of his prey. He said that she would complete his need—or at least it was his hope that she would complete his need.

I wonder who Meredith is, Laura thought drowsily. She slipped into a sleep that was filled with visions of owls gliding toward her from branches, rushing at her, hooting eerily, wings fluttering softly, as she tried to run from them on legs that would not, could not, move.

67

Jean, help me! Please, Jean, help me! Laura's pleading voice, which had sounded so vivid in her head as she sat in the car outside Craig Michaelson's office the day before, began playing over and over again in Jean's mind, as though it was an echo of the doubts Alice had expressed about the authenticity of the fax.

For long minutes after she said good-bye to Alice, Jean sat at the desk, Laura's voice haunting her, as she tried to decide rationally whether Sam and Alice were right. Perhaps she had rushed to accept the fax as real because she needed to believe that Lily was safe.

Finally she got up, went into the bathroom, and for long minutes stayed under the shower, letting the water splash over her hair and face. She shampooed her hair, kneading her scalp as though the pressure of her fingers might unscramble the confusion in her mind.

I need to go for a long walk, she thought, as she wrapped her terry cloth robe around her body and turned on the hair dryer. That's the only way I can possibly clear my head. When she was packing for the weekend, she had impulsively thrown her favorite red jogging suit into her suitcase. Now she was grateful to be able to reach for it, but remembering how cold it had felt with the window open, she took the precaution of wearing a sweater underneath the jacket.

She noted the time as she put on her watch. It was ten-fifteen, and she realized she had not had a cup of coffee. No wonder my brain is muddled, she thought ruefully. I'll get a container to go from the coffee shop and drink it while I'm walking. I'm not hungry, and I feel as if the walls of this place are closing in on me.

As she zipped up the jacket, an uneasy thought crossed her mind. Every time I leave this room, I'm taking the chance of missing a call from Laura. I can't stay here day and night. But wait a minute! I think I can leave my own message on the room phone.

She read the instructions on the phone, picked up the receiver, and pushed the message record button. Taking care to speak clearly, and with the volume of her voice slightly raised, she said, "This is Jean Sheridan. If it's important that you reach me, please call me on my cell phone, 202-555-5314. I'll repeat. That is 202-555-5314." She hesitated, then added in a rush, "Laura, I want to help you. Please call me!"

Jean replaced the receiver with one hand and dabbed her eyes with the other. All the earlier euphoria of thinking that Lily was completely safe had evaporated, but something inside her stubbornly refused to believe that the fax had not come from Laura. The room clerk who took the first phone call from Laura had said she sounded nervous, Jean reminded herself. Sam told me that Jake Perkins, who managed to listen in on that call, had agreed. Robby Brent's call to me imitating Laura and saying that everything was fine was another one of his tricks. He probably talked Laura into this publicity scheme, and now she's afraid of the fallout. And I believe that if she didn't threaten me about Lily herself, then she knows who *did*. That's why I've got to make her realize I want to help her.

Jean got up, reached for her shoulder bag, but decided she didn't want to be bothered carrying it. Instead she put a handkerchief, her cell phone, and her room key in her pocket. Then, as an afterthought, she plucked a twenty-dollar bill from her wallet. This way, if I want to stop somewhere and get a croissant when I'm out, I can do it, she thought.

She started to leave the room, then realized she was forgetting something. Of course, her sunglasses. Annoyed at her inability to concentrate, she went back to the dresser, pulled the glasses out of her bag, walked quickly to the door, opened it, and with a decisive snap, pulled it closed behind her.

The elevator was empty when it stopped at her floor—not like the weekend, she thought, when every time I stepped into it, I bumped into someone I hadn't seen in twenty years.

In the lobby, banners welcoming the Top 100 Sales Representatives of the Starbright Electrical Fixtures Company were being tacked over the front desk and dining room doors. From Stonecroft to Starbright, Jean thought. I wonder how many honorees *they* have, or are all one hundred of them honorees?

The clerk with the large glasses and soft voice was behind the front desk, reading a book. I'm sure she's the one who got the call from Laura, Jean thought. I want to talk to her myself. She walked over to the desk and glanced at the name tag on the clerk's uniform. It read "Amy Sachs."

"Amy," Jean said with a friendly smile, "I'm a good friend of Laura Wilcox, and like everyone else, I've been terribly concerned about her. I understand that you and Jake Perkins were the ones who spoke to her on Sunday night."

"Jake grabbed the phone when he heard me say Ms. Wilcox's name." Amy's defensive tone raised the level of her voice to near normal range.

"I understand," Jean said soothingly. "I've met Jake and know how he operates. Amy, I'm glad that he heard Laura's voice. He's smart, and I trust his impression. I know you hardly met Ms. Wilcox, but do you absolutely believe you were speaking to her?"

"Oh, I do, Dr. Sheridan," Amy Sachs said solemnly. "Don't forget, I was very familiar with her voice from watching her on Henderson County. For three years I never missed that program. Like clockwork, Tuesday nights at eight o'clock, my mother and I were in front of the television to see it." She paused, then added, "Unless I was working, of course, which I tried not to do on Tuesday nights. But sometimes they'd have to ask me to come in because someone was sick, and then my mother would tape the program for me."

"Well then, I'm sure you would know Laura's voice.

Amy, will you tell me yourself how Laura sounded to you on that call?"

"Dr. Sheridan, I have to tell you she sounded *funny*. I mean funny *different*. Just between us, my first impression was that maybe she was hungover, because I know she had a drinking problem a couple of years ago. I read about it in *People*. But now I really think Jake was right. Ms. Wilcox didn't sound like she'd had too much to drink; she sounded nervous—very, very nervous."

Amy's voice lowered to its usual near-whisper. "In fact, Sunday night, after I talked to Ms. Wilcox, when I went home I told my mother that she reminded me of the way I used to sound when our elocution teacher in high school was trying to make me talk louder. I was so scared of her that my voice would start to quiver because I'd be trying not to cry. That's the best way I can describe how Ms. Wilcox sounded to me!"

"I see." *Jean, help me! Please, Jean, help me!* I was right, Jean thought. This is *not* about a publicity stunt.

Amy's triumphant smile at being able to describe her reaction to Laura's voice vanished almost before it appeared. "And, Dr. Sheridan, I do want to apologize that your fax yesterday got caught in Mr. Cullen's mail. We pride ourselves on our prompt and careful delivery of faxes that come in for our guests. I have to be sure to explain that to Dr. Fleischman when I see him."

"Dr. Fleischman?" Jean asked, her curiosity aroused. "Is there any reason why you would explain that to him?"

"Well, yes. Yesterday afternoon, when he came in from his walk, he stopped at the desk and phoned your room. I knew you were in the coffee shop and told him that he could find you there. Then he asked if you had received any new faxes, and he seemed surprised when I said you hadn't. I could tell he knew you were expecting one."

"I see. Thank you, Amy." Jean tried not to show how shocked she was at what the desk clerk had told her. Why would Mark ask a question like that? she wondered. Forgetting that she had intended to get a container of coffee, she walked numbly through the lobby and out the front door.

It was even colder outside than she had expected, but the sun was strong and there was no wind, so she decided she would be okay. She slipped on her sunglasses and began to walk away from the hotel grounds, headed no place in particular. Her mind was suddenly filled with a possibility she did not want to accept. Was Mark the person who had been sending the faxes about Lily? Had he sent Lily's hairbrush to her? Mark, who had been so comforting when she had confided her anguish to him, who had covered her hand with his and made her feel that he wanted to share her pain?

Mark knew I was dating Reed, Jean thought. He told me himself that he saw us when he was jogging at West Point. Did he somehow find out about Lily? Unless he's been sending the faxes, why would he be concerned that I hadn't received one by mid-afternoon yesterday? Is he behind all this, and if he is, would he hurt my child?

I don't want to believe that, she thought, agonized by the prospect. I *can't* believe that! But why would he ask the clerk if I'd received a fax? Why didn't he ask me?

Not thinking about where she was going, Jean walked through streets that she had known intimately as a child. She passed Town Hall without seeing it, went as far along Angola Road as the turn-off from the highway, retraced her steps, and finally, an hour later, went into a combination delicatessen–coffee shop at the end of Mountain Road. She sat at the counter and ordered coffee. Dejected and once again deeply worried, she realized that neither the cold air nor the long walk had succeeded in helping to clarify her thinking. I'm worse off than when I started, she thought. I don't know who to trust or what to believe.

According to the large red stitching on his jacket, Duke Mackenzie was the name of the scrawny gray-haired man behind the counter. He obviously was in the mood to chat. "You new around here, Miss?" he asked as he poured the coffee.

"No. I grew up here."

"By any chance, were you with that twenty-year reunion group from Stonecroft?"

There was no way of not answering the man. "Yes, I was."

"Where in town did you live?"

Jean gestured toward the back of the store. "Right up there on Mountain Road."

"No kidding? We weren't here then. Used to be a dry cleaner on this spot."

"I remember." Even though the coffee was almost too hot to drink, Jean began sipping it.

"My wife and I liked the town and bought this place

about ten years ago. Had to do a complete renovation. Sue and I work hard, but we enjoy it. Open at 6:00 A.M. and don't close till 9:00 P.M. Sue's back there in the kitchen right now, making all the salads and doing the baking. We just do short-order stuff at the counter, but you'd be surprised how many people stop in for a quick cup of coffee or a sandwich."

Only half-listening to the torrent of words, Jean nodded.

"Over the weekend some of the Stonecroft alumni dropped in here when they were walking around town," Duke continued. "They couldn't believe how property values have gone up. What number did you say you were on Mountain Road?"

Reluctantly, Jean told him the address of her childhood home. Then, anxious to get away, she gulped most of the rest of the coffee, even though it was burning her mouth. She stood up, put the twenty-dollar bill on the counter, and asked for a check.

"Second cup's free." Duke was clearly anxious not to lose her ear.

"No, that's fine. I'm running late."

While Duke was at the cash register making change, Jean's cell phone rang. It was Craig Michaelson. "I'm glad you left a forwarding number, Dr. Sheridan," he said. "Can you talk without being overheard?"

"Yes." Jean stepped away from the counter.

"I have just spoken to your daughter's adoptive father. He and his wife are coming into this area tomorrow and would like to have dinner with you. Lily, as you called your daughter, knows she is adopted and has always expressed an interest in knowing her natural mother. Her parents want that to happen. I don't want to go into too much detail over the phone, but I will tell you this much: it is virtually impossible that your daughter ever met Laura Wilcox, so I think you have to assume the last fax is a hoax. But because of her present location, you can be assured that she is safe."

For a moment, Jean was so stunned that she could not say a single word.

"Dr. Sheridan?"

"Yes, Mr. Michaelson," she whispered.

"Are you free for dinner tomorrow night?"

"Yes, of course."

"I will pick you up at seven o'clock. I suggested that having dinner at my home would give the three of you privacy. Then, very soon, perhaps as early as this weekend, you will meet Meredith."

"Meredith? Is that her name? Is that my daughter's name?" Jean realized her voice was suddenly high-pitched, but she could not control it. I'm going to see her soon, she thought. I'll be able to look into her eyes. I can put my arms around her. She did not care that tears were streaming down her cheeks or that Duke was staring at her and absorbing every word she said.

"Yes, it is. I didn't mean to tell it to you now, but it doesn't matter." Craig Michaelson's voice was kind. "I understand how you feel. I'll pick you up at the hotel tomorrow evening at seven."

"Tomorrow evening at seven," Jean repeated. She

clicked off the phone and for a moment stood perfectly still. Then, with the back of her hand, she brushed away the tears that were streaming down her cheeks. *Meredith, Meredith, Meredith,* she thought.

"Looks like you got good news," Duke volunteered.

"Yes, I did. Oh, dear God, yes I did." Jean picked up her change, left a dollar on the counter and, in a joyful trance, walked out of the delicatessen.

———

Duke Mackenzie watched intently as Jean Sheridan left his shop. She looked pretty glum when she came in, he thought, but from the way she looked after she got that phone call, you'd think she won the lottery. What the heck did she mean when she asked what her daughter's name is?

He watched from the window as Jean began to walk up Mountain Road. If she hadn't left so fast, he'd have asked her about that fellow with the dark glasses and cap who had been coming in the last couple of mornings, right after they opened at six o'clock. He always ordered the same thing—juice, a buttered roll, and coffee to go. When he got back in his car, he drove up Mountain Road. Last night he came in again, just before closing time, and ordered a sandwich and coffee.

That guy's a funny duck, Duke thought as he wiped the already spotless counter. I asked him if he was part of the Stonecroft reunion, and he gave me a wiseguy answer. He said, "I *am* the reunion."

Duke ran the sponge under hot water and squeezed it. Maybe, tomorrow, if he comes in, I'll tell Sue to wait on him, and I'll sit in the car and follow to see who he's visiting on Mountain Road, he thought. I wonder if it's Margaret Mills. She's been divorced for a couple of years, and everyone knows she's looking for a boyfriend. Won't hurt to check it out.

Duke poured a cup of coffee for himself. Lots going on around here since those reunion people showed up last week, he thought. If that quiet guy stops in tonight for a sandwich and coffee, I'll ask him about the gal who was just here. I mean she's from the reunion and she's really attractive so he must at least know who she is. It's crazy that she had to be told her own daughter's name. Maybe he knows what's up with her.

Duke chuckled as he downed another swig of coffee. Sue was always telling him that curiosity killed the cat. I'm not curious, Duke reassured himself. I just like to know what's going on.

68

At twelve o'clock Sam Deegan tapped on the door of the district attorney's office and walked in without waiting for a response.

Rich Stevens was poring over notes on his desk and looked up, his expression showing irritation at the abrupt interruption.

"Rich, sorry to barge in, but this is important," Sam told him. "We're making a big mistake if we don't take the threat to Jean Sheridan's daughter seriously. I had a message to call Craig Michaelson, the lawyer who handled the adoption. We just connected. Michaelson has been in touch with the adoptive parents. The father is a three-star general at the Pentagon. The girl is a second-year cadet at West Point. The General called her and asked if she had ever met Laura Wilcox. The answer is absolutely not. And she doesn't remember where she lost the hairbrush."

There wasn't a trace of annoyance left in Rich Stevens' expression as he leaned back in his chair and entwined his fingers, always a sign to those who knew him that he was deeply concerned.

"That's all we need," he said, "to have the daughter of a three-star general being threatened by some nut. Are they putting a bodyguard on the girl at the Point?"

"From what Michaelson tells me, she has two big exams, one tomorrow, one Friday. She laughed at the suggestion that she'd leave the grounds. The father didn't want to upset her by telling her about these threats. He and the mother are flying up tomorrow to meet Jean Sheridan. The General wants to come in here and talk to you Friday morning."

"Who is he?"

"Michaelson didn't want to give that information over the phone. The girl knows she's adopted, but until this morning the General and his wife had no idea of the identity of the natural parents. Jean Sheridan swears she never told anybody about the baby until she started getting the faxes. I say whoever found out about the baby and knew who had adopted her, learned it at the time she was born. Michaelson is sure his records were never seen by anyone. Jean Sheridan suspects the leak occurred in the doctor's office where she was a maternity patient, which at least gives us a starting point in trying to figure out who might have had access to the records."

"Then if Laura Wilcox isn't involved in the threats and didn't send that last fax apologizing for them, I've stuck my neck out by calling her disappearance a publicity stunt," Rich Stevens said bitterly.

"We can't be sure about that part of it yet, Rich, but we can be pretty damn sure that she's not the one threatening the girl. Which raises the question, if Laura *didn't* send that fax, was it sent to make us drop the investigation?"

"Which is what I told you to do. All right, Sam. I'll pull you off the homicides. I wish we knew the name of the cadet. I'll ask you again: Is the General *positive* that she's safe?"

"According to Michaelson, she is because of the tests. He says that if she's not in class, she's studying in her room. She assured her father she wouldn't leave the West Point campus."

"Then with all the security at West Point, she should be all right, at least for the present. That's a relief."

"I'm not so sure about that. Being on the grounds of West Point didn't save her natural father's life," Sam said grimly. "He was a cadet. Two weeks before graduation he was the victim of a hit-and-run driver. They never found the person who killed him."

"Any question that it wasn't an accident?" Stevens asked sharply.

"From what Jean Sheridan tells me, it never occurred to anyone that Reed Thornton—that was his name—was deliberately run down. They believed the driver panicked and then was afraid to turn himself in. But in light of all that's been happening, it wouldn't be a bad idea to look at the file on that case."

"Run with it, Sam. God Almighty, can you just see what the media will do if they ever get their hands on this? Three-star general's daughter, a West Point cadet, threatened. Her natural father, a cadet, died in a myste-

rious accident at the Point. Her natural mother is an acclaimed historian and a best-selling author."

"There's more," Sam said. "Reed Thornton's father
is a retired brigadier general. He still doesn't know he
has a granddaughter."

"Sam, I'll ask you one more time: Are you sure, are
you positive that the girl is safe?"

"I have to accept the fact that her adopted father is
satisfied that she's safe."

As Sam got up, he noticed a pile of notes on Rich
Stevens' desk. "More tips about the homicides?"

"Sam, in the couple of hours you've been out, I've
lost count of how many calls have poured in about sus-
picious-looking men. One of them came from a woman
who swore she'd been followed out of the supermarket.
She got the guy's license plate number. The suspect
turned out to be an FBI agent who's visiting his mother.
We've had two calls about strange cars in schoolyards.
Both of them turned out to be fathers waiting for their
kids. We have a nut who confessed to the murders. The
only problem is he's been in jail for the last month."

"Any psychics call yet?"

"Oh, sure. Three of them."

The phone on Stevens' desk rang. He picked it up,
listened, then put his hand over the speaker. "I'm holding for the governor," he said, raising his eyebrows.

As Sam left the room, he heard the district attorney
saying, "Good morning, Governor. Yes, it is a very serious problem, but we're working round the clock to . . ."

To find the perpetrator and bring him to justice, Sam thought. Let's hope that happens before any more pewter owls get planted on dead women.

Including a nineteen-year-old West Point cadet— that chilling possibility darted through his mind as he walked down the corridor to his own office.

69

"Lily . . . Meredith. Lily . . . Meredith," Jean whispered over and over as she walked up Mountain Road, her hands in her pockets, her sunglasses hiding the tears of happiness she could not stop shedding.

She wasn't sure why she had wandered up that street except that when she rushed out of the coffee shop, she knew she wasn't ready to go back to the hotel. She passed houses that had belonged to neighbors years ago. How many of them still live here? she wondered. I just hope I don't run into anyone I know.

She slowed her step as she came near the house she had lived in. When she had driven by on Sunday morning, she hadn't had the chance to really study what the present owners had done with it. She glanced around. There was no one on the street to observe her. For a moment she stopped and put her hand on the split rail fence that now enclosed the property.

They must have added at least two more bedrooms when they renovated, she decided as she studied the house. When we lived here, there were only three bedrooms, one for each of us—Mother, Dad, and me. When we were kids, Laura used to ask me about that:

"Don't your mother and father sleep together? Don't they *like* each other?"

I had read in an advice column in one of those women's magazines that no woman should have to sleep in the same room with her husband if he snored a lot. I told Laura my father snored a lot. She said, "So does mine, but they still sleep together."

I said, "Well, mine do, too, sometimes." But they didn't. Now she looked up at the second floor at the two center windows. Those are the windows of my room, Jean thought. God, how I hated the flowered wallpaper. It was so busy. When I was fifteen, I begged Dad to cover the walls with bookshelves. He really was handy with projects like that. Mother objected, but he did it anyhow. After that, I called my room the library.

I remember the first day I was sure that my period was late and the days that followed when I prayed it would come. I promised God I'd do anything He wanted if I could just not be pregnant.

Well, now I'm glad I was, Jean thought fiercely. Lily . . . Meredith. I may meet her as soon as this weekend. At some point I'll probably slip and call her Lily, then have to explain, although maybe by then she'll understand. I wonder how tall she is. Reed was over six feet, and he told me that his father and grandfather were taller than he was.

Lily is safe—that is absolutely the most important thing in the world. But Craig Michaelson is sure that she never met Laura. So how would Laura know about the faxes?

Jean had intended to turn and start back to the Glen-Ridge but instead impulsively walked past her old house, up to Laura's former home. She stopped and stood in front of it.

As she had observed from the car on Sunday morning, the house and grounds were being maintained regularly. The house looked freshly painted, the flagstone walk was bordered with autumn flowers, and the lawn was swept free of leaves. Even so, with the shades drawn in every window, the house had a closed, unwelcoming look. Why would anyone buy a house, renovate it, keep it up, and not enjoy living in it? Jean wondered. She had heard a rumor that Jack Emerson owned it. He's supposed to be quite the ladies' man. I wonder if he's kept it as a love nest for his girlfriends. If he does own it, now that his wife has moved to Connecticut, it would be interesting to see if he still needs it.

Not that I care, God knows, Jean thought as she turned and started back to the hotel. With a conscious effort she tried to put her anticipation about meeting Lily aside and concentrate on Laura and the new scenario that had been evolving in her mind.

Robby Brent.

Had Robby Brent been behind the faxes about Lily? she asked herself, trying to reason through that scenario. Maybe he's the one who found out I was pregnant. Maybe now he realizes that he could be prosecuted for sending those threats and wants Laura to take the blame because he suspects I would feel sorry for her.

It's possible, Jean decided as she passed the delicatessen and reluctantly waved to Duke, who was tapping on the window and waving at her. Robby Brent is just nasty enough to have somehow found out about Lily, and then, when the reunion came up, have sent those faxes as a cruel joke. I understand that he does a couple of benefits a year. It's possible he met Lily's family that way. Look how rotten he was, the way he ridiculed Dr. Downes and Miss Bender at the dinner. Even the way he presented his check to Stonecroft was an insult.

It was a scenario that made sense to her. If Robby sent those faxes and the hairbrush, he had to be worried about criminal prosecution, she reasoned. If he planned the publicity stunt with Laura, then that has backfired. In that case, he probably will be in touch with his producers to figure out a story. The media are going to hound them for an explanation.

On the other hand, Jack Emerson worked evenings in Dr. Connors' office and might have gotten into his files. Besides that, I need to know why Mark asked the clerk about my receiving a fax and then was disappointed to learn I didn't get one. Well, at least I can find that out fast enough, Jean thought as she turned onto the walkway that led to the Glen-Ridge.

When she stepped into the lobby, the warmth inside enveloped her, and she realized that she had been shivering. I ought to go up and soak in the tub, she reflected. Instead, she went to the front desk where a now busy Amy Sachs was checking in the early arrivals of the Starbright Electrical Fixtures Company event. She picked up the in-house phone, but when the customer Amy was waiting on was searching in his bag for his wallet, Jean managed to catch the clerk's eye and ask, "Any mail?"

"Not a bit," Amy whispered. "You can count on me, Dr. Sheridan. No more mistakes with your faxes."

Jean nodded as she gave the operator Mark's name. He answered on the first ring. "Jean, I was worried about you," he said.

"You've been worrying me, too," she said in an even tone. "It's nearly one o'clock, and I haven't had anything but half a cup of coffee all day. I'm going to the coffee shop. I'd be glad if you'd join me, but don't bother to stop at the desk and check to see if I've had any new faxes. I haven't."

70

True to his word, when he left President Downes' office, Jake Perkins went directly to the classroom that had become headquarters for the newspaper. There he dug through the files of *Gazette* pictures that had been taken during the four years that Laura Wilcox had been a student at Stonecroft. In preparation for the reunion, he had looked through the yearbooks and found pictures of her. But now he wanted to get others, maybe some that were a little more candid than the yearbook shots.

In the next hour he found some photos that were right on target. Laura had been in a number of school plays. One of them was a musical, and he found a great picture of her performing in a chorus line, a standout in a Rockette-like group, with her high kick and dazzling smile. No question, she was a knockout, Jake thought. If she were in school now, there isn't a guy I know who wouldn't be trying to get her attention.

He snickered to himself as he thought of the way in which a boy would have tried to win favor with a girl back then, probably by offering to carry her books. Today he'd offer to drive her home in his Corvette, he thought.

It was when he came across the graduation picture of Laura's class that Jake's eyes widened. He used a magnifying glass to examine the faces of the graduates. Laura, of course, looked beautiful, with her long hair spilling over her shoulders. She even managed to be attractive while wearing that stupid mortarboard. It was Jean Sheridan's picture that shocked him. Her hands were clasped together. There were tears welling in her eyes. She looks sad, Jake thought, really sad. You'd never guess she'd just walked off with the History medal and a full scholarship to Bryn Mawr. From the expression on her face, you'd swear she'd just been told she had two days to live. Maybe she was sorry to leave this place. Go figure.

He moved the magnifying glass from one to the other of the graduates, looking for the honorees. One by one he picked them out. They've all changed a lot, he thought. A couple of them looked like real losers back then. Gordon Amory, for example, was almost unrecognizable. Boy, was he ugly, he thought. Jack Emerson was Fat Boy even then. Carter Stewart needed a haircut—no, make that a total makeover. No-neck Robby Brent was already going bald. Mark Fleischman looks like a beanpole with a head on it. Joel Nieman was standing next to Fleischman. Some Romeo, Jake thought. If I were Juliet, I'd have killed myself at the thought of being stuck with him.

Then he noticed something. Most of the graduates had inane grins on their faces, the kind people save for group pictures. The biggest smile, however, was on the face of one guy who wasn't looking directly at the camera but instead was staring at Jean Sheridan. Talk about contrasts, Jake thought. She looks as if she's lost her last friend, and he's wearing an ear-to-ear grin.

Jake shook his head as he looked at the pile of pictures on the table in front of him. I have enough now, he thought. Next he would talk to Jill Farris, the teacher in charge of the *Gazette*. She's a good sport, Jake thought. I'll convince her to let me use the picture of Laura dancing on the front page of the next issue, and the graduation picture on the back page. Between them, they bring out the theme of the story — the had-it-all girl who's now on the skids and the nerds who made it big-time.

His next stop was the studio where the camera equipment was kept. There he ran into Ms. Farris, who let him sign out the heavy old-fashioned camera that he delighted in using when he was on a photo shoot. In his opinion it had a sharpness that no digital camera could possibly match. The fact that it was a backbreaker did not faze him when he was on an important assignment, especially since this assignment was one he had dreamed up himself.

He did admit to himself that his newly acquired driver's license and the ten-year-old Subaru his parents had bought for him made his jaunts around town considerably easier than when he used to play roving reporter on his bicycle.

Camera over his shoulder, notebook and pen in one pocket, recorder in the other in case he happened to run into someone worth interviewing, Jake was on his way.

Can't wait to do the house where Laura Wilcox grew up. I'll shoot from both the front and the back. After all, it was the house where that medical student, Karen Sommers, was murdered, and the police were sure then that the killer went in the back door. That will add another human interest touch to the story, he decided.

71

Carter Stewart spent the better part of Wednesday morning in his suite at the Hudson Valley Hotel. He had arranged to meet that afternoon with Pierce Ellison, the director of his new play, and would be going to Ellison's home. They were scheduled to discuss fixes the director wanted, but first Stewart wanted to make some script changes on his own.

Thank you, Laura, he thought, smiling maliciously as he made subtle alterations to the character of the scatterbrained blonde who is murdered in the second act. Desperation, he thought—that's what I was missing. On the surface she's twinkling, but we've got to feel how frantic and frightened she really is, that she'll do anything to save herself.

Carter despised interruptions when he was writing, a fact his agent, Tim Davis, knew very well. But at eleven o'clock the jarring ring of the phone shattered his concentration. It was Tim.

He began with a profuse apology: "Carter, I know you're working, and I promised I wouldn't bother you unless it was absolutely necessary, but—"

"It had *better* be absolutely necessary, Tim," Carter snapped.

"The thing is, I just got a call from Angus Schell. He's Robby Brent's agent, and he's going nuts. Robby promised to send in his edits on the scripts for his new TV show by yesterday at the very latest, and they still haven't arrived. Angus has left a dozen messages for Robby but hasn't heard from him. The sponsor is already furious about the publicity stunt the media say Robby is pulling with Laura Wilcox. They're threatening to bail out on the series."

"Which is of no importance to me whatsoever," Carter Stewart said, his tone frigid.

"Carter, you told me the other day that Robby was going to show you the edits he made. Did you see them?"

"No, I did not. As a matter of fact, when I took the trouble to go over to his hotel for the purpose of reviewing those edits, he was not there, nor have I heard from him since. Now, if you'll excuse me, I was working very well until you interrupted me."

"Carter, please. Let me get this straight. You think that Robby *did* make the edits he promised the sponsor?"

"Tim, try to get *this* straight. Yes, I assume Robby made the edits. He told me he had. He asked me to look at them. I told him I would look at them. Then he wasn't there when I went to his hotel. In other words, to repeat in order to make myself perfectly clear, he made the edits and he wasted my time."

"Carter, I'm sorry. Look, I'm really sorry," Tim Davis said, anxious to placate his client. "Joe Dean and Barbara Monroe have already been cast for running parts and it means the world to them to get that series on the air. From what we read in the papers, both Wilcox and Robby left just about everything in their rooms at that hotel. Could you, would you, I beg you, could you see if by any chance he left the scripts there? The last time I spoke to Robby, he bragged that his rewrites were going to make the scripts hilarious. He hardly ever used that word, and when he did, he meant it. If we can get our hands on them by overnight mail, we might be able to salvage the show. The sponsor wants a surefire comedy, and we all know Robby is capable of delivering it."

Carter Stewart said nothing.

"Carter, I don't like to overplay my hand, but twelve years ago when you were still knocking on doors, I took you on and got your first play produced. Don't misunderstand me. It's been great for me ever since, but right now I'm calling in that chip, not for myself but for Joe and Barbara. I gave you your break. Today I want you to give them the chance to have theirs."

"Tim, you are so eloquent, you almost bring tears to my eyes," Carter Stewart said, his tone now reflecting amusement. "Surely there's something in all of this for you besides friendship for your old buddy Angus and paternal feelings for young talent. Someday you must tell me what it is. However, since you have totally ruined my creative concentration, I will go over to Robby's hotel now and see if I can bludgeon my way into his room. You might prepare the way by phoning ahead, claiming you're his agent, and explaining that Robby has instructed you to send me to pick up the scripts."

"Carter, I don't know how—"

"To thank me? I'm sure you don't. Good-bye, Tim."

Carter Stewart was wearing jeans and a sweater. His jacket and cap were on the chair where he had thrown them earlier. With an irritated sigh he got up, put on the jacket, and reached for the cap. Before he could leave the room, the phone rang. It was President Downes, inviting him to cocktails and dinner at his residence at Stonecroft.

The last thing on God's earth I need, Carter thought. "Oh, I'm sorry," he said, "but I do have dinner plans"— with myself, he added silently.

"Then perhaps just for cocktails," President Downes suggested nervously. "I would consider it a great favor, Carter. You see, I will have a photographer here to take pictures of you and the other honorees who are still in town."

The other honorees who are still in town—that's a good way to put it, Carter thought sarcastically. "I'm afraid—" he began.

"Please, Carter. I won't keep you long, but in light of the events of the past few days, I do need to have photos of the four truly distinguished recipients of our plaques of honor. I need them to replace the group pictures we took at the dinner. You can understand how very important that will be as we launch our building drive."

There was no hint of mirth in Carter Stewart's bark-like laugh. "It seems to be my day to atone for the many sins of my life," he said. "What time do you want me to be there?"

"Seven o'clock would be ideal." President Downes' voice was bubbling with gratitude.

"Very well."

———————

An hour later Carter Stewart was in Robby Brent's room at the Glen-Ridge House. Both Justin Lewis, the manager, and Jerome Warren, the assistant manager, were in the room with him, and both were visibly distressed at what they considered to be the potential liability to the hotel for allowing Stewart to take anything from the room.

Stewart went over to the desk. A thick pile of scripts was stacked on top of it. Stewart flipped through some of the pages. "There," he said. "As I explained to you, and as you can see, these are the scripts Mr. Brent edited, the ones that the production company needs immediately. I won't take possession of them for even an instant." He pointed to Justin Lewis. "You pick them up." He pointed to Jerome Warren. "You hold the express envelope to drop them in. Then you can decide between you who addresses it. Now, are you satisfied?"

"Of course, sir," Lewis said nervously. "I hope you understand our position and why we have to be so careful."

Carter Stewart did not answer. He was staring at the notation Robby Brent had propped on the desk phone: "Made appointment to show scripts to Howie Tuesday, 3:00 P.M."

The manager had seen it, too. "Mr. Stewart," he said, "I understood that you were the one who had the appointment to go over these scripts with Mr. Brent."

"That's right."

"Then may I ask who is Howie?"

"Mr. Brent was referring to me. It's a joke."

"Oh, I see."

"Yes, I'm sure you do. Mr. Lewis, have you ever heard the saying that he who laughs last laughs best?"

"Yes, I have," Justin Lewis said, bobbing his head in confirmation.

"Good." Carter Stewart began to chuckle. "It applies in this situation. Now let me give you that address."

72

After Sam left Rich Stevens' office, he went down to the coffee shop in the courthouse and ordered coffee and a ham-and-Swiss on rye to go.

"You mean 'with shoes,' " the new counterman said cheerfully. Noting Sam's bewildered expression, he explained, "You don't say 'to go' anymore. You say 'with shoes.' "

I could have lived the rest of my life without knowing that, Sam thought when he got back to his office and was taking the sandwich out of the bag.

He placed his lunch on his desk and turned on his computer. An hour later, the sandwich eaten, the last sip of coffee forgotten in the container, he was putting together all the information he had gathered on Laura Wilcox.

I have to acknowledge that you can find a lot on the Internet, Sam thought, but you can also waste a lot of time in the process. He was looking for the kind of background that would not be found in Laura's official biography, but so far he hadn't uncovered anything that was helpful.

Because there was a depressingly long list of Laura Wilcox references, he began to open the ones that he thought might prove revealing. Laura's first marriage, when she was twenty-four, had been to Dominic Rubirosa, a Hollywood plastic surgeon. "Laura is so beautiful that in our home my talent will be wasted," Rubirosa was quoted as saying after the ceremony.

Sam grimaced. Isn't that touching, especially since the marriage lasted exactly eleven months. I wonder what happened to Rubirosa? Maybe he's still in touch with Laura. He decided to look him up and found an article showing a picture of him and his second wife at their wedding. "Monica is so beautiful that she will never have need of my professional services" was the quote attributed to Rubirosa that day.

"A little variation but not enough. What a jerk," Sam said aloud as he clicked back to the spread on Laura's first wedding.

There was a picture of her parents at the ceremony—William and Evelyn Wilcox of Palm Beach. On Monday, when Laura hadn't shown up, Eddie Zarro had left a message on her parents' phone, asking them to contact Sam. When there was no response, he'd had a Palm Beach policeman go to the house. A gossipy neighbor told the cop that they were on a cruise, but she wasn't sure which one. She volunteered that they kept to themselves, "were kind of cranky old people," and that she got the impression they were angry at some of the stuff that came out in Laura's messy second divorce.

Cruise ships get the news, Sam thought. With all the media coverage about Laura these past few days, you'd think they'd make some inquiries. It's odd that we still haven't heard from them. I'll see if the Palm Beach cops can't dig deeper and find out what cruise they're on. Of course, it's just possible that Laura tipped them off not to worry about her.

He glanced up as Joy Lacko came into his office. "The boss just pulled me off the homicides," she said. "He wants me to work with you. He said you'd explain." From her expression it was clear to Sam that Joy was not happy about being reassigned.

Her annoyance faded as Sam filled her in on what he had learned about Jean Sheridan and Lily, her daughter. The fact that Lily's adoptive father was a three-star general aroused her interest, as did the realization that it seemed impossible Laura Wilcox had sent the last fax to Jean Sheridan, the one that claimed that she had been behind all the threats. "And I still cannot believe that five women from the same lunch table at Stonecroft Academy died in the order in which they sat at the table," he concluded. "If it isn't one of those incredible strokes of fate, it would mean that Laura is destined to be the next one to die."

"You mean you have two celebrities missing, which may or may not be a publicity stunt; you have a West Point cadet, the adopted daughter of a general, being threatened, and you have five women dead in the order they sat at the table at school. No wonder Rich thinks you need help," Joy said matter-of-factly.

"I *do* need help," Sam admitted. "Finding Laura Wilcox is top priority, both because she's obviously in danger if those five deaths can be proven to be homicides, and because she may have known about Lily and told someone else about her."

"What about Laura's family? How about her close friends? Have you talked to her agent?" Lacko had her notebook out. Pen in hand, she waited for Sam's answers.

"You're asking the right questions," Sam said. "On Monday I put in a call to her agency. It turns out Alison Kendall had handled Laura herself. It's been a month since Kendall died, but no one at the agency has been assigned to take her over."

"That's unusual," Joy said. "I'd think that would be one of the first things they'd do."

"Apparently the reason is that she's in debt to them; they'd been giving her advances. Alison had been willing to carry her, but the new chief executive isn't. They promised to get back to us if they hear from her, but don't hold your breath. I get the distinct feeling that the agency is not really very interested in Laura."

"She hasn't appeared in anything significant since *Henderson County*, and that's been off the air for a couple of years. With all the twenty-year-old pop-tarts in the news, I guess she's considered a senior citizen by Hollywood standards," Joy observed dryly.

"I think you're right," Sam agreed. "We're also trying to locate her parents to see if she's talked to them. I've already spoken to the guy in California who investigated Alison Kendall's death, and he says there's no indication of foul play there. But I'm not satisfied. When I told Rich Stevens about the lunch table girls, he put in an order to get the files on all the deaths from the police who handled the investigations on each of them. The oldest goes back twenty years, so it may take the rest of the week to get everything. Then we'll go through the files with a fine-tooth comb and see if anything jumps out at us."

He waited while Joy jotted some notes in her book. "I want to go to the Website of the local papers where the so-called three accidents occurred and see if there were any questions raised in them at the time about the deaths. The first was in the car that went off the road into the Potomac; the second was the one who disappeared in the avalanche at Snowbird; the third was killed when the plane she was piloting crashed. Alison was the fourth. Finally, I want to see what was written about the supposed suicide of the girl from that lunch table."

He anticipated Joy's next question. "I have their names, the dates, and where they died listed here." He pointed to a typewritten sheet on his desk. "You can copy it. Then I want to find what the Internet will spit out about Robby Brent that might be helpful. I warn you, Joy. Even with two of us working on this, it will take a lot of time to get it done."

He got up and stretched. "When we're finished with all that, I'm going to call the widow of a certain Dr. Connors and tell her that I need to pay her a visit. He was the doctor who delivered Jean Sheridan's baby. Jean met Mrs. Connors the other day and had the distinct feeling that she was holding back some information, something that made her very nervous. Maybe I can get it out of her."

"Sam, I'm good at getting stuff from the Internet, and I'm probably one hundred times faster than you at it. Let me take over doing the research, and you visit the doctor's wife."

"The doctor's widow," Sam said, and then he wondered why he had found it necessary to correct Joy. Maybe it was because Kate had been on his mind all day. I'm not Kate's husband, he thought. I'm her widower. There's a difference of day and night.

If Joy was annoyed at the correction, she did not show it as she picked up the list on the table. "I'll see what I can find. Talk to you later."

Dorothy Connors had been reluctant to meet with Jean, and when Sam phoned, she adamantly insisted that she had no information that would be helpful to him. Realizing that he had to be tough with her, he finally said, "Mrs. Connors, I have to be the judge of whether or not you can assist our investigation. I want no more than fifteen minutes of your time."

Reluctantly, she agreed to let him come to see her that afternoon at three.

His phone rang as he was straightening the top of his desk. It was Tony Gomez, the police chief of Cornwall. They were old friends. "Sam, do you know this kid Jake Perkins?" Tony asked.

Do I? Sam thought as he rolled his eyes in the general direction of heaven. "I know him, Tony. What about it?"

"He's been going around town taking pictures of homes, and I have a complaint from a couple of people who thought he might be setting them up for a robbery."

"Forget it," Sam said. "He's harmless. He has delusions of being an investigative reporter."

"It's more than a delusion. He says he's working on the Laura Wilcox disappearance as your special assistant. Can you verify that?"

"My special assistant? For God's sake!" Sam began to laugh. "Throw him in jail," he suggested. "And when you do, try to lose the key. I'll talk to you, Tony."

73

"Jean, I had a very good reason for inquiring at the desk about whether or not you had received a fax," Mark said quietly as he joined her in the coffee shop.

"Then explain it to me, please," she said, her tone equally subdued.

The waiter had placed her at the same table where they had sat for several hours the day before. But today the warmth and sense of developing intimacy that had characterized their earlier meeting was missing. Mark's expression was troubled, and Jean knew that she was conveying to him the doubt and mistrust of him that had been building in her mind.

Lily—Meredith—is safe, and I am going to meet her soon, she thought. That was the essential, the alpha and omega of what mattered right now. But receiving the hairbrush in the mail last month, then the threatening faxes, and finding the rose on Reed's grave—each and every incident had torn her apart with worry.

I should have had that last fax by mid-afternoon yesterday, Jean remembered as she looked across the table at Mark. She felt as if they were taking each other's measure, seeing each other today in a different light. I thought I could trust you, Mark, she thought. Yesterday you were so sympathetic, so understanding when I told you about Lily. Were you only mocking me?

Like her, he was wearing a jogging suit. His was dark green and seemed to make his eyes seem more hazel than brown. The expression in them was troubled. "Jean, I'm a psychiatrist," he said. "My job is to try to understand the workings of the mind. God knows you've been going through enough hell without my adding to it. Frankly, I was hoping you would continue to hear from whoever is sending those messages to you."

"Why?"

"Because it would be a sign that he or she wants to stay in touch. Now you've heard from Laura, and you're satisfied that she wouldn't hurt Lily. But the point is that she communicated with you. That's what I was looking for yesterday. Yes, I was troubled when the desk clerk said that nothing had come in. I was worried about Lily's safety."

He looked at her, and his expression of concern changed to astonishment. "Jean, were you thinking that I'd been sending those faxes to you, that I *knew* the one you got late yesterday should have arrived earlier? Were you *really* entertaining that thought?"

Her silence was his answer.

Do I believe him? Jean wondered. I don't know.

The waiter was standing at the table. "Just coffee," Jean said.

"I seem to recall that on the phone you told me you haven't eaten all day," Mark said. "Back at Stonecroft you liked grilled cheese and tomato. You still like that?"

Jean nodded.

"Two grilled cheese and tomato sandwiches and two cups of coffee," Mark ordered for both of them. He waited until the waiter was out of earshot before he spoke again. "You still haven't said anything, Jeannie. I don't know whether that means you believe me or you don't believe me or you're not sure. I admit I find that pretty damn disappointing but certainly understandable. Just answer me this: Are you still satisfied that Laura has been sending those faxes and that Lily is safe?"

I am not going to tell him about the call from Craig Michaelson, Jean thought. I can't afford to trust anyone. "I am satisfied that Lily is safe," she said cautiously.

Mark obviously realized that she was being evasive. "Poor Jean," he said. "You don't know who to trust, do you? I can't say I blame you. But what are you going to do now? Just wait here indefinitely until Laura surfaces?"

"At least for the next few days," Jean said, intent on being as vague as possible. "What about you?"

"I'll stay till Friday morning, then I must get back. I have patients I need to see. Fortunately I had shows already taped, but now I can't delay work on the new ones. Anyhow, as of Friday my room has been reserved by someone attending the lightbulb convention, or whatever it is."

"One hundred top sales reps are being honored," Jean told him.

"More honorees," Mark said. "I hope all one hundred make it home safely. I assume you're going to respond to President Downes' plea to be at his place for cocktails and a photo shoot tonight."

"I don't know a thing about it," Jean protested.

"He's probably left a message on your phone. It shouldn't take too long. From what Downes said, he wanted to make it a dinner, but Carter and Gordon already have dinner plans. Actually, I do, too. My father wants me to have dinner with him again."

"Then I guess your father answered the questions you said you were going to ask him," Jean suggested.

"Yes, he did. Jeannie, you know half the story. You deserve to hear the rest of it. My brother, Dennis, died a month after he graduated from Stonecroft. He was supposed to start Yale in the fall."

"I know about the accident," Jean said.

"You know *something* about the accident," Mark corrected. "I had just finished the eighth grade at St. Thomas and was starting at Stonecroft in September. My parents gave Dennis a convertible for his graduation. You probably didn't know him, but he excelled in everything. He was number one in his class, the captain of the baseball team, the president of the student council, great-looking and funny, and a genuinely nice guy. After four miscarriages my mother had managed to produce the golden child."

"Which was hard for you to compete with, I would think," Jean observed.

"I know people believe that, but actually, Dennis

was great to me. He was my big brother. Talk about hero worship."

It seemed to Jean that Mark was talking more to himself than to her. "He played tennis with me. He taught me how to play golf. He took me for rides in that convertible, and then, because I bugged him so much, he taught me how to drive it."

"But you couldn't have been more than thirteen or fourteen," Jean said.

"I was thirteen. Oh, I never drove on the street, of course, and he was always in the car with me. Our house has quite a bit of property. The afternoon of the accident, I had been pestering Dennis all day for a ride. Finally, around four o'clock, he tossed me the keys and said, 'Okay, okay, get in the car. I'll be right there.'

"I was sitting, waiting for him, counting the minutes till he got in so I could be the hotshot driving the convertible. Then a couple of his friends showed up, and Dennis told me he was going to shoot some baskets with them. 'I promise you'll have your chance in an hour or so,' he said. Then he called out, 'Turn off the engine and be sure to put on the parking brake.'

"I was disappointed, and I was mad. I slammed into the house. My mother was in the kitchen. I told her that I'd be glad if Dennis' car slid down the hill and crashed into the fence. Forty minutes later it did slide down the hill. The basketball net was at the base of the driveway. The other guys got out of the way. Dennis didn't."

"Mark, you're the psychiatrist. You *have* to know that it wasn't your fault."

The waiter was back with the sandwiches and coffee. Mark took a bite of his sandwich and sipped the coffee. It was obvious to Jean that he was struggling to keep his emotions in check. "Intellectually, yes, but neither of my parents was ever the same toward me after that. Dennis was the Christ child in my mother's eyes. I can understand that. He had everything. He was so gifted. I heard her tell my father that she was sure I had deliberately left the brake off, not to deliberately hurt Dennis but hoping to pay him back for disappointing me."

"What did your father say?"

"It's what he *didn't* say. I expected him to defend me, but he didn't. Then some kid told me that my mother had said that if God wanted one of her boys, why did it have to be Dennis?"

"I heard that story," Jean admitted.

"You grew up wanting to get away from your parents, Jean, and so did I. I always felt we were kindred spirits. We both threw ourselves into academics and kept our mouths shut. Do you see your parents much?"

"My father lives in Hawaii. I visited him there last year. He has a lady friend who's quite nice, but he proclaims from the rooftops that one marriage cured him of ever walking down the aisle again. I spent a few days around Christmas with my mother, who seems genuinely happy now. She and her husband have visited me a few times. I admit that it does make me gag a bit to see the two of them holding hands and nuzzling each other, when I think of how she behaved with my father. I guess

I'm over resenting them, except for the fact that at age eighteen I didn't think I could turn to them for help."

"My mother died when I was in medical school," Mark said. "I wasn't told that she'd had a heart attack and was dying. I would have jumped on a plane and come back to say good-bye to her. But she didn't ask for me. In fact, she said she didn't want to see me. It felt like the final rejection. I didn't attend the funeral. After that I never came home again, and my father and I have been on the outs for fourteen years." He shrugged. "Maybe that's why I decided to be a psychiatrist. 'Physician, heal thyself.' I'm still trying."

"What were the questions you asked your father? You told me he answered them."

"The first one was why he didn't send for me when my mother was dying."

Jean wrapped both hands around the coffee cup and picked it up. "What was his answer?"

"He told me that my mother had become delusional. Shortly before she had the heart attack, she had gone to a psychic who told her that her younger son had deliberately released the brake because he was jealous of his brother and wanted to hurt him. Mother had always believed in the possibility that I had wanted to damage Dennis' car, but the psychic put her over the edge. That may even have brought on the heart attack. Want to hear the other question that I asked my father?"

Jean nodded.

"My mother couldn't stand any kind of drinking, and my father liked to have a drink in the late afternoon.

He'd sneak into the garage where he kept some booze hidden on the shelf behind the paint cans, or he'd pretend to be cleaning the inside of his car and have a little cocktail party of his own. Sometimes he'd sit in Dennis' car and have his nip. I know I left that brake on. I know Dennis didn't go near the car. He was playing basketball with his friends. Certainly my mother wouldn't get into the convertible. I asked my father if he had sat in Dennis' car that afternoon, having his couple of scotches, and if so, didn't he think it was possible he might have released that brake accidentally?"

"What did he say?"

"He admitted that he was in the car and got out of it only a minute or so before it rolled down the hill. He never had the courage to tell my mother, not even when that psychic poisoned her mind about me."

"Why do you think he admitted it now?"

"I was walking around town the other night, thinking of how people go through life with unresolved conflicts. My appointment book is filled with patients who are living examples of that. When I saw my father's car in the driveway—that same driveway, incidentally—I decided to go in and, after fourteen years of silence, have it out with him."

"You saw him last night, and you're seeing him again tonight. Does that mean a reconciliation?"

"He's going to be eighty years old soon, Jean, and he's not well. He's been living a lie for twenty-five years. He's almost pathetic, talking about how he wants to make it up to me. Of course he can't, but maybe seeing him will help me understand and put it behind me. He's right about the fact that if my mother knew he had been drinking in the car and had caused the accident, she would have gotten rid of him that same day."

"Instead, on an emotional level she withdrew from you."

"Which, in turn, contributed to the total sense of inadequacy and failure that I remember feeling at Stonecroft. I tried to be like Dennis, but I certainly wasn't as good-looking. I wasn't an athlete, and I wasn't a leader. The only time I felt any sense of camaraderie was when some of us worked a job together in the evenings our senior year. We'd go out afterward and have a pizza. Perhaps the good part is that I learned compassion for kids who have it tough, and as an adult I have tried to make their paths a little smoother."

"According to what I hear, you're doing a good job of it."

"I hope so. The producers want to move the show to New York, and I've been asked to join the staff of New York Hospital. I think I'm ready to make the change."

"A new beginning?" Jean asked.

"Exactly—where what can't be forgiven or forgotten may at least be relegated to the past." He raised his coffee cup. "Shall we drink to that, Jeannie?"

"Yes, of course." As badly as I was hurt, it was worse for you, Mark, she thought. My parents were too busy hating each other to understand what they were doing to me. Your parents let you know they preferred your brother, and then your father deliberately let your mother believe the one thing that she could never for-give you for. What did *that* do to your soul?

Her instinct was to reach across the table and lay her hand on his, the same gesture with which he had com-forted her yesterday. But something held her back. She simply could not trust him. Then she realized she wanted to pick up on something he had just said. "Mark, what was the evening job you worked at during senior year?"

"I was with the office clean-up crew in a building that has burned down since then. Jack Emerson's father got a bunch of us jobs there. I guess you weren't around when we were joking about it the other night. Every one of the guys who is an honoree pushed a broom or emp-tied wastebaskets over there."

"*All* of you?" Jean asked. "Carter and Gordon and Robby and you?"

"That's right. Oh, and one more. Joel Nieman, a.k.a. Romeo. We all worked with Jack. Don't forget, we were the ones who didn't have to practice for games or travel with teams. We were perfect for that job." He paused. "Wait a minute. You should know that building, Jean. You were Dr. Connors' patient."

Jean felt her body turn icy. "I didn't tell you that, Mark."

"You must have. How else would I have known it?"

How else, indeed? Jean wondered as she pushed her chair back. "Mark, I have a few phone calls to return. Do you mind if I don't wait while you get the check?"

74

Ms. Farris was in the studio when Jake returned to school. "How'd you make out, Jake?" she asked as she watched him struggle to close the door while he carefully juggled the heavy camera, moving it off his shoulder and onto the desk.

"It was an adventure, Jill," Jake admitted. "I mean Ms. Farris," he quickly amended. "I decided to do a chronological womb-to-the-present account of Laura Wilcox. I got a great long shot of St. Thomas of Canterbury Church, and as luck would have it, there was a baby carriage outside. I mean a *real* baby carriage, not one of those strollers or rollers or whatever they stick kids in these days."

He was taking his recorder out of his pocket as he took off his coat. "Freezing out there," he complained, "but at least the police station was warm."

"The police station, Jake?" Jill Farris asked cautiously.

"Uh-huh. But let me explain in chronological order. After the church, I got some background pictures, to give people who don't live here a sense of the community. I realize I'm doing this story for the *Gazette*, but I fully expect it to be picked up by larger publications and to find a wider audience."

"I see. Jake, I don't want to rush you, but I was just leaving."

"This will only take a minute. Then I photographed Laura's second house, the McMansion. It's quite impressive if you like that sort of tacky grandeur. It has a big front yard, and whoever lives there now has stuck a few Grecian statues on the lawn. In my opinion they look pretentious, but it will make readers understand that Laura did *not* have a 'surprise lunch' childhood."

" 'Surprise lunch' childhood?" Jill Farris asked, bewildered.

"Let me explain. My grandfather told me about a comedian named Sam Levenson who said his family was so poor that his mother bought cans off a pushcart for two cents each. They were that cheap because the labels had fallen off, and nobody knew what was inside them. She'd tell her kids that they were having a 'surprise lunch.' They never knew what they were going to eat. Anyhow, the pictures of Laura's second house reflect a solid middle-class, even slightly upper-middle-class upbringing."

Jake's expression darkened. "After I took some long shots of the houses surrounding Laura's former home, I drove across town to Mountain Road where she had lived for the first sixteen years of her life. It's a very pleasant street, and, frankly, the house is more to my taste than the one with the Grecian statues. Anyhow, I'd barely begun to shoot when a squad car pulled up and a most aggressive policeman wanted to know what I thought I was doing. When I explained that I was exercising my right as a private citizen to take photographs in the street, he invited me to get in his squad car, and he drove me to the station house."

"He *arrested* you, Jake?" Jill Farris exclaimed.

"No, ma'am. Not exactly. The captain questioned me, and since I felt I had been of valuable service to Investigator Deegan when I alerted him that Laura Wilcox sounded extremely nervous when she called to ask the hotel to hold her room, I felt I had the right to explain to the captain that I was a special assistant to Mr. Deegan in the investigation of Laura's disappearance."

I'm going to miss this kid when he graduates, Jill Farris thought. She decided that it wouldn't hurt to be a few minutes late for her appointment at the dentist. "Did the captain believe you, Jake?" she asked.

"He called Mr. Deegan, who not only did not back me up but suggested that the captain should toss me in jail and then lose the key." Jake looked hard at his teacher. "It's not funny, Ms. Farris. I feel Mr. Deegan broke a trust. The captain, as it turns out, was much more sympathetic. He was even kind enough to say that I could finish my photos tomorrow, since I got to take only a few pictures of the house on Mountain Road. He *did* warn me that I'd better not trespass on anyone's property. I'm going to develop today's film now, and with your permission, I'll sign the camera out again tomorrow and finish my shoot."

"That'll be fine, Jake, but remember, those older cameras aren't being made anymore. Don't let anything happen to it, or I'll be the one in trouble, not you. Now, I've got to run."

"I'll guard it with my life," Jake called after her. I mean it, he thought as he rewound the roll of film and removed it from the camera. But even though the captain warned me not to set foot on anyone's property, for the sake of getting proper coverage for my story, I have to commit an act of civil disobedience, he told himself. I intend to get pictures of the back of Laura's house on Mountain Road. Since no one is living there, I'm sure I won't be noticed.

He went into the darkroom and began developing the pictures, one of his favorite tasks. He found it thrilling and creative to watch people and objects begin to emerge from the negatives. One by one he clipped the prints on a clothesline to dry, then got out his magnifying glass and studied them carefully. They were all good—and he didn't mind saying so himself—but the single shot he'd been able to take of Laura's house on Mountain Road before the cop showed up was the most interesting of the lot.

There's something about that house, Jake thought. It makes me want to put my head under the covers and hide. What *is* it? Everything is in shipshape condition. Maybe that's it. It's too neat. Then he peered closer. It's the shades, he thought triumphantly. The ones in the bedroom at the end of the house aren't the same as the others. In the picture they come through a lot darker. I didn't notice that when I was shooting, but the sun was pretty bright then. He whistled. Wait a minute. When I looked up the Karen Sommers story on the Internet, I think I remember that she was murdered in the corner bedroom, on the right-hand side of the house. I remember a picture of the crime scene with those windows circled.

Why not show a separate picture of just those two windows in my story? he asked himself. I could point out that there is a dark aura surrounding the fatal room where one young woman was murdered and where Laura slept for sixteen years. It would give it a nice, eerie little touch.

To his disappointment the enlargement of the photograph revealed that the difference in color was probably caused by interior dark shades that had been drawn behind the decorative ones visible from the street.

Or *should* I be disappointed? Jake asked himself. Suppose someone is staying there who doesn't want a light to show? It would be a great place to hide. The house has been renovated. There's furniture on the porch, so I assume it's furnished. No one lives there. Who bought it anyhow? Wouldn't it be a scream if Laura Wilcox owns her old house and is holed up there now with Robby Brent?

It's not the dumbest hunch I've ever had, he decided. Should I bounce it off Mr. Deegan? he asked himself.

The heck I will, he decided. It's probably a crazy idea, but if there's anything to it, it's my story. Deegan told the captain to toss me in jail. Now he can just go fly a kite. He gets no more help from me.

75

Sam's visit to Dorothy Connors' home lasted exactly the fifteen minutes he had promised her. When he saw how infirm she was, he proceeded gently, and he quickly surmised that the concern she had shown was for her late husband's reputation. Knowing that made it easier for him to get to the point.

"Mrs. Connors, Dr. Sheridan spoke to Peggy Kimball, who at one time worked for your husband. To assist Dr. Sheridan in finding her daughter, Ms. Kimball stated that Dr. Connors on occasion may have circumvented the rules governing adoptions. If that is your concern, I can tell you right now that Dr. Sheridan's daughter has been located and the adoption was absolutely legal. In fact, Dr. Sheridan is going to have dinner with the adoptive parents this evening and will meet her daughter very soon. That part of the investigation is over."

The naked relief reflected in the woman's expression was confirmation that he had dispelled her concerns. "My husband was such a wonderful man," she said. "It would have been awful if ten years after his death, people began to think he had done something wrong or illegal."

He did, Sam thought, but that's not why I'm here. "Mrs. Connors, I promise you that nothing you tell me will ever be used in a way that could sully your husband's reputation. But please answer this question: Do you have any knowledge whatsoever of how someone might have had access to Jean Sheridan's maternity file in your husband's office?"

There was no trace of nervousness left in Dorothy Connors' voice or manner when she looked Sam straight in the eye. "You have my word of honor that I have no knowledge of any such person, but if I did, I would share it with you."

They had been sitting in the sunroom that Sam suspected was where Mrs. Connors spent most of her time. She insisted on walking him to the door, but as she opened it, she hesitated. "My husband handled dozens of adoptions during the forty years he practiced medicine," she said. "He always took a picture of the baby after it was born. He put the date of birth on the back of each picture, and if the mother had named the baby before she signed it away, he wrote that down, too."

She closed the door. "Come with me into the library," she said. Sam followed her through the living room, continuing through French doors that led to an alcove filled with bookshelves. "The photo albums are in here," she said. "After Dr. Sheridan left, I found the picture of her baby with the name Lily inscribed on the back. I confess, I was terribly afraid that hers might have been one of the adoptions that couldn't be traced. But now that Dr. Sheridan has located her daughter and is going to meet her, I'm sure she would like to have a picture of Lily when she was three hours old."

Stacks of photo albums took up one entire section of the shelves. The section had been labeled with dates going back forty years. The album Mrs. Connors pulled out had a page marker in it. She opened it, slid a picture from its plastic covering, and handed it to Sam. "Please tell Dr. Sheridan how happy I am for her," she said.

When Sam got back to the car, he carefully tucked away in his inside breast pocket the picture of a wide-eyed infant with long lashes and wisps of hair framing her face. What a beauty, he thought. I can only imagine how rough it must have been for Jean to give her up. I'm not that far from the Glen-Ridge. If she's there, I'll drop it off for her. Michaelson was going to call Jean after he spoke to me, so she's probably all squared away about meeting the adoptive parents.

When Sam called up, Jean was in her room and readily agreed to meet him in the lobby. "Give me ten minutes," she said. "I just got out of the tub." Then she added, "Nothing is wrong, is it, Sam?"

"Nothing wrong at all, Jean." Not at the moment, at least, he thought, even though a pervasive sense of unease would not leave him.

He had expected Jean to be radiantly happy at the prospect of meeting Lily, but he could see that something was troubling her. "Why don't we go over there?" he asked, nodding his head toward a far corner of the lobby where a sofa and chair were unoccupied.

It did not take long for Jean to tell him her concern.

"Sam, I am beginning to believe that Mark is the one sending the faxes," she said.

He saw the pain in her eyes. "Why do you think that?" he asked quietly.

"Because he let slip that he knew I was a patient of Dr. Connors. *I* never told him that. There's more. He was inquiring at the desk yesterday to see if I had received a fax and apparently was disappointed that it hadn't come in. That was the one mistakenly included with someone else's mail. Mark told me he worked at Dr. Connors' office in the evening during the time I was seeing the doctor. Finally, he admitted he saw me at West Point with Reed. He even knew Reed's name."

"Jean, I promise you, we'll take a very close look at Mark Fleischman. I'll be honest. I haven't been happy that you've been confiding in him. I hope you didn't pass on to him anything that Michaelson told you this morning."

"No, I didn't."

"I don't want to alarm you, but I think you need to be careful. I bet we're going to find that the person sending the faxes is someone from your graduating class. Whoever it turns out to be—Mark or one of the others who attended the reunion—I don't believe anymore that it's about money. I think we're dealing with a psychotic and a potentially dangerous personality."

He studied her for a long minute. "You were beginning to like Fleischman, weren't you?"

"Yes, I was," Jean admitted. "That's why it's hard for

me to believe that he may be a totally different person from how he appears on the surface."

"You don't know that yet. Now I have something that may perk you up." He took Lily's picture out of his pocket, explaining what it was before he handed it to her. Then from the corner of his eye, he saw Gordon Amory and Jack Emerson coming through the front entrance of the hotel. "You may want to take it upstairs before you look at it, Jean," he suggested. "Amory and Emerson just showed up, and if they see you, they'll probably come over."

Jean quickly whispered, "Thanks, Sam," took the picture from him, and hurried to the elevator.

Sam saw that Gordon Amory had spotted her and was going to try to catch her. He hurried to intercept him. "Mr. Amory," he said, "have you decided how long you'll be staying here?"

"I'll be leaving by the weekend, at the latest. Why do you ask?"

"Because if we don't hear from Ms. Wilcox soon, we are going to treat her as a missing person. In that case we'll need to speak at greater length to the people who were around her just before she disappeared."

Gordon Amory shrugged. "You'll hear from her," he said dismissively. "However, for the record, if you wish to contact me, I expect to be in the general area even after I check out here. Through Jack Emerson, as our agent, we are making an offer on a large tract of land where I plan to build my corporate headquarters. So when I leave the hotel I plan to stay in my Manhattan apartment for several weeks."

Jack Emerson had been speaking to someone near the desk. Now he joined them. "Any news of the toad?" he asked Sam.

"The toad?" Sam raised his eyebrows. He was perfectly aware that Emerson meant Robby Brent, but he wasn't about to let on.

"Our resident comedian, Robby Brent. Isn't he smart enough to know that all guests, missing or otherwise, like fish, smell after three days? I mean, enough already with the publicity stunt."

Emerson's had a couple of shots of whiskey for lunch, Sam thought, noting the man's flushed complexion.

Ignoring the reference to Brent, he said, "Since you live in Cornwall, I assume you'll be available if I need to talk with you about Laura Wilcox, Mr. Emerson. As I just explained to Mr. Amory, we will be listing her as a missing person if we don't hear from her soon."

"Not so fast, Mr. Deegan," Emerson said. "The minute Gordie—I mean, Gordon—and I have finished putting this deal together, I'm out of here. I have a place in St. Bart's that it's time for me to visit. Putting this reunion together was a lot of work. Tonight we take some more pictures at President Downes' house, have a drink with him, and then this reunion is *really* over. Who gives a damn whether or not Laura Wilcox and Robby Brent ever show up? The Stonecroft Academy building committee doesn't need their kind of publicity."

Gordon Amory had been listening with an amused

smile on his face. "I must tell you, Mr. Deegan, that I think Jack has put it very well. I tried to catch Jean, but she was in the elevator and I missed her. Do you know her plans?"

"I don't," he said. "Now if you'll excuse me, I have to get back to my office." I wouldn't tell any of those guys what Jean is doing, he thought as he crossed the hotel lobby, and I hope she heeds my warning not to trust any of them.

His cell phone rang as he was getting into his car. It was Joy Lacko. "Sam, I've got a hit," she told him. "On a hunch I checked out the report on Gloria Martin, the suicide, before I started researching the accidental deaths. At the time of her death there was a big article about Martin in her local newspaper in Bethlehem."

Sam waited.

"Gloria Martin killed herself by putting a plastic bag over her head. And, Sam, get this: When they found her, she had a small pewter owl clutched in her hand."

76

To Duke Mackenzie's delight, at five minutes of nine that evening the taciturn participant in the Stonecroft reunion stopped in again. He ordered a grilled cheese and bacon sandwich, and coffee with skim milk. While the sandwich was grilling, Duke hastened to start a conversation. "A lady from your reunion was in this morning," he said. "Said she used to live on Mountain Road."

He could not see past the man's dark glasses, but something in the way his body stiffened made Duke sure he had gotten his attention.

"Do you know her name?" the visitor asked casually.

"Nope, sir, I don't. I can describe her to you though. Really pretty, with brown hair and blue eyes. Her daughter's name is Meredith."

"She told you that!"

"No, sir. Don't ask how it happened, but someone she was talking to on the phone told her that. I could tell she was all shook up about it. I can't figure out why she wouldn't know her own daughter's name."

"I wonder if she was talking to someone else from our reunion," the visitor mused. "By any chance did she mention the name of the person she was talking to?"

"No. She did say that she'd see them—I mean him or her—tomorrow night at seven o'clock."

Duke turned his back to the counter, picked up a spatula, and removed the sandwich from the grill. He did not see the cold smile on his customer's face, nor did he hear him whisper to himself, "No, she won't, Duke. No, she won't."

"Here you go, sir," Duke said cheerfully. "I see you're taking your coffee with skim milk. They say that's healthier, but for me, I like good old-fashioned cream in my coffee. Figure I don't have to worry. My father was still bowling a great game at eighty-seven."

The Owl tossed money on the counter and left with a mumbled good night. He felt Duke's eyes following him as he walked to the car. I wouldn't put it past him to follow me, he thought. He's just nosy enough. He doesn't miss anything. I can't stop there anymore, but it really doesn't matter. By this time tomorrow it will be finished.

He drove slowly up Mountain Road but decided not to turn into the driveway at Laura's house. Funny, I still call it that, he thought. Instead, he drove well past it and watched in the rearview mirror until he was sure he was not being followed. Then he made a U-turn and started making his way back, always watching for the headlights of other cars. When he was at his destination, he switched off his headlights, made a sharp turn into the driveway, and drove to the comparative safety of the enclosed backyard.

Only then did he allow himself to concentrate on

what he had just heard. *Jean knew Meredith's name!* It had to be the Buckleys that Jean was going to be meeting tomorrow night. Meredith couldn't have remembered where she lost the hairbrush, or by now that detective, Sam Deegan, would have been knocking at his door. It meant he had to move more swiftly than he had anticipated. He would have to enter and leave this house several times tomorrow in broad daylight. But he simply could not leave this car parked outside. That was out of the question. Even though the backyard was enclosed, a neighbor might spot it from a second-story window and phone the police. Laura's house was supposed to be uninhabited.

Robby's car, with his body in the trunk, took up half of the garage. The first rental car that might have left telltale tire tracks at the place where he had taken Helen Whelan's body was in the other parking space. He had to get rid of one of those cars so he could have access to the garage. The rental car would be traced back to him, he reasoned. I have to keep that until it's safe to return it.

I've come so far, The Owl thought. The journey has been so long. I can't stop now. It must be completed. He looked at the sandwich and coffee he had bought for Laura. I didn't have any dinner, he thought. What difference does it make if Laura eats or doesn't eat tonight? She won't have that long to be hungry tomorrow.

He opened the bag and ate the sandwich slowly. He sipped the coffee, reflecting that he preferred it black. When he was finished, he got out, unlocked the door to the kitchen, and went inside. Instead of going up the stairs to Laura's bedroom, he opened the door from the kitchen to the garage and deliberately slammed it behind him as he pulled on the plastic gloves he always kept in the pocket of his jacket.

Laura would hear the sound and begin to tremble with the agony of uncertainty that this might be the time he had come to kill her. But she also would be hungry by now and would be anticipating what he had brought her to eat. Then, when he didn't come up the stairs, both the fear and anticipation would build and build until she was broken, ready to do what he wanted, ready to obey.

In a way he wished he could reassure her that soon it would be over, because to reassure her was to reassure himself. He understood that the pain in his arm was distracting him. The dog bites had seemed to be healing, but now the worst one had become inflamed again.

He had left Robby's keys in the ignition of the car. Repelled at the thought of Robby's lifeless body, covered by blankets and sprawled in the trunk, he clicked the garage door open, got in Robby's car, and backed it out. In a few minutes, which seemed like an eternity, he had his second rental car safely hidden in the garage.

With the headlights off until he was halfway down the block, The Owl began driving Robby Brent's car the few miles to its final destination in the Hudson River.

Forty minutes later, his task accomplished and having walked from the spot where he had sunk the car, he was safely back in his room. His mission tomorrow would be treacherous, he reflected, but he would do his best to minimize the danger. Before daybreak he would walk back to Laura's house. Maybe he would have Laura call Meredith and say she was her birth mother. She would ask to meet her outside West Point for just a few minutes after breakfast. Meredith knows she's adopted, The Owl thought. She talked about it freely enough to me. There's no nineteen-year-old who wouldn't jump at the chance to meet her birth mother, he was confident of that.

And then when he had Meredith, Laura would phone Jean for him.

Sam Deegan wasn't stupid. Even now he might be delving into the deaths of the other girls from the lunch table, investigating the accidents that hadn't been accidents. It wasn't until Gloria that I began to leave my signature, The Owl thought, and the irony is that the first one had been a trinket the stupid woman bought herself.

"You've really made it big, and to think we used to call you 'The Owl,'" she'd said with a laugh, a little drunk, still totally insensitive. Then she showed him the pewter owl, still wrapped in plastic. "I happened to see it at one of those places in the mall that sell this kind of junk," she explained, "and when you phoned to say you were in town, I went back and bought one. I thought we'd have a good laugh about it."

He had a lot of reasons to be grateful to Gloria. After she died he'd bought a dozen of those five-dollar, inch-long pewter owls. Now there were three left. He could get more, of course, but when he had used the three he still had, it might be the end of his need for them. Laura and Jean and Meredith. One owl for each.

The Owl set his alarm for 5:00 A.M. and went to sleep.

77

To sleep, perchance to dream, Jean thought as she restlessly turned on her side and then onto her back. Finally she turned on the light and got out of bed. The room felt too warm. She walked across the room and opened the window wider. Maybe I'll get to sleep now, she thought.

The baby picture of Lily was on the night table. She sat on the edge of the bed and picked up the photograph. How could I have let her go? she agonized. *Why did I let her go?* She felt as if she was on an emotional roller coaster. Tonight I'm going to meet the man and woman who were given Lily right after she was born. What do I say to them? Jean wondered. That I am grateful to them? I am, but I'm ashamed to admit that I'm also jealous of them. I wanted to experience everything that they experienced with her. Suppose they change their minds and decide that I shouldn't meet her yet?

I need to meet her, and then I need to go home. I want to get away from all the Stonecroft people. Last night the atmosphere at President Downes' cocktail party was dreadful, she thought as she turned off the light and lay down again. Everyone seemed to be uptight, but each in a different way. Mark—what is going on inside him? she wondered. He was so quiet and went out of his way to avoid me. Carter Stewart was in a foul mood, growling that he'd lost an entire day's work chasing after Robby's scripts. Jack Emerson had an edge on him and was gulping double scotches. Gordon seemed okay until President Downes kept trying to show him blueprints of the proposed new building. Then he practically exploded. He pointed out that at the dinner he had presented a check for $100,000 for the building fund. I can't believe the way he raised his voice and asked if anyone had noticed that the more you give, the more people try to drag out of you.

Carter was just as rude. He said that since he never made donations to anything, he didn't have that problem. Then Jack Emerson followed those two by bragging that he was donating half a million dollars to Stonecroft for the new communications center.

Only Mark and I said nothing, Jean thought. I will make a donation, but it's going to be for scholarships, not buildings.

She didn't want to think anymore about Mark.

She looked at the clock. It was a quarter of five. What should I wear tonight? I didn't bring all that many changes. I don't know what kind of people Lily's adoptive parents are. Do they dress casually, or do they tend to be more formal? The brown tweed jacket and slacks I wore on the drive might be the best choice. It's a sort of in-between outfit.

I know those pictures the photographer took at President Downes' house are going to be awful. I don't think one of the men even attempted a smile, and I felt as if I were grinning like the Cheshire cat. Then, when that nervy kid Jake Perkins showed up and asked to take a picture of all of us for the *Gazette*, I thought President Downes would have a heart attack. But I felt sorry for the poor kid because of the way Downes practically threw him out.

I hope Jake doesn't have Georgetown on his list of colleges he wants to attend, although he certainly does make life interesting.

Thinking about Jake brought a smile to Jean's lips, relieving for the moment the tension that had been building up since she had heard she was going to meet Lily's adoptive parents.

The smile disappeared as quickly as it came. Where *was* Laura? she thought. This is the beginning of the fifth day since she disappeared. I can't stay here indefinitely. I have classes next week. Why do I persist in believing that I'll hear from her?

I am not going to be able to go back to sleep, she finally decided. It's much too early to get up, but at least I can read. I hardly opened yesterday's newspaper and don't know what's going on in the world.

She went back across the room to the desk, picked up the newspaper, and brought it back to the bed. She propped up the pillow and began to read, but then her eyes started to close. She did not feel the newspaper slip from her grasp, as she finally fell into a heavy sleep.

At a quarter of seven her phone rang. When Jean saw the time on the clock next to the phone, her throat closed. It has to be bad news, she thought. Something has happened to Laura — or to Lily! She grabbed the receiver. "Hello," she said anxiously.

"Jeannie, . . . it's me."

"Laura!" Jean cried. "Where are you? How are you?"

Laura was sobbing so violently that it was hard to understand what she was saying. "Jean, . . . help me. I'm so scared. I've done such a . . . crazy . . . thing. . . . Sorry. . . . Faxes . . . about . . . about Lily."

Jean stiffened. "You never met Lily. I know that."

"Robby, . . . he . . . he . . . took . . . her . . . brush. It . . . was . . . his . . . idea."

"Where is Robby?"

"On . . . way . . . California. He's . . . blam-blaming . . . me. Jeannie, meet me . . . please. By yourself, just by yourself."

"Laura, where are you?"

"In . . . motel. . . . Someone . . . recognized me. I have to . . . go."

"Laura, where can I meet you?"

"Jeannie . . . the Lookout."

"You mean Storm King Lookout?"

"Yes . . . yes."

Laura's sobs became louder. "Kill . . . myself . . ."

"Laura, listen to me," Jean said frantically. "I'll be there in twenty minutes. It's going to be all right. I promise you, it's going to be all right."

At the other end of the line, The Owl swiftly disconnected the phone. "My, my, Laura," he said approvingly. "You are a good actress after all. That was an Academy Award–winning performance."

Laura had slumped back against the pillow, her head turned from him, her sobs subsiding into quivering sighs. "I only did it because you promised that now you wouldn't hurt Jean's daughter."

"So I did," The Owl said. "Laura, you must be hungry. You haven't had a thing since yesterday morning. I can't guarantee the coffee. The counterman in the delicatessen down the hill was getting too inquisitive about me, so I went to another place. But see what else I brought."

She did not respond.

"Turn your head, Laura! Look at me!"

Wearily she obeyed. Through swollen eyes she could see that he was holding up three plastic bags.

The Owl began to laugh. "They're presents," he explained. "One is for you, one is for Jean, and one is for Meredith. Laura, can you guess what I'm going to do with them? *Answer me, Laura! Can you guess what I'm going to do with them?"*

78

"Sorry, Rich. No one will ever tell me that it's only a bizarre coincidence that Gloria Martin, one of the Stonecroft lunch table girls, had a pewter owl in her hand when she died," Sam said flatly.

It had been another sleepless night. After the call from Joy Lacko, he had gone straight back to the office. The file on Gloria Martin's suicide had come in from the Bethlehem police department, and together they had analyzed every word of it, as well as the newspaper accounts of her death.

When Rich Stevens got to the office at 8:00 A.M., he called them in for a conference. After listening to Sam, he turned to Joy. "What do you think?"

"At first I thought it was a slam dunk, that The Owl nut case had been killing girls from Stonecroft for the past twenty years and is back in this area," Joy said. "Now I'm not so sure. I talked to Rudy Haverman, the cop who handled Gloria Martin's suicide eight years ago. He did a very credible investigation. He told me that Martin was into that kind of junk. She apparently was big for picking up cheap tchotchkes of animals and birds and such. The one she was holding when she died was still in its plastic wrap. Haverman found the vendor who sold it to her in the local mall; she distinctly remembered Martin telling her that she was buying it as a joke."

"You say the blood-alcohol level shows that she was smashed when she died?" Stevens asked.

"She was. It registered at .20. According to Haverman, she started drinking after she was divorced, and she went so far as to tell her friends that she didn't have anything to live for."

"Joy, have you found anything in the files of the other women from the lunch table indicating that one of those pewter owls was found in their hands or in their clothing when their bodies were examined?"

"Not so far, sir," Joy admitted.

"I don't care whether or not Gloria Martin bought that owl herself," Sam said stubbornly. "The fact she had it in her hand says to me that she was murdered. So what if she told her friends she was depressed? Most people feel depressed after a divorce even if they're the ones who wanted it. But Martin was very close to her family and knew how devastated they'd be if she killed herself. She didn't leave a suicide note, and from the amount of alcohol she'd imbibed, it's a miracle to me that she managed to get the bag over her head and still hang on to the owl."

"Do you agree with that assessment, Joy?" Rich Stevens snapped.

"I do, sir. Rudy Haverman is convinced it's a suicide, but he hasn't dealt with two other bodies with pewter owls in their pockets."

Rich Stevens leaned back and folded his hands.

"For the sake of argument, let's say that whoever killed Helen Whelan and Yvonne Tepper *may*—and I repeat *may*—be involved in the death of at least one of the deceased Stonecroft lunch table girls."

"The sixth, Laura Wilcox, is missing," Sam said. "Which leaves only Jean Sheridan. I warned her yesterday to trust no one, but I'm not sure if that's going far enough. She may need actual protection."

"Where is she now?" Stevens asked.

"At her hotel. She called me around nine o'clock last night from her hotel room to thank me for something I gave her yesterday. She'd been at a cocktail party given by the president of Stonecroft Academy, and was having dinner sent up to her room. She's meeting her daughter's adoptive parents tonight and said she hoped she'd be able to calm down and get a good night's sleep."

Sam hesitated, then continued. "Rich, sometimes you've got to trust your instincts. Joy is doing a great job digging through the files on the Stonecroft deaths. Jean Sheridan would turn me down flat if I suggested she get a bodyguard, and she'd feel the same way if you offered her protection. But she likes me, and if I tell her I want to hang around with her whenever she leaves the hotel, I think she'd go along with it."

"I think that's a good idea, Sam," Stevens agreed. "All we need is to have something happen to Dr. Sheridan."

"One more thing," Sam added. "I'd like to put surveillance on one of the reunion guys who's still in town. His name is Mark Fleischman, Dr. Mark Fleischman. He's a psychiatrist."

Joy looked at Sam, her eyebrows raised in astonishment. "Dr. Fleischman! Sam, he gives the most sensible advice I've ever heard from anybody on television. A couple of weeks ago he did a program warning parents about kids who feel rejected at home or at school, and how some of them grow up damaged and emotionally warped. We see enough of that, don't we?"

"Yes, we do. But from what I understand, Mark Fleischman got badly hurt both at home and in school," Sam said grimly, "so maybe he was talking about himself."

"See who's available for surveillance," Rich Stevens said. "One more thing—we'd better list Laura Wilcox as a missing person. This is the fifth day she's been gone."

"I think that if we were being totally honest, we'd be listing her as 'missing, presumed dead,'" Sam said flatly.

79

After she hung up from Laura, Jean splashed water on her face, ran a comb through her hair, threw on her jogging suit, dropped her cell phone in her pocket, grabbed her pocketbook, and rushed out of the hotel to her car. Storm King Lookout on Route 218 was fifteen minutes from the hotel. It was still early, and traffic would be light. Normally a careful driver, she pressed her foot on the accelerator and watched the speedometer climb to seventy miles an hour. The clock showed that it was two minutes past seven.

Laura is desperate, she thought. Why does she want to meet me there? Is she planning to hurt herself? The mental image of Laura getting there first and maybe being desperate enough to climb over the railing and throw herself off haunted Jean. The Lookout was hundreds of feet above the Hudson.

The car skidded on the final turn, and for a frightening moment Jean was not sure if she could straighten it, but then the wheels righted and she could see that a car was parked near the telescope at the observation site. Let it be Laura, she prayed. Let her be there. Let her be all right.

Her tires screeched as she pulled into the parking

area, turned off her engine, got out, and rushed to fling
open the passenger door of the other car. "Laura—"
Her greeting died on her lips. The man behind the
wheel was wearing a mask, a plastic mask that was the
face of an owl. The eyes of the owl, with black pupils set
in pools of yellow iris, were surrounded by tufts of white
down that gradually changed in color, deepening to
brown around the beak and lips.

He was holding a gun.

Terrified, Jean turned to run, but a familiar voice ordered, "Get in the car, Jean, unless you want to die here.
And do not speak my name. It is forbidden."

Her car was only a few feet away. Did she dare try to
run for it? Would he shoot her? He was raising the gun.

Numb with fear, she stood uncertainly; then, playing for time, she slowly started to put her foot into the
car. I'll jump back, she thought. I'll duck. He'll have to
get out to shoot me. I may be able to get back in my car.
But in a lightning-quick gesture, he grabbed her arm,
and pulled her the rest of the way into the car, then
reached past her and slammed the door.

In an instant he was backing up, turning onto Route
218, heading toward Cornwall. He ripped off the mask
and grinned at her. "I am The Owl," he said. "I am The
Owl. You must never call me by any other name. Do
you understand?"

He's insane, Jean thought as she nodded. There
were no other cars on the road. If one came along,
could she lean over and blow the horn? Better to take
her chances here on the road than let him get her alone

someplace where she couldn't get help. "I am . . . an . . . ow–owl . . . and . . . and . . . I . . . lllive . . . in . . . a . . ." he chanted. "Remember, Jeannie? Remember?"

"I remember." Her lips began to form his name and then froze before any sound came. He's going to kill me, she thought. I'll grab the wheel and try to cause an accident.

He turned and smiled at her, an openmouthed smirk. The pupils of his eyes were black.

My cell phone, she thought. It's in my pocket. She shrank back against the seat and fumbled for it. She managed to slide it out and edge it to her side where he couldn't see it, but before she could attempt to open the cover and dial 911, The Owl's right hand shot over.

"We're getting into traffic," he said. His strong fingers, crooked like talons, flew to her neck.

She jerked back away from him and, with her last conscious thought, pushed the cell phone between the seatback and the cushion.

When she woke up, she was tied to a chair; there was a gag on her mouth. The room was dark, but she could make out the figure of a woman lying on the bed across the room, a woman in a dress that sparkled and caught the tiny glimmers of light that broke through the sides of the thick shades.

What happened? Jean thought. My head hurts. Why can't I move? Is this a dream? No, I was going to meet Laura. I got in the car and—

"You're awake, Jeannie, aren't you?"

It was an effort to turn her head. He was standing in

the doorway. "I surprised you, didn't I, Jean? Do you remember the school play in the second grade? Everybody laughed at me. You laughed at me. Remember?"

No, I didn't, Jean thought. I felt sorry for you.

"Jean, answer me."

The gag was so tight that she wasn't sure if he could hear her response: "I remember." To be sure he understood, she nodded her head vigorously.

"You're smarter than Laura," he said. "Now I must go. I'll leave you two together. But I'll be back soon. And I'll have someone with me you've been *dying* to see. Guess who?"

Then he was gone. From the bed Jean heard a whimpering sound. Then, her voice muffled by the gag but still audible, Laura began moaning: "Jeannie, . . . promised . . . wouldn't hurt Lily . . . but he's going . . . going to kill her, too."

80

At a quarter of nine, on his way to the Glen-Ridge House, Sam decided that it was not too early to call Jean. When she didn't answer her room telephone, he was disappointed but not worried. If she had dinner in her room last night, she has probably gone to the coffee shop for breakfast. He debated about calling her on her cell phone but decided against it. By the time I place the call, I'll be there, he thought.

The first sense that something might be wrong came when he could not find her in the coffee shop, and again when she did not answer her room phone. The desk clerk could not be sure if she had gone out for a walk. He was the man with the funny colored hair. "That's not to say she *didn't* go out," he explained. "Early morning is a busy time for us, with people checking out."

Sam saw Gordon Amory coming out of the elevator. He was dressed in a shirt and tie and an obviously expensive dark gray business suit. When he saw Sam, he went over to him. "By any chance have you spoken to Jean this morning?" he asked. "We were supposed to have breakfast together, but she didn't show up. I thought she might have overslept, but she doesn't answer in her room."

"I don't know where she is," Sam said, trying to hide his growing anxiety.

"Well, she was tired when we all got back here last night, so maybe it slipped her mind," Amory said. "I'll catch her later. She said she'll be around until tomorrow anyhow." With a brief smile and a wave of his hand he was on his way to the front door of the hotel.

Sam took out his wallet and looked for Jean's cell phone number but couldn't find it. Exasperated, he decided that he must have left it in the pocket of the jacket he'd been wearing the day before. There was one person he knew, however, who might have it—Alice Sommers.

As he dialed Alice's number, he realized again how much he anticipated hearing the sound of her voice. I had dinner with her the night before last, he thought. I wish we had plans for tonight.

Alice did have Jean's number and gave it to him. "Sam, Jean called me yesterday to say how excited she is about meeting Lily's adoptive parents. She also said there was a chance that over the weekend she'll actually meet Lily. Isn't that wonderful?"

A reunion with the daughter you haven't seen in nearly twenty years. Alice is thrilled for Jean, but it has to be one more kick-in-the-teeth reminder to her that Karen's been gone practically the same amount of time, Sam thought. He was disappointed to realize that whenever he was emotionally touched, he covered himself by sounding somewhat abrupt. "It's great for her. Alice, I've got to run. If you happen to hear from Jean, and I haven't spoken to her, ask her to give me a call, okay? It's important."

"You're worried about her, Sam, I can tell. Why?"

"I'm a *little* concerned. There's a lot going on. Listen, she's probably just out for a walk."

"Let me know the minute you hear from her."

"I will, Alice."

Sam snapped the phone closed and walked over to the hotel desk. "I'd like to know whether Dr. Sheridan ordered room service this morning."

The answer came quickly: "No, she did not."

Mark Fleischman was walking through the front door into the lobby. He spotted Sam at the desk and went over to him. "Mr. Deegan, I want to talk to you. I'm worried about Jean Sheridan."

Sam looked at him coldly. "Why do you say that, Dr. Fleischman?"

"Because in my opinion, whoever is communicating with her about her daughter is dangerous. With Laura missing, Jean is the only woman of the so-called lunch table girls who is both alive and unharmed."

"I've thought about that, Dr. Fleischman."

"Jean is angry with me and doesn't trust me. She misread my reason for speaking to the clerk about a fax. She won't listen to anything I say to her now."

"How did you know that she was Dr. Connors' patient?" Sam asked bluntly.

"Jean asked me that, and I told her initially that I'd heard it from her. I've been thinking, however, and I know now where it came up. When the other honorees—I mean Carter and Gordon and Robby and I—were joking with Jack Emerson about working on the office clean-up crew for his father, one of them mentioned it. I just don't remember which one."

Was Fleischman telling the truth? Sam wondered. If so, I've been barking up the wrong tree. "Go over that conversation, Dr. Fleischman," he urged. "It's very, very important."

"I will. Yesterday Jeannie went for a long walk. I suspect she has done the same thing again this morning. I checked her room—she's not there—and I don't see her in the dining room. I'm going to drive around town and see if I can find her."

Sam knew it was too soon for the investigator assigned to surveillance on Fleischman to have arrived. "Why don't you wait a little while and see if she shows up," he suggested. "The odds are that driving around, you'll miss her."

"I don't intend to sit around and do nothing when I'm worried about her," Fleischman said abruptly. He handed Sam his card. "I'd very much appreciate it if you'd let me know when you hear from her."

He walked swiftly through the lobby toward the entrance of the hotel. Sam watched him go, conflicted in his reaction to the man. I wonder if you took any drama medals at Stonecroft, he thought. Either you're on the level, or you're one hell of a good actor, because outwardly you appear just as worried about Jean Sheridan as I am.

Sam's eyes narrowed as he watched Fleischman swiftly depart through the front door. I'll give it a little while longer, he thought. She may just be out for a walk.

81

The chair he had tied her to was against the wall, next to the window, and facing the bed. There was something about the room that was familiar. With growing horror and the sense of being in the midst of a nightmare, Jean strained to hear Laura's muffled outpourings. She mumbled almost constantly and seemed to be slipping in and out of consciousness as she tried to talk through the gag that gave her voice an eerie, throaty tone. The result was a sound that was almost a growl.

She never used his name. "The Owl" was how she referred to him. Sometimes she would recite his line from that second-grade play: "I am an owl, and I live in a tree." Then she would suddenly lapse into a disquieting silence, and only an occasional shuddering sigh told Jean that Laura was still breathing.

Lily. Laura had said that he was going to kill Lily. But she was safe. Surely she was. Craig Michaelson had promised her that Lily was safe. Was Laura delusional? She must have been here since at least Saturday night. She keeps saying that she's hungry. Hasn't he fed her? She must have had something to eat.

Oh, my God, Jean thought as she remembered Duke, the counterman at the deli–coffee shop at the bottom of the hill. He had told her about a man from the reunion who stopped in regularly to pick up food—Duke was talking about *him*!

She twisted her hands in an effort to see if she could pull the cords apart, but they were too tight. Was it possible that he had killed Karen Sommers in this same room? Was it possible that he had deliberately run over Reed at West Point? Had he killed Catherine and Cindy and Debra and Gloria and Alison, as well as those two women in this area who were murdered this week? I saw him drive into the hotel parking lot early Saturday morning, Jean thought, with his headlights turned off. Maybe if I had told Sam about that, he would have investigated him, *stopped* him.

My cell phone is in his car, Jean thought. If he finds it, he'll throw it away. But if he *doesn't* find it, and if Sam tries to locate it the same way he did the phone Laura used to call me, maybe we have a chance. Please, God, before he hurts Lily, let Sam try to trace my phone.

Laura's breathing became gasping gulps, then formed into barely coherent words: "Cleaner's bags . . . cleaner's bags . . . no . . . no . . . no."

Even with the dark shades over the windows, a little light managed to seep into the room. Jean could see the outline of plastic bags suspended by hangers that had been hooked over the arm of the lamp by the bed. She could see writing across the front of the one directly facing her. What was it? Was it a name? Was it . . . ? She couldn't quite make it out.

Her shoulder was touching the edge of the heavy shade. She threw her weight to one side, then to the other, until the chair moved a few inches, and the shade caught on her shoulder and was tilted away from the window frame.

The added light made the thick black marker pen writing on the plastic bag clear enough to be read: LILY/MEREDITH.

82

Jake could not skip his first class at 8:00 A.M., but as soon as it was over, he rushed to the studio. In his opinion the prints of the pictures he had taken yesterday looked even better in daylight than they had under the overhead light in the late afternoon. He congratulated himself as he studied them.

The McMansion on Concord Avenue really looks so "see me, I'm rich," he thought. The house on Mountain Road is such a great contrast to it—middle-class, comfortable suburban, but now with a mystique about it. At home that evening he had checked the Internet and confirmed that Karen Sommers had been murdered in the corner bedroom on the right side of the second floor. I know Dr. Sheridan used to live next door when she was growing up, Jake thought. I'll stop at the hotel and see if she can confirm that was Laura's room. It probably was. According to the floor plan of the Sommers murder on the Internet, it's the other large bedroom on that floor. It makes sense that precious only-child Laura got it. Dr. Sheridan will probably tell me. She's been nice—not like old "Throw-Him-in-Jail" Deegan.

Jake put the prints of yesterday's pictures in the bag

with his extra film. He wanted to have them available while he was shooting, in case he needed them for comparison.

At 9:00 A.M. he was approaching Mountain Road. He had decided that it wouldn't be smart to park in the street. People noticed strange cars, and that cop might recognize his pride and joy. At times like this he wished he hadn't painted it with zebra stripes.

I'll have a soda and a Danish, leave my car at the deli, and walk up to Laura's house, he decided. He had borrowed one of his mother's oversized shopping bags from Bloomingdale's. There'd be no car and no camera in sight. I can sneak down Laura's driveway and get my pictures of the back of the house. I hope the garage doors have windows. That way I can tell if there are any cars parked inside.

At 9:10 he was sitting at the counter of the delicatessen at the foot of Mountain Road, chatting with Duke, who had already explained that he and Sue, his wife, had owned the place for ten years, that it used to be a dry cleaner, that they were open from 6:00 A.M. to 9:00 P.M. and that they both enjoyed being here. "Cornwall is a quiet town," Duke said as he whisked an imaginary crumb from the counter, "but a nice town. You say you go to Stonecroft Academy? That's pretty tony. Some of the reunion people were in here. Oh, there he goes."

Duke's eyes had darted to the window that faced Mountain Road.

"There who goes?" Jake asked.

"The fellow who's been coming in early mornings

and some late evenings to pick up coffee and toast or coffee and a sandwich."

"Know who he is?" Jake asked, not really caring.

"Nope, but he's another one of your reunion people, and he's been coming and going all morning. I saw him go out in his car, come back a little while later, and now he's on his way again."

"Uh-huh," Jake said as he got up and pulled some squashed dollar bills out of his pocket. "I feel like stretching my legs. Is it okay if I leave my car outside for about fifteen minutes?"

"Sure, but not more than that. As it is, we don't have enough parking spots."

"Don't worry. I'm in a hurry, too."

Eight minutes later Jake was in the backyard of Laura's former home, taking pictures. He photographed the back of the house and even took a couple of shots of the kitchen through the door. A grill covered the glass pane over the door, but looking in, he could see a fair amount of the room. It could be a display kitchen in Home Depot, he thought. The counters that he could see were bare—no toaster, no coffee pot, no canisters, no cutsie-pie plates or trays or radio or clock. Absolutely no sign of occupancy. I guess for once in my life I was wrong, he decided reluctantly.

He studied the tire tracks on the driveway. There have been a couple of cars here, he thought. But that could be from the guy who rakes the leaves. The garage doors were closed and didn't have windows, so he couldn't check for cars.

He went back up the driveway, crossed the street, and took several more pictures of the front of the house. I guess that'll do it, he thought. I'll go and develop them right away. Then I'll phone Dr. Sheridan and ask her if she remembers which bedroom was Laura's when they were kids.

It would have been more fun to have found Laura Wilcox and Robby Brent holed up here, he thought as he put the camera back in the shopping bag and started down the hill. But what can you do? You can cover a story, but you can't invent one.

83

After her first class, West Point yearling Meredith Buckley rushed to her room for a final review of her notes for the exam in linear algebra, the course that was proving to be the toughest of her second year at West Point.

For twenty minutes she focused intensely on the notes. As she was putting them back in the folder, the phone rang. She was tempted not to answer it, but thinking that it might be her father calling to wish her luck on the exam, she picked it up and then smiled. Before she could speak, a cheerful voice was saying, "May I have the pleasure of inviting Cadet Buckley, daughter of the distinguished General Charles Buckley, to share another weekend with her parents and myself at my home in Palm Beach?"

"You don't know how wonderful that sounds," Meredith said fervently as she thought of the glamorous weekend she had enjoyed with her parents' friend. "I'll come anytime except, of course, when West Point has other plans for me, which is just about always. I hate to seem rude, but I'm heading into an exam."

"I need five, make that three, minutes of your time. Meredith, I was at a class reunion at Stonecroft Academy in Cornwall. I think I mentioned to you I was going to it."

"Yes, you did. I'm so sorry, but I simply can't talk now."

"I'll be fast. Meredith, a classmate of mine who attended the reunion is an intimate friend of Jean, your birth mother, and has written a note to you about her. I promised to deliver the note to you personally. Tell me when to be in the museum parking lot, and I'll be waiting for you with it in hand."

"My *birth* mother? Someone who was at your reunion *knows* her?" Meredith could feel her heart pounding as she gripped the phone. She looked at the clock. She absolutely *had* to get to class. "I'll be finished with my exam at eleven-forty," she said hurriedly. "I could be in the parking lot at ten of twelve."

"That works out for me. Ace your exam, General."

It took all of Cadet Meredith Buckley's training to force herself to put out of her mind the realization that in a little more than an hour she would know something tangible about the girl who at age eighteen had given birth to her. The only information she had so far was that her mother had been about to graduate from high school when she learned she was pregnant and that her father had been a college senior who was killed in a hit-and-run accident before she was born.

Her parents had talked to her about her birth mother. They had promised Meredith that after she was graduated from West Point, they would try to learn her identity and then arrange a meeting between them.

"We have no idea who she is, Meri," her father had told her. "We do know, because the doctor who delivered you and arranged the adoption told us, that your birth mother loved you deeply and that giving you up was probably the most unselfish and difficult decision she would ever have to make in her whole life."

All this ran through Meredith's mind as she tried to concentrate on the linear algebra exam. But she could not block out the awareness that every tick of the clock brought her closer to greater knowledge of the mother she now knew as Jean.

As she handed in her exam and rushed toward Thayer Gate and the military academy museum, she realized that the reference to Palm Beach had solved the question her father had asked her yesterday on the phone. *That's* where I lost my hairbrush, she remembered suddenly.

84

A stony-faced Carter Stewart came into the hotel at ten o'clock, while Sam was sitting in the lobby. Sam made a beeline for him, catching him at the desk. "Mr. Stewart, I'd like to have a word with you if I may."

"In a minute, Mr. Deegan." The clerk with the wood-chip-colored hair was behind the desk. "I need to see the manager, and I need to get into Mr. Brent's room again," Stewart snapped at him. "The production company has received yesterday's package. Apparently there is one more script that is vitally needed, and I have been asked to do the proverbial good deed once more. Since the script was not on top of the desk, it will involve going *through* the desk."

"I'll summon Mr. Lewis immediately, sir," the clerk said nervously.

Stewart turned to Sam. "If they do refuse to let me go rummaging through Robby's desk, I don't care. I will have paid the debt of gratitude that my agent insists I owe him. He has now agreed that it has been paid in full. He doesn't know it yet, but that gives me the moral right to fire him, which I intend to do this afternoon."

Stewart turned back to the clerk. "Is the manager here, or is he out in the field picking flowers?"

What a nasty human being, Sam thought. "Mr. Stewart," he said, his tone icy, "I have a question, and I need to know the answer to it. A few nights ago, I understand you, Mr. Amory, Mr. Brent, Mr. Emerson, Dr. Fleischman, and Mr. Nieman were joking about working together on the evening cleaning crew of an office building managed by Mr. Emerson's father."

"Yes, yes, something about that came up. That was the spring of our senior year. Another tender memory of my glorious time at Stonecroft."

"Mr. Stewart, this is very important. Did you hear anyone mention that Dr. Sheridan had been a patient of a Dr. Connors who had an office in that building?"

"No, I did not. And, besides, why would Jean have been a patient of Dr. Connors? He was an obstetrician." Stewart's eyes widened. "Oh, my. Have we a little secret about to come out, Mr. Deegan? Was Jeannie a patient of Dr. Connors?"

Sam looked at Stewart with loathing. He wanted to kick himself for the way he had framed the question, and he wanted to punch Stewart for his leering response to it. "I asked you if someone had made that statement," he said. "I did not for one instant suggest that it was true."

Justin Lewis, the manager, had come up behind them. "Mr. Stewart, I understand you wish to go into Mr. Brent's room and go through his desk. I am afraid that I really can't allow that. I spoke to our law firm yesterday after I let you take those scripts, and they were quite upset about it."

"There we are," Stewart said. He turned his back on the manager. "My business here is pretty well wrapped up, Mr. Deegan," he said. "My director and I have completed going over his suggested changes for my play, and I have had quite enough of hotel life. I'm going back to Manhattan this afternoon, and I wish you good luck waiting for Laura and Robby to bob to the surface."

Sam and the hotel manager watched him exit the lobby. "That is one nasty guy," Justin Lewis told Sam. "It's obvious that he hates Mr. Brent."

"Why do you say that?" Sam asked quickly.

"Because a note Mr. Brent left on his desk referring to Mr. Stewart as 'Howie' obviously got under his skin. From what Mr. Stewart said, it was Mr. Brent's idea of a joke, but then Mr. Stewart asked me if I knew that saying about 'he who laughs last laughs best.' "

Before Sam could comment, his cell phone rang; the caller was Rich Stevens. "Sam, we have a call in from the Cornwall cops. A car was spotted in the Hudson. It was partially submerged, but caught on rocks, which is why it didn't go all the way down. There's a body in the trunk. It's Robby Brent, and it appears he's been dead for a couple of days. You'd better get over there."

"Right away, Rich." Sam snapped his phone closed. *"He who laughs last laughs best."* When *Laura and Robby* *"bob to the surface."* Bobbing, as in water? he wondered. Was Carter Stewart, once known as Howie, not only a celebrated playwright but a psychopathic killer as well?

85

At ten o'clock Jake was back in the darkroom at the school, developing his latest set of pictures. The ones he had taken of the back of the Mountain Road house really didn't contribute anything to his story, he decided. Even the door with its decorative grill had a Norman Rockwell, down-home feeling. The shot into the kitchen wasn't bad, but who wanted to look at bare countertops?

This morning was basically a waste, Jake decided. I shouldn't have bothered cutting my second class. As the quick shot he had taken of the house from the front began to develop, he could see that it was a little out of focus. He might as well deep-six it. He'd never use it in the article.

He heard his name being called from outside the darkroom. It was Jill Farris, and she sounded upset. She couldn't be mad at me, he thought—it wasn't her class I cut. "I'll be right out, Ms. Farris," he called.

As soon as he opened the door he could tell by the look on her face that something had really shaken her up. She didn't bother to say hello to him. "Jake, I took a chance you might be in there," she said. "You interviewed Robby Brent, didn't you?"

"Yes, I did. A good interview if I do say so myself."

She's not going to kill it, is she? Jake thought with dismay. Old Downes probably wants to forget that Brent and Laura Wilcox ever set foot in Stonecroft.

"Jake, it just came over the news. Robby Brent's body was found in the trunk of a car submerged near Cornwall Landing."

Robby Brent dead! Jake grabbed his camera. I still have a lot of film left, he thought. "Thanks, Jill," he yelled, as he raced out the door.

86

The car with Robby Brent's body had gone into the Hudson at Cornwall Landing. The normally tranquil park, with its benches and weeping willows, was now the center of police activity. The area had been hastily taped off to hold back the curious bystanders who, like the media, were gathering in ever-increasing numbers.

When Sam arrived at ten-thirty, the body of the late Robby Brent had already been placed in a body bag and in the morgue wagon. Cal Grey, the medical examiner, filled Sam in. "He's been dead at least a couple of days. Stab wound in the chest. Went right through his heart. I have to wait till I can take measurements, but I've got to tell you, Sam, that it appears to be the same kind of jagged-edge knife that killed Helen Whelan. From what I can see, whoever murdered Brent was either a lot taller or was standing on something like a staircase where he was above the victim. That knife went in at a distinct angle."

Mark Fleischman is tall, Sam thought. Talking to Fleischman, he could understand why Jean had been drawn to him. He had a plausible explanation for the reason he had inquired about the fax and for his knowledge

that Jean had been a patient of Dr. Connors. Was he
being honest, or was he a little too glib? Sam wasn't sure.

Before coming to the crime scene, Sam had called
Jean on her cell phone, but she had not answered. He
left her an urgent message to call him and then dialed
Alice Sommers again.

Alice had partially reassured him. "Sam, when Jean
was talking about meeting Lily's adoptive parents
tonight, she mentioned that she wished she had brought
more clothes with her. Woodbury Mall is less than half
an hour away. I wouldn't be surprised if she simply decided to ride over there and do some shopping."

It was a reasonable supposition, and it had helped to
partially allay Sam's concern for Jean. But now the concern was building, and he knew it was his instinct warning him not to wait any longer to begin an active search
for her.

"Robbery wasn't the motive," Cal Grey was saying.
"Brent was wearing an expensive watch and has six hun-
dred bucks in his wallet and a half-dozen credit cards.
How long has he been missing?"

"He hasn't been seen since after dinner on Monday
night," Sam said.

"My bet is that he didn't last long after that," Grey
commented. "Of course the autopsy will pin down the
time of death much more accurately than I can now."

"I was at that dinner," Sam said. "What was he wearing when you got him out of the trunk?"

"Beige jacket, dark brown slacks, and a brown turtleneck sweater."

"Then unless he slept in his clothes wherever he went, he died on Monday night."

Cameras were flashing as photographers behind the tape took pictures of the car that had been Robby Brent's coffin. A salvage truck had hoisted it out of the river, and now, still attached to the cable, it was standing on the bank, dripping water as technicians continued to photograph it from every angle.

A local policeman filled Sam in on the details, sketchy as they were. "We think the car may have been dumped around ten o'clock last night. A couple who live in New Windsor were jogging past here at about a quarter of ten. They say they saw a car parked near the railroad tracks and that someone was in it. They turned and started back about half a mile down the road. When they reached this point again, the car was gone, but a man was walking fast along Shore Road."

"Did they get a good look at him?"

"No."

"Did they mention if he was tall? I mean *really* tall?" Sam asked.

"They can't agree. The husband said the guy was average size; the wife thought he was pretty tall. Both of them wear distance glasses and admit they barely got an impression of the guy, but they are sure that a car was parked here, that ten minutes later it was gone, and that someone was leaving this area on foot and in a big hurry."

God deliver me from eyewitnesses, Sam thought. As he turned back, he spotted Jake Perkins pushing his way to the front of the group behind the tape. He was carrying a camera that reminded Sam of the kind he had seen in a book about the great World War II photographer Robert Capa.

I wonder if that kid has the gift of bilocation, Sam thought. It's not only that he *seems* to be everywhere; he *is* everywhere. His eyes met Jake's, but Jake looked away immediately. He's sore at me for telling Tony to throw him in jail after he claimed to be my special assistant investigating Laura's disappearance, Sam thought. I could have given him a break and at least said that he's trying to be helpful, because he was. After all, he was the one who tipped me off that Laura sounded nervous on that phone call.

He was debating whether to go over and speak to Jake when his cell phone rang. He snapped it out of his pocket, hoping the call would be from Jean. Instead it was from Joy Lacko. "Sam, a call came into 911 a few minutes ago. A BMW convertible registered to Dr. Jean Sheridan has been parked at Storm King Lookout on 218 for a couple of hours. The call was made by a salesman who drove past it around seven-forty-five and then again twenty minutes ago. He thought it seemed odd that the car was there so long and decided to check to see if there was a problem. The keys are in the ignition, and her pocketbook is on the passenger seat. It doesn't look good."

"That's why she hasn't been answering her phone," Sam said heavily. "My God, Joy. Why didn't I insist that she have a bodyguard? Is the car still at the Lookout?"

"Yes. Rich knew you'd want to look over the location before we moved it." Joy's voice was sympathetic. "I'll keep in touch, Sam."

The vehicle with Robby Brent's body was starting to back up. Three bodies in less than a week in that meat wagon, Sam thought. Don't let the next one be Jean Sheridan, he prayed. Please don't let the next one be Jean.

87

Jake Perkins had immediately regretted not acknowledging Sam Deegan when their eyes met. It was one thing not to give the detective any information he might come across, but it was another thing to cut off all contact with him. No good reporter, no matter how insulted he'd been, would ever do that.

He would have loved to ask Deegan for a statement about Robby Brent's murder, but he knew better than to do that. He knew what the official line would be—that Brent was the victim of a homicide by person or persons unknown. They hadn't released the cause of death, but it was a cinch it wasn't suicide. Nobody climbs into the trunk of a car while it's rolling into the river.

Maybe Deegan knows where Dr. Sheridan is, Jake thought. He had tried to phone Jean, but there was no answer in her room. He did want to get confirmation from her that Laura Wilcox had slept in the murder bedroom on Mountain Road.

Struggling with the heavy camera, Jake worked his way through the crowd of photographers and reporters and caught up with Sam at his car. "Mr. Deegan, I've been trying to get in touch with Dr. Sheridan. Do you by any chance know where I could reach her? She doesn't answer her phone."

Sam was about to get into his car. "What time did you try her?" he asked sharply.

"About nine-thirty."

That was the same time I tried her, Sam thought. "I don't know where she is," he snapped as he got in his car. He slammed the door closed and turned on the siren.

Something's up, Jake thought. He's worried about Dr. Sheridan, but he's not making the turn back to the hotel. He's going too fast for me to follow him. I might as well go back to school and clean up the darkroom. Then I'll head over to the Glen-Ridge and see what's going on.

88

On the way to the observation point, Sam phoned the Glen-Ridge House and asked to be put through to the manager immediately. When Justin Lewis got on, Sam said, "Look, I can get a subpoena for your phone records, but I can't waste the time. Dr. Sheridan's car has just been found, and she is missing. I want you to give me right now a list of the phone numbers of all calls received by Dr. Sheridan between ten o'clock last night and nine o'clock this morning."

He had been prepared for an argument but did not get one. "Give me your number. I'll call you right back," the manager said crisply.

Sam put his cell phone on the passenger seat as he raced toward Storm King Lookout. He rounded the bend and saw Jean's blue convertible with a policeman standing beside it. He pulled up behind it and had his notebook and pencil out when Lewis called back. The man obviously had understood the need for urgency. "Dr. Sheridan received seven phone calls this morning," he said crisply. "The first came at quarter of seven!"

"At quarter of seven?" Sam interrupted.

"Yes, sir. It was made on a cell phone from this area.

The name of the subscriber was not given. The number is . . ."

Stunned and disbelieving, Sam wrote down the number that he recognized as the same one Robby Brent had called from on Monday night when he had imitated Laura's voice on the call to Jean.

"The other calls have been identified as coming from a Mrs. Alice Sommers and a Mr. Jake Perkins. They both tried to reach Dr. Sheridan several times. There are two from your own number."

"Thank you. You've been very helpful," Sam said abruptly, and he clicked off. Robby Brent has been dead for a couple of days, he thought, but someone used the phone he bought in the drugstore to entice Jean Sheridan to leave the hotel. She must have rushed out right after that call came in. Her car was spotted here at 7:45 this morning. Who was she expecting to meet here? She had promised to be careful, and there were only two people she would have met without question. Sam was sure of it.

He was aware that the cop standing by Jean's car was giving him a curious stare, but he ignored him. Jean expected to meet either her daughter, Lily, or Laura, Sam thought as he looked blankly at the mountains on the other side of the river.

Had she been forced from her car at gunpoint, or had she walked over to another vehicle on her own?

Whoever this psychopath is, he has Jean. Is Jean's daughter *really* safe? Sam wondered suddenly. He opened his wallet, raced through the cards inside, found the one he wanted, tossed the others on the passenger seat, and dialed Craig Michaelson's cell phone. After five rings a computer voice advised him to leave a message. Swearing under his breath, he dialed Michaelson's office.

"I am so sorry," his secretary apologized. "Mr. Michaelson is in a conference at another attorney's office and cannot be interrupted."

"He's got to be interrupted," Sam snapped. "This is a police matter—a matter of life and death."

"Oh, sir," the manicured voice chided, "I'm sorry, but—"

"Listen to me, young lady, and listen hard. You get Michaelson, and you tell him that Sam Deegan phoned. Tell your boss that Jean Sheridan has disappeared and that it is *imperative* he contact West Point immediately and warn them to put a bodyguard on her daughter. Do you understand me?"

"Of course I do. I will try to reach him, but—"

"No buts. *Reach him!*" Sam shouted, then snapped his phone closed. He got out of the car. I have to put a track on Robby Brent's phone, he thought, but it probably won't do any good. There's only one hope.

He brushed past the policeman, who started to explain that he knew the salesman who had alerted them to the car being there and that nobody could be more reliable. Jean's shoulder bag was on the seat.

"Nothing has been taken out of it?" he snapped.

"Of course not, sir." The young policeman was clearly offended at the suggestion.

Sam didn't bother to assure him that he meant nothing personal by the question. He dumped the contents of Jean's bag on the passenger seat, then searched the glove compartment and all the storage areas inside the car. "If it's not too late, we may have gotten the break we need," he said. "She was probably carrying her cell phone. It's not here."

It was 11:30 A.M.

89

It was 11:45 A.M. before Craig Michaelson phoned Sam, who by then was back in the Glen-Ridge House. "My secretary tried to get me, but I had left the meeting and forgot to turn on my cell phone," he explained hurriedly. "I just got to the office. What's going on?"

"What's going on is that Jean Sheridan has been abducted," Sam said tersely. "I don't give a damn if her daughter is in West Point and surrounded by an army. I want you to be sure that a special guard is put on her. We have a psychopath running loose around here. The body of one of the other Stonecroft honorees was pulled out of the Hudson a couple of hours ago. He'd been stabbed to death."

"Jean Sheridan is missing! The General and his wife are on the eleven o'clock shuttle from Washington right now, on their way to have dinner with her tonight. I can't get in touch with them while they're on a flight."

Sam's pent-up worry and frustration exploded. "Yes, you can," he shouted. "You could get a message through the airline to the pilot, but it's too late for that now anyway. Give me the name of Jean Sheridan's daughter, and I'll call West Point myself. I want it now."

"She is Cadet Meredith Buckley. She's a second-year student, a yearling. But the General assured me that Meredith would not leave the West Point campus either Thursday or Friday because of the tests she has scheduled."

"Let's pray the General is right," Sam snapped. "Mr. Michaelson, in the unlikely event I meet any resistance when I call the superintendent at the academy, please be available for an immediate phone call."

"I'll be in my office."

"And if you're not, make sure your cell phone is on."

Sam was in the office behind the hotel's front desk, the place where he had started the investigation into the disappearance of Laura Wilcox. Eddie Zarro had joined him there. "You want to keep your cell phone line open, don't you?" Eddie asked.

Sam nodded, then watched as Eddie dialed the West Point number. While waiting for the call to go through, he frantically searched his memory for anything that might suggest another path of action. The technical guys were triangulating on Jean's cell phone, something they expected to complete within minutes. When they did, they'd be able to pinpoint the exact location of the phone. That should help—assuming it isn't in a garbage heap somewhere, Sam thought.

"Sam, they're ringing the superintendent's office," Eddie said. Sam's tone when he picked up the phone was only slightly less forceful than the one he'd used with Craig Michaelson. When he spoke to the superintendent's secretary, he did not mince words. "I am Detective Deegan from the Office of the District Attorney of Orange County. Cadet Meredith Buckley may be in serious danger from a homicidal maniac. I need to speak to the superintendent immediately."

He did not have to wait more than ten seconds before the superintendent was on the phone. He listened to Sam's brief explanation, then said, "She's probably in an exam right now. I'll have her brought to my office immediately."

"Just let me be sure that you have her," Sam asked. "I'll hold on."

He held the phone for five minutes. When the superintendent came back on, his voice was charged with emotion. "Less than five minutes ago, Cadet Buckley was seen leaving Thayer Gate and going over to the parking lot of the Military Academy Museum. She has not returned, and she is neither in the parking lot nor in the museum."

Sam didn't want to believe what he was hearing. Not her as well, he thought, not a nineteen-year-old kid! "I understood that she promised her father she wouldn't leave West Point," he said. "Are you *sure* she went outside?"

"The cadet didn't break her word," the superintendent said. "Although it's open to the public, the museum is considered part of the West Point campus."

90

Jill Farris was in the studio when Jake got back to Stonecroft. "Robby Brent's body was in the meat wagon by the time I got there," he said, "but they'd pulled the car out of the water. He was found in the trunk. I bet President Downes is having a heart attack or at least a bleeding ulcer. Can't you see the publicity we'll be getting now?"

"The president is very upset," Jill Farris admitted. "Jake, are you through with the camera?"

"I think so. You know, Jill—I mean Ms. Farris—it wouldn't have surprised me if Laura Wilcox was found in the trunk of that car with Brent. I mean, what's happened to her? I'd bet the ranch that she's dead, too. And if she is, the only one at that lunch table still alive is Dr. Sheridan. If I were her, I'd hire a bodyguard. I mean, when you think how many so-called celebrities won't stir unless they're surrounded by a couple of muscle men, why wouldn't someone like Dr. Sheridan, with a *real* reason to worry, not get some protection?"

It was a rhetorical question, and Jake was already on his way into the darkroom, so he got no answer.

He wasn't sure what he would do with his shots of the crime scene. It was unlikely that they'd ever see the light of day in the *Stonecroft Academy Gazette*. Still, he was certain that he'd eventually find a place for them, even though he hadn't yet received an offer to be a roving reporter for the *New York Post*.

When the pictures were developed, he viewed them with intense pleasure. From different angles he had caught the starkness of the car with its sides dented from hitting a rock pile in the river and its open trunk, dripping water. He also had gotten a good shot of the meat wagon, its lights flashing as it backed away.

The pictures he had taken in the morning of the Mountain Road house were still clipped and hanging on the line. His gaze fell on the last one, the out-of-focus picture of the front of the house. As he looked closely at it, his eyes widened.

He grabbed the magnifying glass, studied the picture, then unclipped it and rushed out of the darkroom. Jill Farris was still there, grading papers. He dropped the picture in front of her and handed her the magnifying glass.

"Jake," she protested.

"This is important, really important. Look at this picture and tell me if something looks out of place or different. Please, Ms. Farris, really look."

"Jake, you'd drive anyone crazy," she said with a sigh, taking the magnifying glass from him to study the print. "I guess you mean that the shade on that window on the second floor in the corner is kind of lopsided. Is that it?"

"That's *exactly* it," Jake exulted. "It wasn't lopsided yesterday. I don't care how empty that kitchen looks— somebody's living in that house!"

91

Sam had returned to the Glen-Ridge House rather than go back to the office in Goshen because he was beginning to feel certain that one of the honorees, or perhaps Jack Emerson or Joel Nieman, was responsible for the threats to Lily. All of them had worked in the building where Dr. Connors' office was located. At some point over the weekend, one of them had referred to Jean as having been his patient. But which one he hadn't yet determined.

Fleischman had insisted he heard one of those other men mention that Jean was Connors' patient. Of course, he could be lying, Sam thought. Stewart denied ever hearing the remark. And he could be lying, too. But at least at the Glen-Ridge he could keep an eye on Fleischman and Gordon Amory, who were still checked in there. The fact that Jean was missing would be picked up by reporters and be broadcast, and he'd bet anything that the news would bring Jack Emerson rushing there as well.

He'd already asked Rich Stevens to put surveillance on all of them. That would kick in soon.

At ten after twelve he got the call he was hoping to

receive from the technical guys. "Sam, we have a fix on Jean Sheridan's phone."

"Where is it?"

"In a moving car."

"Can you tell where the car is?"

"Near Storm King, heading toward the Cornwall area."

"He's coming from West Point," Sam said. "He has the cadet. Don't lose him. Don't lose him."

"We don't intend to."

92

"Please turn the car around," Meredith said. "I am not permitted to leave the grounds. When you asked me to sit in the car, I thought you meant just to talk for a minute. I'm sorry you left the letter about my mother in your other pocket, but I'll have to wait to get it. Please, I must go back, Mr. —"

"You were about to use my name, Meredith. I don't want you to do that. You must refer to me as Owl or The Owl."

She stared at him, fear suddenly gripping her. "I don't understand. Please take me back." Meredith grasped the handle of the passenger door. If he stops for a light, I'll jump out, she thought. He's different. He even looks different. No, not just different—crazy! Questions of doubt, unanswerable questions, flitted through her mind. Why did Dad ask me to promise I wouldn't leave the grounds? Why did he ask me about the hairbrush that I lost? What does this have to do with my birth mother?

The car was speeding north along Route 218. He's going way over the speed limit, Meredith thought. Please, God, let us pass a cop. Let a cop see us. She considered grabbing the steering wheel, but there were cars coming in the other direction; somebody in one of them might get killed. "Where are you taking me?" she demanded. Something was pressing into her back. She moved forward in the seat, but it was still there. What was it?

"Meredith, I lied when I said I met your mother's friend at the reunion. I met your *mother* there. I'm taking you to see her."

"My mother! Jean! You're taking me to see her?"

"Yes, I am. And then the two of you are going to join your birth father in heaven. You'll have a wonderful reunion, I'm sure. You look a lot like him, you know. At least you look as he did before I smashed into him on the road. You know where that happened, Meredith? On the road near the picnic grounds at West Point. That's where your real daddy died. I wish you'd had a chance to visit his grave. His name is on the tombstone: Carroll Reed Thornton, Jr. He would have graduated one week later. I wonder if they'll bury you and Jeannie beside him. Wouldn't that be nice?"

"My father went to West Point, and *you* killed him?"

"Of course I did. Do you think it was fair for him and Jean to be so happy and leave me out in the cold? *Do you think that was fair, Meredith?*"

He turned his head and glared at her. His eyes were flashing. His lips were pressed together so tightly that his mouth seemed to have disappeared beneath flaring nostrils.

He's crazy, she thought. "No, sir. It doesn't seem

fair," she replied, trying to keep her voice steady. I can't show him how scared I am.

He seemed mollified. "Your West Point training. 'Yes, ma'am.' 'No, sir.' I didn't ask you to call me sir. I told you to call me 'Owl.'"

They had passed the cutoff for Storm King Mountain and were on the outskirts of Cornwall. Where are we going? Meredith wondered. Is he really taking me to my mother? Did he really kill my father and is he planning to kill us now? What can I do to stop him? Don't panic, she warned herself. Look around. See if there's anything you can use to defend yourself. Maybe there's a bottle of water somewhere. I could hit him in the face with it. It might give me enough time to reach the ignition key and stop the car. We're passing enough cars now that somebody might notice a struggle. But as she glanced around, she saw absolutely nothing she could use to defend herself.

"Meredith, I can read your thoughts. Don't even think about trying to attract attention to yourself, because if you do, you will not live to get out of this car. I have a gun, and I will use it. At least I am offering you a chance to meet your mother. Don't be foolish and throw it away."

Meredith's hands were gripped together. What was pressing against her back? Maybe, maybe it was something that would give her a chance to save herself and save her mother. With infinite care she unclasped her hands and moved her right hand slowly to her side. She sat up straighter in the seat as she slid her hand behind her back. Her fingers touched the edge of a narrow object that felt familiar.

It was a cell phone. She had to tug to get it loose, but The Owl didn't seem to notice. They were driving through Cornwall now, and he was looking from side to side as though afraid he'd be stopped.

Meredith moved her hand slowly back, the phone cupped in it. She flipped it open, glanced down, and her finger pressed 91 —

She did not see his hand shoot across the car seat, but she felt it as he grabbed her neck. She slumped forward, unconscious, as The Owl grabbed the phone, lowered his window, and threw it onto the road.

Less than ten seconds later, a mail truck rumbled over it, breaking it into bits of plastic.

"Sam, we've lost him," Eddie Zarro said. "He's in Cornwall, but we're not getting any more signals."

"How did you lose him?" Sam shouted. It was a stupid, useless question. He knew the answer—the phone had been discovered and destroyed.

"What do we do now?" Zarro asked.

"Pray," Sam said. "We pray."

93

Jake again asked permission to leave his car outside the delicatessen, and once more it was granted, but Duke's curiosity was now at a fever pitch. "Who are you taking pictures of, sonny?" he asked.

"Just of the neighborhood. As I told you, I'm doing a little story for the *Stonecroft Academy Gazette*. I'll give you a copy when I finish." Jake had an inspiration. "Better yet, I'll mention you in it."

"That'd be nice. Duke and Sue Mackenzie. No capital *k* in Mackenzie."

"Gotcha."

Jake's cell phone rang as, camera over his arm, he was starting out the door. The call was from Amy Sachs, on duty at the hotel. "Jake," she whispered, "you should be over here. All hell is breaking loose. Dr. Sheridan is missing. They found her car abandoned at Storm King Lookout. Mr. Deegan is in the office here. I just heard him shouting about something being lost."

"Thanks, Amy. I'll be right over," Jake said. He turned to Duke. "Guess I won't need that space after all, but thanks anyhow."

"There goes that fellow from the reunion I was telling you about," Duke said, pointing to the street outside. "He's going kind of fast. He'll get a ticket if he's not careful."

Jake looked out quickly enough to see and recognize the driver. "He's been buying stuff here?" he asked.

"Yup. Didn't come in *this* morning, but most days he'd buy coffee and toast, and sometimes stop by for coffee and a sandwich at night."

Could he have been buying it for Laura? Jake wondered. And now Dr. Sheridan is missing. I've got to call Sam Deegan. I'm sure he'll want to check Laura's old house. Then I'll go up there and wait for him, he decided.

He dialed the hotel. "Amy, put Mr. Deegan on. It's important."

Amy didn't take long to come back. "Mr. Deegan told me to tell you to get lost."

"Amy, tell Mr. Deegan that I think I know where he can find Laura Wilcox."

94

J ean looked up as the door to the bedroom was pushed open. The Owl was standing in the doorway. In his arms he was carrying a slender figure, dressed in the dark gray uniform of a West Point cadet. With a satisfied smile he walked across the room and lay Meredith at Jean's feet. "Behold, your daughter!" he said triumphantly. "Look into her face. See the features that must be familiar to you. Isn't she beautiful? Aren't you proud?"

Reed, Jean thought, it's Reed! Lily is Reed incarnate! The narrow aquiline nose, the wide-set eyes, the high cheekbones, the pale golden hair. Oh, my God, has he killed her? No, no—she's breathing!

"Don't hurt her! Don't you *dare* hurt her!" she cried. When she tried to shout, her voice became muffled. From the bed she could hear Laura's frightened sobs.

"I'm not going to hurt her, Jeannie. But I am going to *kill* her, and *you* are going to watch. Then it will be Laura's turn. Then yours. By then I think I'll be doing you a favor. I can't imagine you would want to live after watching your daughter die, will you?"

At a deliberately slow pace, The Owl walked across the room, removed the hanger with the plastic bag on which he had written "Lily/Meredith," and carried it back. He knelt beside Meredith's unconscious form and slid the hanger out of the bag. "Do you want to pray, Jean?" he asked. "I think the Twenty-third Psalm is appropriate for you to recite at this time. Go ahead—'The Lord is my shepherd . . .'"

Stunned and horrified, Jean watched as The Owl began to slide the plastic over Lily's head.

"No, no, no . . ." Before the plastic reached Lily's nostrils, she tipped the chair, falling forward, protecting her child with her body. The chair hit The Owl on his arm and pinned it. He screeched with pain. As he struggled to pull it loose, he could hear from downstairs the sound of the front door being smashed open.

95

When Sam Deegan got on the phone with Jake after Amy Sachs had explained to him that Jake thought he knew where Laura was being kept, he did not give Jake the chance to deliver the speech he had hastily prepared.

Jake wanted to say, "Mr. Deegan, notwithstanding the fact that you publicly disclaimed my assistance and made me the subject of ridicule, I am being generous enough to help you in your investigation, particularly since I am very concerned about Dr. Sheridan."

He got only as far as "Notwithstanding the fact" when Sam interrupted. "Listen, Jake. Jean Sheridan and Laura are in the hands of a homicidal maniac. Don't waste my time. Do you know where Laura is, or don't you?"

At that, Jake almost tripped over his own tongue as he rushed to tell what he knew.

"Somebody is staying in Laura's old house on Mountain Road, Mr. Deegan, even though it's supposed to be unoccupied. One of the honorees from the reunion has been buying food at the delicatessen down the street from the house almost every day. He just drove by. I think he was on his way to the house." Jake had barely spit out the name of the man before he heard the click of Sam's phone.

That sure got Deegan's attention, Jake thought as he waited on the street near Laura's old house. It wasn't more than six minutes later that Deegan and that other detective, Zarro, were screeching to a stop at the curb, followed by two patrol cars. They hadn't used the sirens to announce their arrival, which Jake had found disappointing, but he supposed they wanted to surprise the guy.

He had told Sam he was sure that whoever was in the house was in the corner front bedroom. Immediately after that, they broke down the front door and rushed in. Sam had yelled to him to stay outside.

Fat chance, Jake thought. He'd given them time to get to the bedroom, then followed, the camera slung over his shoulder. As he got to the top of the stairs, he heard a door slam. The other front bedroom, he thought. Somebody's in there.

Sam Deegan came out of the back corner bedroom, his gun drawn. "Get downstairs, Jake!" he ordered. "There's a killer hiding up here."

Jake pointed down the hall. "He's in there."

Sam and Zarro and a couple of the cops ran past him. Jake rushed to the door of the front bedroom, looked inside, and, after an instant of total shock at what he was seeing, focused his camera and began snapping pictures.

He took a photograph of Laura Wilcox. She was lying on the bed, her gown crumpled, her hair matted. A cop was supporting her head and holding a glass of water to her lips.

Jean Sheridan was sitting on the floor, holding in her arms a young woman dressed in the uniform of a West Point cadet. Jean was crying and whispering, "Lily, Lily, Lily," over and over again. At first Jake thought the girl was dead, but then he saw that she was beginning to stir.

Jake aimed his camera and was able to record for posterity the moment Lily opened her eyes and, for the first time since the day she was born, looked into the eyes of her birth mother.

96

It will be only a matter of seconds before they force open the door, The Owl thought. I came so close to completing the mission. He looked at the pewter owls he had clasped in his hand, the ones he had intended to place with the bodies of Laura and Jean and Meredith.

Now he would never have the chance.

"Give yourself up," Sam Deegan shouted. "It's over. You know you can't escape."

Oh, but I can, The Owl thought. He sighed and took his mask out of his pocket. He slipped it on and looked into the mirror over the bureau to be sure it was properly in place. He put the pewter owls on the dresser.

"I am an owl, and I live in a tree," he said aloud.

The pistol was in his other pocket. He took it out and held it against his temple. "Nighttime is my time," he whispered. Then he closed his eyes and pulled the trigger.

At the sound of the shot, Sam kicked the door and it flew open. With Eddie Zarro and the cops behind him, he rushed inside.

The body was sprawled on the floor, the gun beside it. He had fallen backward, and the mask was still in place, blood seeping through it.

Sam bent down, pulled off the mask, and looked into the face of the man who had taken the lives of so many innocent people. In death the scars from the plastic surgery were clearly visible, and the features that some surgeon had managed to make so attractive now seemed twisted and repulsive.

"Funny," Sam said. "Gordon Amory was the last one I would have figured to be The Owl."

97

That night Jean had dinner with Charles and Gano Buckley at Craig Michaelson's home. Meredith was already back at West Point. "After the doctor checked her over, she insisted on going back today," General Buckley said. "She was still worried about her physics exam tomorrow morning. She is such a disciplined kid. She'll make a great soldier." He was trying not to show how shaken he had been when he learned how near to death his only child had come.

"Like the goddess, Minerva, she sprang full-fledged from her father's brow," Jean said. "It's exactly what Reed would have done." She lapsed into silence. She could still feel the unspeakable joy of the moment when the cop had cut her loose from the chair and she had been able to put her arms around Lily. She could feel the poignant beauty of the sound of Lily whispering, "Jean—Mother."

They had been taken to the hospital to be checked. There, she and Lily had sat side by side talking, beginning to catch up on nearly twenty years. "I always imagined what you looked like," Lily had said. "I think I pictured you just as you are."

"And I you. I'll have to learn to call you Meredith. It's a beautiful name."

When the doctor cleared them for release, he said, "Most women after your ordeal would be on tranquilizers. You two are troupers."

They had stopped in to see Laura. Seriously dehydrated, she was on an IV and sedated into a healing sleep.

Sam had returned to the hospital to drive them back to the hotel. But as they met in the lobby, the Buckleys arrived. "Mom, Dad," Meredith had called, and with sad understanding, Jean had watched her fly into their arms.

"Jean, you gave her life, and you saved her life," Gano Buckley said quietly. "From now on you will always be a part of her life."

Jean looked across the table at the handsome couple. They both appeared to be about sixty years old. Charles Buckley had steel gray hair, piercing eyes, strong features, and an air of authority that was balanced by the charm of his manner and the warmth of his smile. Gano Buckley was a delicately pretty, small-boned woman who had enjoyed a brief career as a concert pianist before she became a military wife. "Meredith plays beautifully," she told Jean. "I can't wait for you to hear her."

The three were going together to visit Meredith at the academy on Saturday afternoon. They're her mother and father, Jean thought. They're the ones who brought her up, cared for her and loved her and made her the marvelous young woman she is today. But at least now I'll have a place in her life. Saturday, I'll go with her to Reed's grave, and I'll tell her about him. She must know what a remarkable person he was.

It was a profoundly bittersweet evening for her, and she knew the Buckleys understood when, pleading exhaustion, she left soon after coffee was served.

When Craig Michaelson dropped her off at the hotel at ten o'clock, she found Sam Deegan and Alice Sommers waiting in the lobby.

"We figured you might want to have a nightcap with us," Sam said. "Even with all the lightbulb people here, they managed to save a table for us in the bar."

With tears of gratitude in her eyes, Jean looked from one to the other. They understand how hard tonight has been for me, she thought. Then she spotted Jake Perkins standing near the front desk. She beckoned to him, and he rushed over to her.

"Jake," she said, "I was so out of it this afternoon that I don't know whether or not I really thanked you. If it weren't for you, neither Meredith nor Laura nor I would be alive today." She put her arms around his neck and kissed his cheek.

Jake was visibly moved. "Dr. Sheridan," he said. "I just wish I had been a little smarter. When I saw those pewter owls on the dresser next to Mr. Amory's body, I told Mr. Deegan that I had found one on Alison Kendall's grave. Maybe if I had told him when I found it, they might have decided to get you a bodyguard right away."

"Never mind that," Sam said. "You couldn't know at that time that the owl meant anything. Dr. Sheridan is right. If you hadn't figured out that Laura might be in

that house, they'd all be dead. Now, let's go inside before we lose that table." He considered for a moment
and sighed. "You come too, Jake."

Alice was standing next to him. Sam could see that
what Jake had just said had startled her.

"Sam, last week on her anniversary, I found a pewter
owl at Karen's grave," she said quietly. "I have it at home
in the curio cabinet in the den."

"That's it," Sam said. "I've been trying to remember
what I noticed in your cabinet that bothered me, Alice.
Now I know what it was."

"Gordon Amory must have been the one who put it
there," Alice said sadly.

Sam put his arm around her as they walked into the
bar. It's been a hell of a day for her, too, he thought. He
had told Alice that The Owl had admitted to Laura that
he had murdered Karen by mistake. Alice was devastated to learn that Karen had been killed only because
she happened to come home that night. But she said
that at least it took the cloud of suspicion off Karen's
boyfriend, Cyrus Lindstrom, and at least now she could
hope for some degree of closure.

"I'll take that owl out of the cabinet when I drive you
home tonight," he said. "I don't want you to look at it
again."

They were at the table. "It's closure for you as well,
isn't it, Sam?" Alice asked. "For twenty years you never
gave up trying to solve Karen's death."

"In that sense it's closure, but I hope it's still all right
with you if I continue to drop in for a visit occasionally."

"You'd better, Sam, you'd just better. You've gotten me through the last twenty years. You can't quit on me now."

At the table Jake was about to sit next to Jean when he felt a tap on his shoulder. "Do you mind?"

Mark Fleischman slipped into the chair. "I stopped at the hospital to see Laura," he told Jean. "She's feeling better, although, of course, she's rocky emotionally. But she'll be okay." He grinned. "She said she'd be glad to go into therapy with me."

Jake took the seat on the other side of Jean. "I believe that if anything, this harrowing experience will prove to be a turning point in her career," he said earnestly. "With all this publicity she's bound to get a lot of offers. That's show business."

Sam looked at him. My God, he's probably right, he thought. And with that realization, he decided to order a double scotch instead of a glass of wine.

Jean had learned from Sam that Mark had driven all over town trying to find her, and then when Sam called him, he had rushed to the hospital where she, Meredith, and Laura had been taken. He had left without seeing her when he was assured that she was going to be released shortly. She had neither seen nor spoken to him all day. Now she looked directly at him. The tenderness with which he was looking at her made her deeply ashamed of the way she had mistrusted him. And at the same time it touched her deeply.

"I'm sorry, Mark," she said. "I'm so terribly, terribly sorry."

He covered her hand with his, the same gesture that a few days earlier had comforted and warmed her and made her feel a spark that had long been missing in her life.

"Jeannie," Mark said, smiling, "don't be sorry. I'm going to give you lots of chances to make it up to me. That I promise you."

"Did you ever suspect that it was Gordon?" she asked.

"Jean, the fact is that under the surface there was a lot going on with all our fellow honorees, not to mention the reunion chairman. Jack Emerson may be a shrewd businessman, but I wouldn't trust him as far as I could throw him. My father told me that Jack is known locally as a womanizer and a mean drunk, although he's never been known to be physically aggressive. They all believe that he burned down that building ten years ago. One of the reasons is that on the night of the fire, a security guard who probably was paid off by him did an unusual walk-through to be sure no one was still in the building. It was a suspicious thing to do, but it does suggest that Emerson has never wanted to kill anybody.

"I really believed for a while that Robby Brent could have been the one who killed the girls at your lunch table. Remember what a surly kid he was? And he was nasty enough at the reunion dinner to make me think he was capable of doing physical as well as emotional harm. I looked up references to him on the Internet. He'd talked to an interviewer about his fear of poverty and claimed that he had money buried all over the country on land that he owned but had registered in fictitious names. He was quoted as saying that he was the dumb kid in his smart family and was considered a nerd at school. He said that he had learned the art of ridicule because he was constantly the butt of jokes himself. He ended up hating just about everyone in town."

Mark shrugged. "But then, just when I was sure he was The Owl, as we now know him, Robby disappeared."

"We think he suspected Gordon and followed him to that house," Sam said. "There were bloodstains on the staircase."

"Carter has so much anger in him that I thought he might be capable of murder," Jean said.

Mark shook his head. "Somehow I never did. Carter continually vents his anger by his nasty attitude and also through his plays. I've read the scripts of all of them. You should read them sometime. You'll recognize some of the characters as people you've known. That's the way he gets his revenge against those whom he regarded as his tormentors. He didn't need to go beyond that."

Jean realized that Sam, Alice, and Jake were listening intently to Mark. "That left only Gordon Amory and you," she said.

Mark smiled. "Notwithstanding your doubts, Jeannie, I knew *I* wasn't guilty. The more I studied Gordon, the more suspicious I became of him. It's one thing to fix a nose that's been broken or to get baggy eyes tightened, but to totally alter your external appearance has always seemed somewhat bizarre to me. I didn't believe him when he said that he'd give Laura a job on one of his TV series. It was obvious to me that he resented her playing up to him at the reunion when he well knew that she was only trying to use him. But then this morning, when Gordon was in the hotel after you disappeared, I thought I had been wrong about him. Quite frankly, when I was driving around looking for you, I was frantic. I was sure that something terrible had happened to you."

Jean turned to Sam. "I know you talked to Laura at the hospital. Did she tell you whether Gordon revealed to her how he had managed to make four of the other deaths look like accidents, and Gloria's death look like a suicide?"

"Gordon bragged about that to Laura. He told her that he had stalked all the girls before he killed them. Catherine Kane's car skidded into the Potomac after he had tampered with her brakes. Cindy Lang wasn't caught in the avalanche—he accosted her on that slope and dropped her body in a crevice. There was an avalanche that afternoon, and everyone assumed that she had been caught in it. Her body was never recovered."

Sam took a slow sip of his scotch, then continued. "He called Gloria Martin and asked her if he could stop by for a drink. By then she knew how successful he was and how handsome he had become, so she agreed. But she still couldn't resist getting in a dig at him and ran out to buy the owl figure. Gordon got her drunk, and when she fell asleep, smothered her with a plastic bag and left the owl in her hand."

Alice gasped. "My God, he was so evil."

"Yes, he was," Sam agreed. "Debra Parker was taking flying lessons at a small airfield. The security there was lax. Gordon had a pilot's license himself, so he knew just how to sabotage her plane before she took off on her first solo flight. And Alison's death was simple — he just held her under the water in her pool."

Sam looked sympathetically at Jean. "And I know, Jean, that he told both you and Meredith that he ran over Reed Thornton with his car."

Mark had not taken his eyes off Jean. "When I saw Laura a little while ago at the hospital, she told me that he had three plastic bags with each of your names on them and that he was going to use them to smother you, Laura, and Meredith. My God, Jeannie, when I think of that, I go crazy. I couldn't bear to have anything happen to you."

Slowly, deliberately, he took her face in his hands and kissed her, a long, tender kiss that said everything he had not yet put into words.

There was a sudden flash, and they looked up, startled. Jake was now standing, his camera still trained on them. "It's only a digital," he explained, beaming, "but I know a good photo op when I see it."

Epilogue

West Point, Graduation Day

"I can't believe it's been over two and a half years since Meredith came back into my life," Jean told Mark. Her eyes shining with pride, she watched as the graduates marched onto the field, splendid in their formal dress uniforms: gray cutaway jackets with bright gold buttons, starched white pants, white gloves, and hats.

"An awful lot has happened in that time," he agreed.

It was a magnificent morning in June. Michie stadium was filled with the proud families of the cadets. Charles and Gano Buckley were sitting directly in front of them. On Jean's other side, retired General and Mrs. Carroll Reed Thornton watched as the granddaughter they had come to adore passed by.

So much good has come after so much pain, Jean thought. She and Mark had just celebrated their second wedding anniversary and the first birthday of their baby son, Mark Dennis. Mothering her baby, sharing with him all the wonderful moments unfolding in his life, was softening the pain of not having been able to take care of Meredith. Meredith was crazy about her little brother, even though, as she had laughingly pointed out, she wouldn't be available for much baby-sitting. When the ceremony was over, she would be a second lieutenant in the United States Army.

She and Jake were little Mark's godparents. Jake's pleasure in the honor was expressed in the barrage of articles on baby care that he was constantly sending them from Columbia University, where he was now a student.

Sam and Alice were seated a few rows away. I'm so glad they ended up together, Jean thought. It's been wonderful for both of them.

Sometimes Jean had nightmares about the horror of that reunion week. But she often reflected that those circumstances had brought her and Mark together. And if she had never gotten those faxes, she might never have known Meredith.

It all began here at West Point, she thought, as the first notes of "The Star Spangled Banner" were sounded by the band.

Throughout the ceremony, her mind kept going back to the spring afternoon when Reed first sat down beside her on the bench and began to talk to her. He was my first love, she thought tenderly. He'll always be in my heart. Then, as Cadet Meredith Buckley's name was called to receive the West Point diploma that Reed had not lived long enough to accept, Jean was certain that somehow he was here with them today.

SIMON & SCHUSTER
PROUDLY PRESENTS

NO PLACE LIKE HOME
MARY HIGGINS CLARK

Now available in hardcover from
Simon & Schuster

Please turn the page for a preview of
No Place Like Home . . .

PROLOGUE

Ten-year-old Liza was dreaming her favorite dream, the one about the day when she was six years old, and she and Daddy were at the beach, in New Jersey, at Spring Lake. They'd been in the water, holding hands and jumping together whenever a wave broke near them. Then a much bigger wave suddenly rushed in and began to break right over them, and Daddy grabbed her. "Hang on, Liza," he yelled, and suddenly they were tumbling underwater and being thrown around by the wave. Liza had been very afraid.

She could still feel the sensation of her forehead slamming into the sand when the wave rolled them onto the shore. She had swallowed water and was coughing, and her eyes were stinging and she was crying when Daddy pulled her close and gathered her in his arms. "Now *that* was a wave," he said, as he brushed the sand from her face, "but we rode it out together, didn't we, Liza?"

That was the best part of the dream—having Daddy's arms around her and feeling so safe.

Before the next summer came around, Daddy had died. After that she'd never really felt safe again. Now she was always afraid, because Mom had made Ted, her stepfather, move out of the house. Ted didn't want a divorce, and he kept pestering Mom, wanting her to let him come back. Liza knew she wasn't the only one afraid; Mom was afraid, too.

Liza tried not to listen. She wanted to go back into the dream of being in Daddy's arms, but the voices kept waking her up.

Someone was crying and yelling. Did she hear Mom calling Daddy's name? What was she saying? Liza sat up and slid out of bed.

Mom always left the door to Liza's bedroom open just a little so that she could see the light in the hall. And until she married Ted last year, she had always told Liza that if she woke up and felt sad, she could come into her room and sleep with her. Once Ted moved in, she'd never gotten in bed with her mother again.

It was Ted's voice she heard now. He was yelling at Mom, and Mom was screaming. "Let go of me!" she cried.

Liza knew that Mom was so afraid of Ted, and that since he'd moved out she even kept Daddy's gun in the drawer of her night table. Liza rushed down the hall, her feet moving noiselessly along the padded carpet. The door of Mom's sitting room was open and inside she could see that Ted had Mom pinned against the wall and was shaking her. Liza ran past the sitting room and went directly into her mother's bedroom. She hurried around the bed and yanked open the night table drawer. Trembling, she grabbed the gun and ran back to the sitting room.

Standing in the doorway, she pointed the gun at Ted and screamed, "Let go of my mother!"

Ted spun around, still holding on to Mom, his eyes wide and angry. The veins in his forehead were sticking out and pulsing. Liza could see the tears streaming down her mother's cheeks.

"Sure," he yelled. With a violent thrust, he shoved Liza's mother at her. When she crashed into Liza, the gun went off. Then Liza heard a funny little gurgle and Mom crumpled to the floor. Liza looked down at her mother, then up at Ted. He began to lunge toward her, and Liza pointed the gun at him and pulled the trigger. She pulled it again and again, until he fell down and then began crawling across the room and tried to grab the gun from her. When it wouldn't fire anymore, she dropped the gun and got down on the floor and put her arms around her mother. There was no sound, and she knew her mother was dead.

After that Liza had only a hazy memory of what happened. She remembered Ted's voice on the phone, the police coming, someone pulling her arms from her mother's neck.

She was taken away, and she never saw her mother again.

1

TWENTY-FOUR YEARS LATER

I cannot believe I am standing in the exact spot where I was standing when I killed my mother. I ask myself if this is part of a nightmare, or if it is really happening. In the beginning, after that terrible night, I had nightmares all the time. I spent a good part of my childhood drawing pictures of them for Dr. Moran, a psychologist in California, where I went to live after the trial. This room figured in many of those drawings.

The mirror over the fireplace is the same one my father chose when he restored the house. It is part of the wall, recessed and framed. In it, I see my reflection. My face is deadly pale. My eyes are no longer dark blue, but black, reflecting all the terrible visions that are leaping through my mind.

The dark blue of my eyes is a heritage from my father. My mother's eyes were lighter, a cornflower blue, picture perfect with her golden hair. My hair would be dark blond if I left it natural. I have darkened it, though, ever since I came back to the East Coast sixteen years ago to attend the Fashion Institute of Technology in Manhattan. I am also taller than my mother was by five inches. Yet, as I grow older, I believe I am beginning to resemble my mother in many ways, and I try to distance myself from that resemblance. I have always lived in dread of someone saying to me, "You look familiar. . . ."

At the time, my mother's image was splashed all over the media, and still turns up periodically in stories that rehash the circumstances of her death, so if anyone says I look familiar, I know it's her they have in mind. I, Celia Foster Nolan, formerly Liza Barton, the child the tabloids dubbed "Little Lizzie Borden," am far less likely to be recognized as that chubby-faced little girl with golden curls who was acquitted—not exonerated—of deliberately killing her mother and trying to kill her stepfather.

My second husband, Alex Nolan, and I have been married for six months. Today I thought we were going to take my four-year-old son, Jack, to see a horse show in Peapack, an upscale town in northern New Jersey, when suddenly Alex detoured to Mendham, a neighboring town. It was only then that he told me he had a wonderful surprise for my birthday, and drove down the road to this house.

Jack is tugging at my hand, but I remain frozen to the spot. Energetic, as most four-year-olds are, he wants to explore. I let him go, and in a flash he is out of the room and running down the hall.

Alex is standing a little behind me. Without looking at him, I can feel his anxiety. He believes he has found a beautiful home for us to live in, and his generosity is such that the deed is solely in my name, his birthday gift to me. "I'll catch up with Jack, honey," he reassures me. "You look around and start figuring how you'll decorate."

As he leaves the room I hear him call, "Don't go downstairs, Jack. We haven't finished showing Mommy her new house."

"Your husband tells me that you're an interior designer," Henry Paley, the real estate agent, is saying. "This house has been very well kept up, but, of course, every woman, especially one in your profession, wants to put her own signature on her home."

Not yet trusting myself to speak, I look at him. Paley is a small man of about sixty, with thinning gray hair, and neatly dressed in a dark blue pin-striped suit. I realize he is waiting expectantly for me to show enthusiasm for the wonderful birthday gift with which my husband has just presented me.

"As your husband may have told you, I was not the selling agent," Paley explains. "My boss, Georgette Grove, was showing your husband various properties nearby when he spotted the FOR SALE sign on the lawn. He apparently fell in love with it immediately. The house is quite simply an architectural treasure and it's situated on ten acres in the premier location in a premier town."

I know it is a treasure. My father was the architect who restored a crumbling eighteenth-century mansion, turning it into a charming and spacious home. I look past Paley and study the fireplace. Mother and Daddy found the mantel in France, in a chateau about to be demolished. Daddy told me the meanings of all the sculptured work on it, the cherubs and the pineapples and the grapes . . .

Ted pinning Mother against the wall . . .
Mother sobbing . . .
I am pointing the gun at him. Daddy's gun . . .
Let go of my mother . . .
Sure . . .

Ted spinning Mother around and shoving her at me . . .
Mother's terrified eyes looking at me . . .
The gun going off . . .
Lizzie Borden had an axe . . .

"Are you all right, Mrs. Nolan?" Henry Paley is asking me.

"Yes, of course," I manage, with some effort. My tongue feels too heavy to mouth the words. My mind is racing with the thought that I should not have let Larry, my fist husband, make me swear that I wouldn't tell the truth about myself to anyone. Not even to someone I married. In this moment I am fiercely angry at Larry for wringing that promise from me. He had been so kind when I told him about myself before our marriage, but in the end he failed me. He was ashamed of my past, afraid for the impact it might have on our son's future. That fear has brought us here, now.

Already the lie is a wedge driven between Alex and me. We both feel it. He talks about wanting to have children soon, and I wonder how he would feel if he knew that Little Lizzie Borden would be their mother.

It's been twenty-four years, but such memories die hard. Will anyone in town recognize me? I wonder. Probably not. But though I agreed to live in this area, I did not agree to live in this town, or in this house. I can't live here. I simply can't.

To avoid the curiosity in Paley's eyes, I walk over to the mantel and pretend to study it.

"Beautiful, isn't it?" Paley asks, the professional enthusiasm of the real estate agent ringing through his somewhat high-pitched voice.

"Yes, it is."

"The master bedroom is very large, and has two separate, wonderfully appointed baths." He opens the door to the bedroom and looks expectantly at me. Reluctantly, I follow him.

Memories flood my mind. Weekend mornings in this room, I used to get in bed with Mother and Daddy. Daddy would bring up coffee for Mother and hot chocolate for me.

Their king-size bed with the tufted headboard is gone, of course. The soft peach walls are now painted dark green. Looking out the back windows I can see that the Japanese maple tree Daddy planted so long ago is now mature and beautiful.

Tears are pressing against my eyelids. I want to run out of here. If necessary I will have to break my promise to Larry, and tell Alex the truth about myself. I am not Celia Foster, nee Kellogg, the daughter of Kathleen and Martin Kellogg of Santa Barbara, California. I am Liza Barton, born in this town and, as a child, reluctantly acquitted by a judge of murder and attempted murder.

"Mom, Mom!" I hear my son's voice as his footsteps clatter on the uncarpeted floorboards. He hurries into the room, energy encapsulated, small and sturdy, a bright quickness about him, a handsome little boy, the center of my heart. At night I steal into his room to listen to the sound of his even breathing. He is not interested in what happened years ago. He is satisfied if I am there to answer when he calls me.

As he reaches me, I bend down and catch him in my arms. Jack has Larry's light brown hair and high forehead. His cornflower blue eyes are my mother's, but then Larry had blue eyes, too. In those last moments of fading consciousness, Larry had whispered that when Jack attended his prep school, he didn't want him to ever have to deal with the tabloids printing stories about me, or digging up those old stories. I taste again the bitterness of knowing that his father was ashamed of me.

Ted Cartwright swears estranged wife begged for reconciliation . . .

State psychiatrist testifies ten-year-old Liza Barton mentally competent to commit crime . . .

Was Larry right to swear me to silence? At this moment, I can't be sure of anything. I kiss the top of Jack's head.

"I really, really, really like it here," he tells me excitedly.

Alex is coming into the bedroom. He planned this surprise for me with so much care. When we came up the driveway, it had been festooned with birthday balloons, swaying on this breezy August day—all painted with my name and the words "Happy Birthday." But the exuberant joy with which he handed me the key and the deed to the house is gone. He can read me too well. He knows I'm not happy. He is disappointed and hurt, and why wouldn't he be?

"When I told the people at the office what I'd done, a couple of the women said that no matter how beautiful a house might be, they'd want to have the chance to make the decision about buying it," he said, his voice forlorn.

They were right, I thought as I looked at him, his reddish brown hair and brown eyes. Tall, with wide shoulders, Alex has a look of strength about him that makes him enormously attractive. Jack adores him. Now Jack slides from my arms and puts his arm around Alex's leg.

My husband and my son.

And my house.

2
—

The Grove Real Estate Agency was on East Main Street in the attractive New Jersey town of Mendham. Georgette Grove parked in front of it and got out of the car. The August day was unusually cool, and the overhead clouds were threatening rain. Her short-sleeved linen suit was not warm enough for the weather, and she moved with a quick step up the path to the door of her office.

Sixty-two years old, Georgette was a handsome whippet-thin woman with short wavy hair the color of steel, hazel eyes, and a firm chin. At the moment, her emotions were conflicted. She was pleased at how smoothly the closing had gone on the house she had just helped sell. It was one of the smaller houses in town, it's selling price barely breaking the seven figure mark, but even though she split the commission with another broker, the check she was carrying was manna from heaven. It would give her a few months' reserve until she landed another sale.

So far it had been a disastrous year, saved only by her sale of the house on Old Mill Lane to Alex Nolan. That one had caught her up on overdue bills at the office. She had very much wanted to be present that morning when Nolan presented the house to his wife. I hope she likes surprises, Georgette thought for the hundredth time. She worried that what he was doing was risky. She had tried to warn him about the house, about its history, but Nolan didn't seem to care. Georgette worried also that since he'd put the house in his wife's name only, if she didn't like it, she might be wide open to a violation suit.

It was part of the real estate code of New Jersey that a prospective buyer had to be notified if a house was stigmatized property, meaning one that might be impacted by a factor that, on a psychological level, could cause apprehension or fears. Since some people would not want to live in a house in which a crime had been committed, or in which there had been a suicide, the real estate agent was obliged to make a prospective client aware of any such history. The statute even required the agent to reveal if a house had the reputation of being haunted.

I tried to tell Alex that there had been a tragedy in the house on Old Mill Lane, Georgette thought defensively as she opened the office door and stepped into the reception room. But he had cut her off, saying that his family used to rent a two-hundred-year-old house on Cape Cod, and the history of some of the people who lived in it would curl your hair. But this is different, Georgette thought. I should have told him that around here the house he bought is known as "Little Lizzie's Place."

She wondered if Nolan had become nervous about his surprise. At the last minute he had asked her to be at the house when they arrived, but it had been impossible to change the other closing. Instead, she had sent Henry Paley to greet Nolan and his wife, and to be there to answer any questions Mrs. Nolan might have. Henry had been reluctant to cover for her, and in the end she had been forced to remind him, rather sharply, not only to be there, but to be sure to emphasize the many desirable features of the house and property.

At Nolan's request, the driveway had been decorated with festive balloons, all painted with the words "Happy Birthday, Celia." The porch had been draped with festive papier-mâché, and he also had asked that champagne and a birthday cake and glasses and plates and silverware and birthday napkins be waiting inside.

When Georgette pointed out that there was absolutely no furniture in the house, and offered to bring over a folding table and chairs, Nolan had been appalled. He rushed to a nearby furniture store and ordered an expensive glass patio table and chairs, and instructed the salesman to have them placed in the dining room. "We'll switch them to the patio when we move in, or if Celia doesn't like them, we'll donate them to a charity and take a deduction," he had said.

Five thousand dollars for a patio set and he's talking about giving it away, Georgette had thought, but she knew he meant it. Yesterday afternoon he had phoned and asked her to be sure there were two dozen roses in every room on the main floor, as well as the master bedroom suite. "Roses are Celia's favorite flowers," he explained. "When we got married, I promised her that she'd never be without them."

He's rich. He's handsome. He's charming. And he's clearly devoted to his wife, Georgette thought as she stepped inside and automatically glanced around the reception room to see if any potential clients were waiting there. From half the marriages I've seen, she's a damn lucky woman.

But how will she react when she starts hearing the stories about the house?

Georgette tried to push the thought away. Born with a natural ability to sell, she had progressed rapidly from being a secretary and part-time real estate agent, to founding her own company. Her reception room was a matter of special pride to her. Robin Carpenter, her secretary-receptionist, was positioned at an antique mahogany desk to the right of the entrance. On the left, a brightly upholstered sectional couch and chairs were grouped around a coffee table.

There, while clients sipped coffee or soft drinks or a glass of wine in the early evening, Georgette or Henry would run tapes showing available properties. The tapes provided meticulous details of every aspect of the interior, the exterior, and the surrounding neighborhood.

"Those tapes take a lot of time to do properly," Georgette was fond of explaining to clients, "but they save you a lot of time, and by finding your likes and dislikes, we can get a very good idea of what you're really looking for."

Make them want it before they set foot in it—that was

Georgette's game plan. It had worked for nearly twenty years, but in the last five years it had gotten tougher, as more and more high-powered agencies had opened in the area, their young and vigorous brokers panting for every listing.

Robin was the only person in the reception area. "How did the closing go?" she asked Georgette.

"Smoothly, thank God. Is Henry back?"

"No, I guess he's still drinking champagne with the Nolans. I still can't believe it. A gorgeous guy buys a gorgeous house for his wife for her thirty-fourth birthday. That's exactly my age. She's so lucky. Did you ever find out if Alex Nolan has a brother?" Robin sighed. "But on the other hand, there can't be two men like that," she added.

"Let's all hope that after she gets over the surprise, and has heard the story of that house, Celia Nolan still considers herself lucky," Georgette snapped nervously. "Otherwise, we might have a real problem on our hands."

Robin knew exactly what she meant. Small, slender, and very pretty, with a heart-shaped face and a penchant for frilly clothes, the initial impression she gave was that of the air-headed blonde. And so Georgette had believed when she applied for the job a year ago. Five minutes of conversation, however, had led her not only to reversing that opinion but to hiring Robin on the spot and upping the salary she had intended to pay. Now, after a year, Robin was about to get her own real estate license, and Georgette welcomed the prospect of having her working as an agent. Henry simply wasn't pulling his weight anymore.

"You *did* try to warn the husband about the history of the house. I can back you up on that, Georgette."

"That's something," Georgette said, as she headed down the hall to her private office at the rear of the building. But then she turned abruptly and faced the younger woman. "I tried to speak to Alex Nolan about the background of the house one time only, Robin," she said emphatically. "And that was when I was alone in the car with him on our way to see the Murray house on Moselle Road. You couldn't have heard me discussing it with him."

"I'm sure I heard you bring it up one of the times Alex Nolan was in here," Robin insisted.

"I mentioned it to him once in the car. I never said anything about it to him here. Robin, you're not doing me or, in the long run, yourself any favors by lying to a client," Georgette snapped. "Keep that in mind, please."

The outside door opened. They both turned as Henry Paley came into the reception room. "How did it go?" Georgette asked, her anxiety apparent in the tone of her voice.

"I would say that Mrs. Nolan put up a very good act of seeming to be delighted by her husband's birthday surprise," Paley answered. "I believe she convinced him. However, she did not convince me."

"Why not?" Robin asked before Georgette could frame the words.

Henry Paley's expression was that of a man who had completed a mission he knew was doomed to failure. "I wish I could tell you," he said. "It may just be that she was overwhelmed." He looked at Georgette, obviously afraid that he might be giving the impression that he had somehow let her down. Henry was acutely aware that he had not managed to close a single sale in months. "Georgette," he said apologetically, "I swear, when I was showing Mrs. Nolan the master suite, all I could visualize was that kid shooting her mother and stepfather in the sitting room years ago. Isn't that weird?"

"Henry, this agency has sold that house three times in the last twenty-four years, and you were involved in at least two of those sales. I never heard you say that before," Georgette protested angrily.

"I never got that feeling before. Maybe it's because of all those damn flowers the husband ordered. It's the same scent that hits you in funeral homes. I got it full force in the master suite of Little Lizzie's Place today. And I have a feeling that Celia Nolan had a reaction like that, too."

Henry realized that unwittingly he had used the forbidden words in describing the house on Old Mill Lane. "Sorry, Georgette," he mumbled as he brushed past her.

"You should be," Georgette said bitterly. "I can just imagine the kind of vibes you were sending out to Mrs. Nolan."

"Maybe you'll take me up after all on my offer to back you up on what you told Alex Nolan about the house, Georgette," Robin suggested, a touch of malice in her voice.

3
—

"But Ceil, it's what we were *planning* to do. We're just doing it a little faster. It makes sense for Jack to start pre-K in Mendham. We've been cramped for these six months in your apartment, and you didn't want to move downtown to mine."

It was the day after my birthday, the day following the big surprise. We were having breakfast in my apartment, the one that five years ago I had been hired to decorate for Larry, who became my first husband. Jack had rushed through a glass of juice and a bowl of cornflakes, and hopefully was now getting dressed for day camp.

I don't think I closed my eyes all night. Instead I lay in bed, my shoulder brushing against Alex, staring into the dark, remembering, always remembering. Now, wrapped in a blue and white linen robe, and with my hair twisted into a bun, I was trying to appear calm and collected as I sipped my coffee. Across the table, impeccably dressed as always in a dark blue suit, white shirt, and figured blue and red tie, Alex was rushing through the slice of toast and mug of coffee that was his everyday breakfast.

My suggestion that, while the house was beautiful, I would want to be able to completely redecorate it before we moved in had met with resistance from Alex. "Ceil, I know it was probably insanity to buy the house without consulting you, but it was exactly the kind of place we both had in mind. You had agreed to the area. We talked about Peapack or Basking Ridge, and Mendham is only five or ten minutes from both of them. It's an upscale town, convenient to New York, and, besides the fact the firm is moving me to New Jersey, the added plus is that I can get in some early morning rides. Central Park just doesn't do it for me. And I want to teach you how to ride. You said you'd enjoy taking lessons."

I studied my husband. His expression was both contrite and pleading. He was right. This apartment really was too small for the three of us. Alex had given up so much when we married. His spacious apartment in SoHo had included a large study, with room for his splendid sound system and even a grand piano. The piano was now in storage. Alex had a natural gift for music, and thoroughly enjoyed playing. I know he misses that freedom. He's worked hard to accomplish all he has. Though a distant cousin of my late husband, who himself had come from wealth, Alex was decidedly a "poor relation." I knew how proud he was to be able to buy this new house.

"You've been saying that you want to get back to decorating," Alex reminded me. "Once you're settled, there'd be plenty of opportunity for that, especially in Mendham. There's a lot of money there, and plenty of big houses being built. Please give it a try, for me, Ceil. You have a standing offer from the people next door to purchase this apartment at a nice profit to you, you know that."

He came around the table and put his arms around me. "Please."

I hadn't heard Jack come into the dining room. "I like the house, too, Mom," he piped up. "Alex is going to buy me my own pony when we move there."

I looked at my husband and son. "It looks as though we have a new home," I said, trying to smile. Alex is desperate to have more space, I thought. He loves the idea of being near the riding club. Eventually I'll find a different house in one of the other towns. It won't be hard to persuade him to move. He *did* admit that it was a mistake to buy without consulting me, after all.

One month later the moving van was pulling away from 895 Fifth Avenue and heading for the Lincoln Tunnel. Its destination was One Old Mill Lane, Mendham, New Jersey.

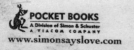